the Sherlockian

the Sherlockian

?

GRAHAM MOORE

**VIKING
CANADA**

VIKING CANADA

Published by the Penguin Group

Penguin Group (Canada), 90 Eglinton Avenue East, Suite 700, Toronto, Ontario, Canada M4P 2Y3
(a division of Pearson Canada Inc.)

Penguin Group (USA) Inc., 375 Hudson Street, New York, New York 10014, U.S.A.
Penguin Books Ltd, 80 Strand, London WC2R 0RL, England
Penguin Ireland, 25 St Stephen's Green, Dublin 2, Ireland (a division of Penguin Books Ltd)
Penguin Group (Australia), 250 Camberwell Road, Camberwell, Victoria 3124, Australia
(a division of Pearson Australia Group Pty Ltd)
Penguin Books India Pvt Ltd, 11 Community Centre, Panchsheel Park, New Delhi – 110 017, India
Penguin Group (NZ), 67 Apollo Drive, Rosedale, North Shore 0745, Auckland, New Zealand
(a division of Pearson New Zealand Ltd)
Penguin Books (South Africa) (Pty) Ltd, 24 Sturdee Avenue, Rosebank,
Johannesburg 2196, South Africa

Penguin Books Ltd, Registered Offices: 80 Strand, London WC2R 0RL, England

Published in Canada by Penguin Group (Canada), a division of Pearson Canada Inc., 2010
Simultaneously published in the United States by Twelve, an imprint of Grand Central Publishing,
Hachette Book Group, Inc.

1 2 3 4 5 6 7 8 9 10 (RRD)

Copyright © Graham Moore, 2010

Manufactured in the U.S.A.

ISBN: 978-0-670-06520-2

Library and Archives Canada Cataloguing in Publication data available upon request to the publisher.
American Library of Congress Cataloging in Publication data available.

Visit the Penguin Group (Canada) website at **www.penguin.ca**

Special and corporate bulk purchase rates available; please see
www.penguin.ca/corporatesales or call 1-800-810-3104, ext. 2477 or 2474

The Sherlockian is a work of historical fiction. All of the contemporary characters in the novel are the product of the author's imagination.

For my mother, who first taught me to love mysteries when I was eight years old. We lay in bed passing a copy of Agatha Christie's A Murder in Three Acts *back and forth, reading to each other. She made all of this possible.*

the Sherlockian

CHAPTER I

The Reichenbach Falls

So please grip this fact with your cerebral tentacle
The doll and its maker are never identical.
—Sir Arthur Conan Doyle,
London Opinion, December 12, 1912

August 9, 1893

Arthur Conan Doyle curled his brow tightly and thought only of murder.

"I'm going to kill him," Conan Doyle said as he folded his arms across his broad frame. High in the Swiss Alps, the air tickled Arthur's inch-thick mustache and seemed to blow straight through his ears. Set far back on his head, Arthur's ears always appeared to be perking up, listening to something else, something distant and behind him. For such a stocky man, he had a nose that was remarkably sharp. His hair had only recently begun to gray, a process that Arthur couldn't help but wish along. Though he was but thirty-three years of age, he was already a celebrated author. An internationally acclaimed man of letters with light ocher hair would not do so well as a wizened one, now, would he?

Arthur's two traveling companions ascended to the ledge on which he stood, the highest climbable point of the Reichenbach Falls. Silas Hocking was a cleric and novelist well known as far away as Arthur's London. His recent offering of religious literature, *Her Benny*, was a work Arthur held in high regard. Edward Benson was an acquaintance of Hocking's and was much quieter than his gregarious friend. Though Arthur had met the two men only this morning, over breakfast at the

Rifel Alp Hotel in Zermatt, he felt that he could confide in them safely. He could tell them of his mind, and of his dark plans.

"The fact is, he has gotten to be a kind of 'old man of the sea' about my neck," continued Arthur, "and I intend to make an end of him." Hocking huffed as he stood beside Arthur, gazing at the vast expanse of the Alps before them. Tufts of snow melted yards beneath their feet into a mighty stream of water that had, millennia ago, driven a path through the mountain as it poured loudly into the frothing pool below. Benson silently pressed a mittenful of snow into a tight ball and dropped it whimsically into the chasm. The force of the wind tore bits off the snowball as it fell, until it disappeared in the air as a series of white puffs.

"If I don't," said Arthur, "he'll make a death of me."

"Don't you think you're being rather rough on an old friend?" asked Hocking. "He's given you fame. Fortune. You two have made a handsome couple."

"And in plastering his name across every penny dreadful in London, I've given him a reputation which far exceeds my own. You know I get letters. 'My beloved cat has vanished into South Hampstead. Her name is Sherry-Ann. Can you find her?' Or, 'My mum had her purse snatched exiting a hansom in Piccadilly. Can you deduce the culprit?' But the thing of it is, the letters aren't addressed to me—they're addressed to *him*. They think he's real."

"Yes, your poor, admiring readers," pleaded Hocking. "Have you thought of them? People seem so terribly fond of the fellow."

"More fond of him than of me! Do you know I received a letter from my own Mam? She asked—knowing I would of course do anything she ever required—she asked that I sign the name Sherlock Holmes to a book for her neighbor Beattie. Can you imagine? Sign his name rather than my own. My Mam speaks as if she's *Holmes's* mother, not mine. Gah!" Arthur tried to contain his sudden burst of anger.

"My greater work is ignored," he continued. "*Micah Clarke*? *The White Company*? That charming little play I concocted with Mr. Barrie? Overlooked for a few morbid yarns. Worse still, he has become a waste of my time. If I have to concoct another of those tortuous plots—the bedroom door always locked from the inside, the dead man's indecipherable final message, the whole thing told wrong end first so that no one can guess the obvious solution—it is a drain." Arthur looked to his boots, showing his weariness in his bowed head. "To put it frankly, I hate him. And for my own sanity, I will soon see him dead."

"How will you do it, then?" teased Hocking. "How does one go about killing the great Sherlock Holmes? Stab him in the heart? Slit his throat? Hang him by the neck?"

"A hanging! My, are those words a balm upon my mind. But no, no, it should be something grand—he is a hero, after all. I'll give him one final case. And a villain. He'll be in need of a proper villain this time around. A gentlemanly fight to the death; he sacrifices himself for the greater good, and both men perish. Something along those lines." Benson pounded another snowball into being and lobbed it gently into the air. Arthur and Hocking watched its open-ended arc as it vanished into the sky.

"If you want to save on funeral expenses," Hocking said with a chuckle, "you could always toss him off a cliff." He looked to Arthur for a reaction but found no smile on his face. Instead Arthur curled his brow in the tight-faced frown he wore when he was in the midst of his deepest thinking.

He gazed at the jaws of the chasm below. He could hear the roar of the falling water and the violent crush it made at the mouth of the rock-speckled river. Arthur felt himself suddenly terrified. He imagined his own death on those stones. Being a medical man, Arthur was more than familiar with the frailty of the human body. A fall of this height... His corpse banging, slapping against the rocks all the way down... The dreadful cry caught in his mouth... Torn limb from limb on the crust of the earth, the wisps of grass stained with his blood... And now, in his thoughts, his own body vanished, replaced by someone leaner. Taller. A thin, underfed ribbon of a man, in a deerstalker cap and long coat. His hard face obliterated, once and for all, on a spike of gunmetal stone.

Murder.

CHAPTER 2

The Baker Street Irregulars

*"My name is Sherlock Holmes. It is my business
to know what other people don't know."*
—Sir Arthur Conan Doyle,
"The Adventure of the Blue Carbuncle"

January 5, 2010

The five-penny piece tumbled into Harold's palm. The coin felt heavy
as it landed, heads up, and Harold closed his fingers around the worn
silver. He squeezed for a few seconds before he realized that his hands
were shaking. The room exploded in applause.

"Hurray!"

"Welcome aboard!"

"Congratulations, Harold!"

Harold heard laughter, and more clapping. A hand slapped him
on the back, and another rubbed his shoulder warmly. But all Harold
could think about was the coin in his own right hand. In his left, Harold gripped his new certificate. The coin had been glued, poorly, to the
lower left corner and had become unattached when Harold overexcitedly
grasped the paper. The coin had fallen off, and Harold had caught it
midflight. He looked down at the tiny silver piece. It was a Victorian-era
shilling, worth only five pennies in its day. It would be worth a lot more
than that now, and to Harold it was worth a fortune. He blinked away
the moisture that had formed in the corners of his eyes. The coin meant
that he had arrived. That he had achieved something. That he belonged.

"Welcome, Harold," said a voice behind him. Someone tousled the deerstalker cap on his head. "Welcome to the Baker Street Irregulars."

These words, which Harold had hoped to hear for so long, sounded foreign and strange now as he finally heard them. All these people— two hundred bodies, laughing and joking and patting backs—they were all clapping for Harold. This Harold. Harold White, twenty-nine years old, with the slight belly, with the thick eyebrows, with the astigmatism, with the sweaty, shivering hands.

Harold couldn't believe that he really deserved all this. But he did. He belonged here.

The Baker Street Irregulars were the world's preeminent organization devoted to the study of Sherlock Holmes, and Harold was its newest member. Harold had published his first article in the *Baker Street Journal*, the Irregulars' quarterly publication, two years earlier. "On the Dating of Bloodstains: Sherlock Holmes and the Founding of Modern Forensics," Harold had titled the piece. It had explored the historical connections between Holmes's first experiments in *A Study in Scarlet* with the work of Dr. Eduard Piotrowski. ("Dr. Piotrowski, practicing in Kraków in the 1890s, beat in the heads of baby rabbits and recorded the patterns made by the blood bursting from their skulls. Holmes's experiments were similarly gory, though he at least had the decency to use his own blood, as well as the labors of his own skull," Harold had written. He thought this was his most amusing line in the piece.) Harold had published two other articles after, in smaller Sherlockian magazines. Tonight was his first time at the Irregulars' invitation-only annual dinner. Just to be included among the guests at the Irregulars' dinner was an immense honor—but to be offered membership, at such a young age, with such a small history of scholarship to his name? Harold couldn't think of another Irregular who'd been offered membership this quickly, after only one dinner.

Harold White, in the cheap black suit that hung loosely on the shoulders, in the chicken-stained tie, was in the middle of the proudest moment of his life. He adjusted the plaid deerstalker hat that rested magnificently on his head. The hat was by far his favorite possession. He'd owned it since he was fourteen years old, since he had first become obsessed with Sherlock Holmes and dressed as the famed detective for Halloween. As his love of Holmes grew from childish infatuation to mature study, what had once been a costume prop eventually became day-to-day clothing. He'd worn the hat proudly at his graduation from Princeton, even temporarily sewing a tassel on top for the occasion. As Harold moved from his nervous teens to his tedious twenties, the hat served him well through the cocktail parties, the autumn picnics, the friends' weddings that cropped up more and more often. He had worn it when he accepted his first career-oriented job as a New York publisher's assistant. He had worn it as he separated from his longest-lasting girlfriend, Amanda, about whom Harold never spoke.

The Irregulars' dinner, held this year at the Algonquin Hotel on Forty-fourth Street, fell amid a grand week of Sherlockiana. For four days around January 6, Holmes's birthday, all the world's societies devoted to the celebration of Sherlock Holmes gathered in New York. Lectures, tours, book signings, sales of Victorian antiques and first-edition printings—for a Sherlock Holmes devotee, it was heaven.

Of the hundreds of Sherlockian societies in attendance, however, the Baker Street Irregulars were by far the oldest, the most senior, and the most exclusive. Truman and FDR had claimed membership, as had Isaac Asimov. Only the Irregulars, and their few guests, could attend the annual dinner, and their rare invitations were the object of heated cravings from Sherlockians the world over. The Irregulars were even responsible, as everyone knew, for deducing January 6 as the day of Holmes's birth. Sir Arthur Conan Doyle had never actually written the date January 6 in the "Canon"—that is, the four novels and fifty-six short stories that make up all the original adventures of Sherlock Holmes. But an extensive, Talmudically deep reading of these tales allowed Christopher Morley, one of the founding Irregulars, to propose January 6 as the most likely candidate for Holmes's birthday. All the other organizations were considered "scion" groups of the Irregulars and needed an official sanction from the Irregulars in order to form. Applications for membership in the Irregulars did not exist—if you distinguished yourself in the field of Sherlockian studies, they would find you. And if the leader of the Irregulars deemed you qualified, you would be presented with a shilling piece as a sign of your membership—like the coin, the faded and ancient silver, that Harold squeezed between his whitening knuckles.

The applause dissipated into chatter. Chairs were pushed back from the dining tables, white linen napkins draped across the plates of half-eaten chickens and boiled vegetables. Tumblers of scotch were downed in long gulps. Hands were shaken. Good-byes were offered.

Harold felt suddenly foolish, clutching his shilling. He had fantasized about this moment since he'd first learned of the Irregulars. And now it was over. He wondered what he would have to do next to have this feeling back. He wanted so much to hold on to his successes and not let them fade away into the dull clamor of normal life. Harold watched servers collect the silverware, sweeping the dirty forks and dull butter knives into plastic tubs.

Harold lived in Los Angeles and worked as a freelance literary researcher. His primary employers were movie studios, whose legal departments hired him to defend against charges of copyright violation. If an angry novelist sued the makers of the summer's biggest action blockbuster, claiming that they had stolen the idea from his little-read political thriller of twenty years back, it was Harold's job to write a brief saying that no, in fact *both* works took their basic plot elements from a lesser-known Ben Jonson play, or one of Dostoyevsky's difficult short stories, or another work that was similarly obscure and similarly in the public domain. Harold's name was well used and well lauded in the legal departments of the studios, except in the rare cases when they would sue one another.

Harold's main qualification for this position was that he had read everything. He had simply read more books—more fiction—than anyone else whom either he or his employers had met. This had been accomplished, at his age, via an acute ability to speed-read. As a child, as he ploddingly read through the pages of every Sherlock Holmes mystery, his desire—his animal need—to know what happened next posed a problem: It took him longer to get through the stories than he could bear. So he taught himself to speed-read from a mail-order self-help book. His fellow students would tease him about this ability, as they found it unthinkable that anybody could read a four-hundred-page novel in two hours and still have any significant amount of information retention. But Harold could. And he would prove it to them, reading books alongside his peers and letting them quiz him about plot elements and descriptive passages. Sure enough, Harold retained more information, more quickly, than anyone he had met at his grade school in Chicago, in his college years at Princeton, or in his adult life since.

"Harold!" came a deep and resonant voice from behind. A set of hands squeezed Harold's shoulders. He turned and looked up into the face of Jeffrey Engels. A snow-haired Californian with a nearly permanent grin etched into his cheeks, Jeffrey was easily the best-liked and most respected Sherlockian in the room. Harold suspected that it was Jeffrey, in fact, who had campaigned for Harold's investiture in the Irregulars. But he knew better than to ask, as Jeffrey would never tell him, one way or the other.

"Thank you," said Harold.

Jeffrey ignored Harold's comment. His usual grin was gone, replaced with a dour stare.

"This affair has taken a grave turn," said Jeffrey quietly.

"To what?"

"To murder!" replied Jeffrey.

CHAPTER 3

The Final Problem

*"You know a conjuror gets no credit
when once he has explained his trick."*
—Sir Arthur Conan Doyle,
A Study in Scarlet

September 3, 1893

Arthur killed Sherlock Holmes by the light of a single lamp.

Encased behind the heavy wooden doors of his study, Arthur wrote quickly. The oil lamp atop his writing desk glowed pale yellow over the book-lined walls. Shakespeare, Catullus, even, as Arthur would admit freely, Poe. His favorites were all there, but Arthur rarely consulted them. He wrote confidently. He was not the sort of writer who spread his sources across his desk like bedsheets, clinging to them tightly, consulting, soiling, pinching. *Hamlet* lay on its shelf—third from the bottom, a quarter of the way around the room clockwise from the door—and if, when Arthur quoted it for another pithy aphorism from Holmes, he quoted inaccurately . . . well, such was fiction.

Murder tasted sweet on Arthur's lips. He salivated. His pen, heavy between his stubby fingers, did not scratch the paper. It stroked the pages, filling each one top to bottom with black ink. The plot, the confounding little puzzle of tricks and then treats, had been worked out well in advance.

At this, the middle point of his career, Arthur was unquestionably

England's great composer of the mystery story. Indeed, as the States had failed to produce a mystery author of any caliber since Poe had invented the form, Arthur thought it not unreasonable to say that he was the most accomplished in the world. There was a trick to mystery stories, of course, and Arthur wasn't embarrassed to admit that he knew it. It was the same trick practiced by a thousand amateur parlor magicians and face-painted circus jugglers: misdirection.

Arthur laid the facts of the crime before his readers clearly, calmly, and efficiently. No important detail was left out, and—yes, here was the mark of the true craftsman—not too many unimportant details were left in. It's an easy feat to confuse the reader with a mountain of unnecessary characters and events; the challenge, for Arthur, was in presenting a clean and simple tale, with only a few notable characters to keep straight, and yet still to obscure the solution from the reader. The key was in the prose, in the way the information was laid out. Arthur kept the reader's mind on the exciting, exceptional, and yet fundamentally *unimportant* facts of the case, while the salient details were left for Holmes to work upon, as if by magic.

It was a game for Arthur, putting together these plots. It was he against his audience, the writer locked in endless combat with his readers, and only one would emerge victorious. Either the reader would guess the ending early or Arthur would confound him to the final page. It was a test of wits, and a war that Arthur did not often lose.

Why, of course, if the reader were smart enough, he could figure the whole thing through after just the first few pages! But in his heart Arthur knew that his readers didn't really *want* to win. They wanted to test their wits against the author at full pitch, and they wanted to lose. To be dazzled. And so Arthur's struggle was long, and moreover it was bloody exhausting. He had come to realize that putting together a decent mystery was an infernally tedious affair. And, his having labored at this mill for some years now, the tedium had engendered in him such a hatred for Holmes as he could no longer contain. Now his hatred extended beyond just the rat-faced detective: It carried over to the readers who adored him so. And now thankfully, at last, in his final Holmes story, Arthur would be done with them all for good.

Late as the hour was, Arthur heard the rambunctious banging of children upstairs. He could hear, faintly, the maid Kathleen telling them to hush up before they woke their mother. Touie would be sound asleep by now, as she had been most of the day. Her consumption was not much worsening, but the clean Swiss *föhn* had done little to improve her health. She rarely left the house. Journeys into the city were simply out of the question. Against her frailty, though, Arthur had become determined. He would take care of poor, dear Touie, his bride since she was nineteen. And if they should have to keep separate bedrooms, for her health, and if nannies would be required to look after the children, and if she had now wilted into the winter of her own private quarters...well, so be it. Arthur would write. He had liked to keep regular, daytime hours for his work, but tonight was different. Some writing one had to do in the dark.

Arthur's pen did not hasten as he moved on to the final page. He made the same broad strokes he always had. The words came to him, first in his head—the orderly noun, the clarifying verb, the occasional but welcome adjective—one by one, and he dutifully recorded them onto the darkening sheet. He did not go back over his sentences once they were on the page. He did not scratch out words, like his good friends Mr. Barrie and Mr. Oliver, endlessly replacing them with their freshest *mot juste*. Such was the mark, Arthur felt, of an indecisive hand. He did not consult his previous paragraphs for where to go next. He simply knew.

His fingers were steady as he came to the last bit of his story. A letter from beyond the grave, to be opened after its sender had passed on. "The best and the wisest man whom I have ever known," Arthur wrote. A fitting tribute; a fine farewell. He placed a light period after "known" and turned the sheet onto its predecessors. He carefully pressed the stack into a tidy, perfect rectangle and flipped the pages over. "The Final Problem," read the title at the top of page one. *Indeed*, thought Arthur. And then, queerly, he smiled. He even allowed himself a chortle, as he was alone. Without his wife, or his children, or even his mother knowing, Arthur was, for the first time in years, finally free.

He stood. He stumbled happily to the door. And then— Oh! He'd almost forgotten.

Arthur practically skipped back to his desk. What had come over him? You'd be excused for thinking he was a love-struck teenager, on his way to call on his *amore*.

Arthur unlocked the bottom-left drawer beneath his desk and removed one dark, leather-bound book from a stack of many. He opened the book and flipped through to the bottom of a page already quite filled with his ink. He plucked up his pen and recorded the date. And then, though most evenings Arthur would spend an hour recording all the day's events and all of his most private thoughts, tonight he committed only two words to his diary.

"Killed Holmes," he wrote.

Arthur felt light. His shoulder muscles loosened. He closed his eyes and inhaled the dark air. He was so happy.

He was careful to lock his precious diary back in the desk before stepping out into the hallway in search of brandy.

CHAPTER 4

The Lost Diary

*"Watson here will tell you that I can
never resist a touch of the dramatic."*
—Sir Arthur Conan Doyle,
"The Naval Treaty"

January 5, 2010, cont.

"To murder!" repeated Jeffrey Engels for emphasis, back in the Algonquin Hotel.

Harold paused. Something was very wrong here.

"The affair has taken a grave turn? To murder?" Jeffrey said again, with a touch of hesitation.

Harold laughed. "The quote is from 'The Adventure of the Six Napoleons,'" he said. "You owe me a drink."

"Well done!" Jeffrey beamed. "So I do."

"But I think you owe me two drinks. The quote isn't quite right. It should be 'the affair has taken a *very much graver* turn,' not 'a *grave* turn.'"

Jeffrey thought for a moment.

"My, you've been invested in the Irregulars all of two minutes and look at you! Picking nits at an old man already. Well, very well. I'll keep you in scotch until dawn at this rate."

Harold had initially encountered this Sherlockian quotation game at the very first meeting he'd attended. Four years ago, before he had written anything for the *Baker Street Journal* or met any of the Irregulars, he found himself at the meeting of the local Los Angeles "scion" society, the Curious Collectors of Baker Street. They were a small group, considerably less prestigious than the Irregulars. Meetings were open to the public. In an oak-lined bar, over glasses of peat-smelling scotch—all Sherlockians seemed to think that ice cubes were made from poison and were therefore to be distrusted, as far as Harold could tell—they called out quotes from Sherlock Holmes stories. One member would holler a quote—"'I never guess. It is a shocking habit, destructive to the logical faculty,'" for instance. Then the man or woman to his right would have to provide the name of the story from which it came—in this case *The Sign of the Four.* If he answered correctly, it would then be his turn to yell out a quote, and then the turn of the Sherlockian to his right to supply the answer. Whoever erred first would find the next round on his or her tab. Given most Sherlockians' fondness for high-quality scotch, and for voluminous quantities of same, new and inexperienced members would find their American Express cards pressed to their limits.

"It's my first night as an Irregular," said Harold. "And my guess is, you're more than a little responsible for that. I think I'm the one who owes you a drink."

Jeffrey's grin returned. "I haven't the faintest idea what you're talking about, kid. Now let's make use of the bar."

A few minutes later, Harold sat on the stool beside Jeffrey, sipping bourbon. A group of revelers had staged a nonviolent coup over the bar's piano and were sing-chanting an old Sherlockian ditty. The bartender regarded them with equal parts disapproval and bemusement.

"To all our friends canonical / On both sides of the crime / We'll take the cup and lift it up / To Holmes and Watson's time," sang the drunken group, to the tune of "Auld Lang Syne." It was both off-key and arrhythmic, though Harold had to admit that he wasn't sure he'd *ever* heard a Sherlockian song sung with much regard for proper pitch.

Harold and Jeffrey were soon talking about the diary, which Harold suspected was all anyone was talking about that night. The singing and drinking were a distraction, but there was really only one thought haunting the minds of the hundreds of Sherlockians in the Algonquin Hotel: the lost diary of Sir Arthur Conan Doyle. The lost diary that had finally been *found*.

After Conan Doyle died, one volume of his diaries had gone missing. The author had kept a detailed daily diary of his activities for his entire life, and yet when his wife and children surveyed his papers after his death, one book was strangely not present. No worn, ink-drenched leather journal for the period from October 11 through December 23, 1900, could be found. And in the century that had passed since that day, not one of the hundreds of scholars and family members who had tried to find it had been able to do so. The lost diary was the holy grail of Sherlockian studies. It would be worth a fortune—perhaps as much as $10 million, if it ever went up for sale at Sotheby's. But more importantly, it would provide a window into the mind of the world's greatest mystery writer, at the height of his powers. For a hundred years, scholars had theorized about what was in the diary. A manuscript for a lost story? Some secret confession from Conan Doyle? And how on earth had it vanished so completely?

Three months before the dinner at the Algonquin, each member of the Irregulars had received a tantalizingly brief e-mail from Alex Cale, a fellow Irregular. "The great mystery is solved," it had read. "I have found the diary. Please make all necessary arrangements that I might present it, and the secrets contained within, at this year's conference."

It was a delicious mystery, even for Alex, who had a particular fondness for this sort of drama. Quickly, a flurry of e-mails skittered across the globe: "Is he serious?"..."He can't mean THE diary, can he?"... "He's been looking for that damned thing for twenty-five years; he only just found it NOW?" The Baker Street Irregulars reacted with incredulity only to buffer themselves from their forthcoming shock; the next three months would see them through stages of exhilaration, anxiety, twitchy anticipation, and, from some darker corners, jealousy.

Alex Cale was already the most accomplished of the Sherlockians. It was difficult to argue that he was not the world's greatest expert on Sherlock Holmes, though the Irregulars boasted more than a few experts who might be inclined to disagree. But of course, his rivals had said, of course it would be *Alex Cale* who found the missing diary of Arthur Conan Doyle. With his money. With his free time. With dear dead Daddy's seemingly never-ending trust fund behind him.

And yet the question currently foremost in the minds of Harold, Jeffrey, and the hundreds of other Sherlockians drinking, laughing, sleeping, or, less commonly, making love in the Algonquin Hotel was this: Where *had* Alex found the diary? And how had he found it?

After his initial message, Alex stopped responding to his e-mails. He returned no phone calls. He answered no letters, even though the craft of old-fashioned letter writing had always been one in which he'd taken some pride. Finally, after a number of attempts at communication from Jeffrey Engels, Alex wrote back a message. If one could even call it that.

"Am being followed," Alex wrote to Jeffrey. "Will update soon." It had the clipped syntax of a telegram, and as a result Jeffrey couldn't tell whether Alex was joking or whether he was losing his mind. He forwarded Alex's message around, and the consensus was that Alex was having a little too much fun with all of this, taking the fantastical mystery a bit too far. Certainly the diary would be valuable, but who— what shadowy figure—would trail Alex around his London home? Cale must be teasing, they thought. Though Harold, prone to fantasy as he was, harbored fears. Was it possible that someone really *was* trying to hurt Alex Cale?

"My best guess?" said Jeffrey. "It's a story. A lost manuscript. Conan Doyle must have decided it was garbage and hidden it away. He wouldn't have wanted anyone to find and publish his subpar work."

"Maybe," said Harold. "But Conan Doyle published a lot of material in his life. And look, not to be blasphemous or anything, but they're not all gems. 'The Lion's Mane'? 'The Mazarin Stone'? I mean, really."

Jeffrey laughed.

"I always took the view that Conan Doyle didn't even write those awful late stories himself. They don't quite sound like him. But the diary is from the fall of 1900. He was preparing to write *The Hound of the Baskervilles*. Probably his best work, if you ask me."

"Yeah," said Harold. "I'm not sure... I just don't think it's a story, for some reason. I think it's..." Harold drifted off. He felt silly saying this out loud.

"It's...?" prompted Jeffrey.

"I mean, that it's... That the diary has a secret in it. Something he didn't want anyone to know. Something he wrote down for himself. And only himself. He was a writer. He was a devout diarist. He liked to put things on paper. It's therapeutic. But then he didn't want the world knowing whatever is in that thing."

Jeffrey's phone went off. The sound was somewhere between a squeak and a beep. He looked at the screen and, motioning an apology to Harold, answered his phone.

"Yes?" was all Jeffrey said, and then, after a moment, "Thank you." Harold looked at him quizzically.

"So you think there's a secret in that diary?" said Jeffrey. "Well then, kid, why don't we find out?"

Harold was still just as confused.

"That was the concierge," continued Jeffrey. "I told him to contact me as soon as Alex Cale checked in." He smiled again, pleased with himself. "Cale is in the lobby. Want to go solve a mystery?"

Harold narrowly avoided knocking his drink over as he jumped up from his stool.

He bounded out of the wide double doors like Holmes on the trail of Professor Moriarty. Jeffrey, still smiling, followed into the radiant lobby.

Alex—Jeffrey was right, that was actually Alex Cale signing his name for the desk clerk—wore a thick trench coat, buttoned to the top, and held a heavy-looking briefcase in his right hand. He transferred the case to his left hand while he finished with the hotel forms. Effete but friendly, Alex was the kind of man who hosted as many parties as he attended and who had a knack for making sure that everyone was satisfied with a drink at even the parties for which he wasn't responsible. Harold had met Alex at previous Sherlockian events, and of course he'd known Alex's name almost as long as he'd known the name Sherlock Holmes, but he did not know him well.

"Alex, my old friend, you're here!" bellowed Jeffrey. Alex turned but didn't seem entirely happy to see the two men heading toward him.

"Gentlemen," said Alex quietly. His accent—English—was rare among the Irregulars, most of whom were American. Alex neither set down the case nor moved to embrace his two colleagues in any way. He stood there like a wet paper towel, damp and used. A storm must have kicked up outside. Harold hadn't noticed. Alex's pupils were wide, as if from lack of sleep. He seemed to gaze right past them.

"Where have you been all week, you old dog? We've missed you. Yesterday we had the most marvelous talk from Laurie King about the Woman—her role in the Great Hiatus, all that. Fascinating."

"Sorry I missed it," said Alex with obvious insincerity. He must know, thought Harold, that they did not want to talk to him about any of this. They wanted to talk to Alex about what everyone wanted to talk to Alex about: The diary. Tomorrow's lecture. The solution to a hundred-year puzzle.

"Who are you?" asked Alex. He didn't even bother to look Harold in the eye as he said it.

"Harold. I'm Harold White. I was just invested in the Irregulars tonight." Harold reached out for a shake, but Alex made no move to take his hand. "We actually met once before. In California. You were at UCLA, giving a talk?"

"Right, yes," said Alex. "I remember. Pleasure to see you again." Alex clearly did not remember, nor did he seem particularly pleased.

"They get younger every year, don't they?" said Jeffrey warmly.

Harold tried not to take offense.

"I'm not really that young," countered Harold. "I've already—"

"Do not turn around," said Alex abruptly.

Harold was confused. "I'm sorry?"

"Do not turn around," repeated Alex. Both Harold and Jeffrey were facing away from the hotel's front doors, though both instinctively started to cheat their heads to the side. "There's someone outside. Through the window. *Do not turn*, what's-your-name—Harry?—what did I just say to you? Now, I'm going to shift slightly to my right. Yes. Now you two do the same. Yes. Again. Can you see anyone? There at the window?"

Harold tried to move his eyes without moving his head, which gave him a slight headache. He saw thick waves of rain batter the tall windows. He saw dull streaks of white light on the glass from the streetlights across Forty-fourth Street. He did not see anything like a face in the window, peering sinisterly into the lobby.

Harold was confused, and he was becoming concerned as well— though for Alex's sanity rather than for his safety. Jeffrey did not appear to see anything untoward outside the hotel either, and he seemed equally uncertain about how to respond.

"C'mon now," said Jeffrey. "Quit putting us on. Come and let's have a drink. You can tell us about your adventures."

Alex either ignored or didn't hear him, searching the rest of the lobby in quick, sharp glances.

"Tell us what's in the diary," Jeffrey continued. "Please. Give us a sneak peek, before tomorrow."

Alex stared at Jeffrey for a silent moment. He appeared genuinely confused.

"You really want to know what's in this diary?" said Alex.

The question was so simple, and the answer so obvious, that it took them a few moments to respond.

"Yes," said the two men, in approximate unison. For the first time, Alex made eye contact with Harold. The effect was unnerving.

"I wonder if you do," said Alex. "When you're presented with a problem, it's only natural to want to know the answer. But if you think you can manage to sleep tonight, then sleep on this: Is the mystery sometimes more pleasurable than the solution? Are you sure that finding out what's in this diary will be as satisfying as forever wondering about what's in this diary?" He stepped back, away from them, switching his briefcase from one hand to the other. He pulled it to his chest, tapping it lightly with his free hand. "I suppose you'll see tomorrow, then."

As Alex walked quickly away across the hardwood floor, Harold noticed the line of wet footprints he left in his path. The shoe-shaped puddles quickly streaked and pooled, their original shape lost into a thin watery sheen.

From around the lobby, Harold could hear murmuring. Sherlockian heads were turning. Wait, was that just Alex Cale, standing there? The man with the briefcase? But before anyone else could approach him, Alex disappeared into an elevator.

"Jesus," said Harold. "What do you think he meant by that?"

"That by this time tomorrow," answered Jeffrey, "we'll have solved the last great mystery of Arthur Conan Doyle."

CHAPTER 5

Mourning

*Petty thefts, wanton assaults, purposeless outrage—to the man who
held the clue all could be worked into one connected whole. To the
scientific student of the higher criminal world, no capital in Europe
offered the advantages which London then possessed.*
—Sir Arthur Conan Doyle,
"The Adventure of the Norwood Builder"

December 18, 1893

Arthur emerged from the orange glow of the Charing Cross Station
into the dry Christmastime cold. Despite being well into winter, London had experienced little snowfall. Thus everyone expected a huge
storm any day now. The cold bashed against Arthur's long coat, wheedling its way into the sleeves, slipping between the laces of his leather
shoes, poking at his earlobes, and, after a few moments, painting the
tops of his ears blush red.

In the second week of this snowless December, Arthur's murder—
and he thought of it as such in no uncertain terms—of Sherlock Holmes
had become public. "FAMED DETECTIVE PERISHES," blared the
headline in the *Times*. Arthur was embarrassed by this supreme foolishness. The dolts even printed an obituary for the man. *An obituary
for a fictional character.* In a newspaper, no less. It was sign enough,
thought Arthur, that things had indeed gotten out of hand with the
fellow. Ending it was clearly the right thing to do. He was a nuisance,
and the good people of London would be better served by some higher

fiction. At least, at last, the madness would die down. Some new adventurer would pop up from the pages of the *Strand* and onto the national stage; perhaps it would be that Raffles character, the one Willie Hornung had been writing about. Sherlock Holmes would be forgotten in a year's time. Arthur was sure of it.

Two and a half years earlier, Arthur had moved from his cramped quarters in Montague Place to a lovely suburban four-story, eight miles away in South Norwood. He certainly didn't miss the noise, or the streetwide bustle you had to mash against each time you left the house. But he did miss walking past the British Museum each day, idling along the great stone wall that enclosed the museum in a squared-off letter U. He had occasionally taken the long way about, peering into the gaping expanse of gray stone as the wall opened to reveal a forest of Ionic columns beneath a simple architrave. The cornice above was so wide and thin that when Arthur glanced at it, he always thought it was as if the clouds above formed the right hand of God, pushing down on the museum, pressing it deeper into the soil of Britain.

South Norwood was nonetheless an improvement. One didn't have to choke through the city smoke every day—"London saves a man a fortune on tobacco," he would joke to Barrie, who would laugh kindly—and it was only a few minutes into Charing Cross by train. He bought a tandem tricycle for himself and Touie, who managed the exercise very well. They could cycle fifteen miles before dinner, if they got started right after tea. The house even had room for Arthur's sister Connie, after Arthur and the Mam put an end to her gallivanting in Portugal. She made an excellent governess for Roger and Kingsley, Arthur's children, the latter of whom was still, at one year of age, no bigger than a throw pillow.

Arthur left the mall in the center of the street, heading south, away from the Charing Cross Hotel. He passed a one-legged news vendor, who shook the day's papers at him. They did not make eye contact.

A line of cabs creaked and rattled along the Strand. The horses made grumbling noises in the cold, like old men, tired and cantankerous.

Boys flitted about delivering notes in all directions at once. The smooth lines of the three- and four-story buildings that bordered the avenue were abutted by bright red "TO LET" signs, offering rooms above the telegraph office, above the shops, above the solicitors' long row. Arthur turned his back to Trafalgar Square and strolled.

The suburbs were a treat, of course, but Arthur missed the city. He loved coming into town for his errands, which he would perform leisurely. He would soak up the city's energy, its squealing and squawking, and then return with a full belly to Norwood. To Touie. To his tricycle.

He was content in this moment. He even swung his stick as he made his way a few paces along the Strand. He would have been in the mood for whistling had he been the sort of man who whistled. It was a fine morning.

"YOU BRUTE!" an old lady shouted as she struck Arthur's head full force with her handbag, bruising his nose and knocking off his hat. Arthur stumbled, unhurt but considerably shocked. She could not have been under sixty years old if she was a day. Her body was hunched, shoulders right above the tips of her toes. She looked more frail than anything else. It wasn't quite clear from where she summoned up the strength to hit Arthur. She wore a thin black armband over her dark coat as if she were in mourning. He stammered.

"I...madam, I...I'm sorry, have I...I've offended you in some way?"

"YOU MONSTER!" she barked before taking aim again with her bag. Heavy, it made a long, slow arc against the sky, the blue of the bag standing out against the thick cloud cover. Aware at least of her presence this time, Arthur stepped back, avoiding the blow. He raised his stick for a moment, assuming a defensive position, and then felt mortified enough to set it back on the pavement. He was an athletic man. He couldn't very well raise his walking stick against a confused, elderly woman.

"Ma'am, I don't know who you think I am, but I assure you I've never met you before in my life."

A page boy stopped his hurried running to take in the scene. He was joined by a tall gentlewoman in a fashionable hat, who carried her sun umbrella outstretched despite the cloudy, wintry day. One turned head led to another. A crowd began to grow.

"I know full well who you are, Dr. Doyle, and don't think I don't know what you've done." Arthur was less confused by her double negative than by her use of his family name. Arthur was not used to being recognized, even though there had been photographs of him in the papers last year. David Thomson had taken a very nice one of Arthur writing at his desk for the *Daily Chronicle*.

Arthur could hear a mumbling emerge from the gathering crowd. "Doyle...Doyle...Doyle..."

"I'm sure I don't know what you're on about," he pleaded. He looked toward the crowd for support, for confirmation of his own sanity against the madness of the crone. Below their twittering jaws, Arthur saw that many in the crowd wore identical black armbands. A whole city in mourning. He could swear on the Holy Book that he'd seen today's papers... Was there some sad news that he'd missed? The passing of some great statesman? Cecil was old, to be sure, but not so old that... Well, the Queen Mother? No, no. Surely he would have heard!

"You killed him, you killed him just as I'm standing here," hissed the old woman.

"Why'd you do it?" barked someone—it could have been anyone—from the crowd.

"I killed...?" sputtered Arthur as the horrible, unthinkable thought appeared behind his eyes. "You don't mean to say that you're angry because I—"

"You killed Sherlock Holmes."

At first Arthur was purely dumbfounded. He didn't speak, didn't move as the old woman whapped him again across the midsection. A few members of the crowd, to their credit, suggested that she stand down, though others were more concerned with Arthur. They wanted an answer. There was none to give.

Arthur's cheeks swelled with rage.

Two months earlier, in October, his father had died in a mental hospital in Crichton, about eighty miles south of Arthur's childhood home in Edinburgh. Charles Doyle's lunacy, combined with his drink, had kept him from ever being close to his elder son. For years Charles had sent Arthur mail from the asylum. Arthur would tense up when he saw the scribbled envelopes on his doorstep, with their telling postmark: Dumphries. His father never sent proper letters, only drawings. Macabre portraits of himself, of Arthur, of animals. Fairies mingling with enormous insects. Grotesquely large centipedes riding cruel, dark blue jays. News of his father's passing initially brought a certain relief. But as Arthur rarely went to visit, he didn't learn until after Charles's death of the detailed log his father had kept of Arthur's achievements. Charles had clipped reviews of each and every one of Arthur's novels and kept them in a scrapbook on which he'd sketched scenes of his family around the table, in the kitchen of their old Edinburgh two-story. The Mam, who despite the alcoholic fits and mad ravings had remained loyal to her husband, found the book among Charles's things and sent it to Arthur without comment. It was only then that Arthur realized what he'd lost. Did Papa even know, before he died, that Arthur was married? That Arthur had two children? That the second child was born premature and spent two months swaddled in the hospital before Arthur took him home?

A week after Charles's death, dear Touie spent a long afternoon with the family doctor. At the end of their meeting, the doctor slowly descended the steps from Touie's second-floor bedroom to tell Arthur that the cough in her lungs was incurable. Tuberculosis. She would be gone within months, most likely. The man was courteous and effortlessly professional, which only compounded Arthur's shame. A medical man himself by training, and yet his own wife had lain stricken with tuberculosis for years and Arthur had thought it nothing but a natural weakness after the birth of their son. His shame threatened, on some days, to overpower his grief. There would be more rides into the country on their tricycle. Arthur would pedal harder. Every trip mattered.

Charles Doyle was real. Touie was real. Their deaths were tragedies. Sherlock Holmes was a bit of imagination. His death was a petty amusement. The old chattering woman and the growing crowd behind her did not know about Arthur's father—they didn't even know his name. The death of Charles Doyle did not merit a single sentence in the *Times*, the *Daily Telegraph*, or even the *Manchester Guardian*. Touie's illness would remain a secret for years. No, these people—these wretched, detestable people—knew nothing of Arthur. They knew only Holmes.

Arthur remained mute to the abuse until a nearby constable meandered over.

"Go along, now, go along," he instructed the crowd, with more understanding than belligerence in his voice. They complied, though the old woman cursed Arthur's name with every breath as she walked away. The constable—short, slim, professional—retrieved Arthur's hat for him.

"Thank you, sir," said Arthur, his consciousness returning to his surroundings.

"Don't you worry about all that, Dr. Doyle," said the constable. "I think you gave old Mr. Holmes a right fine farewell. Just a pity to see him go." And with a tip of his cap, the constable walked away.

Chapter 6

... *Until Now*

The world is full of murderers and their victims;
and how hungrily do they seek each other out!
—Commonly attributed to Ambrose Bierce,
perhaps apocryphally

January 6, 2010

Harold entered a second-floor reception room of the Algonquin Hotel to the sound of ducks in heat. The assembled Sherlockians were quacking at one another in anticipation. They were also "assembled" only in the sense that they were in fact all within the same four walls. They guffawed, hollered, and called to their friends like a rabble. They did not possess even a semblance of assembly.

Hundreds of Sherlockian luminaries were in chairs, though none really sat: To Harold they seemed to vibrate about an inch above their seats. They hovered, inquiring of their neighbors for rumor with sharp torques from side to side. Harold caught the scattered nouns from a half dozen different chatterings: "late," "Alex," "missing."

On his way to an open chair, Harold poked the shoulder of an older English attendee whose name he couldn't remember. The woman turned, her tight gray hair spinning round to reveal glasses thicker than one would think a woman could get away with wearing. Somehow she did.

"Is something up?" asked Harold, trying to seem both nonchalant and not hopelessly uninformed.

"Alex is late," she said quickly. "There was an attempt to ring his room, but the phone is off the hook. He's gone missing."

"Jesus," said Harold.

He thought of Alex's nervousness the night before. Of Alex's belief that he was being followed. It couldn't be...

A small, youngish woman whom Harold didn't recognize sat down to his left. As she turned, a wave of her curly brown hair swept to the side and Harold saw her eyes, opened wide as if taking in the world were a constant act of discovery. Her light blue dress made her appear to be a bit younger than she probably was. She wore a pink and yellow banded scarf around her neck, making her look, for a second, like an unwrapped bonbon.

"Gosh, what a commotion!" she said. Was she speaking to Harold? Her head faced forward as she continued scanning the room.

"Yeah," said Harold, too quietly.

She turned to face him, and the sharp eye contact startled him a bit.

"Excuse me," she said with a friendly tone in her voice. "Did you say something?"

"I...umm, yes. Yeah."

"Sorry, I didn't hear you with all the noise in here. What did you say?"

"Yeah."

She paused. "Yeah?"

"Yeah, I said...Yeah. As in, yes, there's quite a commotion. In here."

She looked at him for a long moment, sizing him up.

"Right," she said. She turned away again.

Harold blushed. Then he started saying things, as was his compulsion. He had a terrible habit, when he became nervous and didn't know what to say, of saying a few unrelated things in rapid succession, as if hoping that at least one of them might take hold.

"Did you come here for the lecture? I'm Harold. Is it still raining out? Harold White."

The woman raised her eyebrows in thought; she was probably trying to figure out which of Harold's prompts to respond to.

"Harold," she said. "Do you know Alex Cale?" Apparently she'd chosen none-of-the-above.

"We're friends," he replied, excited to have somehow begun the conversation with what for him was a solid subject. "Well, we're friendly. I saw him last night. In the hotel."

"He was here last night?"

"Yes. He got caught in the rain." Harold chided himself silently for continuing to focus on the rain. He was sure there was something more interesting he could say to this woman. "He seemed nervous, actually. Said someone was following him. But you know— He's got a flair for the dramatic."

The woman looked up at Harold's deerstalker hat. She gestured to it with her right eyebrow.

"It looks to me like you both do. Do you think someone was following him?"

This was a difficult question. It was probably the most difficult question she could have asked.

"No. Maybe. I mean, wouldn't that be fantastic? Well, not fantastic, not if something bad happened, but…noteworthy. You know what I mean." Something about her just made Harold want to talk—and keep talking. It was an appealing trait. A handy one for a…*journalist*?

After Alex Cale had announced his discovery, those months before, the Baker Street Irregulars had received a deluge of requests from reporters looking to attend this January's convention. Well, "deluge" by Sherlockian standards. Professional Sherlock Holmes obsessives tended not to garner much attention from the media. But they still had firm rules about this sort of thing—no one who was not a member of an accredited Sherlockian organization was allowed to attend the weekend's lecture. All requests were denied.

"Excuse me," said Harold, interrupting himself. "Who are you?"

"Sarah Lindsay," said the woman buoyantly. "Nice to meet you!" She extended her hand for a shake.

"Which organization are you a member of?"

29

"Oh, none," she said. "I'm a reporter. I'm doing a story on Alex Cale and the missing diary."

"How did you get in here?"

In response Sarah shrugged. "Jeffrey Engels," she said. "We e-mailed back and forth for a while, and he let me in."

Harold thought this was a little strange—if Jeffrey had decided to make an exception for Sarah, wouldn't he have mentioned something about it?

"He's such a sweet guy, Jeffrey," she continued. "Are you an Irregular, too?"

"Yes." Harold realized that he had already spilled every secret he might know about Alex—his odd behavior last night, his paranoia. Sarah would make Alex, and the Irregulars, look like fools. She would mock their bits of period costuming, their occasionally self-serious lapses into indecipherable scholarship, their "flair for the dramatic," as Harold had just said. He made a nervous face.

"Are you worried about my being here? You don't need to be, I promise."

"No, I...I don't know what you're talking about. It's just, we have rules about reporters. Strangers of any kind, actually. I didn't—"

"Harold, it's okay. What were you worried about? That I'd tease you about your hat? Or those little pipes that half of the men here are carrying in their coat pockets?"

Harold smiled. She was funny.

"Look," he replied, "we're at a Sherlock Holmes convention. If I *wasn't* wearing a deerstalker cap, don't you think that would be a little weird?"

"Very. If you're going to be an expert on nineteenth-century detective fiction, I say you should dress the part. But aren't you a little... *young* to be an Irregular?"

"I might be the youngest Irregular, but I know this stuff as well as anyone."

"I believe you," she said. "And I might just ask you to prove it."

They were interrupted then by a sound from the front of the room. At the podium, Jeffrey was testing the microphone.

"Yes. Testing. One-two, or some such. Yes? You can hear me? Good." Jeffrey took a deep breath and spread some notes out in front of him. "Ladies and gentlemen, while we wait for the belated appearance of this morning's honored guest, Alexander Cale, let me say a few introductory words. I'd planned to go through this once he'd arrived, but I'm sure Mr. Cale doesn't need to hear yet another recitation of his exploits, or to bide his time while I make still more saucy jokes about a particular evening of drink we shared in Sussex many summers ago."

There were a few giggles throughout the room, and more knowing chortles.

"It's a funny story," Harold explained to Sarah. "There was a poorly planned late-night visit to the stables."

"When Sir Arthur Conan Doyle passed from this consciousness to the next, as he would have put it, on July seventh, 1930, he left behind twenty-eight novels, well over a hundred short stories, seven books of essays on spiritualism, four memoirs, and, of course, a voluminous collection of letters and diaries, which immediately fell into the care of an eager network of scholars. From his letters and diaries, we've gotten to know a Conan Doyle quite different from his public persona: We've seen him as the eternal schoolboy, ever imagining himself to be a knight-errant jumping to the defense of helpless, hapless maidens. We've seen him as the conflicted romantic, embroiled in a passionate mental affair with a younger woman—which from all evidence never became physical—while his invalid wife slowly passed. And we've seen him as jealous creator, raging against his brightly shining creation in page after page of broad, precise script. With this wealth of material, scholars have been able to piece together a fine variety of excellent biographies." Jeffrey leaned forward. "That more than a few of these scholars happened to be members of this august institution is a small matter in which I personally take some great pride. Andrew Lycett, John Dickson Carr, Martin Booth, and, perhaps most definitively, Daniel Stashower have all crafted masterful portraits of John Watson's friend and literary agent."

Sarah made a curious face. "Friend and literary agent?"

"Yes, welcome to Jeffrey being politic," whispered Harold. "Most Sherlockians sort of…uh, *pretend*…that Holmes was real and that Conan Doyle had his adventures published as fiction to preserve his privacy. The rival Doyleans, as they call themselves, think the Sherlockians are stupid. If Jeffrey acknowledged Doyle as the *author* of the stories, half the room would bleat blasphemy. Better to side with the Sherlockians. The Doyleans are less prone to rebellion."

"It's a good thing I didn't come to make fun of you," said Sarah.

"…was a testament to Stashower's work in putting together the most detailed account of Doyle's life and times that we've seen," continued Jeffrey. "But a truly complete biography of the man has always remained out of reach. His diary from October through December of 1900 was not among his papers, all the rest of which were found neatly arranged in his study at Undershaw after his death. Rumors circulated, of course, that various of his children might have hidden it away somewhere, to sell privately. But no substantiation for such claims ever materialized. Indeed, beyond a few quickly unmasked forgeries, there has been no trace of the diary over the past eighty years." Jeffrey paused, took a deep breath, and smiled. "Until now."

The room erupted in applause. Jeffrey said it again triumphantly, for effect: "Until now! Mr. Alexander Cale, known to many of you personally, and known to all of you professionally as an unparalleled Sherlockian scholar and critic, has been on the hunt for this diary for over twenty years. He has made it his life's work to solve Conan Doyle's final mystery. And recently he has done so. He is here today"—and with that, Jeffrey looked behind him, to see if Alex had come in; he had not—"to present the disappearing, reappearing diary to us and to unburden it of its secrets. Foremost, of course, are why this diary wasn't among the others and where has it been hiding all this time? But perhaps even more profoundly for the future of Holmes studies is the question of what Conan Doyle had gotten up to in this brief period.

"Our gap in knowledge occurs just after Conan Doyle returned from South Africa, plying his medical trade among the wounded British soldiers in the Boer War. Ever the patriot, Doyle had done a tour as a medical doctor and, in the summer, returned to England to convince his countrymen of the justness of the British cause. He ran for Parliament in Edinburgh, his hometown, and lost, narrowly. He was focused on politics, on his historical novels and plays. Sherlock Holmes had been dead for seven years, and according to everything we know of Conan Doyle, his presence had not been missed by the great writer.

"Then, suddenly, in March of 1901, we have a letter received by H. Greenhough Smith at the *Strand* magazine. Conan Doyle wanted to serialize a new Holmes tale, set before his death. This story, 'The Hound of the Baskervilles,' marked a new high point in the Canon. Next came a short story that would drive London wild: 'The Adventure of the Empty House,' set in 1894, brought Sherlock Holmes back to life. In it we learn that Holmes had faked his own death in 1891 to foil Moriarty's henchmen, traveled the world anonymously for three years, and was now back to set things right. This magical, perplexing interlude in which Holmes was in exile, presumed dead, we call, as you know, the Great Hiatus. But we know much more of Holmes's activity during this Hiatus than we do of Doyle's. What great change had occurred in him that would move him to bring Holmes back? He certainly had no need of money, though publishers had been banging at his door for another Holmes mystery. So why just then? And why so suddenly? Why return to the mystery stories—to the 'cheap penny dreadfuls,' as he'd call them—and to the hero for whom he felt, we must acknowledge, no little antipathy? It is at this moment when we would most like to peer into the mind of Conan Doyle that his thoughts are closed to us. Until now."

"Didn't he say that already?"

"Shhh."

But there wasn't much more to hear. Jeffrey looked behind him one final time, confirming that no, Alex had not in fact entered the ballroom. As the ducks began to quack again, Jeffrey turned around, back to the podium, allowing his calm to massage the room.

"Ladies and gentlemen, it seems we now have a fresh mystery on our hands!" There was a smattering of chuckles and smiles around the room. "If you'll pardon the further delay, I shall commence the investigation at once."

Before Jeffrey had even stepped off the dais, a fresh gaggle of chatter had washed over the room. A handful of excited Sherlockians stood and then realized they had nowhere to go. Harold recognized Satoru Ishii, the quiet head of Tokyo's largest Sherlockian group. He stood at full attention near the front of the crowd, practically bursting from the need for something to do.

"Well, it looks like you have some excitement for your story," said Harold to Sarah. Only, when he turned, Sarah wasn't there. Perking up his head, he whipped around to see her click-clacking across the slippery wood in her clunky flats. Her brisk walk was aimed unmistakably at Jeffrey, who, ever polite, was trying to back his way out of the room and fend off the rowdy queue of Sherlockians all waiting to ask him the same questions.

Harold was not conscious of making the decision to take off behind Sarah. He would tell himself, later, that he did so in order to be useful to Jeffrey—it wouldn't do to have her pestering him with her questions just now—but in truth Harold had a distinct urge to be useful to *her*.

Facing the emboldened horde of inquiring mystery enthusiasts, Sarah quickly changed course and slipped quietly out between the solid doors. Harold gingerly maneuvered down the aisle, tiptoeing between the feet of a woolly-bearded German before stretching across the lap of a petite, professorially tweeded American. Harold's quiet excuse-me's and sorry's added little to the general clamor.

As he shimmied between the closing doors, the corridor beyond seemed shockingly silent. There was no sign of Sarah.

Harold didn't see her at any point along the labyrinthine hallway or in the bustling lobby into which it fed. But there, by the elevator bank, he glimpsed her hair bobbing in between the opening elevator doors. Harold was in—of all things—hot pursuit.

Accelerating, he was at a near gallop by the time he got to the elevators. There was a curious sensation in his calves, shooting up to his knees. Thinking it over, he believed, not from any recent experience, that that must be called "running." He huffed and puffed his hand between the elevator doors just in time, and delighted at the satisfying *ding!* he heard as the doors began reopening.

"Are you following me?" she asked.

Panting, Harold stepped into the elevator and steadied himself on the golden railing.

"Deep breaths," she added. "You'll be okay."

"We…humph…we should…humph…back downstairs…hunnnh," was about all Harold could manage in response.

"Well put." Faced with Sarah's implacability, Harold decided to gather himself before again trying to dissuade her from heading upstairs. But as his breathing slowed, another mechanical *ding!* announced their arrival on the eleventh floor. Sarah made her way through the bright padded corridor, and Harold followed suit.

Arriving at the door of Room 1117, Sarah gave two quick, friendly raps near the eyehole. A "Privacy, Please" sign hung from the doorknob. They waited.

"How did you know what room he's in?"

Sarah smiled. "I asked politely."

She rapped again, perkily. "Alex?" she said, as if nothing were at all the matter. Harold joined in.

"Alex, it's Harold White! Are you awake?" Again the door gave them nothing in return. Harold stared at the privacy sign, and it seemed to stare back, taunting him with its bland efficiency.

As the stillness became, to Harold, increasingly disconcerting, he heard a shuffling down the hallway. Harold and Sarah turned to see a man in a dark suit. Jeffrey followed a pace behind the man, as Harold had followed Sarah. *He must be the hotel manager,* thought Harold.

"Who are you?" asked Jeffrey of Sarah.

"Hi," she replied. "I'm Sarah Lindsay. We e-mailed back and forth, about this weekend."

Jeffrey made a sour face. "We did," he said. "And I remember telling you, in no uncertain terms, that you were not permitted to attend today's lecture. What are you doing here?"

In response Sarah simply smiled.

"Reporters," said Jeffrey. "Can't take no for an answer, can you?"

She turned to Jeffrey's companion. "There's no answer at the door, Jim." The man didn't reply but merely stepped forward next to Sarah and gave the door his own series of firm knocks.

"Mr. Cale?" he said. Another long, uncomfortable pause. "Mr. Cale, this is Jim Harriman, I'm the Quality of Stay Director at the hotel."

Harold supposed that this was another way of saying "manager."

"Your friend Mr. Engels tells me you're late for an appointment, so I'm going to come in there to make sure nothing's the matter. Mr. Cale?" Still nothing. Jim removed a bar-coded electronic key card from his wallet and slid it in and out of the lock.

"If you'll all excuse me," said Harriman, his hand waiting on the knob.

"Come on now," said Sarah. "These are his friends. If something's the matter, maybe they can help."

Harold couldn't help but notice that there was no mention of her own role in this.

Harriman examined Sarah's earnest face and looked to Jeffrey for a reaction. He didn't find one. The manager thought for a moment, then pressed the hook-shaped doorknob down.

Harold felt a coldness begin in his shoulder muscles and shiver down his back, tingling all the way to his toe tips and newly frigid fingers. Even before the hall light jumped into the dim gray air of the room, he knew. Something was wrong.

When his eyes adjusted, Harold saw the disheveled dresser, its drawers yanked out and overturned. He saw the tipped-over lampshade and the dark splotches of what must be dress shirts on the taupe carpet. He saw the half-open closet door, the pile of clothes hangers on the floor, the fanned-out papers sprinkled like snowflakes.

Harold stepped inside, behind Sarah, Jeffrey, and Harriman the manager. The stiff-legged four moved almost in unison.

"Alex?"

"Alex."

"Al…ex…"

"…Alex." They each took turns calling the name, as if the word itself would make him appear. It became a chant, a round, and an incantation.

The mess accentuated the smallness of the room. The heavy blinds were shut tight, locking in the darkness. Harriman stepped through a narrow entryway past the bathroom door and the closet, toward the dresser against the wall on the right, and the wooden desk in the far corner. Ahead to the left, the room appeared to blossom out in open space—the bed must be in that direction.

Harold watched Jim slow down midstep as he turned the corner, then watched as Jeffrey did the same. Jeffrey's brow furrowed and shook with his head, as a slight tremor reverberated through the older man's body. Sarah stepped beside Jeffrey, turned, and inhaled sharply. Her face was blank, smoothed into soft focus by the darkness.

Harold looked down for a moment and steadied his nerves before taking his next step. Coming to a stop behind Sarah as he turned, he subconsciously crouched down an inch. He peeked over Sarah's shoulder—she suddenly seemed so tall.

His gaze started at the unmade bed and the pillows unsheathed from their cases. It moved to the nightstand and the khaki-colored hotel phone, the receiver off the hook, the red message light blinking in a long rhythm, roughly at the pace of Harold's breath. Then to the lounge chair and matching ottoman, soiled with more scattered paper, a pair of work pants, and a few books. And finally, then, to the floor, and the dead body of Alex Cale.

CHAPTER 7

The Bloodsucker

"[He is] a loyal friend and a chivalrous gentleman,"
said Holmes, holding up a restraining hand.
"Let that now and forever be enough for us."
—Sir Arthur Conan Doyle,
"The Adventure of the Illustrious Client"

December 18, 1893, cont.

London had become an alien land for Arthur, full of strange people going about their strange ways. He felt like Captain Nemo, adrift from civilization and surrounded by monsters. As he tumbled through the rest of this perverse day, eyes seemed to trail him all the way down the Strand, even into Simpson's, where he stopped for his dinner. Inside, they flicked at him from every dim corner as he ate his kidney pie and read the papers. He flipped through the *Times'* back pages to find that even London's cartoonists had drawn their share of blood. A crudely rendered image showed a young boy reading the final Holmes tale, his face contorted in grief and disillusion. Arthur was now accused of shattering a generation's childhood.

He sputtered at the drawing and spilled a droplet of kidney juice onto the paper. The hot beefy broth blotted out the face of the young boy, smudging the ink and distorting his features. The child's skin turned brown. Curiously, Arthur took his spoon, scooped up another helping, and after pushing two peas and a mushy carrot sliver back onto the plate, he dribbled a few more drops of hearty brown juice onto the newspaper. And then a few more. And then a whole spoonful, until the cheap, soggy paper wrinkled and tore from the liquid.

Arthur glanced around Simpson's to see if anyone had witnessed his petulant antics. No one had. Or everyone had, and they were presently gossiping in angry whispers about him. It was impossible to tell.

On the streets, Arthur wobbled through his errands. His solicitor. The pharmacy. There was some vital shop he knew he'd intended just hours before to visit but whose identity he could no longer seem to recall.

A mystifying sensation of loneliness shook him. Arthur had been alone before, to be sure, but to be alone while surrounded by people, the one sane man in a mad place—*that* was loneliness. Of course there had been in his years long bouts of solitary hours. In the first—very well, the only—years of Arthur's medical practice, he logged interminable afternoon after interminable afternoon in his bright, empty office. He would sit at his cheap desk, waiting in vain for patients to arrive on his doorstep. So he made use of the time by writing stories: a long novel called *The White Company* and a handful of short tales that marked the first appearance of a certain consulting detective. They were such pleasant trifles then—his brooding, cantankerous detective and the oblivious, dim-witted assistant. Holmes was too cold-blooded, too remote for Arthur to become attached to him. But Watson! Well, Watson one could come to love. *He* was Arthur's stand-in, not Holmes; it was Watson who shared the author's biography, the author's voice, the author's hotheaded romantic afflictions. Watson was the one he would miss now. But hunched over that desk with his stories, Arthur had never, in all that time he spent patiently hoping to hear the sound of the visitor's bell, been this alone.

He made his way to the Lyceum Theatre and stepped across the long shadows etched onto the cobblestones by the Lyceum's six tall stone columns. It was dark under the broad portico, as the roof shielded Arthur from the late afternoon. It felt warmer in the shadows.

"My, my," crowed a ghostly voice from behind. "You look a fright. Has someone died?"

Arthur turned. A thick, wide-shouldered man emerged from the third pillar back, materializing into the sunlight like a spirit made flesh. His beard was cropped tightly to his cheeks, his unfashionably short hair pasted across his scalp from a deep part far to the left. He wore coat and tails, and shoes of such deep black that they sparkled directly into Arthur's eye. He was dressed for a state funeral—or, more likely in his case, for opening night. After a few seconds had passed and Arthur had recovered from the shock, he recognized his old friend.

"Bram," said Arthur with a deep, steadying inhale. "You gave me some start."

"My deepest apologies," said Bram Stoker as he came forward to shake Arthur's hand. "It's only that you look so pale—I almost didn't recognize you."

"Do I?" Arthur leaned against the freezing Lyceum wall. "It has been . . . It has been a curious day." The great center door to the theater opened suddenly, and a radiant woman bounced onto the portico.

"At six, then?" she called to Bram, her frizzy brown hair shaking free at the sides of her cap as she trotted down the steps. She gave Arthur a smile and a knowing raise of her dark eyebrows.

"Six," responded Bram firmly. The woman—Arthur could not help but admit that she was indeed quite handsome—continued on to the Strand. Just before she merged into its pace and disappeared in the crowd, Arthur caught a glimpse of a black mourning band round her arm. He ground his teeth together.

"You must remember Ellen Terry," asked Bram after she was out of earshot. "I'm sure you've seen her on the stage a dozen times."

"Oh. Yes. Of course. Certainly, yes."

"The woman's going mad with this Juliet." He grinned. "Henry's getting all the press with his Romeo, and the poor girl's a bit starved for attention. Mind you, not that Henry's press is good enough for him either."

This was typical conversation for Bram. His life consisted of placating the raging egos of the actors in his care as manager of the Lyceum—especially Henry Irving, whom Bram managed personally.

As Irving got older, he became more dictatorial in his manner, and ever more vain in his person. At fifty-five, he was perhaps long in the tooth to take the stage as Romeo, but he would hear none of Bram's objections. When the reviews came in—Arthur had read them, of course— and Bram's position was vindicated...well, that only served to further enrage the aging actor. Bram was a dutiful servant, who'd been in thrall to his master since the day they'd met, though Arthur suspected that his friend had not known a happy moment in the fifteen years since he'd accepted this position.

Bram had always wished to be a writer. That was the issue, Arthur felt. That accounted for the very slight bitterness he'd occasionally find in his friend. Underneath the burdens of his thankless, spirit-wearying job, Bram held firm to a passion for the literary life that he rarely shared publicly. He would wake early in the mornings. Before heading to the Lyceum to solve the day's budgetary crisis and flatter Irving until he grew sore in the throat, Bram would scribble such macabre and fantastical stories—truly bloody stuff—and then squirrel them away in a drawer. He showed some to Arthur only once, and Arthur was shocked by the violence Bram could commit only in fiction, and only in secret. On an occasional evening of drink, Bram would describe for Arthur his work on a longer piece, a perpetually half-written novel of undead ghouls and some bloodsucking count from the Continent. For a man so meek and—dare he say it?—sinfully effeminate, Bram had quite a heart for the grotesque.

They'd met two years earlier, when Bram had bought a play of Arthur's, a one-man show for Henry Irving to perform. Over the long nights of rehearsals, and the still-longer nights of burgundy after the play had gone up, they'd become fast friends. Irving was a pompous buffoon, but in this gentle manager with a hidden drawerful of ghost stories, Arthur had found someone who understood him. And just because the man's yarns hadn't netted him more than a halfpenny over the years, while at the same time Arthur had become financially quite comfortable, that was no reason for any tension between the two.

"Do you have a moment?" asked Arthur.

"For you?" replied Bram. "Always. Now, what is afflicting you?"

"I hate him!" Arthur barked suddenly.

Bram laughed. "This is your Holmes we're talking about?"

"I hate him more than anyone! If I had not killed him, he certainly would have killed me. And now these . . . these people act as if the man were *real*, as if I'd murdered *their* father, *their* wife." Arthur spoke faster, the anger welling up inside him. He began ranting to Bram about the unfairness of it all, about how Holmes had distracted the public from better things, about the myriad ways in which, once loosed, the creation begins to dwarf its creator. Arthur's breath puffed into the frigid air like smoke from a pipe.

Finally Bram began to laugh, the sound somewhere between a cackle and a feline meow. Arthur stopped, derailed from his anger.

"I hate him," Arthur repeated.

"You're the one who tossed the poor sod off a cliff," said Bram. "Imagine how he feels about you!"

CHAPTER 8

The Darkened Room

"You know my methods. Apply them!"
—Sir Arthur Conan Doyle,
The Hound of the Baskervilles

January 6, 2010, cont.

In the darkest corner of a darkened room, all Sherlock Holmes stories begin. In the pregnant dim of gaslight and smoke, Holmes would sit, digesting the day's papers, puffing on his long pipe, injecting himself with cocaine. He would pop smoke rings into the gloom, waiting for something, anything, to pierce into the belly of his study and release the promise of adventure; of clues to interpret; of, at last he would plead, a puzzle he could not solve. And after each story he would return here, into the dark room, and die day by day of boredom. The darkness of his study was his cage, but also the womb of his genius. And when into that room—

Harold shuddered, and his thoughts snapped back from such fancies to Room 1117, to his sneakers on the plush carpet, to Sarah's shoulder a hairsbreadth from his face, and to the dead body not ten feet in front of him.

Alex Cale's corpse—and to merely glance at it was to tell it could not be anything other than a corpse—was pressed, like dough, into the carpet. He wore a black two-button suit, his wide black tie only slightly undone. He looked, to Harold, perversely like an undertaker. Except that his shoes were off and resting neatly by his side, revealing thin dress socks that almost matched the black of his suit. Was he dressing when he was killed, getting ready to lace his shoes?

Harold stepped forward, past Sarah, toward Alex. Despite the hundreds of blood-soaked stories he had read, Harold had never been in the presence of an actual dead body before. It was both more and less shocking than he might have imagined. The lifelessness of a man Harold had known—not well but at least in the flesh, so to speak—watered his eyes, and forced him to bite the inside of his lower lip. And yet the sensation of standing straight-backed and alert above the scene of the crime felt shamefully natural.

"I'm calling the police," said the manager. He reached for the phone on the nightstand and then stopped abruptly, his hand an inch from the receiver. The blinking red message light gave his face a demonic glare. He thought better of disturbing the scene. "Please don't touch anything," he said with unexpected force, before slipping out of the room, off to the house phone in the hall.

"Let's go," said Jeffrey, his eyes glassy and wet.

Harold knew that a smart man would quietly walk out the door this instant, head bent low with the gravity of death. A normal man, even, would defer to the police and await news of their investigations in the coming morning papers. A sane man would, under no circumstances, approach the dead body of Alex Cale.

Harold stepped forward.

"Harold, no." The strain in Jeffrey's voice was manifest.

"What would Sherlock Holmes do?" asked Harold. He was deliriously earnest. He had to do this, he had to see if he could.

"Holmes would crawl back onto the page from which he came, because he's made of ink and pine-tree pulp."

"If he were real. If the stories were real. What would he do?" Harold couldn't help his curiosity.

"Harold, this is sick. I will not be a part of this."

"Search the floor for footprints! That's what he does. In the very first Holmes story, *A Study in Scarlet*, the first act of detection he ever does is to examine the ground for footprints."

"It's carpeted," responded Jeffrey.

Harold looked down. Indeed, the entire floor was covered in a plush, taupe carpet. There were no footprints in sight. Sherlock Holmes was not real. Harold was not a detective.

"But Holmes always finds footprints," pleaded Harold. He couldn't stop himself.

Sarah looked at him with a mixture of wonderment and stupefaction.

"You're serious," she said with a growing smile. Behind her raised eyebrows and open mouth, Harold could see her mind flying in a thousand directions at once, working out the angles.

"You can't be serious," said Jeffrey. "This is deranged. You're a literary researcher, not a goddamned detective."

As Harold's eyes swept from Jeffrey to Sarah, desperate for support, he caught a brief glimpse of himself in the tall mirror that hung on the back of the open bathroom door. He saw his own dirty sneakers and the dead body behind them. He followed his straight spine to the deerstalker cap on his head. Harold paused for a moment, transfixed by the image.

He looked at Sarah as if he were a small child, hoping for even the slightest approval.

"What's the second thing Holmes does?" she asked.

Harold and Jeffrey stared at each other for a long moment, Harold daring Jeffrey to say the answer out loud.

"Don't," Jeffrey said firmly. "Damn it, don't you dare."

"'Sherlock Holmes approached the body, and, kneeling down, examined it intently,'" Harold quoted.

He leaned over, bending from the waist like a ballet dancer. Alex's left eye was almost closed, but his right eye was opened surprisingly wide, more than Harold thought normal—though, truth be told, what exactly was normal supposed to be here? Alex's bushy light brown hair squatted on his head like a chicken laying an egg, an impression made stronger by the near-translucent whiteness of his face. He still wore his millimeter-thin titanium glasses, unbent and unbroken. A rainbow of red-purple streaks wrapped around his neck, swirling with tiny color variations and forming an impressive impressionist bruise. Hanging loose around the purple neck was a slender black cord. It appeared soft, like cloth. Harold dropped to one knee to examine it, and only then did he finally catch the light scent of feces circulating in the air. From the body, Harold thought. As he died.

"What's that around his neck?" asked Sarah as she knelt by Harold's side. She both repudiated Jeffrey's caution and encouraged Harold's examination.

Harold peered closer and reached out to touch the cord.

It felt, on his fingertips, like cotton, and as he ran his hand along it, he found a plastic tip clasped to one end.

"It's a shoelace," said Harold. As Sarah reached out to feel it herself, Harold looked over at Alex's shoes, which sat symmetrically by the side of the body. Sure enough, the left shoe was without a lace.

"It's *his* shoelace," said Harold.

There is an undeniable exhilaration in the moment of even the smallest discovery—the house keys unearthed from the deep pockets of yesterday's pants; the mysterious recurring tinkle you hear as you fail to fall asleep explained, upon examination, by the dripping bathroom faucet; the digits of your mother's old telephone number recalled, magically, from some moss-covered Precambrian mental arcadia. The human mind thrills at few things so much as making connections. Discovering. Solving. Harold quivered all over.

"What did Holmes do next?" Sarah asked.

"Don't encourage him!" barked Jeffrey. "The police are coming. And they will have real detectives. With real tools. This is a murder scene, Harold—you can't just go on touching things. Holmes didn't have fingerprint analysis, but we do."

"Good point," said Harold thoughtfully. "But Holmes did pretty well without it, didn't he? Nowadays we've got CSI teams and electrostatic print lifting. But New York City's murder clearance rate is…what, sixty percent? I think Holmes did substantially better, don't you?"

"This is *insane*," pleaded Jeffrey. "You're in shock. Fine. Alex is dead and you're in shock. But don't you dare mess up this crime scene so the real police can't find the killer. They'll be here any minute."

"You're right," responded Harold. "They'll be here soon. We'd better examine the room before they get here and trample over everything. In *Scarlet*—well, gosh, in half the stories—the police come in and make a mess of the place, obscuring all the real evidence. We don't want to miss any clues."

"Do you hear the words you're saying, Harold? Do you have any idea what you sound like?" Jeffrey grunted out a deep breath. "I never wanted to tell you this, but you have always looked stupid in that hat. Take it off, and let's go."

Ignoring him, Harold moved to the far left corner of the room and, proceeding from the exact intersection of the two walls, began a systematic search of the room's edges.

"Sarah, we don't have a lot of time. Will you look around for the diary? I don't think we'll find it—the killer seems to have gone through the room thoroughly and presumably found what he or she was looking for."

It's not that Sarah didn't need to pause to consider whether or not she should actively displace the contents of a capital crime scene—she did. It's that her pause lasted only a subatomic fraction of a second, a quantum period of decision making. In what seemed to Harold to be an instant, Sarah was among the strewn papers, picking them up in piles and gauging their importance.

"What does the diary look like?" she asked.

Harold considered. "Leather-bound. Old. It'll be the thing that looks like a hundred-year-old diary."

"I thought Holmes spoke in aphorisms, not tautologies."

"I think it'll be pretty obvious when you see it, all right?"

The stray papers that Sarah found contained little of interest to the amateur detectives—pages 709 through 841 of Alex Cale's unfinished Conan Doyle biography, which, by the looks of things, would have been impeccably thorough in its completion. She picked up an antique fountain pen from beside the body and held it up for Harold to see. It

was a Parker Duofold "Big Red" model, probably from the 1920s—
black on the blind cap, red on the barrel. It was the same model that
Conan Doyle would have used to write the final Holmes stories.

She found a handful of hardbound books as well: a complete collection of the Holmes tales, dirty and frayed from overuse and almost
solidly blue with marginal notes from the antique pen. Nearly every
paragraph had words underlined or scrawled exclamations in the margins. She found Cale's briefcase beneath a low chair, and when she
pulled it across the carpet, Harold recognized it from the night before.
It was already open. And empty.

As he searched the floor, Harold adopted a rodent's-eye view of the
area where the taupe carpet met the off-white wallpaper, below the vertical streaks of *fleur-de-lis* patterning that provided most of the wall's
decoration. He reached into his coat pocket and removed the magnifying glass that had previously found use only as a finger toy when he
became nervous or bored.

At the sight of Harold with his glass, Jeffrey shook his head in shame.

Harold began a methodical examination of the hotel room's walls. He
could see puckers in the wallpaper through the lens, as every uneven-
ness in the paper's application to the drywall seemed to pop out like a
series of sand dunes. What was Holmes looking for, when he searched
through that fateful Lauriston Gardens house in his first case? That
room had been dilapidated, dust-covered, and mildewy from years of
inattention. Holmes dug through the dust and shone bright match light
into the darkest corners, discovering the word "*RACHE*"—the German
for "revenge"—written in blood at the bottom of the wall in an empty,
unused portion of the room. But, thought Harold, sensational though
such a clue might be, what was Holmes looking for when he found it?
You couldn't expect a *real* murderer to conveniently leave you a message explicating his motivations, could you? Stepping back, all Harold
saw here was clean hotel wallpaper and freshly vacuumed carpet. He
couldn't possibly hope to find a clue as dramatic as Holmes's, after all;
there would be no bloody messages here. He was being responsible in

his expectations. But Holmes's method—that would work. It simply had to. So what the hell was Harold supposed to be looking for?

Harold's search swung, inch by inch, 180 degrees across the room, to the wooden desk and chair. The top of the desk was a mess of papers and pens—whoever ransacked the room seemed to have been particularly concerned with making sure no lost diaries had been hidden in the hotel's "Guide to Your Pay-Per-View Channels." Harold pushed the chair away and crawled under the desk, continuing his examination. The darkness underneath made this difficult, however, so he reached up and brought the overturned lamp from the desktop to his assistance.

He flicked it on and pointed its bulb at the wall.

Then he dropped it, his body ricocheting as he gave a start. The bulb shattered, rousing both Sarah and Jeffrey from their thoughts and sending them rushing to Harold's side. What they saw at first appeared to be a small, murky, dark stain on the bright, clean wall. Then, as they knelt beneath the desk, they began to make out red-brown letters, messily scrawled above the carpet line, as if by finger painting. No magnifying glass was needed to read the still-drying message.

"ELEMENTARY," it read.

It was written in blood.

CHAPTER 9

Sensational Developments

*"You don't know Sherlock Holmes yet... Perhaps you
would not care for him as a constant companion."*
—Sir Arthur Conan Doyle,
A Study in Scarlet

October 18, 1900

The letter bomb in Arthur's mail did not go off as planned.

Some ten minutes prior to the explosion, he settled down to breakfast by the latticework windows. Gray fall light came through the nine
square glass panes. On days like these, the strips of white wood that
separated the glass seemed brighter to the eye than did the window
light. Arthur dug into his eggs and tomato.

Seven years had passed since the death of Sherlock Holmes. Seven
years of stories, adventures, and a new life Arthur had constructed for
himself far away from his old one. He had left London for Hindhead,
and he had left Holmes for better things. This was the life of which
he'd always dreamed.

He had built this house, named Undershaw, three years earlier.
It was grand then, and as the years passed, it grew grander still. The
estate had the air of a carnival about it. There were great stables, which
attracted friends from the city nearly every weekend; dear children and
distant relatives always scampering around hither and yon; a fireplace
fit for a Hindu bonfire; a dark, quiet billiards room in which Arthur
had already lost games to Bram and James Barrie. The new landau, had

for 150 pounds plus the pair of horses to power it, was having the family crest painted on by the staff. Indeed, Arthur made sure to include the Doyle crest on as many elements of his new home as possible. It reminded him of where he'd come from and of the pride he felt in where he'd arrived. Amazing, really, to think of what a man could achieve with the simple ability to put pen to paper and spin a decent yarn. The house bought on make-believe; the house that a penny dreadful built.

Seven years, and Sherlock Holmes remained blessedly buried below the waters of the Reichenbach Falls. Yes, people still spoke of him. Yes, people—strangers—still wrote of him, discussed him, missed him, and begged for his return in letters to the editors of every magazine in which he'd appeared. But not here. No one dared speak of him in this house. The name Sherlock Holmes was not to be uttered out loud in Arthur's presence, nor in the opulent home for which the detective had paid.

Five minutes before the explosion, Arthur left the breakfast table and went to retrieve the day's post from the small mahogany table near the front vestibule. It was a task he enjoyed performing himself. As he walked the halls of his estate, he felt a pleasant moment of contentment. A small army of children and their attendants rampaged upstairs, trotting heavily between the eight bedrooms. Outside, the stable master fed Brigadier, Arthur's own horse, an eight-year-old of strong Norfolk breeding. Through the front windows, Arthur could see the tall pines rising above his three stories. Perhaps later this winter they might acquire one from the nearby woods for a drawing-room Christmas tree.

He scooped up the morning's postal stack in the crook of his arm and made his way to his study for the inspection. He opened the letters quickly. There was a kind note from Innes about the elections, which he appreciated, though Arthur would have preferred not to think on them. He had run for Parliament in Edinburgh over the last months on a largely anti-Boer platform. When he had returned from the front earlier in the year, Arthur had written a history of the war, from the British perspective, as well as many a pamphlet urging his fellow citizens to support the military effort. Then he had run for office, thinking that his pro-war views would be manifestly useful at Westminster. His platform, aside from a promise to defeat the Boer insurrection at all costs, contained a plan to raise tariffs on foreign foodstuffs imported into Britain that could as easily be produced locally (wheat, meat), while lowering tariffs on imported foodstuffs that could not be locally manufactured (sugar, tea). This plan had failed to rally the electorate in his favor, and he had been drawn into a rather public debate on the tense issue of women's suffrage. Arthur had not intended to campaign on this point, but he was a committed antisuffragist, and when asked, he refused to duck the issue. After exaggerated rumors of Arthur's Catholicism were spread across the district on cheaply printed bills, he lost his hometown seat by a few hundred votes. Rather than fight the slander that he was a papist stooge, Arthur retreated back to Hindhead, and to fiction.

The second letter he opened came from H. Greenhough Smith, the longtime editor of the *Strand*. It offered nine thousand pounds for a new series of Holmes stories—a new high bid. Arthur crumpled the letter and deposited it briskly into the waste bin. He would not even reply. *Collier's Weekly*, in America, had offered twenty-five thousand dollars for the American rights to the same. Arthur, in a show of gentlemanly restraint, simply ignored both requests rather than commit the reasonable response to paper and direct both men to hell.

He had just written two new Brigadier Gerard stories. Where was the demand for them? (The horse he had named for the character, not the reverse.) No matter what feat he accomplished in his life, this Holmes would always be there to drown him in those bloody, sordid adventures which the public—feeble muffs!—so craved. Arthur caught himself and took a few slow, deep breaths. He would not let thoughts of Sherlock Holmes into this house.

He would read no more letters just now. A rather large package lay at the bottom of the mail stack. He would open that instead.

Less than a minute before the explosion, Arthur placed the package before him on his desk. Surprisingly heavy, it was wrapped in cheap brown paper and tied with fraying twine. The postmark read Surrey, but there was no return address.

Arthur cut the twine with a satisfying swipe and carefully removed the brown wrapping. Inside lay a black box. Arthur searched for a note, or a card, or a shop's bill, but found nothing at all to indicate the package's sender or its contents.

As he pulled off the lid, he heard the sound of metal scratching metal and then a sharp click. He looked down to find an inch-thick tube of dynamite nestled in pads of crumpled newspapers, like an infant in a crib.

For an instant, Arthur reconsidered his antipapal position and wondered, political slanders aside, whether a relapse into deep and sincere Catholicism might in fact be just the thing he needed.

He stood motionless for a generation, for an eon, for the longest four seconds of his life. There was no explosion. He did not die. As to whether this should provide confirmation for or against belief in the one true church, Arthur was uncertain.

He also did not feel any particular inclination to move, for fear that any shake of the package might restrike the flint inside, setting off the fuse that, at first glance, miraculously had failed to ignite. What little he knew of bomb making—and his knowledge on the topic was quite limited indeed—had come from his time with anti-Boer regiments in Africa. But the letter bomb was not popular among the rebels, and so a method for defusing such lay well outside of Arthur's ken.

He opened his mouth to call for help but then stopped: What if Kingsley heard the cry and came bounding in, or Roger? What if it were one of the maids? It wouldn't do to risk someone else's life to save his own. On that point Arthur was assured.

He peered down into the package, for clues to its construction and thus to the method of its destruction. A short fuse—it must last for only a few seconds at best, thought Arthur—led from a flint at the top to the stick of dynamite. A few other strands appeared to coil around the explosive, but for what purpose he could not be certain. The crumpled papers that padded the stick trembled, and Arthur quickly realized they did so at the quivering of his own hands. His fingertips clutched the edge of the package, but the shaking seemed to start in his shoulders and move in short waves through his body.

He looked closer at the newspapers. Amid the small print, he made out a drawing. Some pictorial demonstration of the article's topic, he thought. Was it a member of the government? A statesman? Arthur pulled the package closer to his face.

The drawing printed on the paper was of a gaunt, bird-faced man in a long cloak, with piercing dots for eyes and a tall deerstalker cap. It was Sherlock Holmes.

The dynamite wasn't padded with newspapers; it was padded with pages from the *Strand*. Pages of a Holmes story. Arthur's fear began giving way to rage.

If it were done when 'tis done, then 'twere well it be done with quickly, Arthur thought, misquoting as usual.

He placed the package down on the side table, and the dynamite rolled slightly to the right.

But rather than causing an explosion, the movement of the dynamite exposed another piece of paper beneath it. An envelope. Sealed, by the looks of it.

Did he dare reach down and take it? He did.

Arthur gently eased the envelope from underneath the heavy stick. He could see that there were words written across the front of the letter but couldn't yet read them. As he pulled the envelope away, gazing upon it as if it were the proverbial sword pulled from the stone, the dynamite settled back down onto something hard. Something metal.

He heard another scrape, and a click. A second flint, hidden beneath the letter, had lit. The fuse that coiled around the stick was afire.

Arthur did what was then the only sensible thing: He turned on his heels and ran, fast as his forty-one-year-old legs could carry him, in the other direction. He made it to the doorway as the bomb exploded. His ears felt as if they were popping off from the sound. Shreds of mahogany splattered across the study. The windows gave way, their white latticework bursting outward and sprinkling glass everywhere. As Arthur collapsed on the floor, on the other side of the open door, there continued smaller crashes from inside, as vases, books, inkwells, and a never-used gasogene fell from their perches.

He heard an approaching clamor from all directions, his household running to find the cause of so great a disturbance. He dared not look back to see what had become of his study.

Rather, still on the floor, his body tense from the shock, Arthur looked at the envelope safely preserved in his hand. Though crumpled and a touch sweat-smudged from being clutched in his palm, the single word scrawled across the front of the sealed envelope was quite legible.

"ELEMENTARY," it read.

CHAPTER 10

The Applied Science of Deduction

"Crime is common. Logic is rare."
—Sir Arthur Conan Doyle,
    "The Adventure of the Copper Beeches"

January 6, 2010, cont.

Harold did his best to ignore the Sherlockians arguing around him. As the timbre of their voices rose, in both volume and pretension, he focused more intently on the three ice cubes in his lunchtime bourbon. He watched their sharp corners round out as they melted. He shook the glass, splashing fresh liquor up and over the cubes, before taking another long sip from his drink. It was noon somewhere.

The two men behind him stood and pointed their accusatory forefingers at one another. Elsewhere in the hotel, similar arguments formed as the fault lines of every long-standing tension within the organization began to give way. Harold was far from the only attendee to fancy himself an amateur detective on a day like this one. The bar was crowded with theorizing Sherlockians, who in the absence of any actual evidence had created grand machinations to explain the crime. Minor points of canonical disagreement became reasons for brutal murder. Some tried to piece together their theories in small groups, hoping that with enough brainpower and expertise they might arrive at a solution. Others jumped straight over the "investigation" phase and landed square at the end of the story they were creating, instantly accusing the man across the table of some vile treachery. And, moreover, actually employing phrases like "vile treachery" in doing so. Everyone was a suspect. But at the world's largest Sherlockian gathering, everyone was a detective as well.

For his own part, Harold was brain-throttled, reduced to animal needs (food, quiet, bourbon) and animal sounds (monosyllabic assents, guttural baying). He wanted to go home.

He was terrified. The reality of the death wet Harold's scalp with a hot sweat. He nervously popped dry pretzels from the bar top into his mouth, crunching them loudly between his teeth in an attempt to drown out the surrounding conversations. Harold had long noticed that most people lost their appetites when they were scared or preoccupied. He had wished he were the same way every anxious night he'd gorged himself on air-packed snacks amid a crisis. When he was depressed, he could restrict himself to mounds of coconut frozen yogurt. But when he was nervous, he needed salty, bite-size carb products: chips, Goldfish crackers, pretzels. Usually he refrained from drinking in such situations, but in light of his close proximity, in the recent past, to the cold, pale corpse of a man he'd briefly known, Harold gave himself a break and employed the ten-year-old single-barrel in the steadying of his nerves.

Sarah, appearing out of nowhere, slid onto the barstool next to him and rubbed a comforting hand between his shoulder blades. Harold was not particularly fond of being touched by strangers in general, although in this specific instance he found it kind of pleasurable.

"It's eleven-thirty," she said with a smile, nodding at his glass.

"It's been a long morning," Harold responded. Sarah agreed and asked the bartender for some coffee. She stayed silent until it arrived.

"Were the police rough with you? They can sometimes be a little... gruff, if you're not used to dealing with them."

Harold wasn't sure whether "gruff" was the right word to describe the police who had detained him—"petrifying" might be better. When they arrived at the crime scene and found him examining the unused pillows for hair fibers, they had immediately placed him in handcuffs.

Their thorough, two-man frisking did not turn up any evidence, but it did trigger Harold's apprehension at the touch of strangers. His skin curdled as they slapped their hands against his waist and thighs. They led him, still cuffed, into an empty room down the hallway, where they interrogated him about his relationship to Alex and his discovery of the killer's message on the wall for what seemed like the entire day. As Harold grew flustered and hungry, his answers to their questions became more convoluted, and his habit of overtalking garbled the plain fact that not only had he not killed Alex Cale but that he hadn't the faintest idea who did. Finally, having taken all the information from his driver's license and making clear in no uncertain terms that Harold was not to leave the city until their investigation had been concluded, they released him. He learned, very much to his surprise, that the whole interrogation hadn't taken more than ninety minutes.

"Are *you* used to dealing with them?" Harold asked.

"I worked two years at the *Salem News*, outside of Boston, when I was younger. I was on the crime beat, but at a small paper like that, the crime beat mostly means calling up the local chief of police and asking who'd been arrested the night before. The guy was an asshole—always called me 'honey' in front of the other cops. But there wasn't much I could say about it if I wanted quotes from him. Anyway, you learn to smile and make nice and let them feel like they're in charge—and of course they are." She sipped again from her coffee and turned on her stool to face him directly, forcing Harold by the laws of social convention to turn and look her in the eye. "Are you hanging in there okay?"

Harold was not immediately sure how to answer the question. He wasn't quite hanging in there, and he certainly wasn't okay.

"Do you think I'm really a suspect?" he asked.

"I seriously doubt it. I'm sure they just wanted to teach you a lesson about messing around with crime scenes. They were trying to scare you."

"They pulled it off."

Sarah laughed. "Seems like everyone here has a theory about who did it," she said, gesturing around the bar at all of the arguing Sherlockians. "What do you think?"

Harold had been thinking about this a lot, in fact, over the past two hours. But nothing he'd come to in his head had seemed either promising or even pleasant to think about.

"You know, the word 'elementary,' written on the wall...it's only actually used in one Holmes story."

"Really?" said Sarah. "Isn't it one of those famous Sherlock Holmes quotes? 'Elementary, my dear Watson'?"

"Yes, everybody knows that phrase, but it isn't actually from the original stories. It's from the old movie series, and the TV version with Jeremy Brett. In all the books, Holmes says 'elementary' to Watson only once, in 'The Crooked Man.'"

"Huh."

"It's a very specific quote, from a specific story. It's weird. And the location: In *A Study in Scarlet*, the very first Holmes story, he finds a word written in blood on the wall. In the darkest corner of the darkened room."

"The blood used to write that message upstairs wasn't from Alex," Sarah said. "There were no puncture marks on the body, no cuts. I was able to get that much from the cops."

"It's the same way in the story. The blood isn't from the victim; it's from the killer."

Sarah and Harold thought about this silently for a long moment.

"You're going to figure this out, aren't you?" she said at last. "You're going to solve Alex Cale's murder." She spoke as if it were so obvious, and when Harold thought about it, he realized that it was.

Harold was the youngest Baker Street Irregular since Alex Cale himself. And he would bring Cale back by doing what Cale never could, by finishing what he had started. By providing what Cale hadn't—the *solution*.

Sarah smiled. "There are a lot of detectives in the hotel this morning," she said. "But I think you're right. I think you're the one who's going to figure it out."

Harold was touched—and emboldened.

"I need to know who would do something like this...Who would kill Alex?" he said. "And who would kill someone in such an odd, macabre way and then leave a bunch of clues behind that reference Sherlock Holmes stories?"

Sarah swept her eyes across the room at the bickering Sherlockians. Two women had drawn what appeared to be a diagram of the crime scene on a bar napkin and were gesturing at it to one another insistently, as if to prove their respective points about how the crime must have been committed.

"Someone who's read way too many mysteries," said Sarah.

CHAPTER II

Scotland Yard

*"The authorities are excellent at amassing facts,
though they do not always use them to advantage."*
—Sir Arthur Conan Doyle,
"The Naval Treaty"

October 19, 1900

"Look, now," said the hairy-faced inspector. "It doesn't seem that they was actually trying to kill you, like. Rather more likely they was just trying to give you a good scare there, eh?"

Arthur sighed and tapped his fingertips on the inspector's tiny desk. A bronze nameplate rested atop the desk, proclaiming "INSPECTOR MILLER" in freshly minted block letters. Two vertical pips pinned to the man's collar served to further emphasize the seniority of this stupid bobby's rank.

The main offices of the New Scotland Yard, where Arthur now found himself for the first time, were surprisingly quiet on a Wednesday morning. The building was only a few years old and seemed too spacious for its inhabitants. Arthur could hear the various clomps of uniform boots against the floor, both close by and from the distant lengths of long hallways. They added a gentle percussive accompaniment to this otherwise irritating conversation, like a native tribal instrument, something he might have heard in the Transvaal while searching for Boer raiders.

"It was a bomb, sir, that someone put in my mailbox," Arthur said.

"It took off half my writing desk. You can understand my alarm. My family was at home." Arthur was doing his very best to restrain himself. His evident stupidity notwithstanding, it was Inspector Miller's irritatingly sanguine expression which so riled Arthur. Woolly muttonchop whiskers drooped down the inspector's face, giving him the impression of a crisply uniformed beagle.

"Right so, Dr. Doyle. Right so. We at the Yard will do everything in our power to apprehend the rogue what was behind this here outrage. Trust we won't see a moment's rest till he's been fixed in darbies. All's I'm saying, sir, is that you needn't fret yourself. The bomb was built quite poorly. It did a big pop, sure enough, but it were a simple black powder, with an extra dose of sulfur in the mix. I dare say it was more for smoke than fire, if you catch my meaning."

Arthur had never before challenged a man to a duel, but in this moment he understood the magnificent reasonableness of the tradition. It was either that or slugging him outright this very second, which didn't seem nearly so gentlemanly.

Arthur spoke slowly, in order to contain himself.

"And the accompanying letter? What do you make of that?" He picked the envelope up from Inspector Miller's desk and shook it before the man's face like a Chinese fan. The right edge of the envelope had been torn open hastily by Arthur the day before. Inside, he had found not a letter but simply a clipping from the *Times*, a two-week-old issue. It was a short article on a killing in the East End. "Foul Murder in Stepney," ran the headline. "Bride Found Dead in Her Bath." It described a young woman who'd been drowned in the bathtub of a rent on Salmon Street. A cheap wedding dress lay beside her corpse, though no information about her identity, or that of her possible husband, had been found—save, however, for a strange tattoo on the young woman's body. It depicted a black crow with three heads. As anonymous female bodies found in the East End were not so rare these days, this was not a case that would warrant much attention. Given the location of the body and the presence of the tattoo, in fact, the Yard had easily assumed her to be a harlot and let it go as another sad example of society's Great Curse.

"I can't imagine but someone's having a bit of wretched fun with you," replied Inspector Miller. "I don't see how bringing a dead dollymop to the attention of a man of your stature is much but a twist and a folly."

"Might it not be the case that the murderer of this poor unfortunate, whoever she may be, is in fact the selfsame bomber who so tore up my study?"

"As I was saying, Dr. Doyle, an investigation is well under way. You rest assured that the situation is in hand. I dare say we've got our best people on it." Inspector Miller tugged on the bottom of his coat, straightening his appearance as he stood a few inches more erect. The movement served only to make him seem even more youthful in Arthur's eyes. The inspector's crisp dark suit appeared to be an even size too large for his undernourished frame. He looked more like a child playing at dress-up in his father's clothes than he did a soldier of justice entrusted with shielding society from the depravity of the underworld. If Miller was the best the Yard had to offer, thought Arthur, then the darkness of these crimes would never see the light of justice.

"If you don't mind me asking," continued Inspector Miller, "seeing as how you're here anyway and I'm put in charge of getting to the bottom of your case..." He fetched an old, yellowing magazine from beneath some papers and laid it down so Arthur could see. "Well, my boys, you see, they'd right have my whiskers if I didn't ask you for a signature when I've got you plain in front of me."

It was the December 1893 issue of the *Strand*. "The Final Problem" was the lead story. Arthur had not come face-to-face with a copy of his last Holmes story for a number of years. The feelings aroused in him were great and diverse. A sense of pride, a stiffening in his spine on account of the hard-earned fame that preceded him into Scotland Yard this morning, came first. But this quickly gave way to incredulous irritation, which scrunched Arthur's face inward till his mustache tickled against the tip of his nose. Of all stupidities, at a time like this, *Holmes?* He was like one of Bram's dead-undead—a ghastly vampire who followed Arthur everywhere he went and from whose all-seeing malevolence Arthur could never escape. It was not Arthur's acclaim that excited the inspector; it was Holmes's.

Arthur took the magazine from the desk and held it to his face.

"And oh, now, don't think it queer, but mightn't you write, 'To Eddie, from one detective to another,' if you don't think that's too presumptuous, sir. And then, if you could, sign it 'Sherlock Holmes'?"

That was substantially more than Arthur could bear. He slapped the magazine back onto the desk and reared up on his feet like a horse. Arthur looked and spoke down to Inspector Miller.

"Sir, if you will not treat these crimes with the seriousness with which they are due, then I shall be forced to investigate them myself." Arthur snatched up the envelope and placed it triumphantly in his coat pocket before the inspector could object. "I will deduce the identity of the man who killed this helpless young bride and who nearly succeeded in his attempt to kill me. And I will do it without your help. Good day."

Arthur spun on his heels and huffed to the door.

"Dr. Doyle," the inspector began, hoping that Arthur acted in jest. "We don't know a thing about this dead girl. No possessions, no rings or jewelry. Fellow who runs the inn says she— Wait, I have it here somewhere, I even looked up the file for you." Inspector Miller rummaged amid the papers on his desk until he got ahold of what he'd been searching for.

"He says she'd come in the night before with a tall gent, real skinny. Man didn't say a word. The girl paid their thruppence for the night right away. She gave the name of Morgan Nemain. Ran it out, it's most certainly a fake. Nothing in the room to put a name on either the lady or the gent. Just a dirty wedding dress. Lord knows where that's from. And that odd tattoo, the three-headed crow, which she must've had inked on by one of her customers, you ask me. You know how that sort does. They said it was hardly fresh either, which meant she'd been at it for a while. My man took a drawing of it." Inspector Miller held up a piece of white paper, on which was drawn a replica of the dead girl's tattoo. Arthur saw what first appeared to be a large black splotch, but as he looked closer, the splotch assumed the rough shape of a pitch-black crow, with three heads poking out of its neck. One faced left, one forward, one right. Arthur thought of the photographs he'd seen of American Natives at war, paint brushed angrily onto their skin.

"Plus," continued Inspector Miller, "they say you ought to be made a knight of the realm soon enough, I hear. Do you really want to be getting yourself mixed up in such ugliness? And have you even thought about why someone would want to be drowning an East End tart and then blowing up a right gentleman such as yourself? Then letting everyone know he'd done so? Please. Be reasonable."

Arthur stopped, his hand on the doorknob. The inspector had a point. The plot was very dark indeed. The solution lay dim in the distance, and Arthur had not the slightest idea how he'd find his way there.

"It's a case worthy of Sherlock Holmes himself," said Inspector Miller with a smile.

Arthur thought again of dueling. There would indeed be a fight this day. But not with this foolish inspector.

"No," began Arthur. "It is not a case worthy of Sherlock bloody Holmes. It is a case worthy of his creator."

And with that, he marched out, swinging the door shut and leaving Inspector Miller alone to contemplate what mayhem he'd just wrought.

CHAPTER 12

A Proposal

"My professional charges are upon a fixed scale.
I do not vary them, save when I remit them altogether."
—Sir Arthur Conan Doyle,
"The Problem of Thor Bridge"

January 6, 2010, cont.

"It's not a bloody *mystery*," insisted Ron Rosenberg, slapping a sharp palm to the bar top for punctuation. Harold gave a jolt. Ron had a tendency to throw his wiry arms around when he became agitated. The more dire Ron's inflection grew, the more alert Harold had to be for an errant elbow swipe.

"You're going to pin this on me, and I think we both know exactly why," continued Ron.

"Look," replied Harold, "I'm seriously not saying you had anything to do with this. With the murder."

"Hush!" said Ron, flitting his eyes across the hotel bar. "Quietly. This is between us."

Ron swung his elbows out again, and Harold dodged. Ron Rosenberg was not among Harold's favorite Irregulars, and it was moments like this that reminded him why. Ron was in his forties, though he looked older. Squinting eyes gave his face the impression of wrinkles, and the impeccably tailored three-piece suits he wore every day made him look like an aged banker. Which he was not. Harold vaguely remembered something about Ron's owning a small real-estate firm in

London, though he wasn't sure what kind. Harold was sure, however, that Ron was not the focus of anyone's investigations.

Ron had descended upon Harold a few minutes earlier, after Sarah had left to take a phone call, and had immediately begun professing his innocence. He was growing more animated by the minute, even as he was trying to contain their conversation by pressing in close to Harold's shoulder and whispering angrily. The effect was that Harold felt he was chatting with a bee—ever buzzing and vibrating.

"What are you so worried about?" asked Harold.

"He was there when you found the body, wasn't he? What did he say? I know he talked about me, don't bloody lie."

It took Harold a few moments to figure out whom Ron was referring to.

"Jeffrey? You're worried about Jeffrey Engels?"

Ron scanned the bar again for prying ears. Sherlockians still surrounded most of the tables in groups of three or four. Strains of elaborate conspiracy—hushed with gravity and paranoia—wafted toward Harold and Ron.

"You know that he and I have had our...polite disagreements," said Ron. "And, very well, some of them have not been so polite. But they have been civil, as such things go, don't you think? We're friends. I would fairly call us friends. Do you think he knew Cale was dead already when he gave that introduction this morning?"

Harold was briefly stunned by the last question.

"No," he replied. "I don't."

"You know he had his disagreements with Cale as well, don't you? Yes, right, they gave a good show of camaraderie, but it was rubbish. Jeffrey kept pressing him for information about the diary and about what he would say at his lecture, but Cale was mum. Jeffrey wasn't happy about it, I can tell you that."

"Look," said Harold, "I don't think either of you did it, okay?"

Ron made a curious face. He seemed genuinely surprised to hear Harold say that.

"Really?" he replied. "Because one of us must have."

Harold hadn't known all of his fellow members for very long, but he had known them. And he genuinely liked these people. He enjoyed being with them. He felt like he was almost at home among them. In the exchange of the faded shilling the night before, Harold had almost—*almost*—found a place in which he belonged.

He was surrounded by dozens of his colleagues, his supposed friends, and he was alone. One of them was a killer. Maybe more than one, Harold had to reason, if they'd read *Murder on the Orient Express*. Of course they had. They'd all read the same books. They all knew the same stories by heart—Christie, Chandler, Hammett, on and on, the list would fill pages. How could any of them have done this?

For the first time that morning, Harold felt angry. He was angry with the killer for taking Alex Cale, and for taking the diary, but he was also angry at him for taking the Baker Street Irregulars. What would the group be like now? At Harold's last Sherlockian meeting, in Los Angeles, they had stayed up drinking scotch until 2 a.m. and laughing about that one massive plot hole in "The Adventure of the Solitary Cyclist." They would never do that again. How could they?

No one could be allowed to get away with this. These things meant too much to him—the group, the club, the people. No one would be allowed to let Harold slip back into the loneliness of his life.

He felt the narcissism of his growing anger.

"Why *did* Jeffrey give that speech this morning?" Harold said. His thoughts were moving quickly.

Ron smiled. "That's an excellent question," he said. "Why not hold off until he knew where Cale was? Why start expounding on the issue at hand, to a roomful of people who already knew everything he had to say?"

"It's like Jeffrey wanted to make sure that everyone in the building knew that he still believed Alex Cale was alive."

"Harold, I'm glad you're coming round to my way of thinking."

Harold had to pause at this comment. Coming around to Ron's way of thinking? No. This was not a good omen. If Harold were going to do this—and Harold *was* going to do this—then he would have to do it soberly, reasonably. Paranoid theorizing was too easy, too emotionally satisfying.

"I think we should—" Ron clammed up midsentence. He was staring over Harold's shoulder.

A hand tapped Harold from behind. He turned and found himself staring into the eyes of a handsome man a few inches shorter than himself and ten years older. The man's crisp black eyebrows burrowed down toward his thin feminine nose, making him look at once pretty and serious. He was dressed in a wealthy-casual style: unpressed khakis and a black collared sweater. Harold would later notice his bulky watch, undoubtedly made of real gold, as the man's one obvious nod to ostentation.

"Are you Harold White?" said the man, speaking quietly.

"Yes," replied Harold.

"I'll let you two talk," said Ron, slinking away. Why was Ron retreating? Who was this person?

Harold looked over the handsome man's shoulder to see Sarah at the door of the bar. She was watching them.

"Might we go somewhere and chat?" said the man. "My name is Sebastian." He stretched his right hand to enclose Harold's, while his left came over the top to press down on the handshake, solidifying the bond. "Sebastian Conan Doyle."

Arthur Conan Doyle's great-grandson paced across the soft cream carpet in Harold's hotel room. He intertwined his hands behind him, compressing his shoulder blades, and then folded his arms in front of him sternly. He moved back and forth between these two positions as he spoke.

"Look, it's no secret that Cale and I fought. We've argued publicly about that diary for years, and there's no point in pretending we haven't. He mistakenly believed that it was public property and that when he found it, he could donate it to a university or to some museum. Obviously, as I'm sure you'll understand, that diary rightly belongs to me. It was written by my great-grandfather. It is my property. I came to New York to talk some sense into Cale, to explain this fact to him once and for all."

Sebastian Conan Doyle looked to Harold for agreement. Sitting erect on the hard-backed wooden desk chair and listening attentively, Harold had no desire to argue with him on this point and yet didn't feel like he could let it pass.

"I understand your position, Mr. Conan Doyle. And look, I'm no lawyer. I don't know all the fine points of inheritance law. But it doesn't seem like the diary has been in your family's possession for eighty years. It all depends on where Alex found it. And right now no one has any idea. Your claim on it doesn't seem quite so simple, that's all."

Sebastian sighed and shook his head. He turned to Sarah, who sat silently on the edge of the bed. She leaned back on her hands and ever so slightly kicked her legs in the air. She smiled at Sebastian and, while barely moving her head, gave him a look of sympathetic neutrality.

"You're spot-on there," said Sebastian, turning back to Harold. "You're not a lawyer."

Neither was Sebastian, thought Harold, though he had no idea what the man born into a moderate fortune actually did with his days. He did know that Sebastian was the oldest son of the now-deceased Henry Conan Doyle, and while Sebastian had a younger sister, an aunt, and four surviving Conan Doyle cousins, his voice was the one most prominently heard on copyright issues relating to the estate of his great-grandfather. Over the years, there had been tremendous infighting among the family over the literary rights to Holmes and Watson and over the fortune those rights churned out every year. The current state of Conan Doyle family relations was not a happy one, from what

Harold understood. Though Lady Harriet Conan Doyle, Sebastian's aunt, had been generous to scholars and to the public over the years, she and Sebastian were not on speaking terms. Harriet, as well as the younger Doyles, had so far stayed out of the issue of the diary. But just a few days after Alex Cale's initial e-mail announced the discovery, Sebastian and his lawyers had gotten involved.

"The courts will decide this well enough when the time comes," continued Sebastian. "I sued Cale, you know, and if whoever has the diary now tries to donate it away, I'll sue that bleeding fucker as well. But..." And here Sebastian came to a stop in the middle of the room, clicking his heels together like a German general in a World War II movie. "The trouble now, first and foremost, is finding them."

"The police still haven't found anything hidden away in Cale's hotel room?" asked Sarah.

"No. Whoever killed him stole the diary as well. I was able to learn at least that much from them. Plus the basic information they've gotten from the hotel key-card records and the few interviews they've conducted with the hotel staff."

"What do the key-card records show?" asked Harold.

"They show that three people entered Alex Cale's room last night. Here." Sebastian produced a folded piece of paper from his pocket and handed it to Harold.

What the hell was going on? Why was Sebastian Conan Doyle handing him police records from the murder? Harold kept his thoughts to himself and looked down.

The folded paper was a photocopy of a printout from the hotel's security department. It listed all uses of Alex's room key card and every opening and closing of the door to Room 1117. "Cale used his card to first enter his room, after checking in, at 12:46 a.m.," said Sebastian. "Then three other people entered Cale's room, at 3:51 a.m., 4:05 a.m., and 5:10 a.m."

"God! Whose key card was used to open the door?"

"That's the problem. No one's. Each time the doors were opened and closed from the inside."

"So someone knocked and he let them in? Three different times in the middle of the night?"

"Evidently," said Sebastian. "Or someone came in and then left and then came in again. Of the three door openings, we can't say which were comings or goings."

"Did they determine a time of death?"

"Between four and eight in the morning. Any one of those visitors, if there were more than one, could have been the one to kill him."

"What about cameras? In the hallways?" asked Sarah.

"None to speak of. There's a few in the lobby, but they're focused on the front doors and registration desk."

"So who came in the front door?" said Harold.

"A bloody ton of people, Harold. It's a two-hundred-room hotel. It was about two-thirds full on January the fifth."

"Did anyone come into the hotel just before Alex received his first visitor? At 3:40, or 3:45?"

"Good question! I'm so glad I've come to you for help." Harold refused to be perturbed by Sebastian's blatant condescension. His mind was occupied with the details of the case. "No. No one entered the hotel between 3:20, when an out-of-town businessman returned from a strip club, and 4:30, when some Sherlockian stumbled in from the vodka lounge down the street—one of the Japanese ones, I forget his name."

"So whoever killed Alex was staying in the hotel last night?" said Sarah excitedly.

"Indeed," said Sebastian.

"Or," noted Harold quickly, "the killer just entered the hotel hours earlier, during a busy time when there'd be no way to identify him, and waited."

Sebastian considered this. "That's a plausible scenario, I suppose. Interesting." He scratched at his neck thoughtfully. "Let me make this very clear for you, Harold. Someone has stolen my property. I would like to get it back. And I'm willing to spend quite a bit of money to do so. Do you understand?"

"Sure," said Harold. As he returned Sebastian's gaze and the moment stretched between them, Harold realized that there was an unasked question hanging in the air. "Is there something you want me to do about that?"

Sebastian grimaced. He didn't seem like a man who often felt the need to explain himself to those around him, and he looked uncomfortable having to do so now.

"I told him," said Sarah. Harold looked at her and realized that she was addressing him, not Sebastian. "I told Sebastian what you're planning to do. That you're going to solve the case. You are, aren't you?"

"Yes," said Harold warily.

"Good," said Sebastian simply. "Then I'd much like to help you do it. I want you to find the diary. If you'd find the killer as well, fantastic. If not, fantastic. I couldn't give a damn. But recover the diary, and return it to me, its rightful owner. I'll pay you. Well."

Harold looked to Sarah for confirmation that Sebastian was serious about this. Her tiny curl of a smile remained as impenetrable as ever. How did she even know Sebastian?

"Why me?" Harold asked, skipping over the thornier questions for a less prickly one.

"In point of fact, that was Sarah's idea. She's been interviewing me these past few months, for her article. I've been staying at a hotel across town. I rang her as soon as I heard what happened. Sarah told me what you did in Cale's room this morning. I was impressed. Let's be honest— I think one of you people did this. I think one of your giddy, delusional pals killed Cale and stole *my* diary. Probably for some obsessive, arcane, and pointless reason. The twisted tosser is most likely building a shrine to the thing right now, praying to it like a dusty Ganesha. I'm going to need someone who is—how shall I put this?—similarly *disposed* in order to get the diary back. 'Elementary' written in blood on the wall? Come on. It's some sick Sherlockian leaving messages behind for another sick Sherlockian to follow. No offense, of course."

"None taken," said Harold genuinely. Sebastian stepped toward him and, standing before Harold, looked him right in the eye. "I have access to certain... Well, I can get you what you need. Tell me how I can help."

Harold thought of the thrill of discovery he'd experienced in Alex's room. The sensation of finding things out. Of solving the puzzle. He thought of his need to know.

"'My professional charges are upon a fixed scale,'" said Harold. "'I do not vary them, save when I remit them altogether.'"

"Excuse me?"

"It's a quote. It's from 'Thor Bridge.' One of the stories."

Sebastian and Sarah looked at Harold blankly.

"I'll do it," Harold explained. "And I'm not going to charge you. But I'll need a few things."

"Very well," said Sebastian.

"I need copies of the police reports. The autopsy, the full interviews, everything."

"Certainly."

"And a ticket to London. First class. I could sit here interviewing Sherlockians all day, but it won't get me anywhere. They're too smart for that. I think the key to the murder is the diary. In order to find out where the diary is, we need to find out where it came from. Where did Alex find it? *How* did Alex find it? I need to see his home. His study."

"Done." Sebastian positively grinned.

"Two tickets," chimed Sarah. They both turned to her, surprised to hear her voice. "I came here to follow the story. Right now you're it."

Harold had up until this moment not been sure that he trusted Sarah Lindsay. He was now absolutely certain that he didn't.

"You need a Watson, don't you?" she said, registering his apprehension.

Sebastian looked down at his shoes, as if to hide his embarrassment at being a part of this conversation. Thinking it over, Harold could muster up no argument against Sarah's logic. If he were to be Sherlock Holmes, he would indeed need a Watson. And yet...

Sarah smiled broadly at him, and with that went the last of his sensible caution.

"The game's afoot!" Harold said proudly as he rose from his chair. Sarah closed her eyes for a second, withholding a smirk.

CHAPTER 13

The White Dress

*"My revenge is just begun! I spread it over
centuries, and time is on my side."*
—Bram Stoker,
Dracula

October 21, 1900

"Might we run over what exactly it is that I am doing here?" asked
Bram Stoker as they climbed York Street north from the Stepney Station. Though not crowded, the passenger trains along the Blackwall line
were few and far between, and so this afternoon's excursion to the East
End had already proved quite time consuming. "I've a play which needs
attending, mind you. Henry wants a live horse onstage for his *Don
Quixote* tomorrow, so I really must be digging a mare up somewhere."

"Dribbling imbeciles, Bram," exclaimed Arthur as he waded through
the unwashed pedestrians. "I wouldn't trust the Yard to find their own
soiled knickers." He looked up in vain for some sign as to his location.
Merely two blocks from the entrance to Stepney Station, and he was
quite lost. "There's a dead girl in desperate need of assistance. It would
be ungentlemanly to turn away."

"She's dead. I don't know that either of us is in a position to give her
the assistance she might need, unless you've been the recipient of some
ordination of which I'm unaware."

"Justice, then," submitted Arthur. "We'll give her justice."

Bram did not appear convinced.

76

"Someone blew apart my writing desk. My family was in the house. My well-being aside, that of my family's ought to concern you."

Bram sighed. "Arthur, what am *I* doing here?"

Arthur stopped. "I need your help."

"My Lord. You want me to be your Watson, don't you?"

"I don't know what you mean."

"You think that because you squirted life into Holmes from the tip of your pen, you might become him yourself. So you need a Watson, and for some reason known only to yourself, you've chosen me. Why not Barrie or, better yet, Shaw? I'm certain *he* has nothing else to do."

"That's quite a deduction. Perhaps you're the one who fancies himself a detective."

"Very well, if you're to act like that, then yes, let's speak plainly," said Bram. "Watson is a cheap, efficient little sod of a literary device. Holmes doesn't need him to solve the crimes any more than he needs a ten-stone ankle weight. The *audience*, Arthur. The audience needs Watson as an intermediary, so that Holmes's thoughts might be forever kept just out of reach. If you told the stories from Holmes's perspective, everyone would know what the bleeding genius was thinking the whole time. They'd have their culprit fingered on page one. But if you tell the stories from Watson's perspective, the reader is permitted to chase in the darkness with the bumbling oaf. Watson is a comic flourish. He's a gag. A good one, all right, I'll give you that, but I hardly see how you'll be needing one of him."

Arthur addressed his friend as if he were forced to explain for the hundredth time why the sky shone blue. "Look here," he began, "I'm trying to put this with all the respect you're due. I'm not well versed in this—yes, you understand—this *neighborhood*, you see? And I'm no gossiping crone, of course. But, let us speak frankly. I've come to understand that you've spent some time in this neck of the woods, and you might have some experience with the local inhabitants that might prove useful in our investigations. Very good?"

Bram was offended by Arthur's implication.

"You do me wrong, my old friend. I don't believe I can stand here and take your insinuations lightly. You know very well what sort of women call this place home, and what a gentleman like you or me would be looking for if we were to come down this way. I'll have you know that your words are most unkind."

Arthur stared Bram dead in the eyes for a moment. He looked up at the surrounding buildings, finding nothing to provide directions save the advertisements for Duke of Wellington Cigars and Grover's Lime Juice. He looked down at the address he'd printed neatly on a scrap of writing paper and scrunched his face in befuddlement.

"My deepest apologies. I had no intention of giving offense. I most certainly did not mean to imply that you were the sort of fellow who sought comfort in this wretched, ungodly place. Blast it, I'm properly lost. Is this Salmon Street?"

"No," said Bram without pausing to think. "Salmon is the next right up that way. You've wandered onto—" Bram stopped himself, realizing his accidental admission. "Yes, give me a moment. I don't know this area." He made a great show of looking around for street signs as well, and of being surprised to find none.

"Pardon me, ma'am?" said Bram to a passing young woman in a black dress. "Might you know the way to Salmon Street?"

The woman stopped, quickly looked Bram up and down, and smiled flirtatiously. Her cheeks were brighter, as she grinned, than the copper buttons on her dress.

"I do, sir," she said. "Might you be looking to take a trip to Hairy-fordshire?"

Arthur looked genuinely confused; what in the world was she talking about?

"I'm very sorry, ma'am, you've misunderstood me," said Bram in a hurry. "We're just looking for Salmon Street. Is it that way?" He pointed up ahead, in the direction he had already suggested.

Now it was the young woman's turn to look confused.

"Why, yes," she said. "It's just up there, take a right."

"Thank you most kindly," said Bram as he turned to walk in that direction.

"But I do think," said the lady, "that if two right gentlemen such as yourselves are looking to take a trip elsewhere, perhaps somewhere more soothing, threepence apiece might pay your fare."

Arthur figured out what she was driving at. He was shocked by the woman's bluntness.

"Good day, madam," he said simply, and walked away in the direction she, and Bram, had indicated. As Bram trotted behind Arthur, he turned back to the confused young woman and offered her a look of apology for his rude and simple companion. She shrugged and continued on her way.

A few minutes later, Arthur had found the address and rapped at the small door. Begrudgingly, Bram stood at his side, shifting his weight tediously from foot to foot.

Arthur knocked on the door once again, this time banging with the flat, pinkie side of his coiled fist. Paint peeling from its edges, the door creaked open, and a squat, angry man appeared behind it.

"And who all are you lot supposed to be, then?" he barked. He wore britches, and a dull gray vest open over his work shirt. His hair, slicked to the back of his head, receded aggressively from his brow, as if running flat out for the nape of his neck.

"Good sir, we are here investigating the case of the poor girl who was murdered two weeks past in your boardinghouse."

"You don't look like bobbies," he said.

"No, we're not. We're—"

The man quickly shut the door in Arthur's face. Arthur was stunned.

"Sir!" he yelled inside after a moment had passed. "Sir, if you'll open the door again, I give you my word that we won't take up too much of your time. We'd just like to see your rooms for a moment. To get a look at the crime scene, if we might. We—"

"This is Arthur Conan Doyle!" shouted Bram at the stolid door. Arthur turned to his friend, surprised to hear his voice.

"I don't see how that's relevant," Arthur said.

But before he could continue, the door opened halfway and the angry man popped his head out into the street.

"You're Arthur Conan Doyle?" he said to Bram.

"No," Bram replied. "I'm...well, I'm nobody. This"—and here he gestured at Arthur—"this is Arthur Conan Doyle."

The man gave Arthur a long once-over.

"Yes," he said when he'd finished. "That looks like you. I've seen your pictures in the paper, awhile back. You sitting at your writing desk, bent over with pen and paper, looking like a grubby queer."

Focused on the task at hand, Arthur did his best to conceal his annoyance.

"Sir, might we come in and take a look around the room where this girl stayed?" he said.

The little man opened the door a bit farther. "A spiffy gent like yourself, I don't see why not," he said. He turned away, pushing the door open wide behind him as indication for Arthur and Bram to follow. They did, taking care as they stepped in to avoid tripping on the raised door sill. They entered a small kitchen area and felt a slight warmth emanating from the stove on the far side of the room.

"Are you working on a new story?" said the man as he led his guests through the kitchen and up a back staircase.

"Yes," said Arthur. "I suppose you might put it like that."

The man's face sparkled with excitement. "So you're going to do it, then, eh? Bring him back to life?"

"I'm sorry?"

"Sherlock Holmes!" exclaimed the man as he turned at the top of the staircase to look downward at Arthur, circled in a halo of light from windows on the higher floor. "It's about time, you ask me. He was always good for a snort, you know, to get a workingman through the day. I miss him like he were family." The man laughed to himself. "More than my own family, right, if I do say so."

In silence, Bram followed Arthur up onto the second floor. They could hear noises—muffled but close—from behind some of the locked bedroom doors.

"How many people do you typically have staying here?" asked Arthur, desperate for a change in subject.

"Oh, that depends," said the man. "I've got ten or so regulars who lay their heads here every night, and then another five or ten who come and go as the whim pleases them. You'd be surprised, but it's the regulars who give me more trouble. Think they can get a day behind in their rents and I won't notice, or I'll give them credit for another night. They get right indignant when I refuse. The comers and the goers, though, they know damn well they've to pay in advance. Threepence a night, and none of that Jew haggling neither."

"Which sort was the dead woman?" asked Arthur.

"Neither, really," said the man. "She only come that one night. With a gentleman, so I gathered, but I never got much look at him."

"Why was that?"

"She come in first, asking if I had a room for the night for her and her husband. 'Husband,' she says! If I had a shiny copper for every 'husband' jerked out his dirty peter in these—"

"But you never saw his face?" interrupted Arthur, trying to learn as little of the sordid details of the man's business as he was able.

"No, sir. Like I says, she come in first, in that pretty white dress, pocketful of coins, talking about a husband. She's giddy, you know, talking all quick, got a blush in her face. Like my own girl on Easter, knows she's got a fresh sweet orange waiting for her from Mum and Pop when she comes down the stairs. This girl is chock-full of grins. Tells me her name is Morgan Nemain, writes it down in my book and—"

"Might I take a look at that book?" interrupted Arthur.

"Surely, I'll fetch it from downstairs on your way out," said the man.

"Pray continue."

"I show her to the room," the man went on, "and she says a gentleman'll be along shortly. I tend to my affairs, and a few minutes later I'm in Hattie Stark's room, explaining to her why the slavey girl hasn't done her wash yet. She's putting up a fuss, saying she needs her wash, and I'm trying to explain that if she doesn't have it out in the morning before ten o'clock, the slavey can't get to it till the next day." Arthur looked down the hall at the row of locked bedchambers. The room in question was at the far end.

"We're going back and forth, like Hattie will do, when I hear a knock on the front door and a voice calling out to get let in. Thought it was a woman's voice at first, to be honest, it was so high and squeaky, but then the 'bride,' she says that's her husband and she'll let him in.

"She seems like a good enough sort, so I let her do it. And I hear her and the gent laughing, coming up the stairs. I poke my head out of Hattie's room to make sure it's just the two of them—three or more people to a room is extra, you know—and I see her leading a tall fellow into the bedroom. I just see him from behind. Black evening cloak, top hat. Walked like a fine sort. Then I'm back to Hattie and her hollering. Told the detectives from the Yard as much."

Arthur and Bram followed the man into the cramped bedroom. A well-made bed sat in the right corner, low to the floor. A pitcher of water rested on top of a bedside table. A stained bathtub that might one day, long ago, have shone bright white was in the left corner.

There were no bloodstains anywhere. There was no visible echo of the horrible killing that had happened just two weeks before. And yet, standing there, conscious of all that had happened and of the great mystery before him, Arthur shivered. The air seemed to reverberate with a distant death, like far-off explosions from the war in the Transvaal.

"What's your story about?" asked the man as Arthur and Bram surveyed the scene of the murder.

"My story?" said Arthur.

"The one you said you're writing! Is Holmes after another thief? Or is it a murder story? I like the murders the best, if you care for my opinion."

"I can't tell you," said Arthur. "It would ruin the surprise."

The man laughed, slapping at his thigh. He seemed to be enjoying himself.

"You know what I like to do, when I read your stories?" he asked. "I like to try to guess the endings early. To figure out who's done it before Mr. Holmes has."

"And do you manage it?" asked Bram, joining the conversation. "Can you outsmart Sherlock Holmes?"

"Haven't done it yet," said the boardinghouse proprietor. "But I have an idea, you know. For how you could bring him back to life."

"And what's that?"

"You don't need a wizard or nothing," the man said. "How's about maybe Mr. Holmes didn't die at all? Maybe he didn't fall off that ledge into the Reichenbach Falls—what if he faked it? To fool Moriarty, like? And then he's been in hiding, off on adventures all around the globe. You bring him back home to London for a triumphant return. That's the way, I'll tell you. There's no one wants to think of Holmes as being dead. Sits ill in the stomach."

"Is that so?" asked Bram, amused by the man's ramblings.

"Honor bright. You swells, you get so accustomed to your writing you forget to think of how your readers will feel about it. We don't want to see Holmes dead, no matter how good is the battle that does him in. We want Mr. Holmes to live forever."

"How about that, Arthur?" said Bram, needling his friend. "How about pushing aside the rock and resurrecting the divine Sherlock Holmes?"

"Do all your rooms have baths in them?" asked Arthur of the boardinghouse owner. "It seems like a fine feature."

"No, no. Just this one," said the man. "This was a powder room years back, when the place was built. Now I rent it out for extra. For a higher class of customers, you understand."

Arthur walked to the bathtub and ran his forefinger along its smooth rim. It felt thoroughly cold, like a windowpane on a snowy day.

"They found her body here?" he said.

"*I* found her body here, myself. She was laying right in the tub, naked as a baby. Her neck was blue and purple, her eyes all bursting out of her head. Like someone grabbed tight around her tiny throat and squeezed till she was going to pop. The dress was set out on the bed, like it were laid out for somebody to put on."

"Did you notice the tattoo? On her leg? Shape of a crow, black, with three heads?"

"I saw it, yes, sir."

"Ever seen a symbol like that before? Something from the hooligans down by the docks?"

"No, no, I can't say that I have. It was a funny shape, though. Right down on her leg, by her ankle."

"Was anything else found in the room? Anything to indicate who this poor woman was?"

"Not a whit. Just a pretty white dress and a dead, naked molly."

Arthur and Bram spent the next few minutes trying to jog the man's memory for any other clues as to the woman's identity but found no success. Arthur then led Bram on a hands-and-knees inspection of the floor, to which Bram begrudgingly acquiesced, though he spent the entire search complaining about the layer of dirt that was being applied to his trousers in the process. The owner of the house produced his guest book, in which they found the signature of "Morgan Nemain"— tall letters, pressed deeply into the page with a wide, heavy stroke. While Holmes was an expert in handwriting analysis, able to discern the most telling clues as to a person's identity from his or her signature, Arthur was not thus skilled. He closed the book silently, resigned to its secrets.

Finally, and with heavy feet, Arthur and Bram left the boarding-house. Arthur in particular rejoined the frantic thoroughfares of Stepney in a sour mood. This had not gone as planned.

"Well, are you all done now?" asked Bram. He was waiting for an opportune moment to tell Arthur that they were headed in the wrong direction. "Have you had your fill?"

"I won't pretend that the day has gone as I had hoped," said Arthur. "Indeed, this puzzle seems ever darker. My Sherlock had his data with which to work. And what do we have? A dress. An eyewitness who only saw the murderer from behind. A nameless woman of the evening. There must be tens of thousands of them on this block alone. I say this is a mite outside the realm of Sherlock's adventures."

Bram thought for a long moment and then made a very fateful decision.

"Arthur, I don't like that you're doing this, and for my own part I would very much like simply to return to my theater in peace, inasmuch as the theater can ever be described as being 'at peace.' I believe that you're jiggling the lid of Pandora's box and that once you become involved, you have nary a notion of what might pop out. Look at where you are right now. This is not a place for you. You're too good a man, Arthur. Others of us…" Bram paused for a long moment. "Well, not everyone is so good a man as you."

"Thank you," said Arthur, regarding Bram fondly. "But, though I don't yet see the way forward, I am too committed to turn back now."

"Very well," said Bram. "In that case I have precisely two things I need to tell you. In two distinct ways you're headed in the wrong direction. First, literally, we are walking north, and Blackwell Station is behind us." Arthur looked up for confirmation of this, and, finding none, he nodded before turning about and walking back the way he'd come.

"Second," continued Bram as he turned and walked beside Arthur, "the dead girl was not a prostitute."

At this, Arthur stopped abruptly.

"Whatever do you mean? She was found in that house, with a man—"

"Balderdash," said Bram. "What East End prostitute owns a clean white wedding dress? Which of them owns a clean dress of any kind? It's grim work, and not the sort that tends to induce sartorial cleanliness. That horrible little man we were speaking to said that she burst into his boardinghouse, face bright with smiles, and then paid her nightly rent up front. The gentleman followed a few minutes later. If she were whoring, pardon my language, she would have paid the rent with *his* money. Now, tell me, what sort of prostitute takes her gent's money in advance and goes blithely into their flophouse to pay for their hours together? If she were on the clock, so to speak, I tell you she'd have stolen the money and snuck away as soon as the man took his eyes off her."

Arthur thought about this deeply. If the dead girl was not a prostitute…

"If not… Well, if not that, what was she, then?" asked Arthur.

"I can't say for sure," said Bram. "I don't possess the deductive faculties of which you've written so eloquently. But I can't understand why no one seems to think of the obvious."

"The obvious?"

"Yes. That she was exactly who she said she was. A bride."

"If she was a bride," said Arthur, putting it all together in his head, "then he was…"

"Yes," said Bram, leading him through the York Street square, ensuring that Arthur, adrift in his head, wasn't hit by a passing hansom. "Then the murderer was the man who'd married her."

CHAPTER 14

Jennifer Peters in Mourning

*"London, that great cesspool into which all the loungers
and idlers of the Empire are irresistibly drained."*
—Sir Arthur Conan Doyle,
A Study in Scarlet

January 9, 2010

In the chilled belly of a British Airways 767, Harold attempted to find out a little more about Sarah. He was not immediately successful.

"Been to London before?" he asked as they settled into their leather seats.

She was silent for a moment before her face brightened into a wry smile.

"Why don't you tell me?" she replied.

Harold was confused. "What?"

"Isn't that one of those things that's in all the Holmes stories? He looks at strangers and can tell everything about their life from the way that they look? The specks of dirt on their shoes, or the calluses on their hands, that kind of thing."

"So you've read the Holmes stories?" asked Harold.

"Bravo! Your first deduction turns out to be correct."

He could never quite tell whether Sarah was flirting with him or teasing him.

"Only a handful, though," she added. "As prep for my voyage among the Sherlockians. So. Tell me something else about myself."

Harold looked down at her stiletto boots, her dark jeans, her plaid flannel shirt with the upturned collar. He got the impression that she was dressed stylishly, but he couldn't quite say why.

She was right, obviously. Holmes performed these little tricks in practically every story. A new client would enter his drawing room and within moments Holmes would have the gentleman or lady completely sized up. In *The Sign of the Four*, Holmes was able to tell the entire life story of Watson's brother after examining the man's pocket watch alone.

The trick was harder than Harold had imagined. His concentration fixed first on Sarah's clothes, but they didn't tell him much. They didn't look cheap, but they didn't look fantastically expensive either. Her nails were long and uneven, the bright red polish chipped off almost entirely.

"Holmes had an advantage," said Harold.

"Yeah? What's that?"

"He lived in Victorian England. He came from a society so class-stratified that you could tell where people grew up within a few miles by their accent. The word 'Cockney' originally meant someone who lived within hearing distance of the bells at St. Mary-le-Bow. Your shirt cuffs were your destiny. Holmes was able to tell so much about a man's walking stick—in, say, *The Hound of the Baskervilles*—because gentlemen carried walking sticks. There are no more rules nowadays. You have a million options of clothing and style to choose from. If your clothes look expensive, they could still be from a secondhand store. I live in L.A., where the basic code seems to be the more casual you look, the more money you have. We're both Americans, so outside of a few very specific regions, accents tend to move around. Especially among people who actually do move around. You're a reporter—how many different cities have you lived in? Four? Six? You could have been born in any one of them."

"Excuses, excuses," said Sarah. "You're not the only Sherlockian who's off chasing Cale's killer right now. But you're the one I bet on. You don't want me to think I've put my money on the wrong horse, do you?"

"You haven't."

"Good. So, have I been to London before or not?"

Harold paused. A flight attendant deposited plastic champagne flutes on each of their tray tables.

Harold believed in Sherlock Holmes. He knew the stories weren't "real," of course—he didn't believe in Holmes like that. But he believed in what the stories represented. He believed in rationality, in the precise science of deduction. Sherlock Holmes could do this. And so could Harold.

He examined her. Bright blue eyes. Thin nose. Two hoop earrings hanging from her earlobes. Curly brown hair held up in a ponytail, a few loose strands dangling down. Something behind her ear. He leaned in closer, over the gap between the first-class seats. There was a small tattoo behind her left earlobe.

"Yes," said Harold. "You've been to London before."

Sarah smiled. "How did you know?"

"I didn't know. But it was a reasonable guess. You have a small mark on your nose, where a piercing used to be. And there's a tiny tattoo of a musical note behind your left ear. Who gets musical-note tattoos? Musicians, obviously. So you were a musician at one point. I'm going with rock band, because you don't take care of your fingers like a classical musician would, and you used to have a stud in your nose. Bass player? You were dedicated, or else you wouldn't have gotten the tattoo. But then you quit and became a reporter. You're freelance, which means that either you're semifamous or you don't make that much money. I don't think you're famous, or I would have heard of you. So you didn't quit music because you needed the money, and you didn't become a reporter for that reason either. So I don't think you've ever been strapped for cash. You were a rich kid, or at least a relatively well-off one, pursuing a crazy dream to piss off your parents. Between your childhood, with parents who could have taken you on European vacations if they wanted to, and your time in your band, which must have toured if you were that committed, it stands to reason that you would have been through London at one point or another."

Sarah beamed at him, and then pressed her hands together in a play-ful golf clap.

"Accordion," she said. "Not bass. I played accordion in a punk band."

"Your punk band had an accordion player?"

"It was pretty cool. But we never made it out of the East Coast. I grew up near Berkeley, and my parents were 'comfortable,' as they'd put it. They took me to Europe three times when I was a kid. Paris, Madrid, and a week in Italy, traveling from Rome to Cinque Terre by way of Florence. But we never went to London."

"But you said you'd been," said Harold.

"Yes," said Sarah. "I have an ex who's British. Born in London. We met in New York, but we went back to visit his family a few times."

She raised her champagne flute and clinked it against Harold's.

"Cheers," she said before taking a long gulp. "I think you did great for your first time."

―――――――

Alex Cale's sister was crying when they arrived. And judging from the pork-pink bags around her eyes, it looked as though she had been for some time.

Though a few years younger than her brother, Jennifer Peters looked much older when she answered the door to her spacious flat in London Fields, on the third ring, and allowed Harold and Sarah inside. Her short hair looked both shiny and frayed, and as they talked, she kept brushing the ends of her severe bob behind her ears. She wore jeans, a low-necked sweater, and thick red socks—no shoes. She would have appeared Sunday-morning comfortable had she not been so clearly miserable.

Her husband was not in the flat with her, and Harold didn't inquire as to his whereabouts. The couple had no children and spent much of the year abroad. She had arrived in London only the day before, to attend to the disposal of Alex's possessions, to recover his body, and see it interred at Highgate Cemetery, where some generations of their family had been laid to rest. Jennifer was her brother's sole next of kin.

When the three of them sat down, Harold and Sarah on the hard couch and Jennifer on a wide, white plush chair, Harold felt grief lying sickly in the room like mildew. The couch felt sticky and wet.

And Harold felt like a tremendous ass. At least he'd had the good sense to leave the deerstalker cap at the hotel, with all of his bags. (Actually, he did so less because of his good sense and more because of Sarah's gentle urging, but still, he thought he deserved credit for the decision.) He couldn't help feeling like a grave robber as he forced Alex's sister to talk about her dead brother, just when she had to deal head-on with the sensation that she had so very little family left.

"When was the last time you spoke to your brother, before his death?" Harold asked.

"I'm sorry, why are you here, again?" Jennifer responded plaintively.

"He was a good friend." Harold swallowed, embarrassed at the exaggeration. "We're trying to figure out what happened to him."

Jennifer turned to Sarah, then away from them both. She looked puzzled, not at the complexity of the problem but at its simplicity. Her brother had died. That was "what happened to him."

"Harold traveled in the same circles as your brother," said Sarah. "We think he might have some insight into who did this that's not available to the police."

"You're a detective?" asked Jennifer of Harold.

"No. Not exactly."

"What *do* you do, then, exactly?"

"I'm a reader."

"What does that mean?"

"I read books...well, I've *read* a lot of books, past tense, I suppose that's more accurate. See, I'm freelance, I work for the legal departments of most of the major studios, and when someone sues one of them for copyright infringement, I help prepare the defense on the grounds—"

"You're one of Alex's Sherlockian friends?"

"Yes."

She faced Sarah. "And you're a reporter?"

"Yes."

Jennifer sighed and crossed her legs, picking lint specks from her red socks. "I hadn't spoken to my brother for a month or so. We weren't... Well, that's not true. We were close in our own way."

"What did you talk about? Did anything seem out of the ordinary?" said Harold.

"Something was always out of the ordinary with Alex. The Great Game was always on, he was always after some relic or precious document or what-have-you. He was always *this* close, ever the last few inches, from finishing his biography. On that day, if I remember, he said that he had been followed ever since he'd found the diary. I thought he was being characteristically overdramatic."

"Who was following him? What did he say about him—or her?"

"Oh, who the bloody hell knows? It's not like this was the first time Alex thought some mysterious stranger had it in for him. Once, when he was at university, he rang Father in a fit because two rival students were conspiring against him to steal his thesis. It was silly, of course. They weren't doing anything of the sort."

"If he wasn't being followed, then who do you think killed him?" said Harold, surprised at his own boldness.

"Don't you think it's obvious?" said Jennifer. "Isn't that why you're here?"

"What do you mean?"

"One of you lot killed him. You're a herd of jealous children. He had a candy bar, and you all lusted after it. 'Give me, give me.'" She uncrossed her legs, pressing her feet into the floor and leaning forward, hands on her knees. "Which one of your friends do you think it was?"

Harold thought of Ron Rosenberg. Jeffrey Engels. A dozen others. A suspicious chill danced up Harold's spine, but he squelched it with a wiggle in his seat.

"I don't know," he said. "Yet."

Sarah piped up. "Think about your last conversation with your brother. Did he have any details on the man he thought was following him?"

Jennifer Peters thought for a moment. "No," she said.

"We'd like to look at his apartment, if that's all right with you," said Sarah.

"Oh, very well, I suppose. What harm could it do?" said Jennifer after a moment of reflection. "I'll take you now. Let me find some shoes."

Murder was so trivial in the stories Harold loved. Dead bodies were plot points, puzzles to be reasoned out. They weren't brothers. Plot points didn't leave behind grieving sisters who couldn't find their shoes.

"You know, your brother," he began after a few moments, "he was a legend in our organization. And that he finally discovered the lost diary? I don't know if it's much consolation to you, but he achieved his dream. He found what he'd been looking for. He was happy, before he passed."

Jennifer laughed to herself and shook her head.

"Happy?" she said, trying the word out on her lips, listening to its sound. "Do you think people are happy when they finally get the things they've been after?" She absentmindedly fiddled with the wedding ring on her left hand.

"He wasn't, really," she continued. "I remember the day he called to tell me that he'd found the diary. His voice was so quiet I could barely hear what he was saying over the phone. He seemed very distant, very formal. I offered a glass of champagne, said I'd take him out to celebrate, he deserved it. 'That won't be necessary,' he said." Jennifer deepened her voice, mimicking her dead brother. "'That won't be necessary.' Who says that? To his sis?"

Jennifer emerged from a back closet with a pair of comfortable walking shoes and a heavy winter coat. As she covered herself up, the fringe of mink at the top of the coat brushed against her earlobes.

"Did he ever tell you where he'd found it?" asked Harold. He'd been waiting for the right moment to ask this question. There wasn't one, he now realized.

"He never told me," replied Jennifer.

"You asked him about it?"

"I asked him a dozen times. 'Alex, you've been on the bloody hunt for ten years and you won't tell me where it took you?' Nothing. I pieced together that he'd been in Cambridge for a week, not sure why. He did most of his research at the British Library, which has excellent Victorian and Edwardian collections. Do you know, he never even told me that he was particularly close, closer than any of the other times he thought he was onto the damned thing. He just rings one day to say, 'Oh, Jennifer, I've found the diary. It's quite fascinating. I'm going to complete the biography and unveil the whole lot at this year's convention.' He sounded mournful—as if someone he'd known had just died. Like he was about to type up the last rites." She frowned, stopping herself from continuing.

"You don't think finding the diary gave him peace, just a little?" asked Sarah. "It was the culmination of his life's work."

"I think that whatever he found in there made him miserable from the second he laid eyes on it till the day he died. Till the day the diary killed him!" Jennifer said. "I think that finding Conan Doyle's diary was the worst thing that ever happened to my brother. What do you think it's going to do for you?"

CHAPTER 15

The Allegations of Love

"At the same time you must admit that the occasion of a lady's marriage is a very suitable time for her friends and relatives to make some little effort upon her behalf."
—Sir Arthur Conan Doyle,
  "The Adventure of Charles Augustus Milverton"

October 21, 1900, cont.

The tallest spire of Westminster Abbey pierced into the pale yellow orb of the setting sun as Arthur left Waterloo Station. Late-afternoon traffic flowed across Westminster Bridge like a gushing stream— like the dread Reichenbach itself, pouring pedestrians and clattering broughams east into the dense city center. Big Ben announced five and twenty.

Somewhere in this city hid the murderous husband of "Morgan Nemain," and Arthur was going to find him. His first stop was the vicar-general's office, which issued more than two thousand marriage licenses on behalf of the archbishop of Canterbury every year. Typically, couples were married by their local diocese, but if the man and woman came from different parishes, then by law only the archbishop of Canterbury had the authority to legalize their union. This in turn meant that if someone was looking to get married clandestinely, the vicar-general's building near Waterloo was the place to do it. It was an open secret, and a rather public irony, that the most ungodly marriages in society were granted by the church's most senior office.

Marriage records were eventually sent to the library for safekeeping, but if the dead girl had wedded just weeks earlier, there was a great chance that Arthur might find a copy of her license still at the vicar-general's.

Arthur and Bram had worked all this out on the train back in from Blackwall, before Bram had begged off the hunt and returned to his Lyceum, to manage his theater and his actors. He had to round up that godforsaken live horse for *Don Quixote*. Egos required tending.

On Westminster Bridge, Arthur was struck by the brightness of the streetlamps running across like a formation of stars. They shone white against the black coats of the marching gentlefolk and fuller than the moon against the fractal spires of Westminster. They were, Arthur quickly realized, the new electric lights, which the city government was installing, avenue by avenue, square by square, in place of the dirty gas lamps that had lit London's public spaces for a century. These new electric ones were brighter. They were cheaper. They required less maintenance. And they shone farther into the dim evening, exposing every crack in the pavement, every plump turtle shell of stone underfoot. So long to the faint chiaroscuro of London, to the ladies and gentlemen in black-on-black relief. So long to the era of mist and carbonized Newcastle coal, to the stench of the Blackfriars foundry. Welcome to the cleansing glare of the twentieth century.

As Arthur hailed a noisy hansom, he averted his gaze from the New Scotland Yard just across the Thames. Curse them.

The coach led Arthur to Kensington, then turned the sharp right onto Lambeth Road. The Lambeth Palace lay squat and blocky ahead of them, its medieval crenellations anachronistically militaristic in the unfortified modern city. To Arthur, the palace resembled a stout and angry Irishman, ready to pick a fight with the pavilions of St. Thomas's Hospital to the north. And beside it lay the office of the vicar-general.

The grand entrance to the church office was a series of openings shaped like upside-down V's, each a few inches smaller than the preceding one. It felt, to Arthur, like entering into a dark tunnel.

Though not a proper church, the building retained that sense of quiet and majestic stillness with which Arthur had always associated both the Catholic and the Anglican houses. He held suspicions toward the church—indeed, any church—and yet he had to admit that he did love churches. Arthur admired anything that connected him with antiquity, that made him feel like a part of the Britain that stretched back over the millennia. He believed in his people and the ideals of their civilization more than he believed in their God. He had more love for the Saxon than for the Anglican.

Arthur was faintly embarrassed by the loud *clomps* his boots made on the floor as the sound reverberated through the long hallways. Robed friars with thick bellies walked past him and yet didn't seem to make nearly so much noise as they moved.

The friar who attended the marriage desk looked young enough to be Arthur's son. His robes were a muddy brown, and his face appeared open and completely unwrinkled, as if the boy were without a trouble in the world. As he looked Arthur straight in the eye, he did not blink or flick his eyes elsewhere in politeness. He simply stared directly at Arthur, holding his position with the certainty and clear head of the resolutely devout.

"Good day, sir," began Arthur. "I was hoping I might trouble you for a look into your marriage records."

"Is it your daughter?" said the youthful friar pluckily.

"Pardon me?"

"Your daughter. Don't have to be Sherlock Holmes to see that you're married yourself." The friar smiled and directed his gaze down to Arthur's gold wedding band. "Most fellows like yourself—older gentlemen, a few specks of salt in the hair—come in here, they're chasing after a lost daughter. I'm not supposed to let just anyone go digging about in the files, but I tend to make an exception for a kind-looking sort who's after his darling girl. You'd be surprised at how many come in."

Arthur thought about this, and decided quite rationally that lying was by far the best approach to take.

"Yes. My daughter," he said. "She's gone missing. I fear she's run off with her beau, a dastardly fright of a man. Nemain—that's my name. Archibald Nemain. My dear girl is Morgan. Might I give a quick once-over to your records book, to see if she's come through here to be married?"

"I feared as much," said the friar knowingly. "Please follow me. We keep the allegations back here."

The young man led Arthur behind his desk, into a small antechamber of the marriage office. The room was quite cloistered, walled in by massive gray stones. Arthur felt as if they pressed in on him from all sides. He thought of Poe, the sweet horror of "The Cask of Amontillado."

The room's only furniture was a massive wooden chest, pocked with two dozen small sliding drawers. Whatever the chest's original function, it had been at some point more recently converted into a storage space for alphabetically organized wedding allegations—the legal documents that spelled out formally a couple's intention to marry.

As Arthur surveyed the task before him, the murmurings of a young man and woman came from the direction of the friar's desk. He left Arthur alone while he went to attend to their certification.

For the better part of an hour, Arthur sifted through the drawers of allegations. At first his hunt was underscored by the excited giggles of the bride-to-be at the friar's desk and the slow, even responses of her groom, who calmly presented the friar with the necessary details: the couple's names, their parents' names, their places of birth and residence, and the signed approval of the bride's father. After they had left, the friar attended to the further couples and eager young men who entered his office. Some men came to fulfill these duties alone, sparing their fiancées the trouble. Arthur could hear them all come and go like hummingbirds drifting onto a nearby tree—the clicks and clumps of their arrival, the squeaks and cries of their business, the whisks and flaps of their heartened departures.

The handwritten documents before him possessed the romance of governmental bureaucracy. Though each was filled out by the loving right hand of its willing groom, the allegations read less like Shakespeare and more like a will.

"4 October 1900," began the first of many, "which day appeared personally Thomas Stacey Junior of Morden in the County of Surrey, aged twenty-four years and a Bachelor, and alleged he intends to marry with Mary Beach of the County of Norfolk, aged twenty years, a minor and spinster, by and with the consent of Richard Norris, her uncle and guardian lawfully appointed, she having neither father, mother, testamentary or other Guardian whatsoever to her appointed." It droned on for a solid page, ascertaining that neither bride nor groom was married prior, and that no other "impediment by reason of any precontract" existed that would hinder their ability to be lawfully married.

Arthur's mind drifted to his own wedding, sixteen years before—My! Had it really been so long since that sweet August day at Masongill? Arthur had been a poor doctor when he met Touie; poor in both senses of the word. His fledgling practice had yielded but a meager income, though it was only now, years later, that he was able to realize that this might have had something to do with his poverty of talent. He had met his dear Touie—then Louisa Hawkins, a name that now sounded so foreign to Arthur that it might have referred to someone else's wife—when her brother had come to him suffering from cerebral meningitis and had become Arthur's resident patient. Arthur had given him a nightly sedative of chloral hydrate, and the man had died within a week. Occasionally Arthur still wondered, as he had at the time, whether the treatment had actually killed him—most likely not, he assured himself. Sixteen years later, Arthur understood that a dose of chloral hydrate did carry certain risks. But his patient had been wasting away in delirious fits—surely some sedative was necessary? What an imprecise science was medicine. It was more an art than was fiction.

Arthur wondered about the marriages whose first beginnings he now drew from the wooden chest and skimmed over between his thumbs. Were they all as happy as his had been, when he saw his bride at the

altar, when he exchanged a wink with his crying mother in the audience? What would these passions become in a decade and a half?

Love grew docile with age, like a faithful hound. It became precious
and prized, locked away from the world like a jewelry box. Love grew
commendably dependable—love was eggs, love was ham, love was the
morning paper. He loved Touie as much as he ever had. No. *More.* He
would always love Touie. Yes, since she'd gotten sick, those years ago,
they'd refrained from certain intimacies. They would have no more
children—but still Arthur could not be happier with his family. He
felt as if he'd grown up with Touie, even though he'd been twenty-six
when he met her, and she'd been twenty-eight—as if he'd become a
grown man right beside her. As if she were the dear sister from whom
he kept no secrets.

Well, perhaps one secret. There was Jean . . .

Three years earlier, he'd met the beautiful and brilliant Jean Leckie,
and he'd been clocked clean across the jaw by the sparkle of her conversation, by her immodest wit, by the radiant flourishes of her batting
eyelashes. She was young, but she was so wise, so unafraid to think and
wonder and express herself as if she were a man. Arthur had never met a
woman like her, and he felt quite certain that he never would again. Of
course he remained completely pure in his intentions toward her. Their
hands would never even touch. He stretched out his chest when he
walked beside her, holding his arms behind his back at ninety-degree
angles at the elbows. He had taken an oath, the same oath written on
the hundreds of papers that lay across his lap at this moment. He would
never betray it. But he would continue to see Jean, as much as he hon-
orably could. He would take long walks through the countryside with
her. She would cheer him from the stands at his cricket matches.

This, too, was love. And to Arthur's great surprise, the two loves did
not exclude one another. He loved Touie all the more for his loving
Jean. He loved them so differently that they magnified one another,
that they reflected mirror opposite images of the divine into his bulging heart. He thought that he might pop, sometimes, from the gallons

of love that poured into his middle-aged body. The oil and water of separate affections did not mix, but they also did not detonate. They coursed separately and equally through his bloodstream.

How much love could one man store in himself? Did he love more than the fresh-faced grooms who affixed their bachelor names to these allegations? Did he love more than the radiant brides who blushed all the colors of a June rose garden at the thought of becoming the new Mrs. What-Have-You? Did all loves look the same, like plucked and boiled chickens? Or were they different, like corneas, fingerprints, crania?

Arthur thought about the love that had died within the breast of Morgan Nemain. The love that was strangled naked in a filthy Stepney bathtub and left to rot. She had not been dead very long when the boardinghouse proprietor had found her. Her belly might still have been warm to the touch. Her heart had not yet sprouted tiny white-petal maggots.

Arthur furiously flicked through the allegations for some glimpse of the man who had done this. He scanned the pages for revenge.

Sometime later the friar returned. Arthur did not hear him enter, so engrossed was he in his search for names. The boy tapped Arthur on the shoulder to get his attention, and Arthur jumped up, startled. He held his hand to his chest and took a series of deep breaths.

"My apologies, sir!" said the friar. "I had no intention of startling you!"

"Quite all right," huffed Arthur. "I had no intention of being startled."

"How goes your digging?"

"Not well, I fear," admitted Arthur. "I've found no one with the name Morgan Nemain mentioned in any of these documents. She—my daughter—she probably gave a false name."

The friar nodded knowingly.

"I'm rather hard up for clues." Arthur had an offhand thought, and he continued with a smile, "You must see so many young men come and go through your doors... You wouldn't happen to remember the name, or the face, of a fellow with a high whine of a voice. He would have been here two weeks ago Tuesday. Black cloak. Black top hat." Arthur laughed—would there be any way in which he might be *less* specific in his description?

The friar made a face as if he'd just tasted sour milk. He stared at Arthur curiously.

"Funny, sir . . . I think the man you're looking for asked me the very same question."

Now it was Arthur's turn to make an odd face.

"Pardon me?" he said.

"Your fellow. The groom. It was the strangest thing. A man comes in, tight, high little voice, black-on-black clothes, two weeks or so past, like you said. Wouldn't have thought twice about it myself, of course, except that I felt I recognized him. And he saw that I did, and asked me whether I did, and I said yes. I did, and he said I couldn't have, that didn't make sense, and I agreed, and that was that."

"I'm sorry, I have no idea what you're saying."

"I recognized the gent because he'd come in *before*. Some months back. He'd filled out an allegation, and he'd gone off to be married. Then, a few weeks ago, a fellow comes in looks just the same. I smelled, what, *déjà vu*, yes? That's what the French say? I wouldn't have remembered him, except I get this funny feeling in my gut that I've seen him before. I ask him if I have, and he gets just terribly nervous.

"'From when do you think you'd be recognizing me?' he says.

"'I hardly know,' I say. And I have a laugh, jesting with the man. 'Have you ever been married before?' I'm kidding, of course—he was young, not yet thirty, how would he have been? But he becomes frightfully agitated. Flops his arms around like he's a marionette.

"'I am quite certain, my good friar,' he says to me, 'I am quite certain that I haven't the faintest idea to what you might be referring.' His voice gets so high it's like he's playing a William Byrd. Then he goes into it, gives me quite a talking-to. He uses some language which I don't fancy hearing under this roof, you understand? I would have taken umbrage and caused a stir, for my part, but I am in the service of the Lord. I turn the other cheek. He produces his allegation, I sign in my place at the bottom, and he goes on his way."

As Arthur listened to the friar's monologue, he felt a prickly sensation along his spine and a widening of his brow. He felt the intoxicating tingle of discovery.

"Do you recall what name the young man gave?" asked Arthur, leaning forward onto the tips of his toes toward the friar.

The friar looked down. "I don't, sir, I'm sorry to say."

Arthur's mind whirled around like a top, spinning in circles, running through possibilities. "But you say you think he'd been married before?" he asked.

"Well, I hardly thought it too likely at the time, except for the man's surliness," said the friar. "But now... Do you think it's so?"

"I think," Arthur wanted to say but could not, "that whatever this man did to Morgan Nemain he did to another girl *first*."

CHAPTER 16

The Answering Machine

*"Circumstantial evidence is a very tricky thing," answered Holmes
thoughtfully. "It may seem to point very straight to one thing, but if
you shift your own point of view a little, you may find it pointing in
an equally uncompromising manner to something entirely different."*
—Sir Arthur Conan Doyle,
"The Boscombe Valley Mystery"

January 9, 2010, cont.

In the thirty-three-minute cab ride from Jennifer Peters's flat in London Fields to Alex Cale's in Kensington, Harold and Sarah learned much about Jennifer and Alex's family history.

They were both, as anyone could gather, quite wealthy. Henry Cale, their father, had built a shipping fortune from nothing—he had been a hardscrabble Newcastle man, who carried to his death the Geordie provincialism and classist suspicion of the wealthy with which he'd been brought up. He was not a man to sit idly by while his children sat idle. He would not allow them to rest on their family's newish fortune.

Which, Harold gathered from Jennifer's bitter ramblings, largely explained Henry Cale's emphatic annoyance when his children steadfastly refused to make money. Alex and his sister were both next to useless in this regard—fine universities, American graduate schools, any position in the world open to their letters of application. Yet Jennifer dabbled incessantly: a graduate program in the writing of poetry (her father bellowed at her when he heard the news), a teaching position looking over six-year-old tots (her father broke a wineglass that time), an administrative role in a campaign for Third World debt relief (he threatened to remove her from his will), eventually leading to a marriage with one of the campaign's wealthy founders (all threats rescinded, if only because she no longer needed his inheritance anyway). Jennifer now directed her husband's charitable trust.

Alex Cale had been decidedly more driven than his sister, though no less a disappointment to old Henry. He'd been a promising boy—quick-witted, a good head for numbers, sterling marks all around. Things went sour in his third year at university, when he asked to take a leave to finish a novel. His father ended that conversation sensibly by having Ms. Whitman, his secretary, show Alex out of his office.

Henry was encouraged when, a few years later, Alex asked for a loan so that he might open up a bookshop. Henry did not know much about what the market was for a little used-book shop in Chelsea in 1973, but at least the boy wanted to start a *business*. Let us be thankful for small gifts.

The bookshop lasted an unimpressive twenty-eight months before abandoning its lease to an Indian restaurant, the proprietors of which promptly turned Alex's old back office into a delightfully smelly kitchen. Alex would walk past the Indian restaurant in later years and find himself both nostalgic and hungry at the same time. He ate there frequently. Jennifer remembered that he had taken her and her husband out to dinner at the Indian restaurant on the night of its closing, before it gave way to a French-Asian-fusion type of something or other. (Their father had been too busy to attend.) Alex had seemed more upset about losing the Indian restaurant than he'd been at the loss of his own shop.

Further financial misadventures followed, though none with quite so much of their father's money at stake. Poor investments had been made in a fledgling literary magazine, a collection of nineteenth-century antiques, and on an inexplicable six months Alex had spent apprenticing an artisan who built wickerwork furniture. If anyone were to construct a biography of Alex Cale, thought Harold, this might be the detail glossed over because it didn't conform to the general thrust of the man's narrative.

Yet, Jennifer explained as the cab skimmed the southern edge of Hyde Park and Harold looked out at the bark-naked trees, the overarching narrative theme of Alex's life was indisputably Sherlock Holmes. He'd fallen in love as a boy, asking their nanny, Deirdre, to read the stories to him over and over again at bedtime. He'd written on Conan Doyle at school and finally joined the Irregulars when he was only twenty-four. He wrote regularly for the *Baker Street Journal* in every phase of his life. In all of his passions, there was Sherlock.

When Henry Cale died suddenly of a brain aneurysm in 1989, his two children began to drift apart, no longer tethered to the cold steel pole of their disapproving father. They no longer needed one another as protection against him. It was as if they'd been trenchmates in the war, and now that the bombing had stopped, neither knew what to say to the other. Jennifer had her husband and their charity, Alex had his Holmes and his endless research.

It was after his father's death that Alex's quest to find Conan Doyle's lost diary became all-consuming. He was armed now with a figurative fortune in shovels for digging into Conan Doyle's life. There would be no distractions for Alex from then on. There was no one left to tell him no. His father would at last be proved wrong when Alex found the diary and completed his biography; Alex would have amounted to something grand indeed, only not grand in the way his father had hoped. He would have achieved victory and rebellion at the same time.

Harold was surprised by how confessional Jennifer Peters had become, though he was unnerved by the odd rhythms of her speech. She would speak beautifully and painfully of her brother's deepest feelings in one moment and then, in the middle of a sentence, clam up, her thoughts drifting out into the gray winter sky. A minute later she would light up again, and a torrent of words would touch on her brother's childhood and their familial anxieties. She reminded Harold of the locks to the Chicago River, where he'd grown up—closing shut to fill up with water and then swinging open to dump thousands of muddy gallons out of the lake.

The cab pulled up to one of a series of similar-looking three-stories along Phillimore. Tall trees rose from backyards behind the buildings, and Harold could see them poking over the tops of the sharply slanted roofs. Harold paid, with Sebastian Conan Doyle's money, and the three approached Alex's flat.

Jennifer let them into what first appeared to be a carnival's back lot. Fantastical toys and ancient gewgaws littered every available surface. A shimmering silver gasogene, an ornamental saber, a copper lamp, a dozen medicine jars full of heaven-only-knows, a glass-encased revolver, an atomically dainty tea set, a banjo, fourteen flowerless vases in every color, and books, books, books. Books of every size, shape, and design. Books settled neatly on shelves, books strewn in scattered piles, lone books perched improbably off the ends of tabletops and footrests. Neither the books nor anything else within Harold's field of vision seemed in any sort of order—it was a decorative cacophony, an interior designer's manic breakdown.

From hallway to sitting room to dining room to whatever lay beyond, each area had wallpapering of a different color. Yellow, pink, purple. The flat looked like a gigantic piece of candy. Harold imagined that Willy Wonka's private study might have looked similar.

"Wow," was all Harold said.

"I think my brother's... *eccentricities* had become more apparent in recent years," Jennifer responded.

"Do you mind if we look around?"

"Go right ahead," Jennifer said. "Good luck finding anything."

There was no way to perform an organized search of such an unorganized collection—Harold gave in to the randomness at his feet and flitted back and forth like a bee hunting for pollen. He nosed around in the yellow study, picking at a copy of Gibbon's *Decline and Fall of the Roman Empire*. He opened an old cigar box in the purple room to find a collection of foreign currencies, dollars and kroner and four kinds of pesos all collected in clear plastic bags and rubber bands. Sarah searched separately. The two didn't discuss what they were looking for—Harold wouldn't have known what to tell her anyway. He hoped that they would know what it was when they found it.

Sarah picked up a set of matching salt and pepper shakers shaped like cats. She placed them neatly on a table, next to a set of four-by-six photographic prints. She tightened the scattered pile of photographs. Harold began to watch her, soon paying less attention to the detritus at his feet and more attention to the way Sarah searched the room. She was cleaning, almost. When she came to a blue ribbon loosened beside a white cardboard box, she retied the ribbon. She was putting things right. Harold looked down at the mess at his own feet—he was simply picking things up and placing them back down approximately where he'd found them. There was no system to what Harold was doing, only mindless entropy. Everything that wasn't the diary, he treated as dirt. Sarah, on the other hand, was taking the deathly clutter of Alex Cale's apartment into her hands and making something better of it.

They searched in relative silence, punctuated by an occasional story from Jennifer. Harold or Sarah would produce an object—some trinket or faded memento—and Jennifer would do her best to describe its origin. She often did not know where things had come from but would try to interpolate their origins from what sketches she had of her brother's travels. That frozen clock looked South American; Alex had been there in '98 or '99; *ergo*, he must have picked it up in Argentina.

It was Sarah who first noticed the answering machine. She gestured toward the slow, steady blink of its single red light.

"Have you checked his messages?" she asked Jennifer.

"Oh!" Jennifer looked surprised. "I hadn't seen that."

"May I?" inquired Sarah.

Jennifer nodded, and Sarah clicked the Play button. There was a loud click and then a piercing beep.

"One. Message." The anthropomorphic voice of Alex's answering machine was an older woman's, and came out in a broken staccato.

"First. Message. Received at. Seven. Forty-one. P.M. January. Four. Two thousand. And ten." That would be five days ago, thought Harold. Three days before the Irregulars' dinner.

"Mr. Cale, this is Sebastian Conan Doyle," came the new, human voice from the message. Having spoken with Sebastian just the previous day, Harold found it spooky to hear his voice on the crackly tape. Sebastian sounded angry.

"I trust you received the injunction from my solicitors. I know you're hiding from me. You won't answer my letters. You won't return my calls. You think because you dug up the right trunk in some attic somewhere, you're entitled to something which belongs to me. You little wanker. Can you hear me, Cale? Are you there right now, listening to my voice? Pissing your trousers in panic. Well, listen to this: If you give that diary away, you will regret it. I will see to it that you come to hate the very name Conan Doyle."

There was another loud click, and the message ended.

CHAPTER 17

A List of Atrocities

"We must look for consistency. Where there is a want
of it we must suspect deception."
—Sir Arthur Conan Doyle,
"The Problem of Thor Bridge"

October 21, 1900, cont.

Arthur Conan Doyle laid his head down on the messy pile of stranglings and took a deep breath.

Who knew that a detective's work was so infernally tedious?

Arthur had spent most of his day awash in paperwork. He had
learned nothing else of importance from the friar at the vicar-general's
office, despite the young man's eagerness to assist. They had searched
through the allegations together, working into vespers, but nothing
was found which jogged the friar's memory into fixing a name to the
murderous groom. Satisfied that he had exhausted the usefulness of
the vicar-general's, Arthur made the short walk to Scotland Yard in
just a few minutes. Inspector Miller was not in—thankfully!—but the
men who were knew Arthur by reputation and were delighted to be of
service. He had then spent some hours engaged in the examination of
the Yard's criminal files. If the murderer had in fact struck twice, there
must be some record of his earlier crime. And yet, despite the ample
quantity of dead girls found within London proper over the past year,
none had been found in a cheap East End boardinghouse, naked, tattooed, and accompanied by a fresh white wedding dress.

So Arthur concerned himself with the stranglings, hoping to find some sort of pattern amid these dreadful folios. Having killed Morgan Nemain in such a manner, did it stand to reason that the killer would have employed the same technique in his other crime—or, God forbid, his other *crimes*? Arthur was unsure. Did the criminal mind relish consistency? Arthur wondered whether murderers were like craftsmen, each with his own set of favorite tools. The leatherworker had his awl, the blackguard his blade. Or perhaps villains allowed themselves a beastly serendipity, employing whatever devices lay at hand for their slaughters. Arthur wished for some tool to peer inside the skulls of London's killers, to see how their perverted brains led them to evil. If only such a device existed.

He heard the clack of boot against tile and the pleasant jingle of a teacup rattling against its saucer. He looked up from the stack of papers before him to see a young police officer bringing him his tea. Square-faced and professional, the officer presented a welcome sight.

"Your tea, Dr. Doyle?" said the officer as he laid his tray on the desk.

"Thank you," said Arthur as he pushed the papers into order.

The young man hesitated for a moment, waiting for further instructions. When he received none, he turned on his heel and made his way to the door of the large office Arthur had been loaned for the evening. Night had begun sometime ago, and the black sky, which Arthur could see from the window, made the New Scotland Yard building seem even more massive, and even more quiet.

"Officer!" said Arthur, getting the young man's attention. "Officer…?"

"Binns, sir. Frank Binns." He approached Arthur's desk once again.

"Have you ever met a murderer, my boy?"

Officer Frank Binns gave himself a moment to reflect before speaking.

"A few, I'd wager. Just last week I picked up a fellow who'd gotten into a fight down at his pub. Man worked for the railways, if I recall. Got into fisticuffs with another railman and beat him over the head with his pint o' bitters. It was a grim sight."

"Yes, I'm sure," said Arthur, unsatisfied by this response. "But have you ever dealt with a true killer? Someone born for evil?"

"How do you mean?"

"Well now, I'm looking for a man that's killed two—at the very least two—young girls, and in cold blood. He planned it out. He knew what he meant to do in advance. What sort of man would kill a poor *woman* in such a fashion? It defies reason."

Officer Binns helped himself to a chair before he responded. "Do you mind a digression, sir?"

"Not at all," said Arthur, pushing his chair back a few inches from the desk.

"I grew up in Dorset," Officer Binns began. "I had a pal there, Sean Runny. Runny wasn't his real name, mind you, it was the name we boys had given him seeing as his nose was always running—winter, spring, summer, or fall. Anyhow, one year we have a rash of sheep killings in the area. Everyone is up in arms. It goes on for six months. No explanation—someone's sneaking across the fields at night, slitting right into the leg veins of the Border Leicesters we all kept, and standing there while they bleeds to death. Mothers are keeping their kids at home all day for fear the mystery sheep killer is going to switch his tastes to people. It's a long story, but finally the authorities catch him in the act—and what do you know, it's Sean Runny that's been killing the sheep. Sean! I got to see him just once, while he was clapped in the darbies, before they took him away. I ask him why he'd done it. 'Why'd you kill those sheep, Sean?' I ask him. And do you know what he says to me?"

"I don't," said Arthur.

"He stares me right in the eye," said Officer Binns. "And gets this confused look on his face. Like he's thinking it over, thinking real hard. And finally, it's as if he gives up trying to puzzle it out. 'I dunno, Frankie,' he says to me. 'Why do *you* think I did it?'"

Arthur was unsure of how to respond. He remained silent and still.

"My point is, don't fret yourself over the why's, Dr. Doyle. Who knows why people get up to mischief? There's no way to explain what's in a man's head." He tapped on his own head twice, as if to indicate the thickness of the skull. "Best to spend the time worried over the how's. And the who's."

When Officer Binns left, clapping his feet against the floor, Arthur spent a long minute sipping at his tea. It was horrible—watery and cold. He pushed the tray aside and continued sorting through the papers, dividing them into piles.

Stabbed girls. Shot girls. Drowned girls. Strangled girls.

October 24, 1900

There were options, for Arthur. There was a selection of the dead from which he could choose: a tea-shop girl, recently married, stabbed in St. James's Park; a nurse run over by a carriage near University College; not one but two separate governesses beaten and robbed in Kensington. He felt as if he were selecting from a chocolate box of horrors.

Focusing on the girls who'd been strangled, Arthur found a number of intriguing possibilities. In the days following his trip to the Yard, he made his grim rounds. He went to see their families, their homes, the places where they'd been killed. He asked the same questions every time: "Pardon me, but had your daughter married before her death?" and "I hate to disturb you further, but did you by any chance notice a wedding dress in the vicinity of the body?" and "So sorry, but when you discovered your sister, was she in the nude?"

It reminded him of his house calls, back in his medical days. He would ask the same questions in the privacy of each bedroom. "And how are we feeling today?" or "How has your appetite been?" or "Does your tooth still ache? Oh, Mrs. Harrington, tell the truth: Have you been taking the cocaine drops I gave you?" He preferred those medical inquisitions to the criminal ones he now conducted.

His interviews concluded, Arthur would, one by one, cross each girl's name off his list. Within a few days, he had exhausted all of his most likely possibilities. He began exploring the less likely options: Bodies found on the street. More anonymous prostitutes. Even an elderly woman who appeared to have suffocated by accident, in her weakened state, against her own bed pillows.

It was when his options had all but run out that he found himself, on the Friday next, back in the East End. Three months earlier a girl's body had turned up in an alley behind Watney Street, near Whitechapel. The cause of death, as listed in the coroner's report, was uncertain. The girl's trachea had been snapped, and yet there was so much bruising around her body that it was impossible to tell whether the neck injury had killed her or whether it was any one of the other dark blue bruises or deep red cuts spread across her pale body that had done her in. She'd been discovered fully clothed. There was no mention, in the documents retained by Scotland Yard, of a wedding dress among the girl's possessions. They did, however, know her name: Sally Needling. She was a good girl. Her parents had put her up as missing, and when the body had come in, they had taken one look at it and known she was theirs. They lived far away in Hampstead. Twenty-six years old, she was well on her way to being a spinster and still lived at home. They had money. A nice bit of land. Her father was a barrister. The girl was certainly no harlot; moreover, her parents could think of no reason for her to be in Whitechapel at all, as they'd informed the Yard.

Arthur found the alley behind Watney Street. He went about his rounds in the dark and narrow space. A horrible smell seemed to drift outward from deep within. As Arthur walked a few paces into the alley, he realized the cause of the smell: A butcher's shop, on the other side of the alley, had stored half-carved piglets and cattle husks that had gone bad outside the shop's back door. Presumably, Arthur hoped, before they could transport the rotting meat elsewhere. While dim, the alley looked out onto a busy thoroughfare. Arthur could hear the rattling carriages from Watney Street as he walked to the most remote part of the alley. It was indisputably a public place, far removed from the closed-door chambers of the boardinghouse where Morgan Nemain had met her end.

This most likely would not be it, Arthur realized. A girl being strangled in the alley would make so much of a racket that it would easily be heard in the street. Whatever atrocity had been committed here, he felt confident that it had little to do with the mystery at hand.

It was at this moment in his thoughts that Arthur looked up. A line of clothes hung from a string going across the alley, connecting a window of the building on the alley's east side with a hook in the wall on its left. All manner of apparel hung from the line: woolly trousers, bright shirtwaists, leg-o'-mutton jackets, soggy white shirts, stockings of every shape and size imaginable. What an odd assortment!

Arthur exited the alley and looked onto the doorstep of the building to the alley's east side, from the window of which the clothes hung. There was no sign out in front of the four-story brick home. It appeared to be someone's private residence. And yet so many garments dried outside.

Arthur knocked on the door. He heard nothing from inside. He knocked again. Finally an old woman answered the door. She had a mean face—squat nose, deep-set eyes, and beside her lips the lines of a permanent frown.

"Well then? What is it?" she barked.

"Pardon me, ma'am," said Arthur. "Is this your home?"

"No, sir, the queen lives here. She's inside at the moment, tending to the char."

Arthur was unimpressed by the woman's sarcasm.

"I'm in need of a place to rest my head for the night," he replied. "Might you be able to provide me with room and board for a reasonable fee?"

The woman looked up and down the block, as if searching for someone amid the midday traffic.

"What have you heard?" she asked.

"I'm sorry, I don't know what you're talking about."

"Who told you to come here for a bed?"

"No one. I was passing by, and your lovely home appeared so hospitable."

The woman examined Arthur, then sniffed her nose in the air. "From time to time, I rent my rooms out to strangers," she said. "If they look like a responsible sort. You seem halfway decent, I suppose."

The woman turned and led Arthur inside.

"How many rooms do you have here?" he asked.

"I might have a spare one for you, if you behave yourself, and I suggest that's the only room you need concern yourself with." Arthur recognized that the woman's behavior was quite odd, but he said nothing. He was making progress.

She led him through her kitchen into a long hallway. The house seemed quiet, or at least far quieter than Arthur's previous boardinghouse experience. Various rooms flanked the hallway, and Arthur could make out two bedchambers and an indoor water closet through the half-open doors as he passed by. At the end of the hall lay what looked to be the master bedroom. Its doors were swung wide open, and Arthur could see the late-morning light pouring in from outside. As they approached the room, the woman turned left, ascending the first few steps of a long, narrow staircase as she spoke.

"Your room will be upstairs. The ones downstairs are full." As Arthur came to the bottom of the stairs, he glanced to his right, into the bright bedroom. The wide bed was neatly made with white sheets and a blue blanket. An oil lamp rested on the woman's nightstand. And on the far side of the room, a small closet was open—in fact, it was without doors at all, and a pair of useless hinges hung from the wall. As his head turned back toward the staircase, he could just make out the contents of the closet: the dark clothes of a woman who cleaned a large household, the torn dresses, the drab bustles, and one bright white wedding gown.

Arthur stopped at the foot of the steps. He looked back toward the open closet: What in the world was this mean Whitechapel charwoman doing with a dress like that? Arthur planted his feet, refusing to ascend the stairs after the woman.

"Where did you get that?" he asked quietly.

The woman turned. She appeared confused. "Get what, now?"

"You have a sparkling white wedding gown in what I presume is your bedchamber. Forgive my impoliteness, but it is considerably too small for you to wear. Whose is it?"

Suspicion flashed across the woman's face.

"And what's it to you?" she asked, with a note of anger in her voice. Arthur decided that in this instance the truth might serve his case better than a fresh lie.

"My name is Arthur Conan Doyle. I am investigating the murder of Morgan Nemain, and as of this moment I am also investigating the murder of one Sally Needling."

"And what's that to do with me?"

"Sally Needling stayed here on the night that she died, didn't she? She was one of your tenants."

The woman matched Arthur's deep stare as the seconds ticked by. Neither blinked. The woman's brow became cross as she emitted a low snarl.

"Get out, you rotting pego!"

"How did her corpse get from your boardinghouse to the alley behind? I don't believe you killed her—a man did. But you were here when it happened."

"I don't care who you are or what business you're on. The door is thataway. Make use of it."

Arthur was in need of some means to compel this woman to talk. He thought of her strangeness at the door. She had treated her boardinghouse as if it were clandestine. As if she did not want anyone to know what she did in this house.

"You've been keeping lodgers here against the wishes of someone nearby, haven't you? Someone who frequents this very block, I'd wager. Hmmm, now..." Arthur broke eye contact, rubbing his palms together and humming as he pieced together the most likely possibilities.

This woman did not appear to share his regard for the cause of justice. He would have to be more firm.

"Quite a large place, isn't this?" he said. "For a woman such as your-self to possess? You've no ring on your finger…You don't own this house, do you? You're looking after it for someone else and renting out rooms on the side for an extra few shillings a week. But your little busi-ness would be shut down if the house's owner became aware of what you're doing, would it not? I would hate, of course, to be the one to have to tell him."

Arthur adjusted his overcoat and puffed out his chest.

"I won't give it back," said the woman after a long moment, her face falling as she became resigned to confession.

"I truly couldn't care whether or not you do," said Arthur. "But I need to know what transpired here between you and the murdered girl."

"I didn't kill her!"

"I know," said Arthur. "Who did?"

"I hardly got a look at him, he came by so quick. He came in with the girl—Sally, you say? And she was wearing that dress. When was the last time you've seen a dress like that? It sparkled in the light, shined like electricity. The man had on a black cloak, black hat, nothing much out of the ordinary. He kept his head ducked down a lot, hiding his eyes. The girl paid for their room. I showed them upstairs, and that was that." The woman sat down on the staircase, folding her bosom over her knees and holding her legs into her body. It seemed to Arthur as if she were cocooning herself.

"Well, I thought that was that," she continued. "The next morning I go to their door, to ask if they want their breakfast. I'd some porridge, and even some ham from the butcher's across the way. There was no answer, so I opened the door. She was…The girl, you see, she was… And the dress, crumpled up in the corner like it was *trash*…Hell." In the darkened stairwell, Arthur could not tell whether the woman was crying. He suspected that she was.

"You found Sally's body," said Arthur. "She was stark naked. She'd been strangled. The man was gone. The dress was by her side."

The woman said nothing, but she nodded, first once, then many times, as if she were confirming the truth for herself as well as for Arthur.

"Isn't it such a beautiful dress?" she said. "Have you ever seen anything like it?"

"You didn't want it to go to waste. To have the police take it away. You thought that maybe you'd sell it, or maybe you'd keep it for yourself. It must be quite valuable, a dress like that. So you hid it away in your closet. But you had to do something with the body, didn't you?" The woman was definitely crying now. Arthur took the first few slats of the staircase in small steps, ascending foot by foot. He drew a handkerchief from his pocket and handed it to the woman. She used it to smear the tears across her cheeks.

"You took the body and deposited it in the alley just beside your home. You must have brought her down these very stairs—she was heavy, wasn't she? She must have hit every step on the way down. That's why the body was so bruised when the police found her. You realized that a *naked* dead girl would attract rather more attention from the police than a clothed one, so what did you do? You took some skirts from your own closet, didn't you, and wrapped them around her? A fair trade, I suppose, for her lovely white dress."

The woman continued to cry as she buried her head between her knees. Arthur wanted to sit beside her, to give her an arm. But there was no room on the narrow staircase. He was forced to stand above her, looking down while her tears dripped onto her soiled shoes.

"You may keep the dress," he said as he walked backward down the stairs. "And the kerchief."

CHAPTER 18

Pleasure Reading

*"Altogether it cannot be doubted that
sensational developments will follow."*
—Sir Arthur Conan Doyle,
"The Adventure of the Norwood Builder"

January 9, 2010, cont.

After Alex Cale's answering machine clicked off, there was silence in
the cluttered Kensington flat. As the lead detective on the case, Harold
felt it was his duty to say something.

"Well then," he said. "That happened."

"What the bloody hell?" said Jennifer incredulously.

"Let's not overreact."

"Do you know who that was? Do you know that man?"

"Yes. I'm sort of working for him, technically." Harold was treated to
a look of stunned horror from Jennifer.

"His name is Sebastian Conan Doyle," chimed Sarah. "He had been
fighting with your brother publicly."

"We knew he'd been threatening Alex," added Harold, "though in
more of a legal, trading-angry-letters sense. We didn't know that he'd
been *really* threatening Alex, in, like, an I'm-going-to-kill-you sense."

"Let's sit down," said Sarah. "Perhaps we should back up for a minute."

The three sat, and Harold and Sarah spent the next fifteen minutes
trying to explain everything they knew about Sebastian Conan Doyle
and his fight with Alex. They talked about the angry letters back and

forth, about Alex's fear of being followed, and they even explained that they had come to London on Sebastian's dime. Though, Harold was quick to add, they had no allegiance to his side in the argument. They simply wanted to find the truth. And the diary.

Jennifer seemed unconvinced. She quieted Harold by slowly raising her palms in front of her, as if she were feeling her way through a dark room. "Hush," she said. "I need a simple answer. Do you think Sebastian Conan Doyle murdered my older brother?"

Harold and Sarah made a brief moment of eye contact, in which Sarah, ever so slightly, smiled and ducked her chin in deference. This was Harold's department.

"I don't know," he said after a long pause. "He's certainly the most likely suspect. But the most likely suspect at first is almost never the one who's actually done it, right? If this were a Conan Doyle story, I think Sebastian would be a red herring."

The look on Jennifer's face was not one that conveyed to Harold that she placed much value on this analysis.

"Why don't you presume for a moment, Mr. White, that this is *not* a Conan Doyle story? What if you presumed that this was, oh, just for argument's sake, something that happened in the real world, to a real live person? In that case, don't you think I should tell the police about Sebastian's message?"

"Yes, absolutely, tell them about the message. But when you do, maybe don't mention the part about how we were here? Or about how we talked to you at all? The New York police had sort of... well, *asked* that I not leave the state. You know. Just for a while. Not that I'm a suspect or anything, myself. Anyhow. You get the point. I don't mean to give you the wrong impression—"

"Harold," interrupted Sarah. "Take a deep breath. Back to your original train of thought. Why don't you think Sebastian killed Alex Cale?"

"A number of reasons. One, *why* would he do it? Money, sure, yeah, great. But now that Alex is dead, who's he going to sell the diary to? Everyone knows it was stolen. And the only collectors with enough money or interest to buy the thing were all staying in the hotel where Alex died. And *they* all think Sebastian probably killed Alex, too! They'd never buy the diary off of him—they'd much rather turn him in and get to play the hero. Which leads me to point number two: If Sebastian killed Alex, he didn't go to very much trouble to conceal it, did he? If you were planning to murder someone, would you leave a recording of your voice making threats in the possession of your victim? Sebastian is a dick, but he's not an idiot. So. Point number three: *How* did he do it? The hotel had cameras in the lobby. He claims not to have visited the hotel that night, so if the NYPD had found his face on one of the tapes…well, we'd have heard about it by now, because he'd already have been arrested. And how'd he get into Alex's room? The door wasn't forced. Alex opened the door willingly. Three times, even. He knew whoever killed him. If he was as paranoid about being followed as you said he was and…well, as I *know* that he was, because I saw him myself, then do you think he'd just have let Sebastian Conan Doyle into his suite with a smile? He wasn't going to offer to make the guy a hot cup of Earl Grey with milk, right? Plus, okay now, here's point the fourth: The message in blood? The shoelace for a murder weapon? Does that really sound like Sebastian to either of you? And if he left those clues in order to frame somebody—another Sherlockian, somebody like me, frankly—well then, didn't he do a pretty piss-poor job of it? If his goal was to implicate someone else, it's funny that he remains the only one implicated. Why not shoot him on a dark street corner, grab the suitcase with the diary from his hands, and blame it on some mugger? Why not break in to his apartment here in London, steal the diary, and blame it on some crack team of house burglars? If Sebastian did it, then he did it in about the dumbest way possible."

With a great *humph* of an exhale, Harold concluded his monologue. His normally plump, pale cheeks had become taut and red. Both Sarah and Jennifer stared at him, stunned.

"That was shockingly coherent," said Sarah at last.

Harold squeezed his eyes shut for a moment and gave her a look that he hoped would indicate that he did not find her last comment particularly helpful.

"I can see why Mr. Conan Doyle hired you," said Jennifer after another pause. Harold couldn't tell whether or not this was meant as a compliment.

"Ms. Peters," he began, "there is one question I still have for you."

"*One?*" whispered Sarah, *sotto voce.*

"In all the books lying around this apartment, I haven't found a single one written by Arthur Conan Doyle. I haven't found any notes either, or reference materials, relating to the great work of Alex's life, his Conan Doyle biography. I understand why he took the original diary to New York with him, but would he have taken *all* of that secondary material as well?"

"No," replied Jennifer, "he would have kept it in his writing office."

"His writing office?"

"Yes. My brother kept a writing office down the street, in which he worked. He didn't like to write in the same space in which he lived—it made him feel claustrophobic or locked up or something or other."

"What about all of the books in the study, and that great wooden desk? That's not his office?"

"That's his *reading* office. Or maybe it was his pleasure-reading office, I can't remember what he called it. But all of the Sherlock material would be in his writing office. It's literally right down the street. We can head there now, if you like."

While Jennifer gathered her heavy coat and Harold buttoned his, Sarah whispered to him, quietly enough that Jennifer wouldn't hear.

"Just to be clear," Sarah said, "is there one of you people who *doesn't* have obsessive-compulsive disorder?"

The walk to Alex Cale's writing office was indeed brief. It was on the very next block north. Harold couldn't help but notice that the apartment building looked just like that of Alex's other, nonwriting flat—a fact that served only to accentuate the idiosyncratic pointlessness of the expense.

On the front stoop, Harold listened to the midday hum of activity in the building while Jennifer fumbled in her bag for the keys. She removed a collection of personal effects—square black makeup cases, rounded contact-lens holders, curved-steel beautifying apparatuses—and then placed them back in her bag as the rummaging continued. Harold considered offering to help, but wondered whether asking a woman to help sort through her purse might be considered rude. He could never tell about situations like this.

But before he could speak up, the door swung open, seemingly of its own accord. A man emerged from inside, carrying a leather bag, and politely held the door open for Jennifer. Though he looked young—he couldn't be much above thirty—his hairline had already started to recede on the sides, while the center section remained firmly tethered to his brow. His loose jeans were dirty, stained with splotches of blue paint. He sported a nondescript gray sweater and an awful, ill-kempt goatee.

Jennifer smiled at the man as she took the weight of the door from his hand, and he returned a smile as he wordlessly trotted down the front steps.

"I hate goatees, too," said Sarah to Harold, as if reading his mind, when they had entered the building. "It's, like, have a beard or don't, you know?"

By the time they'd reached the door to Alex's writing office, Jennifer had managed to find the proper ring of keys from her bag. But as she held the key up in front of 2L, she stopped suddenly, realizing that it was unnecessary: The door was already ajar.

It looked like an animal's jaw, opening wide to eat them.

"Hello?" called Jennifer, a note of fear in her voice. "Hello?!"

There was no response.

"Is someone inside?"

Harold turned to Sarah for guidance, but her eyes were locked on the open door.

She nodded to herself: This would be *her* department. Without looking at him, she stepped forward, pushing the door open all the way. She entered the bright flat.

It was even more of a mess than Alex's hotel room in New York. The diffuse London sun shone through wide windows onto a sea of books, all of them toppled onto the floor from their rightful shelves. Cushions had been thrown off the couch and the linings cut open. White tufts of down—or whatever couch pillows were stuffed with—were spread around like snowdrifts. As Harold entered, he noticed the freshly emptied wooden bookshelves, the insides of which were colored more darkly than the outsides, having not been exposed to daylight in years. He could see a tiled kitchenette off to one side of the central living space, with its own mess. Plates shattered on the floor, a clattered array of silverware gleaming from the white tiles. Every drawer on the desk at the far side of the room had been opened, and some even removed. Blue ink spilled across the desktop from an overturned bottle.

Jennifer remained in the doorway, too afraid to enter. Sarah took a quick walk through the flat, from end to end.

"No one's here," she pronounced.

Harold watched the blue ink on the desk dribble onto the floor. It was still wet. And still dripping.

"That goatee!" yelled Harold, putting it together. It wasn't blue paint that he'd seen on the man's jeans. It was ink.

He ran past Jennifer into the hallway and down the stairs, taking them three at a time. He popped open the building's front door with a great push. But it was no use. Harold surveyed the long street as he heard the door click shut behind him. He didn't see a soul.

CHAPTER 19

The Broken Hair Clip

*"There's the scarlet thread of murder running through
the colourless skein of life, and our duty is to unravel it,
and isolate it, and expose every inch of it."*
—Sir Arthur Conan Doyle,
A Study in Scarlet

October 27, 1900

The Needling family lived in a mansion called Millhead, which rested
at the bottom of a hill in West Hampstead. Great white pillars shot forth
from the dirt, pressing the sharply angled roof upward, like an arrow to
the heavens. Before the pillars lay a row of delicate hedges, and two empty,
symmetrical flower beds. Into the distance spread a craggy heath, whose
reddish outcroppings of rock stretched into the cloud-covered horizon.

Arthur had sent word of his coming the day before. He'd prepared
the first telegram himself, a "Dear Sir" sort of job to Sally Needling's
father, explaining who he was, how he'd become involved in "the tragedy" and all that, and asking permission to visit the man's home. Then
Arthur had decided it might be odd, to send such a missive without
warning, and so he'd hurried down to the Yard again, to have them
broach the issue. Best to let the authorities handle the awkward bits,
Arthur felt. Inspector Miller had made contact with Sally's father, Bertrand Needling, who quickly assented to a visit. Arthur had sent a brief,
yet polite, note this morning, thanking Mr. Needling for his time and
letting him know that Arthur would be on the 4:05 from King's Cross.

He'd made no mention of Sally directly, nor of her murder, nor of a cheap East End boardinghouse with a white lace wedding dress tucked away in its back bedroom closet.

Arthur clapped the heavy bronze knocker against the front door. He could hear the sound echo throughout the house. After a wait, a servant answered the door and let him inside. The family had been expecting him.

His interview with the family was tense and hushed, their voices quieted to a whisper. Bertrand and Clara Needling sat on opposite ends of the drawing room. Sally's two brothers were out. Arthur never learned where. The talk was punctuated by strange, sudden silences. In the middle of describing some facet of her daughter's brief life, Mrs. Needling would lose the train of her thoughts and her sentence would putter to a halt, like a steam engine cooling to its last breaths. Mr. Needling, a pallid barrister, would not jump in to pick up the thought, however, and Arthur was mindful of interrupting. And thus a lengthy silence would hang, until finally Arthur felt comfortable asking another question, on an unrelated topic so that it seemed he'd received a satisfactory answer before. He found that the household existed in a grief-drunk haze, and he waded through it cautiously and politely.

Sally had been born in '74, in this very house. A happy girl, Mrs. Needling assured Arthur. She used to run up the hill behind the house and then roll down it with the boys. She'd put on her brothers' worn and oversize trousers so she didn't get her dresses dirty. For her eighth birthday, she'd begged and begged for a ruby hair clip she'd seen in a shop window in the city, at Routledge's on Oxford Street. After some pleading with her father, the hair clip had been acquired and presented in a box filled with pink tissue paper to a squealing Sally. She wore it all day long, and her mother had to pry it from her hair that night at bedtime. And wouldn't you know? The next day Sally went up the hill with her brothers, the clip still in her hair. As she rolled down the hill, gay as a bird, the clip broke into a dozen pieces. Sally was devastated. Of course another, identical clip had to be purchased, and it was, the very next day. It had taken only the smallest bit of cajoling of Mr. Needling, his wife explained through her first smile of the afternoon.

"Dr. Doyle doesn't need to be hearing about all this," said Mr. Needling with a terse and quiet ferocity. "He's trying to find out who killed her, not write her biography."

Mrs. Needling began to respond to Mr. Needling's outburst. "Dear, I was just explaining what a . . ." And then she let her sentence go, fading off into the stuffy air.

"Was she fond of any gentlemen that you knew of? Did she have many callers?" said Arthur, again changing the subject. Best to start here and see if this led to a conversation about Sally's single-night marriage.

"No, sir," said Mr. Needling. "She was a quiet girl, you see. Kept to the estate a lot. She was quite fond of her horses."

Arthur nodded that he understood. They didn't know that she'd been married when she died. Her relationship with this man, this killer, had been a secret she'd kept from her family. Should he press further? It is a horrid thing, to tell a mother that she'd missed her murdered daughter's wedding day.

"She did have her friends in the city, though," offered Mrs. Needling. "She'd been spending a lot of her time around them."

"Her friends in the city?" inquired Arthur.

"Janet and . . . Emily. Yes. Janet and Emily—those were the names. Sorry, she only ever mentioned their Christian names in talking about them. And they never came to the house either, Sally always went into the city to see them. They'd attend one of those meetings or some such."

Mr. Needling stirred in his seat, clearly agitated by the direction the conversation had taken. He said nothing, however. Arthur addressed Mrs. Needling, ignoring her husband's discomfort.

"What sort of meetings would those be?" he asked casually.

Mrs. Needling looked to her husband for guidance, but he refused to meet her eyes.

"Perhaps they were more 'talks' than 'meetings,' I should say. Sally wasn't a terribly active member, you understand—she just went for the speeches. And for her girlfriends, of course. She liked meeting the other young women."

"We don't want you to get the wrong idea, Dr. Doyle, that's all!" interjected Mr. Needling. "She was a good girl. Always was. You must remember that."

"Of course, Mr. Needling. I'm sure your daughter was the very flower of West Hampstead. Which is all the more reason for me to find the man who did this vile deed and see that he's punished." Bertrand Needling hardly appeared comforted by Arthur's words. "Now, what were these... these talks your daughter attended with her friends?"

"Voting rights for women," replied Mrs. Needling unabashedly. "She went to the talks about extending the vote to women. She was a suffragist, Sally."

"Now, now," said Mr. Needling. "Let's not overstate the case, shall we, dear? She went to some talks. She had a few friends. It was all relatively harmless. But I'm a Primrose man myself. I'm in the League." Mr. Needling raised his right hand, flashing a silver ring on his index finger. Arthur leaned forward and recognized the familiar five-leaf-rosette shape adorning the ring. "Disraeli right through our Cecil," Mr. Needling continued, "now, those are statesmen. And I'd never have let a daughter of mine go too far into a folly like that. I've read you on the subject as well—of course you agree with me. Understand that it was a youthful diversion for the girl, that's all. Nothing serious."

"She was a suffragist," repeated Mrs. Needling. "She would talk about it whenever she got the chance." Her husband gave a loud cough, and Mrs. Needling became quiet again. Arthur had no urge to get involved in this family's politics. He had a lingering fondness for Disraeli, he had to admit, but goodness, Cecil? The Marquess of Salisbury was a rotten prig. How the Conservatives had atrophied, that he was their new standard-bearer. But Arthur, thankfully, had the good sense to refrain from saying as much.

"Do you know the name of her organization? Or the location of those meetings?"

"She didn't go to meetings," said Mr. Needling. "She traipsed into a few harmless talks. And she was not a member of any organization. These girlfriends may have been, I can't vouch for them, but Sally was *not*. I'm sure I've forgotten the names of the groups, or where she went. Somewhere in London."

"I apologize for bringing up such an unsettling point, but her body was found in Whitechapel," said Arthur. Mr. Needling frowned and gritted his teeth. "Is it possible that your daughter's meetings may have been—"

"My daughter, sir, had no business in Whitechapel, of that you can be most certain. Do you understand me? No business at all." Mr. Needling slapped both his hands down against the arms of his chair. "The police are in error. Or her body was transported to that foul spot by the villain who killed her, in order to obscure his tracks." Her body indeed had been moved, thought Arthur, but, sadly, only from inside the boardinghouse to the alley beside it. The girl had spent her wedding night in Whitechapel.

"Tell me," he began, "did your daughter ever receive any letters from these friends? From Janet and Emily? I suspect that they have information that might be vitally useful to my investigations"—Arthur left aside for the moment what that information might be—"and so finding them is of the utmost importance."

Mrs. Needling considered the question. "I don't believe so," she said. "But if Mr. Needling doesn't object, you're welcome to examine her writing table and see for yourself."

Arthur looked toward Mr. Needling, whose pale face offered neither permission nor disapproval. "I would appreciate that very much, if you don't mind." Mr. Needling nodded and remained seated while his wife took Arthur through the palatial house and up the stairs to Sally's rooms.

As Arthur entered, he was struck first by the immaculate cleanliness of Sally's quarters. Not a speck of dust flew into the air as the door was opened. Not a stitch of the bedspread lay out of place. The servants must still clean it daily, he thought, though the girl had been dead for months.

Arthur stood before the desk. Six small drawers lay atop it, while two wider ones lay below, between the table legs. He reached his hand out to pull one open and then paused, glancing back toward Mrs. Needling in the doorway. She leaned against the doorframe, her left hand reaching across her body and holding on to the wall as if she were pulling it toward her.

Arthur waited, hoping she would excuse herself. His search would take some time, and he preferred to do it alone. Heaven only knew what he might find, and he did not want to excite the poor woman.

She didn't budge, however, but instead looked up to the ceiling. She leaned heavier against the doorframe and cupped the plaster in her glove.

Oh well. Arthur pulled open one of the drawers above the desk, yanking it fully out of its hutch. Envelopes and pens and ink bottles rattled around in the drawer as it landed with a clack on the desktop.

Mrs. Needling shivered, shaken from her haze.

"If you'll excuse me, Dr. Doyle," she said. "I must attend to a supper goose." And with that, she left Arthur alone. He felt like a grave robber. Or a ghoul. Lord, where was Bram when you needed him?

His search was methodical. He read the letters carefully. A handful were from Sally's brothers, who'd been away in the Transvaal the year before. Good lads. Two were from an uncle in Paris. Three from a grandmother in Swansea. Arthur learned much about the weather on the Continent and the Atlantic tides at the Swansea beaches, but little about the secret life of Sally Needling. Who were these girls, Janet and Emily? Exactly what organization had they been a part of? And who was this man who had surreptitiously married Sally without even her parents knowing?

Arthur went through the top drawers one by one until he came to the fifth one in his search. He pulled at the bronze knob. Yet the drawer held firm against his pull. It was locked. He bent over and noticed a small keyhole below the knob. It looked like a purely decorative feature, like the tiny locks affixed to the front of leather-bound diaries. He couldn't imagine that it provided much in the way of security. Arthur pulled again on the knob, harder. The drawer didn't budge.

This was promising.

He went to the bedroom door and closed it quietly. He didn't want the family to hear him at work. He walked back to the dresser and bent over the keyhole once again. He didn't know much about picking locks, but once, over a tall carafe of brandy, Wilde had explained to him how the job was done. How Wilde knew, Arthur could not be certain, but then again, the man was ever a mystery to all his friends. As Arthur took up a pen from the desk, he became sad, thinking of his old friend. What had happened there?

After the arrest, the trial, prison, Wilde had vanished. Where was he now? Arthur hadn't the foggiest. Such a great man, such a warm and broad-smiling soul, brought low by mere vice. Every man knew the dangerous pull of sin. Yes, in honesty, every man experienced certain... *urges*. It was not the feeling them which had brought kind Wilde so low. It was the giving in. The failure born of weakness. To be a man, a *good* man, was to overcome the natural iniquities of one's manhood. Wilde had succumbed to sin, but Arthur did not hate him for it. He was only saddened. He wanted Wilde back—the old Wilde, the good Wilde, the witty and buoyant Wilde who lit up every dinner table at which he sat.

Arthur banished the thought from his head as he jabbed the tip of the pen into the keyhole. Best not to think upon it.

But the pen didn't fit. The keyhole was too small. Arthur tried the other pens at the desk, but none would do the trick. He had to look elsewhere.

The jewelry box next to the mirror was an obvious choice. As he opened it, he blinked at the flare of light that escaped from the glittering jewels inside. Diamonds, opals, golden bracelets and rings of every color. Arthur found three pearl necklaces, and yet the clasps on all of them were U-shaped, and so useless for his purposes. After only a few moments of digging, he found an item with a long, thin clasp. It was perfect for lock picking. He removed it from the pile, clasp first, and stepped toward the desk. He was halfway there when he looked down and saw what he held in his hand: a shimmering, ruby-red hair clip.

Arthur stopped, staring down at it. It was so small in his palm. Two metal bands stretched from end to end, onto which colored stones had been laid. It was ecstatically colorful in the way of all children's jewelry. He could imagine the thrill inside eight-year-old Sally over opening up a wrapped box to find this on the morning of her birthday. He could imagine her crying inconsolably when she rolled to the bottom of the hill and found pieces of the broken clip buried in her hair. He knew why her father had consented to purchasing an identical replacement—the one that Arthur now held—at once.

Arthur inserted the long metal clasp into the keyhole. It fit perfectly. He flicked it up, then down, then side to side, twisting it to find the tumbler. He remembered what Wilde had described to him, how you had to find the tumblers, however many there were, sequentially. You had to press them one by one. Arthur pressed harder into the lock, jabbing for a deeper tumbler, when the hair clip broke. The miniature screws connecting the clasp to the central two bands popped out, and the clip split into two halves. The bands with the colored stones on them fell to the floor, while his push forward threw him slightly off balance. He removed the end he still held, the clasp, from the keyhole, and looked down.

Heavens! He had stepped on the fallen clip while regaining his balance. The bands were shattered into four or five pieces now, and a few stones had broken loose from their holds. A cloud passed outside the tall windows, and beams of light blanketed the room. The stones glimmered on the floor, islands in a wood-brown sea.

Arthur left the wreckage where it lay. The milk, so to speak, was spilt. No use crying now. He turned back to the desk, again inserting the clasp into the keyhole.

Within another minute he'd gotten it open.

Arthur opened the drawer hungrily. He laid it on the desktop and peered down. Inside, there was nothing but a quarter-inch stack of identical white papers. He lifted a handful of them up, and held them to the window light.

The papers were devoid of writing. He flipped through each one and found them all equally blank.

There was no mark on the pages, save one. At the top of each paper, there was the image, printed in black ink, of a three-headed crow. Arthur gave a start. It was the same image that had been found tattooed on Morgan Nemain's leg!

But what did it mean?

He folded the papers and committed them to his coat pocket. He replaced the drawer as he'd found it.

He knelt to the floor and swept the bits of shattered hair clip into his hand before gently depositing them back into the jewelry box and leaving.

There remained no sign, after he left, of his ever having been there.

CHAPTER 20

The Chase

*"At the present moment, you thrill with the glamour
of the situation and the anticipation of the hunt."*
—Sir Arthur Conan Doyle,
The Valley of Fear

January 9, 2010, cont.

"The police are on their way," said Jennifer Peters as she clapped her cell phone shut. Harold and Sarah were looking through the piles of books and papers in the writing office, while Jennifer remained close to the doorway. In the five minutes since Harold had run downstairs and been unable to find any trace of the goateed man, Jennifer had managed to step only a few feet into the apartment. She remained motionless, arms crossed above her belly, as if giving herself a deep hug.

"Look, this is awkward," said Harold, "but I'd rather not speak to the police, if that's okay. I've been at the scenes of two crimes in the last seventy-two hours, and I'd kind of like to avoid another grilling about that. If you don't mind."

Jennifer hugged herself tighter, and spoke curtly. "Fine. Go. I won't tell them you were here."

Harold gave Alex Cale's bookshelves a quick once-over and then motioned to Sarah that they should leave. She closed the drawer of Alex's desk that she'd been rifling through and followed Harold to the door. She gave Jennifer a warm look and placed a hand on the older woman's shoulder as she passed by.

"Thank you," said Harold as they exited into the hallway.

"I'd rather not see either of you ever again, please," said Jennifer.

Harold nodded, and without another word he and Sarah left the building.

After a reflective half minute on the street outside, Harold finally spoke.

"Well," he said, "the bad news: Whoever that guy was, with the goatee, he took everything of any use out of that apartment. No diary, okay, but not even a spare photocopy of the diary. Or any excerpts that Alex had typed up. Or notes on what was in it. Did you notice the laptop power cable beside the desk? Ten to one there used to be a laptop attached to it, and he took that, too. There were plenty of books on Conan Doyle, sure, but not a single piece of information about the diary itself, or how Alex had found it."

"Is there any good news?" asked Sarah as they walked toward Argyll Road.

"Yeah. We've actually laid eyes on someone who's mixed up in this, whatever the hell 'this' is. And we know the guy's not a Sherlockian. Or at least not an Irregular; I'd have recognized him if he was."

"I suppose that's something like good news. But I think I can do you one better." Sarah reached into her coat pocket and removed a thumb-size piece of purple plastic. She handed it to Harold. "A flash drive. It was in one of the drawers on Alex's desk."

"You stole it?"

Sarah just shrugged.

Harold was impressed. He could never tell whether she was two steps behind him or two steps ahead.

"Not sure if anything useful is on it, but we can check it out back at the hotel," said Sarah, turning her head to look behind them once, and then again a few seconds later. "I have some bad news, too."

"What?"

"I think we're being followed."

Harold felt his body grow suddenly tense. "Seriously?" he asked.

"I'm going to kneel down on one knee, as if I'm adjusting my shoe. When I do that, come in front of me and turn to face me, and talk to me as if you're just naturally continuing our conversation. Then look casually behind us and see if you notice a big guy in a leather jacket. Ready? Go."

Sarah dropped her right knee to the pavement, and, leaning over her left, she reached into her left shoe as if she were trying to remove a stone from it. She had on thin black flats, out of which she pulled her heel, running her fingers along the inside lining of the well-worn shoe.

Harold turned to face her, doing his best to seem casual. He placed his hands in his pockets as he spoke.

"Okay, this is me talking to you," he said, "I'm still talking, blah-blah-blah, here I am talking." He gazed past her down the street. Among the throng of pedestrians—a hand-holding couple, a jogger in a tracksuit, an Indian family of four—Harold quickly made eye contact with a large man in a leather jacket and loose blue jeans. He was heavy-set, with a circular head and puffy cheeks. The coat looked flimsy, and the man held his hands in his pockets to keep them from the cold.

Shit, thought Harold, realizing he'd just exchanged a glance with the man. Harold flicked his head abruptly to the right, finding a distant street sign at which to stare.

"We just looked right at each other," he said. "I think he saw me notice him."

"What's he doing now?" asked Sarah as she continued to fiddle with her shoe.

Harold kept his face aimed at the street sign—"KENSINGTON PALACE," it read, accompanied by a tiny picture of a walking man, and an arrow pointing behind Harold's back—while he tried to turn only his eyes to the left, in order to spy on the man. The motion made his eyes hurt. The heavyset man had averted his gaze as well, and he seemed to be occupying himself by staring into the front windows of a tanning shop.

"He's looking away," said Harold. "Definitely seems fishy."

Sarah placed her heel back in her shoe and stood up. She led Harold down Kensington Road with a quickened step.

"What should we do?" Harold finally asked.

Sarah raised her hand and stepped from the curb onto the street. "Get out of here," she said.

A cab came quickly, and the two shuffled inside. It was only after they had shut the taxi's door behind them and the driver had turned his head around to inquire about their destination that they both realized they weren't sure what to say.

"Umm . . . not the hotel?" asked Harold.

"He might know where we're staying already, but just in case, let's not tell him." Sarah raised her voice as she spoke to the driver. "Do you mind just heading straight for a minute while we figure out where we're going?"

By way of response, the driver—a South Asian man with dark hair and a prodigious mustache—shrugged. He switched the car into Drive.

Harold and Sarah both swiveled in their seats and looked out the taxi's rear window. The man in the leather coat was on his cell phone.

As they watched him recede into the distance, however, they saw a quickly moving black car come to a sudden stop in front of him. The man lowered his cell phone. He pulled open the car's door and swung his wide frame inside the car in one continuous motion; it appeared surprisingly graceful for a man of his size. The car sped forward, growing larger in the taxi's rear window. It was headed straight toward them.

Harold turned back to the driver. "Do you mind going a bit faster?" he said.

"Faster?" replied the driver. "Faster to where?"

"Wherever," said Sarah. "Up that way. And faster."

The driver shrugged again, and gave a knowing shake of his head. *Americans!*

Behind them the black car weaved between lanes, aggressively making up the distance between it and the taxi. The side windows of the black car were darkened, so Harold couldn't make out who else might be inside. His view into the car's front window was obstructed by one intermediate car, and then another, until finally he managed to get a second's clear view of the black car's driver: a balding young man in a gray sweater, who sported an awful goatee.

Harold inhaled sharply.

"Holy shit," was all he managed to say.

Sarah saw the Goateed Man at the same time as Harold did. She turned instantly toward the driver.

"Hi," she began, "would you please make a right turn up at that light? Yes, right here."

"Missus," the driver replied, "what is going on?"

"Please turn *right here*, now!" barked Sarah.

The driver switched lanes and took the turn.

"I do not want to be part of any trouble," he said as they headed south past Imperial College.

"Neither do we. So let's try to avoid trouble as much as we can, all right, by making a sharp left up ahead."

"I will drop you off at this corner here."

"No!" interjected Harold. "We're being followed."

"Come on, now," said the driver. "Time to get out."

"Sir, I'm being completely serious. Look at the black car behind us. They've been following us since we got into your cab."

The driver looked up into his rearview mirror. There were more than a few black cars.

"Why would someone follow you? What, you are a famous actor or something?"

"Actually," said Harold as he thought the matter over, "that's a good question. I'm not sure why *they're* following *us*. As far as I can tell, they're the ones who have something we want."

"So maybe I pull over here and you can go to figure out who is chasing who."

"That's not a bad plan," said Harold.

Sarah looked at him strangely. "What?" she asked hesitantly, as if she were afraid of the answer.

"I have an idea," said Harold. He reached into his wallet and removed a tight clump of bills. Without checking to see how much money he was handing over, he folded the clump and handed it to the driver. The cabbie looked pleased as he thumbed through the money.

"I need you to do one more favor for us," Harold continued. "Speed up. A lot. Then pull a quick left up ahead, at"—he squinted to make out the street sign—"Fulham. Then stop abruptly, as soon as you can."

The driver glanced down at his new wad of bills, then shrugged. *Whatever you say*, spoke his gesture.

As the cab accelerated, Harold could feel his back press into the cushioned seat. He looked down to find his hands, of their own accord, gripping the seat below.

The cabbie swung the wheel to the left, diving into a gap between the oncoming cars, and Harold's body was thrown to the right, against Sarah. He could feel her limbs tensing as the cab pulled the turn. When the car straightened itself, he tried to scoot himself politely away from her but ended up pushing with a hand against her upper thigh. She seemed not to notice.

The driver swerved the car to the curb and slapped the brakes with gusto. Without seat belts, Harold and Sarah were jerked forward against the divider. The car came to a stop.

"Wait here for a second," said Harold as he exited the car. He stood outside the open door for a moment, waiting for the black car to pull the same turn and appear in front of him.

He didn't have to wait long. After a few seconds, the car came hurtling through the intersection. But, unlike the cab, it had no plans to stop. It accelerated further as it straightened out on Fulham Street.

Harold, twitchy with adrenaline, stepped out into the street immediately in front of the oncoming car. He could see the confusion on the Goateed Man's face, at the wheel, when he realized what had happened. For a long moment, as the car raced toward Harold, he began to reconsider his plan. If the Goateed Man wanted to kill him, he now had the perfect opportunity. All he had to do was keep his foot on the gas and Harold would be slammed against the front of his car. He could chalk the death up to a simple traffic accident, and no one would ever know the truth. Harold was playing a classic poker move against the oncoming car—he was paying for information, taking a calculated risk not for the purpose of winning but in order to learn something about his opponent. If he lived, it would be because the Goateed Man did not want to kill him. And that was important information. If he died, however... Well, Harold figured, if the Goateed Man really wanted to kill him, then he would have been killed already. Like Alex.

Harold could make out the Goateed Man's grimace as he pressed on the brakes and yanked the car to the left, onto the curb. The metal screech of the wheels pierced through the midday traffic noise. The car turned to its side, front sticking out into the first lane of the street as it slid across the pavement. It finally stopped a few feet in front of Harold.

He looked directly into the face of the Goateed Man in the driver's seat. The man scowled. Harold smiled. The Goateed Man wasn't trying to kill him—in fact, he was going out of his way not to. Harold walked calmly up to the black car and knocked delicately on the passenger-side window.

There was a long, silent pause. The inhabitants of the car seemed not to know what to do. They had signed up for a car chase, not a polite tête-à-tête, and the change of activities was throwing them off their normal role.

Finally the passenger-side window slid down, revealing the man in the leather jacket inside.

"Yes?" said the man, his face glacially serene.

"You don't have the diary, do you?" said Harold, coming to this realization only after he'd spoken it out loud.

The man said nothing while he considered the situation. This pause worried Harold; perhaps this guy was smarter than he'd hoped.

"You don't have it either, then," said the man as his face broke out in a broad smile.

Shit. Harold had given up as much information as he'd gotten. But maybe this trade was worth it. If neither of them had the diary...

"You didn't kill Alex Cale," said Harold. It was not a question.

"You sure about that?" said the man. He reached into his coat pocket and removed a gun. He pointed it straight at Harold's face. It appeared impossibly large as Harold stared down its barrel.

Harold's resolve wavered. How sure was he, really, that this man didn't want to kill him? Harold couldn't think anymore. Logic collapsed. Cool, Sherlockian reason was burned up in the heat of his terror.

"I don't have it," Harold pleaded. "The diary. I don't even know where it is. Or who took it."

Suddenly the black car seemed to shiver. It sighed, then tilted slightly downward, sloping to the pavement away from Harold.

Harold looked over the roof and saw Sarah on the other side of the black car. How did she get there? He saw her rise from a kneeling position by the back tire: She'd punctured it. And, evidently, the front one as well.

"Cab!" she yelled at Harold. "Now!"

Looking down, he could see that the man with the gun was ever so briefly distracted by the commotion. Harold took the opportunity to run as fast as he possibly could.

He yanked open the cab door and flung himself into the backseat. Sarah was half a second behind him.

"Please go now anywhere as fast as you can!" shouted Harold at the driver. There was a recognition in the man's face that something serious had happened. He didn't ask questions, but instead threw the cab back into Drive and kicked at the gas pedal.

Harold looked through the back window. No one had gotten out of the black car. And it didn't give chase. The black car sat motionless, leaning to its left against the curb.

Sarah revealed a small retractable knife in her palm. She folded the blade back into its shell and slipped it into her purse. She looked into Harold's eyes with an impossible cool.

"So," said Sarah, "how'd your plan work out for you?"

CHAPTER 21

Virgil and Dante on the Shores of Acheron

"Abandon all hope, ye who enter here."
—Dante Alighieri,
The Divine Comedy

October 30, 1900

Bram Stoker stood before Aldgate Station, examining the printed image in his hand. It was a three-headed crow, rendered in black ink upon a sheet of clean white paper. The crow's beaks, in the image, were outstretched and open slightly, as if each were about to devour its own succulent prey. The eyes were hollow dots where the white paper showed through. The wings looked like single brushstrokes, or single slices of a knife. The image was menacing. Warlike. Murderous.

Bram handed the paper back to Arthur, who had been waiting in silence while his friend finished his examinations.

"A frightful beast, that one," said Bram in regard to the image. "I've never seen anything like it."

"Nor I," said Arthur with a sigh. "I haven't a clue as to where it comes from or what it's meant to represent."

"Nothing nice, I'd wager. So you discovered these papers in Sally Needling's rooms? And the Yard had described the same image as having been tattooed onto Morgan Nemain's leg?"

"Yes," said Arthur, "and I can tell what you'll want to know next. Did

Sally Needling have the image tattooed on *her* leg as well? The answer, I'm afraid, we don't have. The useless muffs from the Yard didn't note anything about a tattoo in their report on the Needling case. But she was a good girl. From a respectable family. Having found her body in a Whitechapel alley was enough trouble for the police. They might have elected to omit a mention of a tattoo, to save the girl's parents—and themselves, for that matter—a whole lot of bother."

"Indeed. I gather that your impression of the Yard worsens with every passing day."

"My God, man, they're imbeciles! In four days I'm halfway to solving two murders, possibly more, that they'd given up on as lost long ago. They are wretched detectives."

At that, Bram was forced to smile.

"It's a good thing, then," he said, "that we've such a master sleuth at our disposal."

Arthur grimaced. He found Bram to be so flippant sometimes about matters of the utmost seriousness. But he needed the man's help to once again navigate the East End, and so he held his tongue.

"My hope," said Arthur, "is to find the tattooist who inked this design upon the leg of Morgan Nemain, and most likely upon the leg of Sally Needling as well. This image meant something to these girls. They kept these papers imprinted with the image, and at least one of them had it permanently inked onto her skin. Perhaps they told the tattooist what it meant. What it symbolized."

"Have you given any thought to the possibility that the murderer himself drew the tattoo onto Morgan Nemain's skin, after she died?"

"Lord, Bram, but isn't that a gruesome thought? I don't know where you get these ideas. No, I don't find that a likely scenario. In the first place, the Yard man said that the tattoo had not been drawn recently. Moreover, if Sally was in possession of a stack of the same drawing, it seems most probable that whatever involvement these girls had with the crow image, they had it voluntarily, and they had it long before Sally's murder."

"Well reasoned, Arthur. But how do you intend to find the tattooist? There must be a thousand seamen in London who know how to apply ink to a hot needle."

Now it was Arthur's turn to smile. He stepped back and gestured to their surroundings. The midday din of Aldgate descended on them. Carriages rattled and banged their way down High Street. A gang of young boys kicked dirt into the air as they jostled one another and chucked pebbles at the passing horses. Beggars shook their rusted tins, and pickpockets followed quietly behind any man with a decent top-coat. And the stench, that horrid dead-fish stench, drifted across it all in gusts from the docks to the south. Arthur inhaled deeply, sucking in the putrid air and puffing it back out again between his grinning cheeks.

"'Now put yourself in that man's place,'" said Arthur. "'What would he do then?' Or, in our case, she?"

Bram frowned. "That's a quote from something, isn't it?"

"Yes. From *A Study in Scarlet*."

"That's one of your own stories!"

"Indeed. And it's good advice, don't you think? Come." Arthur led Bram east away from the station, along High Street. "Imagine you're a young girl, fresh-faced and twenty-six years of age, from a northern heath. You come into the city occasionally, for shopping, the theater, and perhaps the occasional suffragist lecture. You and your girlfriends have decided to burn ink onto your bodies, in order to symbolize something or other. Where do you go?"

"To the Strand. She would ask about in the shops there, the places she'd been before, about who in the city could draw the tattoo."

"Close, Bram, but I fear not quite right. On the contrary, Sally would have gone anywhere *besides* the Strand. She wouldn't want to be recognized in those familiar shops, asking around for a tattooist. What if her parents discovered her trip? What would they think? It would be a disaster."

"But they say that painting on the body is becoming more common in these late days. I haven't seen a British sailor *without* a burnt mark on his forearms in years. And, not that I listen to such gossip, but they say that even the Duke of York has been tattooed, that it was done up while he was in Malta."

"Yes, yes, of course, George of all people would attract such stories. Bit of an Orientophile, that boy. But behavior befitting the rude men who work on the seas, and the rude heir to Wales, is not necessarily behavior befitting a solicitor's daughter from West Hampstead. If Sally was inked, she was inked in secret."

Arthur thought that Bram seemed impressed by this reasoning, but that he was doing his best to conceal it.

"Why, she'd go to the docks, of course," said Bram. "She could have anything she liked done in secret by the river. This neighborhood's reputation, in matters as unladylike as these, precedes it."

"Very good," said Arthur. "Precisely."

At this, Bram made a strange face, though Arthur had no idea why. He was too busy enjoying the requisite pedantry of detective work. This was ever so much more thrilling than his day at the Yard, sifting through papers. To discover something for oneself was exciting, of course, but to then explain it to a mystified audience... Well, a detective needs an audience. Arthur felt that he understood his old Holmes more and more with every passing day. "Now then, our girl is off into London, headed for the docks. Where does she go?"

"The closest stations are the Shadwell and Fenchurch stations on the Blackwall line, or, better yet, Wapping Station on the East London line."

"Indeed you're right," said Arthur. "That's how a city dweller would get there. But Sally Needling wasn't from the city, was she? To make it to the Blackwall line, she'd have had to muck about between trains at Cannon Street. Frankly, it's confusing, even for someone like me. And she doesn't know the docks at all. She's a simple country girl. Don't you think she'd have taken the simplest route possible to any stop that read as next to the London docks on a rail map?" Arthur produced a rail map from inside his coat pocket and stretched it out between his hands. "See here! She'd have taken the Great Northern to King's Cross, obviously. Then she'd have taken the Metropolitan line here, to Aldgate."

"But the Mark Lane station is closer to the docks."

"Yes, but would she have known that? I suspect not. Examine this map." Arthur stopped walking and turned to face the wall of a tavern. He spread the map flat against the wall with his palms. Inside, he could hear the clinking of pint glasses and the squeaks of boots on beer-sodden boards. It was a tuneful clatter, a song beaten out every afternoon by a drunken rabble on dirty glass and crumbling wood. *The Ballad of the Midday Bitters*, Arthur thought.

"Does it not look," he continued, "from the way the streets are drawn, as if it would be easier to get to the docks from Aldgate Station than Mark Lane? You and I know that in the world as it exists, Mark Lane is closer. But in the world as Sally Needling understood it, Aldgate is the nearer. She'd have looked at this great, wide street right here—the Commercial Road—and decided it was an easier route than the crisscrossing mess she'd have had to dodge through by the Tower. So she'd walk east from the station, to the Commercial Road, and then turn right onto Leman. She'd approach the docks this way, right from Wellclose Square. Come along!"

Arthur hurried, dragging the rail map through the air behind him like a kite. Bram followed along as Arthur dodged his way between the pickpockets and the whores, south toward St. George. As he ran, Arthur observed the shop fronts they passed: tobacconists, public houses, shipping offices, boardinghouses. As they neared Wellclose Square, Arthur veered off east, but a tap on the shoulder from Bram put him back on track to the south, toward the docks. On the corner of St. George and Well Street, just below the Wellclose Square, he found what he'd been looking for: a Far Eastern spice merchant.

"Tang Spice," read the hand-carved sign out front. "Import and Export."

"Aha!" cried Arthur. "Perfect. What does Sally know of tattooing, save that it is an art cultivated in the East? She'd certainly have gone to an Eastern shop to procure its services." He pulled open the crooked front door and entered the spice merchant's shop. Instantly a host of smells washed over Arthur and Bram as they stepped past the doorway. Neither man had the faintest clue as to the origins of these intoxicating scents. Strange perfumes clogged their nostrils and lightened their heads. The sensation was dizzying, but oddly pleasurable.

A small Chinese man, old and frail, appeared from a back room. He had a single scrap of white hair atop his head, and he wore a dirty robe, stained with streaks of bright orange.

"Sirs," whispered the old man. "How do I help?"

"I hope you're able to help me quite a bit," said Arthur quickly. "Do you by any chance work with ink?"

The old man frowned. "Ink? I do not import the ink from China, sirs."

"Not to import, my good man. Rather, to burn it into my skin. I would like a tattoo, you see, and I'm sure that in your days you've drawn more than a few for a lost traveler."

The old man's frown remained for a moment and then dissipated into a shrug.

"Afraid, good sir," he said, "that you are in error. Here I sell spice. Not the skin paintings." He raised his bony right hand, which shook as he raised it. He held his arm straight out, and Arthur could see the twitching of the man's fingers. "Afraid I could not draw one, if even I attempt it." Finally the man lowered his hand.

There was no way this man could hold a hot needle steady enough to ink a tattoo without forever scarring the customer.

"Pardon me," said Arthur, the excitement puffing out of him through a deep sigh. Without another word, he led Bram outside the shop. Though they had been inside for only a short while, they each felt a shock of daylight and fresh air as they stepped back on to the street. The spice smell tingled Arthur's nose hairs as it was sucked away by the wind.

"But I would swear," he said after a moment, "that they must have come by here. They *must* have, Bram, it's the only path that makes sense!"

"She might have found a willing tattooist in any public house between the river and Whitechapel Road," replied Bram. "Or she might have asked any passing sailor on the street to perform the service. There's no way to deduce where she went, my friend."

Arthur considered the problem deeply. Was Bram in the right? Was there truly no way, given the faint information they had, to deduce the thoughts and actions of those girls? If that was true, then the whole process of detective work that Arthur had described in two dozen ripping tales was fraudulent. He had everything he needed to piece the matter together, Arthur felt so in his bones. If he could not do it, then he wouldn't merely be a failed detective—he'd be a failed writer as well. He and Holmes would go down as charlatans together. Arthur's "science of deduction," the ability to reason one's way through the darkest horrors of the human experience, would prove but a dreadful sham. A penny lie, and not worth so much as that.

Another strange thought came to Arthur's mind as he stood on St. George, just below the Wellclose Square. Was this how it felt to be one of his readers? To be lost in the middle of the story, without the slightest of notions as to where you were headed? Arthur felt horrible. He felt as if he had no control of events as they unfolded. What trust his readers must put in him, to submit themselves to this unnerving confusion, while holding out hope that Arthur would see them through to a satisfying conclusion. But what if there were no solution on the final page? Or what if the solution were balderdash? What if the whole thing didn't work? His readers took a leap, did they not? They offered up their time and their money. And what did the author promise them in return?

I am going to take care of you, he wanted to say to them. *I know it seems impossible now, but it will all work out. You cannot see where I'm going, but I can, and it will delight you in the end.*

Trust me.

And so many had honored Arthur with their trust.

He took the map from his pocket. He pulled it wide and sat down on the curb.

Bram gave a look of displeasure. "Arthur, it must be filthy down there—"

"She hadn't a clue where she was going, man! That's the key. If you knew nothing about this area, where would you go?" Arthur traced his fingers across the map as if it were written in braille.

"We walked directly from the Metropolitan Station to the docks, and I didn't see any other spicers along the way."

Arthur looked hard at the map.

"We walked to the docks directly," he said. "Directly! That's it!"

"I have no idea what you mean."

"We walked to the docks directly, by taking the most direct route, because *you* knew how to get here! But Sally would not have known the most direct route. Remember how I stopped at Wellclose Square and started off to the left?"

"Yes," said Bram, beginning to put it together himself. "The street opened out that way. But it doesn't actually lead toward the docks, it only leads east and back up to Cable Street."

"But I didn't know that!" said Arthur with great excitement. "Without you there to correct me, I would have headed into the square!"

He leaped to his feet. He was almost run over by a broad four-wheeler as he dashed into the street. The baying horses missed him by only a few inches. The carriage driver shouted something that sounded like an obscenity, though Arthur wasn't paying enough attention to hear precisely what the man had said. He turned around and raced back north up Leman Street, away from the docks. Bram ran just behind him.

In the center of Wellclose Square, the Danish Church rose two stories above the Neptune Street Prison to its left. A flophouse for sailors, run by the Methodist Mariners Church, lay east of the square, beside the London Nautical School. Looking over the run-down inhabitants of the square, Arthur couldn't help but think that the whole of the East End conformed to the square's odd architectural organization: church, then prison, then slum; church, then prison, then slum.

Between the throngs of dark-faced sailors, Arthur spied another Oriental shop across the square. He ran to it eagerly.

But inside, he found the shopkeeper little more help than the previous one. Though of Eastern descent, the man did not administer tattoos. Arthur left dejected, again shaken in his faith.

"I cannot bear it, Bram. We reasoned it out. My logic is incontrovertible. The steps, as I've described them, are orderly and sequential. As sure as two and two make four, Sally Needling came into this square. It is too reasonable to be untrue."

Arthur sat down again on the cold dirt. He leaned back against the side wall of the mariners' boardinghouse. Two small windows dotted the wall above his head. They were surrounded by wooden placards announcing the rules of the house: "All sailors welcome," said one. "Orientals welcome" and "Alcohol is forbidden on the premises," said others. A warm glow came from inside, illuminating the placards and casting a red backlight on Arthur's hat.

Bram stood before Arthur and gave him a pitying look.

"I'm sorry, my friend. Perhaps reason ends at the Tower, and in the slums of East London we have only madness to guide us.

"Let us go back home," Bram continued, "and get a good night's rest. You look exhausted. Perhaps tomorrow some thought will have burst into your mind which—" Bram stopped speaking. His next words appeared caught in his mouth, before he then swallowed them back down. He had the queerest expression on his face that Arthur had ever seen.

"Bram? Is something the matter?"

"Jesus Christ, my Lord and Savior. *Fuck*." Bram looked positively bewitched.

Arthur sighed, leaning his head against the wall and folding his hands across his lap.

"I'm aware that we're among sailors here," he gently chastised his friend, "but that hardly means you have to speak like one."

Bram responded with a cackle. Arthur was growing concerned. Had Bram suddenly lost his wits?

"I can't believe my own eyes," said Bram through his laughter. "Arthur, stand up."

With a shake of his head, Arthur ascended to his feet. He dusted the dirt off his coat with a few pats of his hand.

"Now, turn around."

Arthur turned around and faced the wall of the mariners' flophouse.

Not six inches from his face was a pen-and-paper drawing of a three-headed crow. It was tacked to one of the wooden placards on the wall, the one that announced "Orientals welcome." The drawing was identical to the one Arthur held in his coat pocket.

"I would very much like to see Sherlock Holmes do that," said Bram slyly. Arthur grinned, feeling devilish in his victory.

"Come along," he said quietly.

Arthur led Bram around the Methodist Mariners' boardinghouse until he found a side entrance, away from the church. A few other placards adorned the outer wall of the building. They were drawn in Oriental characters, each shape a complex array of interlocking strokes. Arthur was reminded of the hedge maze in front of Alnwick Castle.

"They've a separate house set up for the Oriental sailors," said Arthur slowly as he realized what he'd found. "They can stay here for pennies while their ships are docked. And so a little community has formed. The sailors can trade goods with each other, alcohol and tobacco, opium and fresh pipes. And, naturally, they've a tattooist in residency."

Arthur entered the building and was greeted by a wall of noise. Sailors from every port of the Orient shouted at one another in tongues, belting out foreign curses and dissonant chanteys. In one corner, a pile of men lay stacked, as if in a tin. Some puffed opium from three-foot pipes, while others had already fallen unconscious and lay across the floor or on the legs of their fellows. Two massive, bald Orientals held bottles, from which they drew a viscous liquid into glistening syringes. The bottles were small and bore the label "Friedrich Bayer & Co.: Pure

Heroin for the Alleviation of a Child's Bedtime Cough." A nearby group was engaged in similar activities with a heavy jar of morphine. Arthur surveyed the state of international relations: Heroin from the Germans, morphine from the English, opium from the Chinese, and all traded freely until everyone drifted unconscious into his own sweet and vivid chimeras.

Arthur thought of Sally and Morgan entering through these same doors, two virgins crossing the river Styx. He said as much aloud.

"If you're Virgil, does that make me Dante?" Bram joked in response.

"I believe it to be the other way around," said Arthur.

An employee in a crisp black suit approached Arthur and Bram. He was a thin white man, and he spoke with the lilt of the Scottish Highlands.

"And what ship has brought the two of you to my doors?" he said through half a smile.

"Charon's raft, perhaps, but let's leave that aside for now." The house employee did not seem to catch Bram's reference, but his face betrayed no impression either way. "We're looking for some young women."

"So are half the men you see before you," said the employee. "I doubt they've the coin to pay for it. But you two, on the other hand..." He looked Arthur and Bram up and down, from their polished shoes to their ridged hats. "My name is Perry. I'm sure I'll be able to help you find what you require."

"Thank you," said Arthur, "but we're not looking for young women who are here tonight. We're looking for a pair of women who came in here some months, perhaps as much as a year or so, in the past. They made use of your resident tattooist."

Perry frowned. He had hoped to make a tidy profit off these two gents.

"You may find him in the back." He pointed toward a far doorway. "And when you've finished speaking to him, we'll see if there isn't anything in which I can interest you gentlemen."

A velvet curtain, drenched in smoke and pocked with pipe burns, separated the larger room from which Arthur and Bram came and the quieter back room into which they proceeded. Bram pressed the curtain aside.

The haze of smoke was thinner here, and sconces of thick candles were attached every few feet to the walls. On a cushioned table in the center of the room, a foreign sailor with skin the color of an ash tree lay shirtless. He reclined belly-down on the table, his back facing up into the light. A handful of colored designs were imprinted upon the sailor's back and an equal number upon his arms, which hung down at the man's sides.

Before the sailor stood the tattooist himself. He was the largest Japanese native Arthur had ever seen. His head was completely bald, a style made all the more pronounced by the intricate tattoos that were printed onto his scalp. As he turned to face Arthur and Bram, they could see the colored designs running up his neck, across to his ears, and over the top of his head.

The tattooist was dressed in work clothes: wool slacks and a white shirt. Before him he held a long, sloped needle, which he pointed directly at Bram as he spoke.

"You'll wait outside, gentlemen," he said, somewhere in between a question and a statement. His accent was purely native to the London docks, without a trace of his Eastern homeland. His voice was deep and ragged from smoke. Arthur thought that his insides must be as burnt as his skin.

Before Arthur could respond, Bram reached over into Arthur's coat.

He pulled the crow drawing from Arthur's pocket and held it before the tattooist without a word. The tattooist stared at it strangely. Arthur could see the recognition in his face, as well as a sense of pride in his work.

"Aye now!" barked the bare sailor on the operating table. "Let's get on with it, shall we?"

"And where'd you find that, then?" said the tattooist, ignoring his customer.

"A young girl's corpse. This image was printed on her leg."

"A corpse? Somebody killed one of those girls?"

One of which girls? thought Arthur, though he remained silent.

"Yes," said Bram.

"Who?"

Bram paused for a moment, considering. The tattooist stepped backward, toward a small instrument table in the corner of the room. Arthur could see dozens of thin, sharp needles arranged from smallest to largest across the table. Some were straight, the size of clothespins, and others were long and hooked, like the beaks of seagulls. The tattooist stroked his needles menacingly.

"Not you," Bram said at last.

The tattooist smiled. "All right, Smithy, off you go," he said to his customer. "Let me have a minute with my friends here."

With a series of hand gestures, the customer indicated his extreme displeasure at this turn of events. As he left the room, he bent over and spit on Bram's shoe. Bram did not so much as flinch.

Arthur felt it was time to take the lead on the investigation.

"You tattooed a group of girls, at least two, sometime ago?" he said.

"I did," said the tattooist. "Must have been more'n a year. The design was quite simple. No shading, just black ink on those pale little legs. I used..." The tattooist paused and turned to his instrument table. He selected a needle of medium grade, from the middle of the table. He handed it to Arthur.

"...this one." It felt impossibly light in Arthur's palm, as if it weren't even there. The needle was made of ivory and was only as wide as a charcoal pencil. Arthur looked up at the tattooist to find him staring back, waiting for a sign of Arthur's approval. There isn't a craftsman alive who doesn't take pride in his tools.

"It's a lovely...device," said Arthur.

"I carved it myself. In Kyoto." The tattooist sighed, and his eyes went soft. He lost himself for a moment to nostalgic recollection and then quickly returned his mind to his surroundings.

"It was the first and only time a flock of mollies came in for a set of matching ink," he said. "I put that crow there on all four of them."

"Four?" exclaimed Arthur.

"Right so. There were four girls that came in together, with a copy of that drawing on a piece of paper. Just like the one you have now."

"What were their names?"

"Well, let's see, allow me to consult my bankbook. I'm sure they each provided me with a check." The tattooist's voice dropped even lower to convey his icy sarcasm.

"I see," said Arthur. "And how about the drawing itself? I've never seen such a design in my life. What does the three-headed crow symbolize? From where did it derive?"

"I cannot hardly say. Isn't it just the devil's own, that image? The girls brought that paper in here with them, told me how they wanted it inked. I practiced a few times on paper before moving on to the skin. You saw the image I tacked up outside this place? One of my practice drawings. I took a liking to it. The girls never said what it meant." The tattooist gave a chortle. "But do you know? I tacked it to the wall in here, and sailors, they have made inquiries. Off the boat they've come, and when they've seen that design, they've said, 'Aye, paint me up with that.' I moved the sketch outside, since it had become so popular. Don't think they know what it means any more than I do. But it's a spooky shape, isn't it, that crow, and I think it drums me up business."

"What did the girls' conversation consist of, when they were in your shop?"

"I hardly remember, there was so much chattering. They were loud. Giddy, I think, nervous about the pain from the needle. People will go one of two ways when it's their first time. Either they grow quiet like little mice, too scared to speak, or else they talk my ear off, can't shut them up for anything. And they cried out, too, when the needle hit. Had to give them each a double dose." The man gestured to his table, at a hypodermic syringe.

"Morphine?" inquired Arthur.

The tattooist nodded. "And lately I've been adding a shot of that imported heroin. It seems to make the customers less drowsy than the morphine, but just as docile."

"We believe that these girls were part of some club. Or a group of some sort. Can you recall if they spoke at all about women's suffrage?"

"What's that, then?"

"Never mind," said Bram. "Can you recall anything they said? Even the littlest word or phrase could make all the difference."

The tattooist raised his hand to the top of his head while he thought. He tapped idly on his bald scalp. It sounded like the ticks of a clock.

"A faucet," he said at last.

Arthur and Bram exchanged a look.

"A faucet?" said Bram.

"Yes, odd, I know," said the tattooist. "That's why I remember it. One of them would make some joke, and another would say, 'Tell it to the faucet!' And they'd all double over in giggles. They kept repeating the jokes again and again. The morphine will do that to you. Little girls, really, couldn't have weighed more than six, seven stone apiece. Probably should have used less anesthetic. Anyhow, they became quite giggly."

"About a faucet?"

"'I'd like to see the faucet do that!' Or, 'And what'll the faucet say now?' And then, 'Drip, drip, drip!' and they'd flop on the floor with their laughing."

"What in the world does that mean?" asked Bram, a puzzled look across his face.

"It means," said Arthur, "that these girls were disgruntled members of the National Union of Women's Suffrage Societies."

Even the tattooist looked impressed. He and Bram regarded Arthur with cocked heads and raised eyebrows.

"And how do you know that?" asked Bram.

"Because when you're pumped full of opiates, a lot of things seem funny that really are not. Even bad puns. It appears our girls didn't care too much for the leader of the NUWSS, one Millicent *Fawcett*."

"Arthur, my God, you've given Holmes a run for his money today. I'm embarrassed to say I've never heard of this Millicent Fawcett."

Arthur sighed, wishing that he, too, had never heard that woman's name.

"Do you remember my run for Parliament, at the seat from Edinburgh?"

"Of course," said Bram, surprised at the question.

"Do you remember that my candidacy was sunk by a set of vicious rumors as to my alleged papist sympathies?"

"Yes. They were petty drivel. Balderdash."

"Just so. And Millicent Fawcett was the one who spread them."

CHAPTER 22

The Great Hiatus

*"Perhaps the greatest of the Sherlock Holmes mysteries
is this: that when we talk of him we invariably
fall into the fancy of his existence."*
—T. S. Eliot,
from a review of *The Complete
Sherlock Holmes Short Stories*, 1929

January 9, 2010, cont.

Harold and Sarah sat in a run-down Internet café, sipping tea and staring at two dim computer screens. A few computers to their left, a heavy man in his forties clicked through page after page of online porn.

There had been a lengthy debate earlier, in the cab, about the relative safety of returning to their hotel. The driver had seemed remarkably invested in the outcome of their conversation. Both Harold and Sarah eventually came to the conclusion that the men in the black car—the Goateed Man and his associate with the gun—must have known who they were. Who knew how long the men had been following them? The hotel couldn't be regarded as safe. And so, as the first order of business was to access the contents of the flash drive that Sarah had filched from Alex Cale's desk, the cabbie had deposited them at the Kensington Internet Café, where they now searched through the drive's files.

Harold was still impressed with Sarah's cool in the car chase. His body had been practically convulsing, and it was only through the single-minded focus of will that he was able to plant himself in front of the oncoming car. But Sarah had slipped behind and punctured the tires without pause. He felt himself to be an endless buzz of confusion, of questions and doubt and uncertainty. Outside of his books, the whole *world* was a mystery to Harold. And Sarah always seemed to understand. He wished he could be more like her.

He opened up the flash drive and thought he'd hit pay dirt. A massive text file labeled "ACD BIO DRAFT 12.14.09" greeted him promisingly. He opened the document, and there it was—the most recent draft of Alex Cale's long-awaited Conan Doyle biography. Obviously, Harold thought, there must be a lengthy section in the manuscript about the missing diary, where Cale had found it, and what it contained.

Harold spent two hours reading through the entire biography while Sarah sipped green tea and checked her e-mail. She went outside once to make a call, then again when her phone rang and she left to take it.

Harold went through the manuscript quickly. He was already familiar with most of the details of Conan Doyle's life—born in Edinburgh in 1859, studied medicine at the University of Edinburgh, married to Touie in 1885, married to Jean in 1907—and so Harold read even faster than usual.

Alex's tone was loving and deliriously antiquarian. He seemed to mimic the prose of Conan Doyle himself. "Determined was the face, and hardened was the resolve, of Arthur Conan Doyle as he descended from the steps of the P&O ocean liner to the dirty port of Cape Town," opened the passage on Conan Doyle's time in the Boer War. It was pretentious and yet infectious, a delight for Harold to read. His eyes watered as he got to the section on Conan Doyle's death, in his bed, in the loving arms of his second wife. "You are wonderful," were Conan Doyle's final words, whispered to the teary face of his wife of twenty-three years. Harold thought of Alex Cale dying alone, in a sterile hotel room, his eyes bulging from his head and his muscles taut from struggling. Harold realized that in the days since Alex's death he had not paused to mourn. To measure the loss. What would it matter, really, if Harold did find the diary? What difference would it make if he found Alex's killer? If the man were put in jail for the rest of his wretched life?

Alex would never see his own life's work completed or published. He would never be able to undertake a new project. The world had lost his voice, it had forever lost the maker of these sentences—"Defying Conan Doyle's incorrigible belief in the supernatural, Harry Houdini sought to prove to him once and for all that genuine magic did not exist. Houdini did so by performing feat after feat for the author but was confounded to find that Conan Doyle refused to believe, after each card was pulled from the deck, that no magic had transpired. 'I produced your card by sleight of hand, not paranormal force,' one imagines Houdini saying. 'And yet my card is here,' one imagines Conan Doyle responding. 'However it was done, it is magic to me.'" Harold concealed his tears with a napkin, blowing his nose and crumpling the cheap white paper into a tight little ball before flicking it into the trash.

Harold realized for the first time that he wasn't doing this for Alex. He was doing this for himself. He was doing this for the *solution*. The almighty answer that lay just beyond his vision, past the murky clouds and into the heavens. This was not about justice. This was about mystery.

He looked up from his screen to find that Sarah was not beside him. Through the front windows of the café, he could see her on the street outside, talking animatedly into her phone. She had taken a number of these mysterious calls in the last few days, always leaving to talk so Harold couldn't hear. He was trying not to be paranoid, but someone had recently just pointed a gun at him. That had been a singular experience in Harold's life, and he dearly hoped he would not have another like it.

"Who was that on the phone?" he asked Sarah when she returned.

"My editor, back in New York," she replied. "He's very excited about the piece."

"Yeah? What did you tell him?"

"Not much. That we're making progress. That you're a fascinating character to hang the piece on. He'd love to meet you, when we head back to New York."

Harold wasn't sure which he was more flattered by—Sarah's calling him fascinating or the idea that they were headed back to New York. Together.

It did seem odd that she'd have to leave the room to speak to her editor, though. Harold tried to quiet his suspicions.

"I'd love to meet your editor," he said simply. "After all of this is over."

"Speaking of which," she said, "what have you found?"

"There's something weird here."

"Oh, yeah?"

"There's nothing new in here from the section of Arthur's life that the missing diary should cover—October through December of 1900. There's only a few pages on that period of his life, and everything in it comes from the public record. There aren't any secrets." Harold flipped through the pages on the screen. "We learn that Conan Doyle ran for public office back home in Edinburgh, lost miserably, played a lot of cricket, did some consulting for Scotland Yard, and then finally resurrected Sherlock Holmes. Those details have been in a dozen other Conan Doyle bios before. We all knew that already."

"Hold up there," said Sarah. "I didn't know that already. Arthur Conan Doyle consulted for Scotland Yard?"

"Yeah. There are plenty of newspaper accounts of his work at the time. He started to become more . . . let's say more 'eccentric' as the years went on. Somebody made a half-assed attempt to kill him by planting a letter bomb in his mail slot. It didn't work, needless to say. But Arthur started talking to Scotland Yard, and he got quite invested in a few of their cases. At one point there was some serial killer he thought he was chasing, actually, but it never amounted to much."

"He never caught who he was after?"

"No. In fact, I don't even think the Yard regarded it as a serial-killer case. Jack the Ripper had shocked all of London a few years earlier, and I imagine they thought Arthur was letting his literary sensibilities get the best of him. But they were happy for the publicity, happy with the public's knowing that Arthur Conan Doyle was on their side. As the years went on, actually, there would every now and then be this huge public outcry for Scotland Yard to deputize him again on some major case. When Agatha Christie disappeared, in 1926, all the newspapers had editorials asking Conan Doyle to get involved. And you know what's funny? He did. And he *found her*. She had gone off for a drive in the country one day and never returned. Her car was crashed against a tree, but there was no blood or sign of a body."

"Jesus. How'd he find her?"

"He correctly figured that there was only one train station she could have walked to—or been walked to—in the area, and only one train she could have gotten on without being noticed. Somehow, and I honestly forget how, he figured out which stop she would have had to get off at. Sure enough, her husband found her in that town, three days later, living under an assumed name. She'd had a nervous breakdown after catching him in an affair with another woman. It was kind of sad, really."

"Wow. This doesn't have anything to do with the missing diary, does it?"

"No."

"Okay, so...Conan Doyle worked for Scotland Yard, and then— shortly after—resurrected Sherlock Holmes?"

"Yeah. The Great Hiatus came to an end with the publication of *The Hound of the Baskervilles* in March 1901. Sherlock Holmes had been dead for eight years, and suddenly, for no apparent reason, Arthur decided to bring him back. To write more stories about the fictional detective he *loathed*, by all accounts. He told people it was for the money, but that never quite made sense. He had all the money in the world already, plus he'd had blank-check offers from every publisher and magazine in the world for years at that point. Why then? And why bring Holmes back so...so different."

"Different?" said Sarah, intrigued.

"Yeah," said Harold. "After the Great Hiatus, when Holmes returned in those later stories, he was just different. Meaner. Colder. He starts manipulating witnesses for information. Lying to people. Committing crimes himself if he thinks it'll serve his cause. One time he even seduces and proposes marriage to a housemaid in order to get her to let him into her house. Then he never calls on her again. He becomes a real bastard. He also seemed to have lost his faith in the English justice system. All of a sudden, he was acting as judge and jury, even meting out punishments for the criminals he caught. Early on, Holmes worked in conjunction with Scotland Yard, but in the later years he was completely independent. And he'd developed real contempt and animosity toward the police. Sure, the cop characters were always dumb in the Holmes stories, the better to show off how smart he was, but after the Hiatus the cops become obsolete. Holmes wants nothing to do with them at all.

"The question of the Great Hiatus—the question that Alex's biography doesn't seem like it's capable of answering—is, what happened to Holmes while he was gone?"

"It sounds to me," said Sarah, thinking it over, "that the question is, what happened to Arthur Conan Doyle?"

CHAPTER 23

The Suffragists

"Woman's heart and mind are insoluble puzzles to the male."
—Sir Arthur Conan Doyle,
"The Adventure of the Illustrious Client"

November 11, 1900

Arthur fastened the top button of his S-bend corset. He sucked in his belly while he affixed the bottom straps to his garters. The trumpet skirt was loose and wrapped easily around his waist. But as he stood up and the folds of his skirt fell delicately over his white stockings, Arthur felt a sharp pain in his chest and back. The corset hurt already, digging into his rib cage and shoulder blades.

"Ow, Bram, is all this really necessary?" he complained. "My God, it is tremendously uncomfortable." Bram looked up from the more modern, "liberty" bodice around his own belly. Arthur was quite a sight. Clumps of pectoral fat were pressed up by his corset, giving the appearance of a pair of succulent breasts. His skirt, loose in the current style, fit him rather well. The incongruity of Arthur's bushy mustache made Bram laugh out loud, though once he had shaved it, put a wig on, and applied a little makeup...well, Bram didn't think Arthur would look half bad.

"You'll look the image of a proper lady, Arthur, don't you worry." Bram couldn't help smiling as he said it. "Holmes was always putting on some fresh skirts to go undercover in his adventures, wasn't he? Seems a good time for you to give it a try. I've borrowed some stage makeup from Henry's dressing room, and some wigs from the ladies'. They will not mind, and Henry will not notice." Bram pointed to a stained porcelain sink in the corner of the room. The two men dressed before great mirrors, which reflected gaslight from a dozen surrounding lamps. They had taken hold of an abandoned dressing room, deep in the belly of the Lyceum Theatre. None of the actors wanted to use it any longer, because it remained the only dressing room still lit by gas. Bram had been forced to pay for the installation of electric lights in Henry's dressing room shortly after he'd paid for the installation of electric lights onstage. Henry felt that it was inconceivable that he dress by gaslight, if he were to perform by electric light. Shortly thereafter all of the other actors had lodged similar protests, and Bram had the new lights installed throughout the theater, save for this single, faraway dressing room.

"I don't see why I can't continue my investigations in a good pair of trousers," said Arthur. The corset was making him irritable. Even the fastening loops which hung from the back scraped against his skin awkwardly. He would not have a moment's peace in this awful contraption.

"What else would you have us do?" said Bram. "Attend tonight's meeting of the National Union of Women's Suffrage Societies in top hats and tails? I believe they'd notice you in particular, the famed author and celebrated antisuffragist Arthur Conan Doyle. They'd eject us before we'd even made it to our seats. And if we dressed as other, less famous men, we'd still attract rather more attention than we need as a pair of gentlemen at a suffragist rally. If we're to go, and to go unmolested, then we're to go as women."

Arthur knew that Bram was right. But he was still displeased.

"If you like," Bram continued, "I can go to the meeting alone. No one knows who *I* am. I wouldn't need any disguise at all to spend an evening with the ladies of the NUWSS."

Arthur thought he detected a trace of bitterness in Bram's voice. Just because the man's literary career wasn't moving along as he'd hoped, there was no cause for him to take his frustrations out on his more successful fellows.

"No, I need to be there myself. To see Millicent Fawcett and her satin gang. Someone is killing those girls off, and if I'm to protect the rest of them, I'll need to see precisely what they're up to."

"Ever the chivalrous knight, aren't you?" said Bram.

Arthur drew a thin evening shawl over his shoulders and tied it in front of his neck in a double bow. "Chivalry is the very soul of manhood. It is what separates men from beasts."

"It is also," said Bram as he tended to his skirt, "what separates men from women."

"Indeed! As well it should." Arthur toyed with the bonnet in his hand, spinning it around to find the proper straps. "Were men to become women and women to become men, why, that would spell the death of our civilization! It would be the fall of England."

"I take it, then, that you haven't reconsidered your position on granting women the right of suffrage? Come. Sit. Allow me to shave your mustache." Bram led Arthur to a chair by the sink. His tools had already been laid out. Scissors, cream, straight razor. "Unless, of course, you'd like to perform the honors yourself?"

"No," said Arthur. "I don't believe I could bear it. I've had this mustache since I was six and ten years of age, did you know that? I was the first boy in my class to sprout follicles." He sat in the chair, facing his friend, and closed his eyes. "And yes," Arthur continued, "I have certainly reconsidered my position on the topic of women's suffrage. I have considered it again and again, and each and every time I have found the argument of the suffragists to be wanting."

Bram prepared the shaving cream in a clay mortar, whipping it quickly with a feathered brush. "And what is it about the argument for the rights of women which still leaves you unsatisfied?" he said. He took a pair of short steel scissors from the sink.

Arthur flinched. He gritted his teeth but kept his eyes closed. He didn't want to witness the extirpation of his own facial hair.

"It has nothing to do with rights, man," he said quietly, barely moving his lips so that Bram could do his work. "It is about duty. Men have their duties to society, and women have their own. It is thus that the sexes are able to cohabitate happily. Can you imagine what would happen were wives to start voting alongside their husbands? It's no secret that the Conservative Party finds far greater support among the women of England than the men."

"Gladstone said as much when he sank the Reform Bill." Having trimmed Arthur's mustache down to a taut stump, Bram began applying cream with the aid of his brush.

"Quite so," said Arthur. "You've a good memory for politics. The Liberals kicked the legs out from under the suffragists for their own electoral reasons. My larger point remains. Let us say the bill had passed and the society women of England had begun to vote. A young couple, freshly married, goes off together to the polls. The husband votes for, in this case, Gladstone. The wife votes for Cecil, the most honorable marquess of Salisbury. Why, the fights they would have! What a strain it would place on their marriage were the wife to suddenly commence telling her husband how to vote! Or how to tariff this year's French grain! It would be as if men started telling their wives how to keep a soufflé from falling. The rate of divorce in this country would explode."

When Arthur had finished speaking, Bram slid the razor cleanly across his upper lip in a dozen short strokes. Inch by inch, Arthur's mustache was scraped from his face. Bram handed him a hot towel, which he'd taken great care to prepare.

Arthur opened his eyes. He examined his visage in the mirror. He looked so . . . *nude.*

"All right then," said Bram. "Let's get some eye shadow on you. A dab or two of powder to your cheeks and we'll be off."

"How did you come to know so much about ladies' makeup?" asked Arthur as he accompanied Bram to the latter's powder box.

"I work in the theater, Arthur," Bram replied. "And I'm sure I've many talents of which you're most likely unaware."

Arthur held up a pouch of white powder. It looked just like flour, or unmelted cocaine.

"The powder will whiten you out, and then this"—here Bram displayed a razor-thin charcoal pencil—"will darken the lines around your eyes. Now sit, and let's be quick. The lecture begins at eight. Who knows? Perhaps you'll learn something."

───────────

When Arthur and Bram arrived at Caxton Hall in Westminster, they found a mob already assembled. Their brougham joined a column of others along Palmer Street, as each cab deposited a suffragist at the curb. From his window Arthur could see a line of black bonnets stretching north for blocks. The bonnets bobbed up and down like apples in a water bucket as the ladies underneath stopped to greet one another. While Arthur stared, Bram paid their driver, who seemed eager to move along. Arthur was careful, at Bram's urging, to grasp the folds of his skirt as he stepped out of the carriage. He hadn't gone through all the trouble to become a woman only to botch it up by strutting about like a man.

As they approached the ticket booth, Arthur became nervous. This would be the first test of his disguise. So far none of the women who surrounded him had looked at him twice, but when he reached the front of the ticketing queue, he'd be but inches from the face of the young woman behind the glass. She couldn't have been more than sixteen years of age, Arthur noticed. She smiled to each customer merrily, just like a child.

Bram had attempted to enter the queue ahead of Arthur, but he was rebuffed. Arthur would go first. If his disguise were to be found out, it was better that it be done right away.

As he neared the front of the queue, it occurred to Arthur that he would actually have to *speak* to this woman. He had not prepared himself for that. Without moving his mouth, he began to contract his throat, trying to soundlessly practice forming a high and womanly voice. He hadn't the foggiest notion as to whether this would be effective.

Finally he came to the front and stared directly into the eyes of the ticket girl. She beamed at him.

"How many tickets for you this evening?" she said perkily.

Arthur swallowed.

"Two, please," he said, in the highest voice he could muster. Hearing his words out loud, he did not think that he sounded even remotely like a woman, but rather more like a boy of twelve. The ticket girl, however, simply smiled in response.

"That'll be fourpence, ma'am," she said.

Oh, thank goodness, thought Arthur. Without another word, he paid the girl for two tickets, and she passed them to him through a slot beneath the glass. Arthur handed one to Bram, who followed him through the great double doors of Caxton Hall.

Though it was still a quarter to eight, the hall was already full inside. Lines of stiff wooden chairs had been assembled in rows. Each chair squeaked and rattled as the lady upon it shifted back and forth to address her friends. Arthur and Bram spent five minutes searching for empty seats, which they eventually acquired along the far right edge of the audience, most of the way to the rear.

At least two hundred women—and three or four men—sat in the body of the hall. A brass beam ran the length of the stage, separating it from the floor. A squat lectern, no more than a foot high, lay atop a table at the front of the stage. Behind it a line of chairs had been set up facing the audience. A few were occupied by distinguished women of middle age, while others were still empty as ladies walked back and forth greeting one another warmly and pulling one another close for quick, furtive conversations. Banners draped the hall, bearing suffragist slogans. "Thoughts have gone forth whose whispers can sleep no more! Victory! Victory!" read the most prominent of them. In the mezzanine above, at least another hundred women perched along the wooden railing, peering down at the stage. All present were bright-eyed with excitement. The event was soon to begin.

Arthur searched through the crowd for Millicent Fawcett, but he could not find her. He kept his head down as best he could and deliberately avoided eye contact with the woman seated next to him. Though his disguise had fooled the ticket girl, it might not have the same effect on everyone. It was better to be cautious than to be discovered.

Finally one of the women on the stage approached the podium and brought the room to order. She was dressed all in white from head to toe and was one of the very few women in the building who was not sporting a wide-brimmed bonnet. Her brown hair glistened under the stage lights. She slammed a gavel sharply against the podium three times, and the room instantly fell into silence.

When all had taken their seats, Arthur realized that the entire front row of the audience was occupied by men. They rarely looked toward the stage but instead kept their heads buried in tiny notebooks, in which they each scribbled furiously. Reporters, Arthur realized. Here to cover the rally.

The political lecture which followed was both as dreary and monotonous as any Arthur had attended, and at the same time it was bracingly strange in its tone. First, the woman in white thanked them all for their attendance and for their support. She delivered an introduction of such bloodless character that Arthur briefly wondered whether he'd accidentally stumbled into a meeting of some obscure horticulturalist society. It consisted solely of welcomes, and greetings, and let-us-not-forget-the-contributions-of-so-and-so's. This, then, was the timbre of London's most politically revolutionary organization? The woman in white announced that she would be followed by two speakers. The first would be Millicent Fawcett and the second Arabella Raines. At the mention of the name Fawcett, Arthur became rigid in his seat.

When these two women took the stage, they riled the audience into a frenzy almost from their first words. Arthur had thought of this event as a lecture, but what he found was significantly more like a debate. Or perhaps a match of bare-knuckled boxing. Fawcett and Raines—both in black frocks and cream-colored hats—stood on opposite sides of the lectern. They rarely turned to face one another but instead addressed the audience one after the other in five-minute segments as they debated their positions on suffrage.

Millicent Fawcett spoke first, and she did so calmly. Her voice never rose above the level one would use to say grace at the dining table. Everything about her manner was dignified and discreet but at the same time commanding in its sensibility. Her bright flaxen hair was pulled back in a bun. She had dark, deep-set eyes and a hard nose, which only increased the impression of sober seriousness that she conveyed. And yet, before she had gotten to the end of her first sentence, there were grumbles from the crowd. And then, an instant later, halloos of approval. The woman in white had to return to the lectern several times with her gavel in order to quiet the audience.

Millicent Fawcett's argument was actually quite Conservative in its principles, Arthur realized. She acknowledged that men and women were different creatures and had different realms of expertise and interest. Indeed, such was the fundamental principle of her argument for women's suffrage.

"If men and women were exactly alike," she said, "then a legislature composed entirely of men would adequately represent us. But, rather, because we are not alike, that wherein we differ goes underrepresented in our present political system. In our society men are the champions of our statecraft, while women are the champions of our domestic life. This is just."

"Bloody Tory!" shouted an angry woman from the mezzanine.

"We have rights!" cried another.

Millicent Fawcett continued as if there had been no interruption.

"In years past, our government concerned itself solely with the affairs of men. But in recent years, the state has seen fit to involve itself in matters of education, in matters of child rearing, and in matters of the home. The preoccupations of women are becoming the preoccupations of society as a whole. As a result, women must have a say in the conduct of their government. Women now seek to involve themselves in the life of their government because their government has involved itself in their lives! To grant women the right of suffrage will not cause them to abandon their societal obligations but rather cause them to more effectively fulfill them!"

It was a good speech, thought Arthur, one well reasoned and well composed. He had never considered the matter in this light before. He would have to think these points over later, at some time when he was not on the heels of a killer.

When it was Arabella Raines's turn to speak, the crowd was equally rowdy, though for opposite reasons. She was pale and thin, a mere wisp of a woman. She looked like a specter underneath her black clothing. But from her tiny body came a voice so powerful as to cause Arthur to sit up in his chair. Her words carried as if she were on the stage at the Royal Opera House.

She was a student of Mill, clearly, and much more radical, in her Liberal politics, than Millicent Fawcett. Her argument was based solely on the natural rights of women, on their inherent right as human beings to everything that men had. Though she, too, emphasized that there were fundamental differences between the sexes.

"I say not that women are the same as men," she bellowed. "I say that women are *equal* to men. For a century women have been involved in the affairs of the state. They have founded and served in political organizations of every stripe. There are women who march with the Primrose League, just as there are women who march with the Social Democratic Federation. If women are fit to advise, convince, and persuade voters how to vote, they are surely also fit to vote themselves. But allow me to be clear about the principles behind this call for suffrage. They should rightfully extend, by the grace of God, to all of his creatures. As landed women should vote, so should poor women. So should Indian women. So should Negro and Asian women. Our rights derive not from our government, but from our God."

"Radical!" came a shout from high in the hall.

"Suffragette!" came another call. At the word "suffragette," Arabella Raines looked up toward the mezzanine, trying to see who had said it. Her face grew quite stern.

"That is a word used in condescending jest," she said. "It is a taunt thrown at us by the Americans, and by the shortsighted editors of our own *Daily Mail*." Saying this, she gazed down onto the front row and gave a look of extreme chilliness to one of the assembled reporters. "They say we are 'suffragettes' because we play at revolution. I say we are not playing at all, and that this is no game. I say, rather, that we are perfectly serious as to our aims, and that we are perfectly serious as to the means required to achieve them."

At this, the room exploded in a volley of bitter shouts. Unspeakable insults were lobbed back and forth across the hall. The woman in white jumped to the lectern, where she banged her gavel upon the wood again and again, to little use. Millicent Fawcett did not so much as flinch amid all the commotion. She stared out at the crowd, straight-backed and still. Yet Arthur saw something in her eyes, even from as far away as he sat. There was a sadness. Some sense of opportunity lost, perhaps. This was not the meeting for which she had hoped.

Within a few moments, the room had settled down. The two speakers continued their debate, one after the other for an hour. Their points did not change, and their opinions seemed only to have hardened. Though they fought on the same side, as far as Arthur was concerned, the gap between them grew as the hour wore on. Millicent Fawcett remained ever calm and professional, while Arabella Raines allowed herself a greater range of emotions on the stage. Neither granted the other an inch. Only at the very close, in her final statements, did Millicent Fawcett remind the house that despite the barbs flung between them, they were united in their pursuit of women's suffrage. The crowd seemed united only in their disapproval of her gracious attempt at conciliation.

"The suffragists quarrel like the House of Atreus," said Arthur after the speakers had finished. Though the event had concluded, few of the attendees seemed eager to leave. They milled about in small packs, sharing their opinions in hushed tones. "Mrs. Fawcett appears to preside over a divided kingdom. But from what the tattooist told us, I'd wager that our girls were in the anti-Fawcett camp. That they were among the more radical suffragettes."

"I agree," said Bram. Both men kept their faces close together, so as to avoid submitting their costume disguises to unwanted scrutiny. "Let us follow Mrs. Raines and see where she is headed. For if Sally had compatriots among these ladies, they would certainly have been in Mrs. Raines's camp."

Arthur and Bram maneuvered through the crowd toward the stage. A few feet before it, they spied Arabella Raines holding court over a dozen young suffragists. The two huddled by the wall, near Arabella and her associates. They discussed it, and neither felt that engaging a group of real women in conversation was a prudent course of action.

Eventually Arabella Raines, with another girl in tow, headed toward the front door. Without speaking, Bram and Arthur began to pursue the women. They pressed through the crowd after them, which was slow going, as half the women in the hall reached over to shake Arabella's hand or stopped to give her an approving smile.

Arabella's friend, who mingled beside her, was quite small. Arthur thought that the crowd threatened to pour over her like a wave. The girl moved about in quick, nervous motions. Her black hair was falling out of her bonnet and over her ears, while her tiny nose seemed to twitch whenever she spoke. She reminded Arthur of a field mouse.

Just before they left the main hall for the lobby, Arabella and her small friend took a sharp left. They opened a door and went inside, closing it behind them. And it wasn't until Arthur had finally pressed his way up against it that he saw the letters stenciled on the wooden door. "W.C.," it read. With the addendum "Ladies" printed underneath.

"Oh, dear," said Arthur. "Perhaps we should—"

"Oh, come off it, Arthur," said Bram. "Would you like to find your killer or not?" Bram pushed past Arthur and opened the door to the ladies' powder room. Arthur looked around, instinctively regarding this as an unholy act. When no one gave him the slightest bit of notice, he gulped a deep breath and followed in behind Bram. He felt as he were trespassing upon sacred ground.

Inside, Arthur's boots made a heavy clap against the tile floor. Bram hadn't been able to find a pair of ladies' shoes that fit his massive feet, so Arthur had worn a dress that touched the floor in order to cover up his men's boots. But it had never occurred to him that his boots were so much louder than ladies' flats.

The women's W.C. in Caxton Hall was the very image of Dutch cleanliness. Three flushing water closets were separated by dark wood along the right wall. The tiles spread from the toilets to a sink on the left. Of all the public restrooms Arthur had been in, this was by far the most sanitary. Even Bram, who managed his own theater and its rest areas, seemed impressed.

At the sink, Arabella had removed her bonnet and adjusted her hair in the mirror. She turned to Arthur and Bram, nodded at them politely, and returned her gaze to the mirror. She seemed not to give either of them another thought.

A flush from one of the water closets signaled the presence of Arabella's friend. Bram walked into the far closet and shut the door behind him. Arthur was unsure what to do. He wanted to stay close to these women, to hear what they said to one another, and yet he couldn't just stand there staring, could he?

Arthur found his solution near the sink. Two comfortable chairs had been set out, most likely for ladies who needed a place to sit and collect their breath when their corseting grew too tight. Arthur sank into one of the chairs and gave a dramatic sigh. He fanned himself with the sleeves of his frock. Though he was putting on a bit of a show, he had to admit that this clothing did exhaust the wearer. If the day hadn't yet convinced him of the merits of women's suffrage, it had certainly convinced him of the justness of the movement for Rational Dress.

Arabella's mousy friend exited her water closet and moved toward the sink.

"Oh, Emily," said Arabella to her friend, "I'm to join Dot and those Manchester girls for a late supper. I do believe they're plotting something grand for their home town. Care to join us?"

"Thank you, no," said the mousy girl, now revealed to be named

Emily. "I left some work unfinished at home, before I came here. I should return to it."

"A few stitches of knitting?" said Arabella with a laugh.

"Yes," said Emily through a grin. "Some knitting." With that, Emily placed her right foot up on the resting chair next to Arthur's. She lifted her skirt above her knee. Arthur tried to seem uninterested while she adjusted the straps on her garters. Her stocking was white, and quite thin. Arthur could practically see straight through it. He picked a spot on the wall across from him and held his gaze on it. It wouldn't do if she saw him staring. She pinched at her stocking, trying to shift it across her beautiful, pale leg. She moved her knee from left to right as she shimmied the stocking, and the motion hiked her skirt farther up her thigh. Arthur was becoming quite distracted.

He lost track of the spot along the far wall and let his eyes drift to Emily's exposed thigh. He saw her muscles tighten as she leaned her weight into her leg. His eyes traveled down to her dimpled knee, which seemed to pucker out as her leg bent further. His gaze fell to her sleek shin and then around to the long back of her smooth leg and the black splotch upon it. He stared closer. It was a tattoo of a three-headed crow.

Arthur gave a start and almost fell off his chair. Both women immediately turned their heads to him.

"Pardon," he said in his best female voice. "Dizzy." He was trying to minimize his word count, so as to lessen their opportunity to detect the masculine undercurrent to his speech.

"I understand," said Arabella sympathetically. "I used to pass out once a week when I wore corsets like yours. I don't mean to pry, and you're free to wear the clothing you choose, but there is a wonderful sale on now at Whiteley's, on their modern bodices. My very life changed when I switched over myself."

"Thank you," said Arthur.

"I don't see how we're to win our suffrage if we can't draw a decent gulp of air into our lungs. Right, Emily?"

"Yes. Right," said Emily. She regarded Arthur suspiciously. She did not seem so easygoing as Arabella, nor as trusting.

"Well then, I'm off. Do give one of these 'liberty' bodices a try, ma'am, I'm sure it would do you wonders," Arabella said to Arthur. She next turned to Emily. "I'll see you Thursday next? And please, be careful with your . . . knitting. I'd hate for there to be any accidents. In your stitch work." With a gentle bow, she was gone.

By the time Bram flushed and came out of the water closet, Emily had finished adjusting her stocking and replaced her skirt over her leg. She left quickly, without a good-bye to Arthur or even a friendly nod. The very instant she had left the room, Arthur burst up from his chair.

"She has the tattoo!" he cried. "On her right leg! I saw it!"

"Arabella Raines?" said Bram, confused.

"No," said Arthur. "Her friend Emily. The other one. Quickly, man, we've no time to spare!"

Arthur narrowly avoided tripping over his own skirt as he hurried out of the ladies' powder room in full pursuit.

CHAPTER 24

The Bloodstains Bear Fruit

"You have brought detection as near an exact science
as it will ever be brought in this world."
—Sir Arthur Conan Doyle,
A Study in Scarlet

January 10, 2010

Harold woke to the sound of running water. Groggy, he raised his head
and turned to find the source. He gazed across disheveled sheets—deep
blue with red stripes crossing in a grid pattern—to a cream carpet and
a dark wooden desk. Harold had been in so many different hotel rooms
over the past week, hadn't he, and they all looked exactly the same.
Which of them was this?

As he turned to the bathroom door, which could have been any
bathroom door in any hotel room on either side of the Atlantic, Harold
saw wisps of steam escaping from the bottom. The shower was running inside the bathroom. It looked warm. He heard someone move
around inside the shower and realized it was Sarah. The events of the
past night came back to him. Harold was sorry to recall that nothing
thrilling had occurred the night before.

They'd found this hotel after a quick Google search from the Internet café. It was close, it was quiet, and it accepted payment in cash.
They couldn't risk using credit cards.

They had spent the evening separately reading through Alex's Conan
Doyle biography. Sarah had appreciated the chance finally to read it for

herself, while Harold pored over it again and again for any indication of where Alex had found the diary. Or any glimpse as to what was even inside it. No matter how many times he read it, no new facts presented themselves.

The most exciting moment of the evening, for Harold, had come when the two learned that the hotel had a laundry room. They realized that without a return to their previous hotel room they'd be spending another day in the same clothes. They changed into the white robes they found hanging inside the bathroom door and walked, dirty underwear, jeans, and shirts piled in their arms, down the stairs in nothing but the robes. Harold's eyes kept drifting to the folds of Sarah's robe, which swayed to expose her right thigh halfway up to her waist every time she stepped forward. He did his best not to stare. He was pretty sure she didn't notice.

Later that night they slept on opposite sides of the single king-size bed. They wore their robes like pajamas. The whole thing felt disheart-eningly chaste, like a teenage sleepover, and yet Harold still had trouble sleeping. He lay on his side, facing away from Sarah even though he usually slept on his back. He didn't want to risk turning and acciden-tally staring at her. What if she opened her eyes just at the instant that his happened to be on her? She'd think he'd been staring at her the whole night, which he certainly hadn't been. Better not to let his head point anywhere near her direction, for fear of a misunderstanding. So he lay on his right side and felt the weight of his body pressing pain-fully into his shoulder as he failed to fall asleep.

Harold sat up in bed when he heard his BlackBerry buzz from the nightstand. He examined it and found a new e-mail from Sebastian Conan Doyle. Sebastian was in London and wanted to meet with them. "Immediately," Sebastian had insisted.

As Harold set the BlackBerry on the nightstand, he noticed Sar-ah's phone resting beside it. He thought back to her long calls the day before, while they were in the café. He was suspicious. He had no trou-ble admitting that to himself. Whatever affection he might have for

Sarah—however much he might enjoy her teasing and whatever tiny crush he might have on her—he still didn't trust her.

As he took Sarah's phone from the nightstand, he comforted himself with the thought that Holmes hadn't been totally honest with Watson all the time either. He had lied to Watson frequently, in fact, keeping his companion in the dark so that Holmes could solve his cases as he saw fit. In *The Hound of the Baskervilles*, Holmes even had Watson off on a pointless mission for the majority of their investigation, so that Holmes could hide in the shadows and observe the suspects while they were distracted by his bumbling sidekick. Harold wasn't doing anything that Sherlock Holmes wouldn't have done himself.

Harold didn't feel guilty as he examined the call records on Sarah's phone. However, as he heard the shower shut off in the bathroom, he knew he needed to move quickly.

Yesterday afternoon Sarah had exchanged a number of calls with a New York area code. One of the calls had been at 3:03 p.m. They had definitely been in the café then. This must have been the call she made to her editor.

As Harold heard Sarah puttering in the bathroom, he pressed Redial. The seconds stretched interminably as he waited to hear a ring.

A female voice answered quickly. "Silverman, Rummel, Tabak, and Siegler. How may I direct your call?"

"I...ummm..." Harold hadn't considered how he'd respond. "Is this a law firm?"

There was a pause on the other end of the line. "Yes, sir. Can I help you?"

The bathroom door opened suddenly, and Sarah came out fully dressed but with a towel wrapped around her wet hair.

"No, thank you," said Harold into the phone as he hung up.

Sarah stopped when she saw him with her phone in his hand.

"Is something going on?" she asked.

"Who's Silverman, Rummel, Tabak, and Siegler?"

Her first reaction was anger. "You checked my phone? Why would you check my phone?"

"Because you lied to me about calling your editor. At least I know that now. Look, I'm sorry, but between the car chases and the guns and the dead people, I'm a little bit on edge. And you seemed *very* eager to follow me to London."

Sarah sighed. She stared at the floor for a moment, collecting herself, and then sat down on the bed. She curled and uncurled her bare toes on the carpet as she spoke.

"Yes. I lied to you. I didn't want to tell you that...the law firm. They're my divorce attorneys. I'm in the middle of getting a divorce."

Of all the things Harold was expecting her to say, this was definitely not among them. "Marc Epstein. That's the name of my lawyer. You can call him and check. I didn't want to tell you because...well, I don't have an editor. I'm not actually working as a reporter right now. But I used to. I wrote for a bunch of papers, a few magazines—I'm sure you Googled me. But then, after I got married, I sort of stopped. My husband—my ex-husband—made enough, and I ended up moving away from writing. And now that I'm getting divorced, I want to do it again. So I'm writing freelance articles. Or trying to, at any rate. And when I heard about Alex finding the diary, when I started reading about the Irregulars, all of you guys, it just seemed too perfect. Anyone would buy this. It's an amazing story."

"That's why you put me in touch with Sebastian. Why you made all of this happen. You wanted something to write about."

Sarah looked up from her feet for the first time since she'd started talking. Her eyes shone with moisture. "I *needed* it, Harold. I needed this story to happen. I needed to get my life back."

After his shock had subsided, what Harold realized was that he wasn't angry. He understood her, more than he wanted to.

"It's okay," he said. "I get it. We're going to find the diary. I promise. But let's make a deal first. We're in this together. You won't lie to me, and I won't go through your phone logs." He smiled. She smiled back.

In a moment that he would recall fondly later, he even reached out and put his arm around her. She laid her towel-wrapped head on his shoulder.

"Thanks," she said at last.

"No problem. I know what it's like to need to prove yourself. To imagine yourself a certain way in your head for so long, and then to get a chance to put it into action in real life. And real life is a lot trickier than I was hoping for."

Sarah laughed.

"We both need to solve this," Harold added.

"Yes," she replied. "And the funny part is, I think I need to solve this more than you do."

———

Sebastian Conan Doyle's London home was in Holland Park, along Abbotsbury Road. The four-story was tooth white and bracketed on either side by tall plane trees. Harold and Sarah took the few steps from the street to the entryway quickly and gave their names to the doorman. He let them in right away. He'd been expecting them.

The house swallowed Harold within its massive enclosure. The ceilings seemed a few feet taller than they needed to be and the hallways a few feet wider. Even the doorways seemed oversize, stretching almost to the ceiling. Art hung genteelly from the walls. It was all modern, or so Harold assumed, though he didn't know much about art. The paintings seemed structural, architectural, full of simple colored shapes smashing into one another.

Sebastian met them at the upstairs landing. He seemed happy to see them. He shook Harold's hand warmly, and did the same with Sarah. "Come," he said, leading them through the flat into what could only be described as a drawing room.

Sebastian settled onto a large couch, the cushions of which looked as if they'd never before been rested on. Harold and Sarah sat delicately on an opposing couch. Harold felt as if he didn't want to break it, or disturb it, as it looked so pristine. A fat and unmarked manila envelope lay on a coffee table between them.

"Let's get to it, shall we?" began Sebastian quickly. "What have you found?"

Harold and Sarah exchanged a furtive look: What should they tell him? Harold felt it was his duty to be the one to respond.

"First of all," Harold said, "did you get anything from the New York police?"

"Yes, of course," said Sebastian. "I've everything you'd asked for. Autopsy results, police reports, crime-scene photographs. All the bloody horrors." He plucked the manila envelope from the coffee table, then tossed it to Harold.

Harold opened it and began flipping through its contents. Indeed, there were photocopies of the handwritten police reports, computer printouts of the crime-scene photos, hotel manifests, and a thick set of documents labeled "CORONER'S REPORT."

"How did you get these?" asked Sarah.

Sebastian turned to her with a look of pure condescension. He did not respond to her question.

"I've flipped through them myself, out of curiosity," he said. "The photos especially are more gruesome than I'd have thought."

There was something about Sebastian that made Harold uneasy. Something about his casual intensity. His ever-tilted head. Sebastian conveyed the impression that your number was already up and he was just waiting for the right moment to let you know.

"The most interesting bit here," continued Sebastian, "is in the supplemental section of the detective's report. It concerns the DNA test of the blood on the walls."

"Oh?" said Harold as he looked for the page. "The blood in the word 'elementary'? Do they know whose it was?"

"They do. It was Alex Cale's."

Harold stopped flipping through the documents, and looked up at Sebastian.

"Damn," he said. "In the story the blood came from the killer, not the victim."

"There are a whole bunch of departures from the story, though," interjected Sarah. "In *A Study in Scarlet*, the victim is poisoned, not strangled."

Harold turned to Sarah, surprised that she was already so familiar with Conan Doyle's work.

"Jesus," she said in response to his look, "you've been talking about the stories nonstop for the past three days—you can't blame me for wanting to read more of them myself. I read a bit online while we were in the café."

"Did the coroner find any poison in Cale's blood?" Harold asked the room.

"No," said Sebastian. "Alex Cale was strangled to death, no doubt about it."

"What about his nose?" Harold asked strangely.

"His nose?" said Sebastian.

"His *nose*?" said Sarah.

"The blood," said Harold. "Was it from Cale's nose?"

"Harold," said Sebastian, "I'm not a doctor, but I don't think they can tell you where in the body a person's blood came from. They can only tell you that it's someone's blood."

"No, no, the coroner's report…" Harold trailed off, thinking rapidly as he tore through the pages in front of him. He slowed down as he found what he was looking for, trying to read the illegible scribbles of the coroner's handwriting. The photocopy itself was blurry, making the report even more difficult to read than it would otherwise be. "Can either of you tell what this says?"

Sarah leaned in close and ran her fingers down the page. She squinted. Harold could smell the hotel shampoo on her hair as a strand fell across the coroner's report. She flicked it back behind her ear with a swipe of her hand.

"Hemorrhage?" she said. "Something about a hemorrhage?"

"In the nasal cavity. A blood clot in..." Harold again let his sentence collapse halfway through.

"I haven't the slightest idea what you're trying to communicate, Harold," said Sebastian. "So Alex had a blood clot in his nasal cavity? He might easily have smashed up his nose fighting with his killer."

"No. His face wasn't bruised when we found him. His nose wasn't broken. It was more deliberate than that. In *A Study in Scarlet*, the message from the killer, written in blood on the walls—the blood came from the killer's nose. He'd gotten a nosebleed while he argued with the victim."

"So here," said Sarah, "the killer used Alex's blood instead of his own. He made an incision inside Alex's nose, or something along those lines, after he killed him. He was probably worried about DNA evidence. Didn't want to make it too easy for you."

"It's strange," said Harold. "He's not re-creating the story exactly. He's using bits and pieces of it. Is he trying to tell us something, with what he's including? Or is he..." Harold again let his sentence collapse midway through. He exhaled the rest of the air in his lungs through pursed lips.

"Or what?" asked Sebastian.

"Or," finished Harold, "what if the killer didn't actually know the story very well? What if he didn't know it by heart? He killed Cale in haste. He wasn't planning it. They had a fight. Some sort of argument. Had to be about the diary. Then he tried to cover his tracks by making it look like a Sherlockian did it. Dressing the murder up with these Sherlockian clues. He half remembered the beginning of *A Study in Scarlet*, but he got it wrong."

Sarah looked confused.

"So now you think it *wasn't* a Sherlockian who did it?"

"I'm suggesting the possibility," said Harold as he fixed his gaze dead on Sebastian, "that the murderer might have been someone familiar with the Sherlockians and yet not of them."

Sebastian looked down his nose at Harold in silence. Finally he grinned devilishly, his cheeks turning apple red.

"Really, Harold? Is that it? Is that the best you've got?"

Sarah looked back and forth between the two men. She seemed unsure of her position.

"We found the message you left on Cale's machine," said Harold. "You sounded pretty angry."

"Yes, yes, yes, and then after Cale died, I offered to help *you* two silly twats find the killer. And *I told you all about my fight with Cale.* I never made a secret of it."

"Who's following us?" blurted Sarah suddenly.

Now Sebastian appeared confused. "I'm sorry, someone is following you?"

"Yes," she said.

"Someone with a gun," added Harold. "A very large gun. And whoever it is ransacked Cale's office as well."

Harold studied Sebastian's expression as best he could. Sebastian gave every indication of processing this information for the very first time.

"Then don't you think," Sebastian said, "that it's likely that whoever this armed pursuer is, he might be, oh, let's just suppose, Cale's bloody killer?"

"Maybe," said Harold. "Except I don't think that guy has the diary. I think you do."

A long moment of silence followed.

"Perhaps, Mr. White, you've exhausted your usefulness," said Sebastian icily.

Harold braced himself. Would Sebastian lunge at him? Did he have a weapon? Harold stepped back, trying to prepare himself for anything.

"I suggest you leave," continued Sebastian. His voice was firm yet calm. He seemed to be a man easily driven to annoyance, but not to anger.

"I'll be in touch," said Harold as he made his way toward the door. He felt he'd handled that quite well.

"So where'd you get those balls from?" asked Sarah after she and Harold had made it onto the street below. They walked along Abbotsbury, under the older Oriental planes that grew closer to the park. They hadn't discussed where to go, but that didn't stop them from walking. Harold was deep in thought, processing the new information. He felt as if he were at the edge of something, just at the precipice between not-knowing and knowing. He was so irritatingly close to figuring it all out, and yet, damn it, he didn't quite have it.

"Sorry?" said Harold, awakening from his thoughts.

"Balls. All of a sudden. Up there." She gestured behind them toward Sebastian's building. "Do you really think he killed Cale?"

"No," said Harold after a sizable pause. "I don't. I suppose there's a lot of evidence that points to him. Motive, means. And the guy creeps me out, I'll be honest. But I don't think he killed Cale."

"Great way to show it."

"I don't *think* he did, but I could be wrong. And I wanted to see how he'd react. Maybe he'd break down and confess the whole thing. Murderers do that in the Holmes stories all the time, once they've been confronted. Even if there isn't any real evidence against them."

For a few minutes, they walked in silent lockstep. Holland Park turned into Notting Hill and then Bayswater. The buildings grew a few stories taller, and the street noise a few decibels louder.

"So, *déjà vu*, we're being followed," said Sarah suddenly.

"What?" Harold was incredulous.

"Older man. Mud-brown suit. Glasses. Wing tips so loud I can hear them from here."

"Christ," said Harold. "How did they find us? And how are you so good at telling when someone is watching you?"

"I don't know. Maybe they had a man on Sebastian's flat, figuring that ten to one we'd show up there eventually? And you try being a woman walking down a busy street sometime. You become acutely aware of each set of eyes that're on you. It's better training than the CIA."

Having no experience being stared at himself, Harold felt obligated to accept her reasoning. "You said he's older?" he asked as they continued walking, faster now.

"Yes," she replied. "Seventies, maybe."

"Seventies? You don't see a lot of goons in their seventies. Unless...
Unless he's the boss of the operation! He hired them to follow us, they
screwed it up, and now he's doing the trailing himself."

"Shit," said Sarah, suddenly more nervous. "You see the alley up
ahead on the left? Ten paces? Eight?"

"Yeah."

"Turn into it with me. Right... *now.*"

Sarah slid suddenly to her left, and Harold followed into the alley.
In an instant she had thrown out her arm, pressing him up against the
wall. The bricks felt hard and cold against his back. Her arm felt hard
and warm against his chest.

"Don't move," she said.

She reached into her coat pocket and pulled out her retractable knife.
She flipped out the blade. It was dark in the alley, even for a foggy midday, as the tall buildings on either side blocked out the sun. The steel
blade appeared a murky blue in the dim light.

Sarah flattened her own back against the wall, next to Harold but
closer to the alley's entrance. Harold saw her breath in the cold air,
even and measured. He realized then that he'd been holding his breath.
He was too scared to exhale. He heard loud footsteps approaching the
alley. The man's wing tips sounded like hooves on the pavement. Harold let out a tiny wisp of air.

There was an instantaneous flash of violence. The old man turned
into the alley, and Sarah leaped at him. Her movements seemed half
professional and half bestial. Before Harold's single puff of hot breath
disappeared into the cold alley, Sarah had the old man on the ground.
Her knife was pressed into his neck.

The old man clutched at his knee. Sarah must have kicked it.

"Ahhhh!" he yelped.

Harold's eyes settled on the man's face. His big glasses. His patchy
gray skin. His thick, dark eyebrows. His nose, seemingly too large for
his face, looked soft and mushy. As if it were a costume nose, knocked
halfway off in the man's fall... *Oh, Jesus.*

"Don't! Ah! It's me!" yelped the old man again.

"Let him up," said Harold.

Sarah didn't budge, keeping her eyes firmly on the old man and her knife scraping against his neck.

"Harold, please, owww, don't let her kill me!"

"Sarah," said Harold after a deep gulp of oxygen. "It's okay. Let him up." He placed a hand on her shoulder. For the first time, she took her eyes off the old man and looked up at Harold.

"It's okay," said Harold. "It's Ron." His face grew flush with embarrassment. "From the Irregulars. It's Ron Rosenberg."

CHAPTER 25

Surveillance

"Danger is part of my trade."
—Sir Arthur Conan Doyle,
"The Adventure of the Final Problem"

November 12, 1900

Arthur inhaled a deep lungful of Morris tobacco, then coughed it up, sputtering as a mist of gray smoke floated up into the gaslight above him. He leaned against the streetlamp and inhaled again on his cigarette. Arthur was not a regular cigarette smoker, and yet he felt that while one was engaged in the work of surveillance, smoking seemed the only practicable method for passing the time. He glanced across the street, into the third-floor window of a moderate four-story. The lights were on inside, and they shone clear out into the night. He saw a figure move in front of the window, framed in the light like an actor in a Chinese shadow play. Arthur instantly stepped backward, out of the narrow beam of the streetlight above him, and dipped his head. The figure in the window was Emily, the petite suffragist from the night before, and it was of the utmost importance that she not discover Arthur spying on her. She passed out of the window's frame, deeper into her flat and out of Arthur's vision. He took another puff of his Morris, this one a bit less full. Goodness, was not surveillance the most infernally tedious activity to which he'd ever submitted himself?

The "chase" the previous evening had been so utterly typical that

Arthur felt he must have scripted it himself. Emily had dashed into a passing two-wheeler on Palmer Street, and Arthur and Bram had quickly found another free cab behind her. They had shown their driver a handful of coins and let him know that it would be his fee were he to successfully follow the two-wheeler up ahead to its destination. He'd given Arthur a heartening "As you say, ma'am" and whipped at his reins. If the cabbie had any concerns as to the disassociation between Arthur's clothing and his voice, he did not express them.

They had ridden from Westminster all the way to Clerkenwell, as the whole while their driver kept Emily's hansom in view. They arrived at the four-story on Aylesbury Street just as Emily was turning her key in the front door. Arthur had the cabbie stop a few houses before Emily's and then instructed him to pull up outside it after she had entered. They'd waited a few moments, until a light turned on inside the third-floor flat. Arthur and Bram couldn't see far enough into the windows to tell what Emily was doing, but they now knew where she lived.

After they had let the cabbie go, there'd been considerable disagreement over what to do next. Arthur had wanted to bang on the front door, demand to be let up, and then confront this girl as to her role in the affair. Bram noted that this plan carried with it a considerable amount of danger. It was likely that Emily was a clandestine associate of at least two murdered suffragists. She had been involved in the murders of Sally Needling and her friend, and perhaps the letter bombing of Arthur's study. They still didn't know what the tattoos meant. And most importantly, they had no information about the murderous husband they were after. If Emily knew him, or if she even conspired with him, he might come calling on her at any moment. Perhaps it would be helpful to have a little more information before they confronted her.

Arthur had not been entirely convinced by Bram's arguments, though he had been cautioned by them. "Very well," he allowed. "Let us first set up watch over Emily and her quarters. We're going to have to get out of these ridiculous clothes sooner or later, so let's take turns running home for trousers and shirts while the other keeps a view on those windows. If Emily leaves, we shall again give chase. If she stays, we shall do the same. Agreed?"

And so they had proceeded, with Arthur taking the first trip home for a fresh change of clothes. There had been no more trains at that hour, so he had engaged another hansom in the most expensive cab ride of his life. At home he was greeted by the stillness of a sleeping household. At the sound of his key in his lock, at the clap of his shoe on the floor of the front hallway, he had felt suddenly alien. Like a thief in his own home. Not one of the souls peacefully sleeping underneath this roof knew a thing about the quest which had so consumed him over these past weeks. His obsessive machinations were hidden from these drowsy snorers on the second floor. Not his wife, Touie, nor his love Jean, was so alive in his mind as were the dead and their killer.

No one had stirred as he had ascended the stairs to his chambers. Fortunately, he and Touie still kept separate sleeping arrangements, on account of her illness, so he had no need to disturb her slumber as he fumbled about with his corset.

He had returned to Clerkenwell three hours later, riding in the same hansom in which he'd left. It was then Bram's turn to make use of the cab, the driver of which was having the most prosperous of evenings. Arthur and Bram had alternated thus for much of the following day. They took turns sleeping in a nearby hotel, though neither man managed much in the way of decent rest.

And now, at a quarter to six in the evening on the day after the suffragist lecture, Arthur manned his post alone, with only a silver case of Morris cigarettes to keep him company. The night had been long, yes, but the day had been even longer. The midnight chill had kept him awake until dawn, but Arthur was growing disoriented by the day of half-sleeping and half-waking attention to a single window. Pedestrians came and went, yet Arthur remained, forcing himself alert despite the stultifying inactivity. He had heard soldiers in the Transvaal describe sentry duty as being one in which the hour of the day became lost entirely. A second might feel like an hour, and an hour like a second, until one had no idea whether it was noon or night. Arthur found himself having just the opposite experience. He knew precisely what hour it was, and he counted down the minutes to Bram's next arrival on his pocket watch.

At six o'clock exactly, Arthur saw Bram turn the corner onto Aylesbury Street. Bram looked considerably more rested than Arthur, though he seemed no happier about their mission. The men traded pleasantries, though neither seemed in the mood to be particularly pleasant about it.

When the light in Emily's window clicked off, it stole Arthur and Bram's attention toward the darkened flat. They each instinctively stepped away from the streetlight, well outside the range of the gas lamp twelve feet above their heads. After a long few moments, Emily appeared in the building's front door. She carried a heavy purse, into which she deposited her keys after locking the door behind her. At the bottom of the four steps between her front door and the street, she almost smacked directly into an old woman. Emily appeared to blurt out a quick apology and continue on her way, while the old woman regained her balance along the handrail and ascended toward the door of Emily's building.

Arthur turned to Bram. "Do you think we have the same plan in mind?" he asked.

"I'm sure we do not," replied Bram cautiously.

"Then I'll explain in a moment," said Arthur. "For now, come!" Arthur spun around and headed straight for the door to Emily's building. She was walking east and was already approaching the corner. In a few seconds, she would be out of view.

But Arthur paid her no mind. Rather, he hopped up the four steps to Emily's residence while the old woman fumbled with her keys.

"Pardon me," said Arthur to the old woman. "Might I give you a hand with that?"

The woman looked confused as she glanced up from her ring of keys and into Arthur's bright face. He'd shaved at home, but left his upper lip untouched. Not yet twenty-four hours old, Arthur's nascent mustache was ill shaped and splotchy. He looked like a teenager overeager to prove his manhood.

"I..." stammered the old woman. "Well...I...certainly..."

Arthur reached out and snatched the keys from her hand. He found the right one and opened the door to her building. He handed the keys back to her while he held the door open and gestured for her to pass inside.

"After you, madam," he said.

She seemed unsure of how to handle this situation, but years of social training kicked in.

"Thank you, sir," she said, and walked into her building. She moved through the small vestibule, and, the correct key already in hand, she unlocked the door to her flat and went inside. Arthur remained smiling at the building's entryway, continuing to hold open the door as if he were a shoddy butler. As soon as she'd vanished into her flat, Arthur let his smile drop and called outside to Bram.

"What are you waiting for? Let's go!" he cried.

Bram followed Arthur up the building's winding central staircase and onto the third-floor landing. They came to a sturdy door with the letter "C" marked in brass upon its face. Arthur tried the knob, on the off chance that it happened to be unlocked. It was not.

"Well then," said Bram. "Fine work. What now?"

By way of response, Arthur picked up his right leg, leaned back, and kicked at the door with all his might. There was a loud crunching sound, and both men could see the doorframe shake. And yet the door itself did not budge. Arthur kicked again, just beside the knob, and again the hallway was filled with the slap and crunch of boot against wood. But again the door did not give.

They could hear the old woman from downstairs coming out into the hall, drawn from her flat by the noises from upstairs.

"What's going on there?" she shouted up the staircase. Bram and Arthur exchanged a look. What should they say?

"Almost done!" shouted Arthur in response. "We'll be through in a minute!" This did not remotely address the woman's question, but it seemed to provide them with a little bit of time. The old woman seemed not to know what next to say.

Arthur shrugged and then wound himself up for another kick. This one was no more effective than the others.

"You're quite sure there's no problem?" the woman called.

"No, ma'am!" yelled Arthur. As he prepared himself for another kick—his knees were growing sore—Bram stuck out his hand.

"Wait," whispered Bram. "If you really intend to break in to Emily's lodgings by force, then we might as well just see it done." Bram reached a hand into his coat pocket and removed a pearl-handled revolver. He drew back the pin, pointed it at the door, and pulled the trigger.

The whole building seemed to echo from the gunshot. As Arthur's hearing returned, he began to make out reverberations from every corner of the four-story. But it wasn't until the ringing in his ears began to subside that he became fully aware of what had just occurred.

"Sorry about that, ma'am!" Bram yelled down the staircase. "That'll be all for now!"

Arthur looked at the door. The knob hung loose from the door's face, and the lock inside appeared permanently disfigured. Bram easily pushed the door open with one gentle stroke of his hand.

The old woman did not respond, but seemed instead to return to her flat. Or so Arthur could deduce from the sounds he heard burbling up the staircase.

"That was a good bit louder, and rather more sudden, than I might have expected," Arthur said. "Don't think I've ever heard a shot go off indoors before. Frightfully loud."

"If your plan is to search through Emily's lodgings," said Bram, "then I suggest we do it quickly. We'll have inquiries about the noise soon enough." He entered the flat, and Arthur followed.

Inside, they found a mess that had little to do with their break-in. A tea set lay out beside a couch, cups and saucers scattered over every flat surface. Murky liquid, which might once have been called tea, pooled inside the cups. It gave off a gentle whiff of spoiled milk.

Off to one side of the room was an open doorway leading to a cramped bedroom. Arthur could see from the main sitting room that the bed was unmade and that articles of ladies' clothing were strewn about the floor alongside the bedsheets. Though the windows had seemed large from across the street, as they were Arthur's only portals into Emily's world, now that he was inside, they seemed rather small. They mustn't let in much light, even in the daytime. Outside, it was dark, and as Arthur approached the window, he looked down at the lonely streetlamp under which he'd stood. He could barely make it out, given all the fog.

Across from the bedroom door sat a worktable, on which all manner of objects seemed to coexist. There were chemical beakers and test tubes, sacks of colored powders and wide Corning vials, balls of twine and a stack of cheap brown wrapping paper. The work done upon this table was scientific, Arthur could tell at least that much. In the center of the table, a white box lay opened. Arthur peered inside and found himself face-to-face with a tube of dynamite.

It looked identical to the tube he'd found wrapped in a very similar package, in his letter box. Fortunately, in this case the dynamite did not appear to be attached to anything. There was no triggering mechanism in sight. Arthur reached down and turned the package over. On the bottom a label had already been fixed. "Dr. Arthur Conan Doyle," it read. "Undershaw. Hindhead."

Bram joined Arthur at the desk. He merely nodded as he observed the letter bomb, and the name printed on its address label.

"My God," said Arthur. "It was this Emily girl. She was the one who tried to kill me." But before Bram could respond, they heard footsteps at the door to the flat. Both men turned.

Emily stood in the doorway in her colorful coat. Under the crook of one arm, she held a stack of letters. In the other arm, she held a revolver, which she aimed straight at Arthur.

Arthur's mind turned, strangely, not to his family, or his loves, but to Bram. Underpinning Arthur's fear was the thought that he should never have involved a friend so good as Bram in all this. *Bram deserved more*, Arthur realized as he stared into the steel face of Emily's pistol and watched her pull back the pin.

CHAPTER 26

Ron Rosenberg Theorizes

"How do you know that?"
"I followed you," [said Holmes.]
"I saw no one."
"That is what you may expect to see when I follow you."
—Sir Arthur Conan Doyle,
"The Adventure of the Devil's Foot"

January 10, 2010, cont.

With great effort Ron Rosenberg heaved himself onto his feet. He still clutched his knee, his hands rubbing at the spot where Sarah had kicked it. While Ron took a deep breath, Sarah stepped back, giving him space. She continued to hold the knife in her hand, however, its blade outstretched and at the ready.

"Why are you following us?" said Harold.

"And more importantly," said Sarah, "what the hell are you wearing?"

As if suddenly remembering his disguise, Ron reached up to his face and pulled off the costume nose. He removed a pair of fake gray eyebrows and a very convincing gray wig. Bits of leathery fake skin had been dislodged from his cheeks and forehead. They hung off him, making it look as if his face were melting.

"Maybe I should be the one asking questions of the two of you!" he said. "What have you done with the diary?"

"Jesus, Ron, we don't have the diary. Stop." Harold turned to Sarah, addressing her. "The costume, the old man bit... It's a Sherlock Holmes thing. When he was trailing suspects, Holmes would go out in disguise a lot. He often dressed as an old man, or even an old woman. It's in a bunch of stories." He turned back to Ron. "Which doesn't explain what you're doing *here.*"

"I had hoped not to reveal my hand this early, Harold, but you leave me no choice. I think you killed Alex Cale and stole the diary. I think you're in league with Sebastian Conan Doyle and that the two of you planned it together."

Sarah smiled.

Harold rubbed his temples with his hands, more irritated than angry. "Why would I kill Cale?"

"Because you wanted to be number one, Harold. Don't pretend you're not ambitious. You've been an Irregular for, what, a week now? You've already published an article in the *Baker Street Journal.* You've befriended all of the group's luminaries, including me. You made sure to meet Alex Cale the night before his death. Jeffrey Engels sponsored your investiture, you must know that. But did you think he was going to help you cover up the murder, too? Don't be stupid, Harold."

Harold didn't even know where to begin his response. Ron was embarrassing, not just to himself but to Harold. Detective work was serious and difficult and not something to be dabbled in. Ron wasn't cut out for this. This wasn't a time for amateurs.

"I didn't kill anybody," Harold said wearily. "If I was the murderer, then why was I the first person to discover his body? Why am I out here trying to *find* the murderer? Why not go home and enjoy my new ten-million-dollar diary, the one that I just stole?"

"To draw suspicion away from yourself, of course!" replied Ron. He spoke with equal parts professorial condescension and rueful acknowledgment of a skilled adversary. "No one ever suspects that the detective himself is the murderer. It's a brilliant device, but an old one. Agatha Christie used it first, not Conan Doyle. *The Murder of Roger Ackroyd.* Remember, I've read all the same stories that you have, Harold. I know what you're up to."

"Well, if that's true," said Harold, "then since you're the one investigating me, since *you're* the one playing detective, maybe you're the one who killed him."

Ron stood motionless, thinking this over. Harold nodded toward Sarah, who gave Ron a polite smile as the two walked out into the street. Alone, Ron was lost in thought.

CHAPTER 27

The Strange Tale of Emily Davison

"What business is it of yours, then?" [said Henry Wood.]
"It's every man's business to see justice done," [replied Holmes.]
—Sir Arthur Conan Doyle,
"The Crooked Man"

November 12, 1900, cont.

Arthur stood perfectly rigid as his gaze leaped between the hard steel pistol in Emily's hand and the hard steel expression on her face. Her skin was firmed smooth and taut with rage. The millennial seconds drew long. Arthur realized that he was not breathing, though when he attempted to open his lungs to air, his body did not respond. He stood just between Bram and Emily. He could neither hear nor feel his friend behind him, though Bram could not be more than three feet away.

"You bloody butchers!" whispered Emily. "You killed my Sally. And you killed my Anna. You close your evil eyes now, and you picture their faces while you die." She shivered with anger, her right index finger vibrating against the trigger.

"You misunderstand," said Arthur through quivering lips. "We haven't killed anyone." He raised his hands above his head, giving the universal sign for surrender.

Behind him, he thought he could faintly hear the motion of Bram's coat. Bram's revolver, Arthur realized, was back in his pocket. Was he making a go for it?

"I catch you standing here, right here, guilty as sin, and all you can do is lie!" Emily raised her voice as she became more set on pulling the trigger. "I didn't expect to find two of you. But when you're done, I'll still have four bullets to spare. The two of you for two of mine, then? I'll wager the trade is fair."

Arthur hadn't the faintest idea what she was talking about. But from the look in her eyes, he knew she'd kill him whether he understood or not. He heard another rustle of cloth behind him. Bram was going to get them both killed.

"Elementary!" cried Arthur with every bit of air he could muster.

Emily frowned. Her lips pursed, and then loosened, as her face expressed a series of confused expressions.

"Elementary?" she asked.

"I am Arthur Conan Doyle," he said. "And you're the one who's been trying to kill me."

Emily appeared shaken by this information. She stared Arthur dead in the eyes, as if trying to read the truth on his face. Was he really Arthur Conan Doyle?

"I shaved my mustache," he explained. "Yesterday." Emily's rage seemed to subside as she evaluated his statement.

"*You* are Arthur Conan Doyle?" she asked, her whole body twisting with confusion.

"Yes."

"And who are you?" She looked over Arthur's shoulder.

"My name is Bram Stoker." Emily's face gave no sign of recognition as Bram spoke. "I'm a friend of Arthur's."

"Who are you?" asked Arthur of Emily, as if addressing a child.

"Emily...Emily Davison," she replied.

"Miss Davison, you sent a bomb to kill me in the mail," said Arthur. "There was a clipping from the paper attached. The murder of your friend. You wrote 'elementary' on it, I haven't the faintest idea why. I investigated the case. There were clues the Yard had missed. I followed them. To this house. I followed them to you."

Arthur watched Emily Davison inhale deeply, her chest pressing outward as it filled with air. Arthur suddenly noticed the sweat that had formed on his brow and beneath his arms. He felt damp and unclean.

Emily lowered her revolver. Arthur could feel the blood returning to his face. As he blinked, the girl's demeanor changed completely. She flopped herself down on one of the chairs beside the couch and rolled back her head. She looked as if she'd just been holding up a great weight and now she'd let it go.

"I can't believe it worked," she said quietly. "I hoped... my God, I hoped so much that it would. I can't believe... How did you find me?"

"Your tattoo," replied Arthur cautiously. He was unsure of what to make of this woman and her sudden change in demeanor. "We found the man who'd painted it. You and your friends were imprinted with matching tattoos, were you not?"

"Oh, but you *are* good, aren't you? I knew you would be. I prayed you would be. But you weren't supposed to come here. You weren't supposed to find me."

"Who were we supposed to find?" asked Bram.

"The man who killed my friends. The man who killed Sally and Anna. I wasn't trying to hurt you, you must believe me. I was trying to hire you." The girl let herself sink into the massive couch. She discarded her revolver onto a long coffee table as if it were a ring of keys. She appeared suddenly harmless.

Arthur took the opportunity to turn his head around. Behind him Bram inched his hand toward his coat pocket for his revolver. Arthur shook his head at Bram. Bram raised an eyebrow, as if to say, *Are you sure?* Arthur nodded. *Yes.* He was sure. The immediate danger had ended. What was required now was talk, and lots of it.

"Perhaps you had better explain," suggested Arthur.

Emily paused, considering this for a long moment. She looked as if the idea of having to explain herself to Arthur had never crossed her mind. She pursed her lips and made a face that sank with both gravity and exhaustion.

"Yes," she said. "Perhaps I had better. We have much to discuss. May

I offer you gentlemen some tea? Please? It is the least I can do. I'm not sure if I've still got milk, but I know there's some fresh honey in the cupboard."

"Thank you, no," said Arthur as he sat down beside her on the couch. "Did you send a letter bomb to murder me?"

"I wouldn't mind a cup, if you've got one handy," said Bram. He took a seat on an armchair opposite Arthur. Emily stood up and went to her kitchen, where she put on a pot of hot water.

"Yes," replied Emily after she'd returned to the drawing room. "And a thousand apologies for that. But I'd no intention of murdering you, you must believe me." She sighed. "It was just supposed to give a little pop and a burst of smoke. It's only that it was my very first letter bomb. I think I used too much dynamite. I would never have hurt you. Do you understand? Not you." A weariness had crept into her voice, fully replacing the anger which not two minutes before had seemed completely to consume her.

"Might we start from the beginning?" suggested Arthur.

"The beginning?" she said. "But it's so hard to say when that might have been. I've been a woman all my life, you know." At this she smiled ruefully. "But I suppose I've been a suffragist for less time than that."

"Why don't we begin there?" said Arthur reassuringly. "You and your friends Sally and Morgan—er, I believe you said her real name was Anna? You, Sally, and Anna were all suffragists?"

"I'm not ashamed to say I was rather more committed to the cause than those two. But I think that's plain as day, isn't it?" She stopped herself and straightened her back. "Oh, but this is coming out all wrong! You deserve an explanation, Dr. Doyle, and soon you may even deserve my thanks. There were four of us. Sally, Anna, Janet, and, of course, myself. We met at Caxton Hall over the years, as we all went to the meetings. I wasn't yet seventeen when I joined the NUWSS, if you can believe it. The others were older. We'd see one another from time to time at the meetings, and then one evening about two years ago—BANG." Emily clapped her hands together in front of her, giving

Arthur a scare. "We became fast friends. Funny how you can know someone for years and then all of a sudden something passes between you and you become inseparable. That's how it was with us. And it was that way between Janet and me especially. She was by far the most beautiful girl I'd ever seen. She and I simply understood each other, from our first conversation onward, there wasn't a moment of uncertainty or confusion between us. Sometimes people confuse me. I have trouble making out whatever it is that they're saying. But never with Janet. Do you have a friend like that, with whom you can share absolutely anything, and nothing between you is forbidden?"

Arthur thought of Bram. Their relationship, for all of its trust and goodwill, was not exactly that which Emily described. He said nothing, and Emily continued her strange monologue.

"At least I still have my Janet. This man, this detestable creature, whoever he may be, hasn't gotten to her yet."

The kettle crowed, and Emily stood up to prepare the tea. She returned in a few moments with three empty cups, which she laid before her guests along with a steaming pot. She allowed it to steep while she spoke.

"We formed our own group, the four of us. Mrs. Fawcett is daft, and practically a Tory to boot. People like her are not going to win our suffrage. She is weak and fearful, and she is beholden to the society in which we live for her purse, as well as for her husband. She thinks no more highly of England's women than does the stodgiest old anti-suffragist." Emily again smiled bitterly. "Like you! For Fawcett, and for her useless union, our fight is merely one of politics. Can you imagine the shortsightedness? And so we formed a rival organization. We were not by any stretch the first to do so, mind you. You'd be surprised how many splinter groups exist on the margins of Millicent's minions. Those girls from Manchester—you'll be hearing about them soon, I'll promise you that!"

Arthur hadn't any clue as to who these Manchester girls were, but he saw no use in interrupting the flow of her thoughts.

Emily poured three cups of tea, though Arthur had not asked for any. He sipped politely out of habit. When it occurred to him that he was accidentally taking tea with a woman who had nearly murdered him, he felt foolish and returned his cup to the table.

"We named ourselves the Morrigan, after the Irish goddess. She's the goddess of war, and of prophecy. She could assume different forms as well—sometimes she took the shape of an eel, sometimes a wolf, but our favorite was the crow with three heads. We adopted the crow as our emblem and had it painted permanently onto our skin to prove our devotion to the cause. We had such plans as would have sent the kingdom into shock. We were to launch a campaign of pamphlets this fall. We hired a printer and tried out arrangements for our emblem. It took ages. He was most helpful, that printer—he never even charged us for his many hours of work. But pamphlets would not save the country, we knew that. We were prepared for more, if need be. They would be followed by bombs. And if the bombs failed to rouse the public's attention to the cause of England's women...well, then we were prepared to build bigger bombs if it were required. I'd have liked to see the NUWSS do that!"

"You would have bombed London?" said Arthur. "You would have turned your own homeland into a battlefield over legislative politics?"

"There is a war under way in London whether we join it or not!" said Emily forcefully.

She banged her palm down on the table, splashing tea onto the saucers. Bram raised his cup and took a gentle sip.

"England is changing. The Morrigan is not a cause of that change; she is an effect. Have you been to Whitechapel, Dr. Doyle? Have you seen the depredations there? A hundred thousand ladies enslaved as whores. Have you been to Westminster? Another hundred thousand enslaved as chars. The women of England have but three choices in this age. We toil with our hands, we toil with our cunts, or we marry rich and toil with our very hearts. Which would you choose?"

She became more animated as she spoke, the anger again building inside her. Arthur gripped on to the cushions of the couch, afraid and unsure as to where this all was headed.

"I've read your speeches, you know. I've read what you said in Edinburgh. We all have. And I've read your stories. I've read your Sherlock Holmes. Your London died with him, dropped off a cliff and drowned in a pool of frothy water. The Morrigan was to see the deed through."

The girl stared off into the distance, as if at some imaginary horizon. Arthur felt himself to be in the presence of villainy. This was the kind of rage which tore down civilizations.

"You attempted to murder me over a speech?" Arthur asked, as calmly as he could.

"No, no, of course not," she said. "I told you. I never meant to hurt you. I needed your help."

"My help?"

"We never set our bombs. We never even distributed our pamphlets. The NUWSS reigns still as the sole and impotent voice of suffrage in London. Before we could see our plans to fruition, Sally was murdered. And then Anna. I saw that article in the paper, the one I sent you, and I knew it was her. 'Morgan Nemain.' Ha! It was a little joke between us that Anna used for her pseudonym. 'Morgan,' for the Morrigan, and 'Nemain'—that's the name of one of the Morrigan's spirits, in the myth. She was the funny one, Anna was . . .

"Janet, my dear Janet, was so distraught she gave it up. She went away to live with her uncle in Leeds. I wrote to her about my plans. How I would carry on the Morrigan myself. She never even wrote me back."

Arthur saw something new on Emily's young countenance. A great sadness had entered her cheeks, reddening her face and wetting her clear green eyes. "Even dearest Janet left me! This killer took everything, don't you see? He wrenched from my breast every last soul on whose love I depended. I had no one left to turn to. Except for you."

"I'm afraid I don't understand," said Arthur.

"I've read all of your stories. The plots are so good, I can't imagine how you do it. And that Holmes! He is a bitter hater of womankind, but he is also a true genius. Everything seems to come to him so easily, have you noticed that? 'Elementary,' he says; he figures it all out with barely any effort. I'd never be able to find out who killed Sally and Anna on my own. But Holmes could. *You* could. I believed in you, Dr. Doyle. I believed that you were noble and good, that you were the equal of your creation. And I was right. It worked. My Lord, it worked... 'The Crooked Man,' that was my favorite story. Isn't it everyone's? That's where he says 'elementary' to his friend Watson. I put that in the letter to get your attention, to excite your curiosity. And I can see that it did."

"You wanted me to investigate the murders of your friends?" said Arthur, incredulous. It was too fantastical to be believed. This girl was either mad or brilliant. Arthur was unsure of which possibility he found more comforting.

"Well, who else could?" she said reasonably. "The Yard didn't care a whit for my friends. They thought Sally was a cheap harlot, and when Anna's family told them that their daughter had vanished, they spent a few days asking around and then let it go. They never even found her body. To make matters worse, if I told the Yard the truth about our group, they'd have been rather more keen on arresting me than on arresting the murderer of my friends. I thought about sending you money and asking for your assistance, but all of my meager funds have gone toward the bombs. I realized I did have one trick up my sleeve." She gestured to the far table and the long stick of dynamite. "You catch more flies with honey than with vinegar, true, but how many might you be able to catch with a quarter pound of dynamite?" Emily smiled. Arthur did not.

He rose to his feet, standing tall before her like St. Peter at the gates of heaven.

"Miss Davison," he began, "you are a common criminal. You are a thug and a villain, and I will see you punished. Your murdered friends have my sympathies, but you will not. I shall go to Scotland Yard and inform them that it was you who placed a letter bomb in the mail, with me as its recipient. I share your despair at the treatment of young women in Whitechapel; perhaps you can inform me, when you arrive, as to the condition of the ladies at Newgate Prison."

"But, Dr. Doyle!" said Emily as she burst up from her chair. "I realize that I behaved uncharitably toward you. I can understand your anger. But I was desperate. Have you no compassion? Sally and Anna are dead! Murdered! You're not going to find out who killed them?"

"No," said Arthur as he walked toward the door. "I am not. You may expect the police at your doorstep on the morrow. Good evening." Arthur yanked open the door and exited.

Bram finally stood from the couch, resting his teacup gently on its saucer.

"Good evening, Miss Davison," he said. "It was a pleasure to have met you."

With that, Bram followed behind his friend, leaving Emily Davison alone in her drawing room. She did not follow them out.

CHAPTER 28

Thinking

Sherlock Holmes closed his eyes and placed his elbows upon the arms of his chair, with his finger-tips together. "The ideal reasoner," he remarked, "would, when he had once been shown a single fact in all its bearings, deduce from it not only all the chain of events which led up to it but also all the results which would follow from it."
—Sir Arthur Conan Doyle,
"The Five Orange Pips"

January 10, 2010, cont.

It was time for Harold to do some deep thinking.

That's how Sherlock Holmes had done it. He'd sit in his armchair, wearing his dressing gown, puffing away at his pipe, while he kept his eyes closed to all distraction. And he'd methodically, step by step, go through the problem at hand. He would break it down logically and figure out what *had* to have happened. After a few hours, he'd burst up suddenly, without any warning, and he'd have his answer.

That was Holmes's greatest gift, Harold realized. Not his uncanny powers of observation, not his encyclopedic knowledge of footprints and poisons, not his facility with disguises or scent-sniffing dogs. The real trick was concentration. It was his ability to think through a mystery. Reason was his weapon against the unknown.

If Harold was going to become Holmes, or at least a worthy heir, then he'd have to do the same thing. The only trouble was that it was proving harder than he'd hoped.

Harold sat in the red armchair, his elbows resting against the curved armrests. The cushioned seat below him was comfortable, though it pressed his wallet, which was in his right rear jeans pocket, awkwardly into his buttocks.

He should get up and remove it. Then he'd be more comfortable.

Harold was back in the hotel room in which he and Sarah had spent the previous night. She lay on the bed eating a Greek salad while she flipped through the pages of Alex Cale's Conan Doyle biography. Harold could hear the crunching of the romaine lettuce in her mouth and the dull sound of her plastic fork scraping her plastic salad bowl. The noise made it difficult to concentrate.

The wallet in his pocket was really starting to bother him. It tilted the weight of his pelvis so that there wasn't any truly comfortable way to sit. He should get up and take out his wallet so he could get back to thinking. But he'd promised himself that he wouldn't stand up until he had a solution. He would stick to his plan. He would remain seated.

Sarah was chewing again. God, he should have told her to take a walk or something. Since she had nowhere else to go, she had decided to finish Cale's work and have some lunch. She'd asked if he'd mind her hanging around while he did his thinking, and he'd said that he didn't. Harold was very polite, and he liked having Sarah around, a lot. But she was making it very hard to sustain a logical train of thought.

Here was the problem at hand: In October, Alex Cale had announced that he'd found the lost diary of Sir Arthur Conan Doyle. He'd called his sister to tell her the good news, and he'd declined her offer to celebrate. He'd spent the next months reading and studying the diary, preparing to integrate the information gleaned from it into his biography. Though, as of December 14, the manuscript of the biography hadn't been rewritten to include any of it. On January 5, Cale had arrived at the Algonquin Hotel in New York to present the diary to his fellow Sherlockians. He reported being followed, and he seemed afraid. In the middle of the night, his door was opened to visitors three times. There was no clue whatsoever as to who those visitors might have been, and no one had yet claimed to be among them. Between 4 a.m. and 8 a.m., he was strangled to death with his own shoelace.

His own shoelace. That was pretty odd, wasn't it? There weren't any instances of shoelace stranglings in the Canon...

The killer had written the word "elementary" on the wall, in the darkest corner of the darkened hotel room. He'd written it using Cale's blood, which he'd gotten from puncturing the inside of Cale's nose. The room had then been ransacked. The diary was found and removed.

Or, thought Harold, *wait*. What if the diary hadn't actually been removed from the hotel room in New York? What if Alex had left it in his writing office in London? That's why the killer had to break in to that office, to search for the diary there as well! *No. Damn.* That didn't work. Harold knew who'd ransacked the London office: It was the Goateed Man, and his friend with the gun. But the Goateed Man didn't have the diary, because if he did, he wouldn't have asked Harold for it. So the diary hadn't been in the London office. It had to have been in the hotel. Did that mean two different sets of people were searching for it? The killer, who'd taken it from the hotel, and the Goateed Man, who'd failed to find it in London? But if that were true, then what did the Goateed Man know about the true killer? Did he, like Ron Rosenberg, think that *Harold* was the killer? Is that why he'd asked him for the diary? If he—

Sarah crunched loudly into a chunk of crisp lettuce. Harold heard every gnash of her teeth while she chewed. He heard the plastic fork rummage around again in the bowl, and then he heard her bite into something else. It sounded duller...Maybe a cucumber? Or a feta-covered olive?

Harold completely lost track of his thoughts. His concentration had been shot. And now his wallet was bothering him again.

Did Sherlock Holmes have these difficulties concentrating? Did Arthur Conan Doyle? Harold thought of Conan Doyle's attempts at consulting with Scotland Yard. No one seemed to regard them as having been particularly successful. What an ego Conan Doyle must have had, to think that just because he wrote mystery stories, he could solve real-life mysteries.

Harold closed his eyes tighter and focused his thoughts. "We must look for consistency," Sherlock Holmes had said. "When there is a want of it we must suspect deception." So what was inconsistent here? What didn't make sense?

Crunch, crunch, crunch.

For the love of God, thought Harold. *If she doesn't stop chewing that salad like she's operating a trash compactor, there's going to be another murder.* Harold heard her chewing stop, as if she'd read his thoughts. He heard her walk into the bathroom and shut the door. Then he heard the rush of running water. Harold felt he would have only a minute of uninterrupted concentration before Sarah left the bathroom and her chewing started up again.

Even though his wallet was now digging sharply into his backside, he would ignore it. He would give this one last minute of pure mental energy. He was committed to his task, and nothing would keep him from it. So then: *What doesn't make sense?*

That's when he figured it out.

His eyes burst open. He squinted, adjusting his eyes to the daylight. They had been closed for a while. He stood up from his armchair and heard a creak in his knees. He must have been sitting there for hours. He called to Sarah in the bathroom.

"Sarah!" he yelled.

"Yeah?" she called back over the sound of running water.

"Alex Cale never found the lost diary of Sir Arthur Conan Doyle!"

Harold heard the water stop. A second later Sarah emerged from the bathroom, a very strange look on her face.

"Excuse me?" she said.

"Alex Cale never found the lost diary of Sir Arthur Conan Doyle. He lied."

"How do you know that?"

"There's one piece of evidence that doesn't make sense. There's one thing that doesn't belong. Once I figured out what that was, the whole story unraveled."

"And that thing was...?"

"The manuscript! What's the story, as we know it now? Cale spent twenty years working on that thing. It was supposed to be the culmination of a life's work. And then, at long last, he finds what he's been looking for. The diary. After all these years, he can finally complete his manuscript... *But he doesn't?* He's too busy in the three months after he found the diary to include its contents in his masterpiece? It doesn't make any sense."

"But wait, all we have is one backup copy of one draft of his manuscript. Maybe that chapter was in a different file. Maybe it was in a different draft. We have no way of knowing."

"True," said Harold. "But think about this. What did Alex's sister say about his mood after he found the diary?"

Sarah raised her eyes, trying to remember. "She said he didn't want to celebrate," Sarah finally replied. "She said he wouldn't talk about what was in the diary. He didn't tell her anything. She said for those last months, whatever he found in the diary made him nothing but miserable."

"Does that make any sense? Or was it that not finding the diary, and deciding to lie to the public, made him nothing but miserable? In the time since Cale supposedly found the diary, did he ever divulge, to anyone, even the slightest hint about its contents? Or anything about where he'd found it?"

"No."

"Is there any hard evidence, besides Alex's word, that he actually found that diary?"

"No."

"So which is more probable: that Alex Cale solved the greatest mystery in the history of Sherlockian studies, but refused to tell anyone how he'd solved it or what the answer was, and then neglected to write about it in his almost-completed book; or that he lied about finding the diary in the first place?"

Sarah nodded, admitting that Harold had a point.

"Okay then," she said. "If he never found the diary, then who killed him?"

At this, Harold had to smile. The explanations really were the most fun part of being a detective.

"No one," Harold said. "Alex Cale killed himself."

If Sarah had been surprised before, now she was dumbfounded.

"Bullshit," she said.

"'When you have eliminated the impossible, whatever remains, however improbable, must be the truth.'"

"I'm going to assume Sherlock Holmes said that?"

"Yes. And he's right. I know it's improbable, but it's the only way to explain everything."

"Okay then," said Sarah as she plopped herself down on the bed. "Explain everything." She sat looking up at Harold like an eager audience member at the opening curtain of a play. She'd never looked at him like this before. The sensation was exhilarating.

"The first thing that needs explaining is, *why* would Cale lie about finding the diary and then attend the convention? What the hell was his plan? He was just going to show up at the lecture the next morning empty handed and say he was sorry? The suicide explains it. He never intended to make it to the lecture. His plan, from day one, was to announce that he'd found the diary and then kill himself under suspicious circumstances, making it look like the diary had been stolen. He ransacked his own room. He opened and closed the door to his room three times in the night, to simulate having received potentially murderous visitors. And remember, *no one* claims to have visited Cale at any point in the night. Sure, the killer wouldn't, but would two innocent Sherlockians really lie about it to the cops out of paranoia?"

"He strangled himself with his own shoelace?" said Sarah, swinging her feet off the edge of the bed as she spoke. "Is that even possible?"

"The medical community is split about that one," said Harold. "Some think it's possible, some think it isn't."

"How in the world do you know that?"

"I've read a lot of mysteries. This isn't exactly the first time the issue of self-strangulation has come up. Plus, he might have used a tool for help. Do you remember at the crime scene? There was an antique pen on the floor by the body. The same model that Conan Doyle used. What if Cale used the pen to tighten the shoelace around his neck? Then it fell away when he collapsed. The pen would make it easier for him to tighten it initially, before he lost muscle strength."

"But it might not even be possible?"

"You're being kind of glass-half-empty about this, don't you think? It might *be* possible. Neither of us is a doctor. But even if we were, we couldn't rule out the possibility, not for certain."

Sarah smiled. She was enjoying this.

"This happened in a Holmes story, you know. Not the strangulation via shoelace. But in 'The Problem of Thor Bridge,' a woman killed herself in such a fashion that it looked like murder. She did it in order to frame her husband's mistress."

"Doesn't the word 'elementary' appear in a different story? You told me that."

"Yes. It does. When Cale wrote 'elementary' on the wall, he wasn't pointing us toward 'Thor Bridge.' He was pointing us toward *A Study in Scarlet*, like I always thought, which is where the killer leaves a message on the wall in his own blood. And whose blood was on the wall?"

"Alex's!" said Sarah buoyantly.

"And then, secondly, the word 'elementary' is from the story 'The Crooked Man.' To be honest, I have no idea what that story has to do with Cale's death. It's another story where what looks to be murder actually isn't. One Colonel Barclay appears to have been murdered by his wife. But Holmes deduces that the man actually died of shock, and the wife was silent about it because she was with her lover at the time. It's sort of a weaker version of 'Thor Bridge,' really. I don't know what Cale meant by that message. Yet."

"So why'd he do it?" Sarah said. "Why did Alex lie about finding the diary and then kill himself while making it look like the diary had been stolen?"

Harold paused. He realized that he'd been pacing back and forth across the room as he'd been speaking. He planted his feet into the carpet as he continued.

"I have no idea," he said. "That will be the next step in our investigation." *The next step. Our investigation.* Harold liked the promise implicit in those phrases. "But there are a few possibilities that come to mind. What if he did it to frame somebody? Like in 'Thor Bridge.'"

"Who did he frame?" Sarah swung her feet off the edge of the bed as she spoke.

"Sebastian Conan Doyle," said Harold. "Ten to one all the cops think he did it."

"Actually, I'll take ten to one that all the cops think *you* did it, but I see your point."

"Cale hated Sebastian. They'd been fighting for years, with increasing bitterness. They'd been racing each other to find the diary. Maybe, for his final trick, Cale decided to screw Sebastian over once and for all. By announcing he'd found the diary, he'd throw Sebastian off the scent. Then, by killing himself and making it look as if someone else stole it, he'd ensure that Sebastian would go off and spend years trying to find the murderer. He'd spend all this time and energy doing things like…well, like hiring me, but he'd be looking in the wrong place. Because no one stole the diary from Cale. Plus, all the cops would declare Sebastian their number-one suspect. Even if they never arrested him, because he didn't actually kill anyone, he'd be tarred with suspicion for the rest of his life. Cale dies a martyred hero, and Sebastian lives a villain."

Sarah raised her eyes to the ceiling, pondering everything Harold had just said. It was a lot to take in, but she seemed to be reasoning through it in her head, searching for flaws in his logic. Based on her grin, and the constant swinging of her legs off the edge of the bed, it didn't look as if she'd found any.

"That was some productive thinking you did back there!" she said at last.

"I know!" said Harold. He was awfully proud of himself.

"I have two problems with all of that, though," said Sarah. "Problem number one: Why now? Why, after all these years, would Alex Cale abandon his lifelong quest for the diary in order to kill himself and frame Sebastian?"

"I agree," said Harold. "We know what he did, but we're not sure why he did it. We'll need to figure that out."

"Problem number two—and this one is more serious." Sarah took a deep breath. "If Alex Cale lied about finding the diary, and killed himself, and ransacked his own hotel room," she continued, "then who the hell is chasing us?"

To that, Harold had no response.

CHAPTER 29

Arthur Returns to Scotland Yard

*"What is the meaning of it, Watson?... What object is served by this
circle of misery and violence and fear? It must tend to some end, or
else our universe is ruled by chance, which is unthinkable."*
—Sir Arthur Conan Doyle,
"The Adventure of the Cardboard Box"

November 13, 1900

The New Scotland Yard hummed along pleasantly in the morning,
like a gigantic scientific experiment. Identically uniformed constables
streamed in and out of the front gate and up into the five-story as if
they were tiny bubbles of carbon dioxide in a great bunsen burner.
Arthur entered past the wrought-iron fence just at the foot of Big Ben.
The clock above his head announced a quarter to eleven.

He found his way without much difficulty to the office of Inspector Miller. The door was already open, and Arthur walked in without
a knock. The inspector looked up from his papers, and Arthur again
noticed how youthful he appeared behind his thick beard.

"Dr. Doyle!" he exclaimed, setting a few papers aside on his cluttered desk. "I wasn't expecting a visit from you today."

"That's because I hadn't the time to telegraph my intention to visit,"
said Arthur defiantly.

Inspector Miller paused. He had the air of a man who'd been caught
doing something very naughty.

"Right so, then," said the inspector. "It is a pleasure to see you nonetheless." He gestured toward the open chair before his desk. Arthur sat, taking the same position he had when he was last here. Had that been only two weeks past? What speed at which a man's life might be irrevocably altered!

"How goes your...er...your investigation?" said Inspector Miller, feigning curiosity.

"I have found the criminal who attempted to murder me by way of a letter bomb," said Arthur.

Inspector Miller gave a look of surprise. "You have?"

"Yes. I have—"

"Pardon me," came a voice from the doorway. "Do you have a minute, sir?"

Arthur turned in his chair to see a teenage constable at the door. His hat fit him awkwardly, and his messy hair popped loose beneath the brim. The constable paid Arthur no mind.

"I am conducting an interview at the moment," replied the inspector. "I'll be sure to attend to you when it has concluded."

"Yes, well then, right. Very good. Except, you see, it was the chief inspector who sent me down. He said to see if you were busy, and, if not, to send you out on a fresh one. It's just come in."

"As I am quite busy, I'll see to it when I've finished my interview. Thank you, Constable." Inspector Miller turned back to Arthur and gave him a look of understanding weariness. *These new recruits*, said the inspector's face. *Look what I am forced to put up with!*

Yet the young man hung idly in the doorway. There seemed to be some sentiment caught in his throat which he found himself unable to express.

"May I continue?" asked Arthur of Inspector Miller, with more than a trace of sarcasm.

"Please," said the inspector.

"I've caught you a murderer. Or an attempted one, at least. And now I am prepared to reveal her identity."

"Her?" said the inspector.

"Yes. Her. It was a woman who built my letter bomb. She is quite insane, though evidently quite intelligent as well."

Inspector Miller regarded Arthur blankly. "This is Dr. Arthur Conan Doyle," he said to the constable, by way of an explanation.

"Oh!" said the constable. "I see!" He seemed even more embarrassed to have intruded upon this meeting, and yet he still did not turn to leave.

"... So, if you've no objection," said Inspector Miller, "we wouldn't mind getting back to our business. Dr. Doyle and I have much to discuss, you understand."

"Of course! Yes, of course, sir!" The young constable turned to Arthur. "So very pleased to meet you, sir. I'm a great admirer... Well, we all are, aren't we? I don't think I'd be on the force if it wasn't for those stories, you know. Read them when I was but a simple boy from the North Country, and now look at me!"

Arthur looked at him but felt it would be impolite to share his opinion of how far the lad had come.

"It's just that," the boy continued, now addressing Inspector Miller, "I rather got the sense that the chief inspector wanted you to get down there right away."

"Constable!" said Inspector Miller. "I am in the middle of an interview. With Dr. Doyle. I am sure that within the hour I will have the time to—"

"The assistant commissioner CID is already on his way to the scene, sir." After this abrupt outburst, the constable flinched, as if he'd just taken his first shot with a musket and was afraid to see where it had landed.

Arthur could not believe the dysfunction of the Yard. Wasn't this ramshackle conglomeration of incompetents supposed to be a military division? He would love to have seen Lord Kitchener at the helm of this motley lot.

"Damn it!" said Inspector Miller. "Mr. Henry has already left? You stupid fool, why didn't you say so straightaway? I've lost valuable minutes thanks to your mealy-mouthed sputterings!" The inspector shot up from his desk and yanked hold of a coat and hat that had been hung on a set of corner hooks.

"Oh, for pity's sake," said Arthur. "Inspector, I'm sure you have duties to attend to, but this is unbecoming!"

"Dreadfully sorry, Dr. Doyle, it pains me to have to run out in this manner. But you don't know Edward Henry. He's new to the Yard, just come back from India. Straightaway the commissioner has promoted him to the CID, as assistant no less. Some sort of trial run to see how Henry takes to London. I'll tell you how London takes to him, I will. The man's been putting darkies in darbies for ten years, and now he thinks he knows how to handle the British criminal classes. A lot for him to learn, a bloody lot. He wants to reorganize the whole unit, shift the priorities, install a bunch of gadgets in the office to replace honest investigation. Rules and regulations, that's what he's been on about. Waste of bloody time. Do you know what a detective's best tool is, Dr. Doyle?" The inspector tapped at his shiny, knee-high boots. "Boots on the ground, that's what solves a case."

Arthur stood and followed the two of them out into the main corridors of Scotland Yard.

"There is a young girl out there with a mind for bomb making," he said. "I strongly suggest that you arrest her forthwith."

As he walked, Inspector Miller gestured toward the constable. "Certainly. I can have Constable Billings here pick up anyone you like," he said.

"You'll find all the evidence you need in her flat. March in there and you'll catch her red-handed."

"Excellent," said the inspector as he took the building's central staircase in long strides, his boots clopping down two steps at a time. "We'd be happy to pick up anyone you say on your word alone. Whom would you like Constable Billings to arrest?"

Arthur felt suddenly powerful. He knew that the Yard would never care about his ideas or his abilities as a sleuth. And yet he could see how they were nevertheless captive to his name. This entire structure bent at the first gust of the winds of reputation.

"Her name is Emily Davison," said Arthur. "Clerkenwell." He provided the young constable with her address.

"Right on it, sir," said the constable with a pleased deference.

"Now," said Inspector Miller, "to where am I headed?"

Billings produced a folded sheet of paper, which Arthur only then noticed had been in the boy's hand for the duration of their conversation. The constable handed the paper to Inspector Miller, who read its contents as he marched double time to the doors of Scotland Yard.

But then, with his outstretched hand mere inches from the front door, Inspector Miller halted. A perverse look spread across his face.

"Dr. Doyle," said the inspector slowly, his eyes stuck on the paper, "would you mind coming with us to the scene of this fresh crime? I think we may be in need of some assistance, of a sort you may be particularly suited to provide."

Arthur was quite confused by the man's request, but he quickly assented with a nod.

"Of course," he said. "But might I ask why you think I will be able to help?"

"Because," said Inspector Miller as he looked up into Arthur's face, "I've been assigned to investigate the apparent murder of one Emily Davison. Late of Clerkenwell."

Of all the thoughts and sensations which flooded into Arthur's mind at that moment, the one that most consumed him was an awareness of his odd positioning in the lobby of Scotland Yard. A hundred detectives gushed past him on their way out, bumping shoulder to shoulder, while another hundred pushed past him on their way in. Two hundred detectives on two hundred cases, and here was Arthur frozen between them, one middle-aged author fallen into a mystery just deep enough to drown in.

CHAPTER 30

British Birds, Catullus,
and the Holy War

*"It has long been an axiom of mine that the little
things are infinitely the most important."*
—Sir Arthur Conan Doyle,
"A Case of Identity"

January 11, 2010

If you were Alex Cale and you had killed yourself and then left a trail
of Sherlockian clues behind as to your reasons, to where would those
clues lead?

This was the question before Harold and Sarah. They discussed their
options. They could head back to New York in order to have another
look at Cale's hotel room, except that the room would certainly have
been washed clean of evidence by this point. They could return to
Sebastian Conan Doyle's flat to see if anything Cale had said to him
over the past few months provided any hint as to Cale's motivations,
except that their last meeting with Sebastian Conan Doyle hadn't
ended on friendly terms.

So, surveying the absence of excellent investigative options before
them, Harold and Sarah decided to give Alex Cale's writing office
another look. "Cale was trying to leave a series of clues for a fellow
Sherlockian to follow. Any Sherlockian, like me, would have traced

Cale's steps as far back as his writing office. So it stands to reason that a message might be waiting for us there."

Sarah admitted that this sounded as reasonable as any other option available to them.

"But," she added, "the office is a crime scene now. Jennifer Peters called the police. And I don't think she's our biggest fan either. How are we supposed to get in?"

As it turned out, this was less of an issue than they expected it to be. After they'd waited around on the building's front steps for only a quarter of an hour, pretending to search for keys in Sarah's purse, a teenage boy appeared as if from thin air and let them in. The teenager did not make eye contact with either Harold or Sarah but instead kept his chin aimed at the ground while he unlocked the door. Seemingly lost in his thoughts, the boy trudged up the central staircase to his own flat, dragging his feet and slouching his shoulders the whole way up. Harold was glad to note that even across the Atlantic, general sullenness was the basic cloth of teenage attire.

The door to Cale's flat was closed, but when Harold turned the knob, he found that the lock was broken. The Goateed Man must have cracked it when he broke in to search the office, and it looked like the building's owner hadn't put in a replacement yet. Yellow barricade tape crisscrossed the doorway in the shape of an X. Harold and Sarah ducked under it as they entered the flat.

The rooms appeared much as they had left them two days earlier. Though, had it been two days? Or three? Or was it only yesterday that Harold had been here, sifting through the toppled piles of hard-backed books on the floor? He realized that time since the murder had entirely lost its distinction. Strange, he thought, that these, the most noteworthy days in his whole life, would blend together so easily into a mush of adrenaline and intrigue.

He looked over at Sarah, who was wading through her piles of books and papers, searching for God-knows-what. He realized that in the flurry of revelation about her divorce, and her lie, he'd been so satisfied with himself for finding the answer to that small mystery that he hadn't actually asked her much about the divorce itself. He knew nothing at all about her soon-to-be-ex-husband or the pressing legal issues that required heated calls with her attorney. He felt a twinge of jealousy, of course. That's why he hadn't asked about it. He was afraid to learn about the man she must once have loved so much and who now was fighting with her about some obscure and boring financial matter. Harold, for his own part, had never seriously considered marriage. He wasn't averse to the idea: it's just that it had never come up in anything more than a theoretical sense. He always imagined that he'd marry one day—he was still young. Though Sarah didn't seem much older, and she'd already made the leap. Then she'd crashed on the rocks and come drifting to the shore.

He tried to imagine Sarah making coffee on Sunday morning. Doing the crossword puzzle in bed, wrapping the white sheets around her legs while she reminded Harold that "adze" was a four-letter word for a wood-carving tool. The image seemed absurd. He could only picture Sarah attacking the tires on a black sedan with a switchblade, or examining a ransacked crime scene for secret messages. His relationship with her, whatever sort of relationship it was, had existed under rather unusual circumstances, to say the least.

Harold became suddenly sad. As soon as this was over, Sarah would leave and go back to somewhere that wasn't in his life. And then he would have to go back to a sparsely tasteful one-bedroom in Los Feliz, to a small stack of civil-court filings and a larger one of old books, to the local friends he had dinner with once a month each, and to a yearly gala in New York where he could put on his deerstalker cap in public and no one would laugh at him. These days with Sarah were fantasy, and real life would soon return. What a miserable thought. This would not end with slow Sunday-morning coffee. It would simply end.

He'd had a girlfriend, Amanda, just after college. The thing he remembered most about her—more than the eleven blissful days they spent in Buenos Aires or that one night when they'd had sex four and a half times and he'd been seconds away from using the words "soul mate" when she fell asleep—was her ability to live entirely in the present moment. She was able to accept the joys and misfortunes in front of her as they came, without wondering endlessly when the joys would end or the misfortunes would lift.

Harold was paralyzed by endings. He couldn't think about where he was or what he was doing without thinking about when it would end. He would try so hard to experience current pleasures, and to divorce them from the knowledge of a past that was comparatively more or less pleasurable; he would try to separate the present from its eventual conclusion, but he never felt that he was able to accomplish it. He tried in that moment to focus on the books at his feet, on the mystery and adventure around him, and mostly on Sarah's quiet breath, the sound of which he could just make out from across the room. But he couldn't stop thinking about the spoiled milk he'd return to in his fridge in L.A. or the four messages he'd find on his answering machine, none of which he cared to listen to. This, too, would end.

"When does this stop?" Harold asked out loud. He hadn't remembered deciding to speak, and yet there it was. The words had already been loosed.

"What do you mean?" asked Sarah. She plopped the book in her hands down on a pile and crossed her legs in front of her.

He wasn't sure how to have this conversation. And he certainly didn't want to. But he'd started it, improbably, and he knew of no conversational exit.

"Well...when does the investigation stop? What are we even looking for now? It's funny about detective work. It's like it becomes its own self-justifying, self-sustaining machine. You find a clue, you deduce an explanation for something or other, and then you follow that to the next one. And then the next one. And maybe we're making progress somewhere, or maybe being a detective is like being trapped inside a perpetual-motion machine. There's always more to analyze. There's always more to find. We can start analyzing our own analysis. We could run on our own fumes forever!"

Sarah responded with a curious look. "I appreciate that you're feeling very philosophical about this," she said gingerly. "But I'm not sure what you mean."

"What did we set out to do? We wanted to figure out who killed Alex Cale. And we wanted to recover the diary. Well, we know who killed Alex Cale. And we know that the diary can't be recovered, because it was never found in the first place."

"We don't know why Cale did it."

"But does it matter? Do the why's matter if we already know the what's?"

Sarah paused, trying to read Harold's face. He was getting at something, certainly, but neither of them was sure what it was.

"What are you saying, Harold? Do you want to go home?"

"No," he said. "But why are you still here?"

"Why am I still here?" Sarah looked confused by the question.

"I can tell you why I'm still here. Because Alex Cale killed himself in order to leave me a message. But why are you still here?" *For me*, thought Harold. *Say that you're here for me.*

Sarah looked him coolly in the eyes. "For the diary," she said. "I'm here to find the diary. That's my story."

Harold returned her stare and tried to match her expressionless look. He was sure he failed. She must be able to see the sadness he was holding back.

"Alex never found the diary," he said. He did a very good job of minimizing the quivering in his voice.

"No. But you can."

"What're the books you've got there?" he said, gesturing to a pile beside her as if nothing had passed between them.

"Some history," she said. "And poetry. German, Roman."

"Wait. Is the poetry Roman, or is that the history?"

"Umm..." She pulled an old, heavy hardback from the pile. It didn't have a glossy sleeve, just a bruised and black cardboard cover. "*The Poetry of Catullus.* He was Roman, right?"

Harold laughed. "Yeah. And I'll bet there's a military history in there as well—something called *The Holy War*?"

Surprised at Harold's specificity, Sarah looked down at her pile. In a moment she removed another hard-backed book.

"Yes," she said. "How did you know this was here?"

"Open the book."

She did, then looked up at Harold in shock. "The pages are empty!" she exclaimed.

"Yeah. It's a fake. Just a little joke on Cale's part. When Sherlock Holmes came back to life, after the Great Hiatus, he reappeared to Watson disguised as an elderly bookseller. He carried three books with him, which he gave to his unsuspecting friend as a gift. The books were a collection of Catullus's poetry, plus something called *The Holy War*, which so far as we can tell wasn't even a real book, and a nature guide called *British Birds*. I'm sure you'll find that last one in there, too." Sarah began to look through the books in her pile, in search of *British Birds*. "The Catullus part has always been a curious point for Sherlockians. He was one of the most openly sexual of the Roman poets, in both hetero- and homo- varieties. It's a funny thing to give to your best friend after a long absence."

Sarah completed her search of the books beside her and turned to Harold empty handed.

"There's nothing here called *British Birds*," she said.

"I'm sure it's there somewhere."

Harold joined her on the floor, and together they went through the pile again. Nothing.

So they searched the entire flat. They roamed the floor on hands and knees, picking up every book they found along the way. At first Harold took the south end and Sarah took the north, but when they still couldn't find the book, they traded and re-searched each other's section. Again, nothing.

"It's not here," said Sarah finally.

"That doesn't make any sense," said Harold. "There's no way Alex

Cale would have had only two books of this little Sherlockian trilogy. Someone as obsessive as he was? Of course he'd have a copy."

"So the Goateed Man stole it," said Sarah.

Harold thought about this. "Maybe," he said. "It's possible. But why would he think there was anything special about that book? And if he *did* know there was something special about it, then why did he turn the whole apartment upside down?"

"That's a good point."

"And if the Goateed Man didn't steal it..." concluded Harold. "Well...if he didn't steal it, then it was never here. And Alex Cale was trying to send us another message."

CHAPTER 31

Introducing Mr. Edward Henry

*"Criminal cases are continually hinging upon that one point. A man
is suspected of a crime months perhaps after it has been committed.
His... clothes are examined and brownish stains discovered upon
them. Are they blood stains, or mud stains, or... what are they? That
is a question that has puzzled many an expert, and why? Because
there was no reliable test. Now we have the Sherlock Holmes test,
and there will no longer be any difficulty."*
—Sir Arthur Conan Doyle,
A Study in Scarlet

November 13, 1900, cont.

Arthur had quite a bit of explaining to do. This he attempted during
the brief ride to Clerkenwell aboard the Scotland Yard carriage. He and
Inspector Miller traveled quickly, and so Arthur spoke more quickly
still. By the time their carriage, a broad four-wheeler, had pulled in
front of Emily Davison's lodgings, Arthur had given Inspector Miller a
more or less satisfactory summary of his investigations.

Emily Davison's flat was swarming with police. A dozen bobbies
milled about the drawing room as they performed a variety of odd
tasks. Two poured charcoal powder over every available surface, the
lumps of black soot giving the room the appearance of a long-since-
erupted volcano. The men pressed clear glass onto the powder lumps
and then pulled the glass up into the light. They gazed intently at the
kaleidoscopic images produced by the powder on the glass, and then,

seemingly unhappy with their results, they pressed the glass down again to create another image. Another group of investigators hovered in a circle over something on the floor. With their hands full of odd devices, they took turns kneeling down and applying their tools to whatever lay there. As Arthur stepped farther into the drawing room, he could see a pair of stockinged legs on the floor, at the center of the group. Then he could make out a black frock above the legs, torn and folded at a strange angle. This must be the body of Emily Davison, Arthur realized. Through the crush of hovering detectives, Arthur saw one man kneeling beside it. He held a long steel rod, which was curved in the shape of a half-moon. In the center of the rod stood a hinge, which allowed the man to open and close the half-moon shape as if it were the jaws of an animal. He placed the device around Emily's skull and gazed at some sort of scale at the top of the instrument. The kneeling constable barked a series of numbers at the standing ones, who replied by barking the numbers right back at him for confirmation. Arthur realized that the man was measuring the diameter of her cranium.

Into this clamor strode the imposing figure of Assistant Commissioner CID Edward Henry. Though he displayed no identification, Arthur had little doubt as to the man's position. He stood at least half a foot taller than most of his men, held up by long, skinny legs which stretched into his gaunt torso and angular face. All the man's features were hard edges, as if his skin had been pulled up against his bones. Thick eyebrows and a compact mustache gave him a pugnacious glare. As he marched authoritatively toward his men, he called out in a foreign tongue.

"*Jul-dhee kuro! Jana hae!*" said Edward Henry. "What do you have then, boys?"

Each of the dozen constables, plus Inspector Miller, turned to face him. He swept his gaze around the room, from right to left, observing his men as they paused. "It's Hindi, gentlemen. Picked it up in the Bengal inspector-general's office. If you're out to catch a crook, it helps to speak his tongue. Now: Miss Davison's bedchamber contains two used teacups on her nightstand. You and you"—here he pointed at two of his men—"go apply the powders to those cups when you've finished out here. You remember how I showed you? Good."

Inspector Miller turned to Arthur as both men remained near the doorway.

"You see the burden that's been placed upon me?" whispered Inspector Miller. "The commissioner thinks he's some sort of magician. The men all think he's gone native. And I don't take kindly to some new recruit getting promoted to CID and barking Hindu hoodoo at my boys."

At the sound of Inspector Miller's whispers, Assistant Commissioner Henry turned to the doorway to find Arthur and the inspector waiting.

"Inspector Miller," Henry said. "It's a pleasure to see you so far afield."

Miller stepped into the drawing room, standing unnaturally erect as he approached Henry's position. Only the couch separated the two men.

"Are you ordering my constables to pour dust all over the scene?" said Inspector Miller.

"Technically," replied Henry, "they're *my* constables. And you're my inspector."

"My apologies, gents!" said Inspector Miller boisterously. "I wasn't aware we'd gone off to the beach for the day, so that we might play about in this blackened sand!" A few of the constables smiled. Most alternated their attentions rapidly between the two men, unsure in whom to place their allegiance.

Edward Henry stared at Inspector Miller for a long moment, matching his glare second for second.

"Did we find any fingerprints on the cups and saucers down there?" Henry finally said, pointing at the messy pile of tea things on the low table by the couch.

"Yes, sir," said one of the men. "I believe we've isolated a few sets of them curvy smudges you told us to get."

"Brilliant," said Henry. "Now let us see if we can figure out to whom they belong."

"They belong to me," said Arthur.

His voice, unburdened by the tensions of the Yard, burst clear throughout the drawing room. Henry looked Arthur up and down, as if he'd just noticed him there for the first time.

"And your name, sir?" said Henry.

"My name is Arthur Conan Doyle." Every detective in the room, save for Inspector Miller, registered a look of shock. Inspector Miller smiled, claiming Arthur for his own side in the intradepartmental warfare.

"Dr. Doyle is my guest here," said Inspector Miller. "He and I were engaged together on another case, the conclusion of which had brought Arthur—pardon, I should refrain from your Christian name in front of the men—had brought Dr. Doyle to this very door."

"It's an honor, Dr. Doyle," said Edward Henry, with a note of genuine awe in his voice. "When I was in India, I greeted the arrival of one of your stories with a full evening alone, locked inside my study, so that nothing would distract me from it. You'll find no more ready a disciple of Mr. Sherlock Holmes than I."

"I've no doubt," said Arthur succinctly. "Now. What's happened here?"

Arthur could feel the scales of power tip as he walked through the drawing room. As he came to the dead body near the window, the men parted in their huddle to give him space. He thought it humorous that between the two accomplished detectives in the room and himself, the untested amateur, it was he who held the men's respect thanks to the continuing allure of an aged penny dreadful.

"Emily Davison was beaten and strangled," said Henry. "Most likely sometime last night, or into the early dawn. Her neighbor downstairs, one Mrs. Lansing, came up to complain this morning about a bunch of noises she'd heard the evening before. Gunshots, she said they were. She believes she heard them around six in the evening, though she can't be sure of the time. She came up to Miss Davison's flat and found that the front door lock had been shot apart and the door was swinging open from its hinges." *That would be Bram's work*, thought Arthur, though he decided against interrupting Mr. Henry's monologue. "Mrs. Lansing became concerned, and entered the flat. She found Miss Davison's body, and called for the police."

Arthur leaned over the body of Emily Davison and was reminded of whale skin. The way a whale's thick, gunmetal hide punctured by a harpoon just above the surface of the sea spouted blood and water in equal torrents. He had spent a winter hunting whales off the coast of Greenland in his youth. Fifty Scotsmen on a boat, held together by rough language and the strength of their spear arms. By spring they had docked and gone after the smaller meats. They had clubbed seals for a month, chasing the slippery blobs of shiny flesh across the ice floes. Colin, the ship's foremaster, had slipped on seal brains one morning, landing face-first in the thing's moist belly. The men laughed, made jokes, and did their jobs. It was rough work.

He'd been with Emily Davison not twenty-four hours before. He had been so justifiably furious with her then, so full of hot rage over her vile bombing campaign—and now she was but this pale white mess on the floor of her drawing room. Her throat was blotched with red and purple, while her face was equally bruised. Her nose was in tatters, split open and smashed to one side. Her eyelids were red and bulbous, like those of a crushed bug. He noticed that a small stream of blood had run from her left eye onto the wooden floor. It had already congealed and dried into a rubbery black pool. The rage that Arthur had felt toward Emily Davison was no match for what lay in the dark heart of the man who'd done this to her.

"There is a collection of dynamite and wires upon the girl's table," said Edward Henry. "Hard as it may be to believe, given the look of her, it seems this girl was in the business of making bombs."

"I know," said Arthur as he stood to his feet. He would rather not gaze on the body anymore, if he could avoid it.

"The fingerprints my men gather here," said Edward Henry to Arthur, "we will retain for comparison with the killer, when we find him. I've developed a system for classifying all the impressions left by a man's fingers—we imprint all ten onto a sheet of paper and record their most noteworthy features. When we find ourselves a suspect, we can compare the marks on his fingers to those left upon Miss Davison's belongings. And if they match, then *bus sub hoe guy ya*. It is done."

"A method for preserving and recording the prints of a man's fingers?" said Arthur. "It sounds terribly impressive. My, it sounds like something my Holmes would have done. But I'm afraid the prints upon those teacups will be of little use to you. As I said, some of them are mine. And some belong to a dear friend, one Mr. Stoker." Edward Henry looked at Arthur expectantly, at the sight of which Arthur took a deep breath. Again, he had a lot of explaining to do.

In the time it took Arthur to finish telling his story to Henry, the constables completed their measurements of Emily Davison's body. While Arthur talked, Inspector Miller lit a cigarette and coolly smoked it as he stared out the window. Edward Henry provided little in the way of reaction to Arthur's tale. Rather, he interrupted only occasionally to ask for clarification on any point on which Arthur had not been perfectly clear. He would nod when he understood, and he would nod a second time to indicate that Arthur should continue. The man's face betrayed nothing besides a careful and professional consideration of the matter at hand. Arthur couldn't help but be impressed. If ever there were a Yard man who resembled Sherlock Holmes, it was this one.

"Thank you, Dr. Doyle," was the only thing he said when Arthur had concluded. Edward Henry then turned to Inspector Miller. "Were you aware of all this?" he asked his fellow detective.

"Indeed I was. I've been in communication with Dr. Doyle as to these investigations from the start."

"I see," said Henry pensively. "Dr. Doyle, I'm sure that this Stoker fellow you've mentioned will be able to corroborate your story?"

Arthur was unsure of why his "story" required any corroborating. "Certainly," he said. "If you need, I can provide you with his address."

Edward Henry exhaled through his nose and climbed wearily to his feet. He folded his hands behind his back and began to pace. He seemed greatly vexed over some inner dilemma.

"It's a fantastic story," he said after pacing in silence for a few moments. "Rather like something from one of your books, isn't it? But I wonder if the casual reader would even find it credible."

"Sir," said Arthur as he stood to join the detective, "I should like to know what you mean by that."

"I mean," said Henry, "that you would have me believe that you deduced, through only a lengthy chain of logical reasoning and a brief evening in a skirt, the identity and location of the woman who tried to murder you. That you then went to her lodgings to confront her, but, finding the door locked, you—or this friend of yours—drew a pistol and shot through the lock. When you then came face-to-face with your attempted murderer, you argued with her briefly, sat down to a bit of tea, explained to her the error of her ways, and left. That you then went home, got a good night's rest, and called upon our dear Inspector Miller the next morning to explain the whole affair. And that *someone else* snuck into this flat soon after you'd left and beat this poor, unfortunate girl into the floor like she was wet laundry? It's a good story you've concocted, Dr. Doyle, and it explains every bit of your involvement in this matter that we were sure to discover otherwise. It seems to have thrown Inspector Miller off the hunt, hasn't it?"

Arthur was aghast. It had never occurred to him that the Yard would suspect him, of all people, in Emily's murder. It was hideous that anyone could believe him capable of such a thing.

Inspector Miller abandoned his perch by the window. Arthur couldn't help but think that the inspector had a slight smile on his face.

"You cannot possibly be accusing Arthur Conan Doyle of murder!" said Inspector Miller. "They say he'll be knighted soon enough. If you accuse him falsely, it will be rot on your promising career."

"I don't accuse anyone," said Henry. "I merely suggest that we will have to follow up on his story. And that we may have to submit Dr. Doyle to a more thorough interrogation."

"How dare you!" said Arthur. He was suddenly quite angry. His blood had not boiled slowly, like water in a kettle, but rather it had gone hot all at once. In just an instant, he found himself shouting at A.C. Henry. "Do you see her face? Could *I* have done this? Could I have done that with these hands?"

What happened next Arthur would always regard as the strangest of accidents. He raised his knuckles to Edward Henry's face, understandably trying to show how soft and gentle they were. These were the hands of a writer, not a butcher, and Arthur had simply wanted to show the detective that. But at the sight of Arthur's knuckles just inches from his face, Edward Henry batted Arthur's arms down with a sweep of his hand. Feeling himself attacked, Arthur then did what any warm-blooded man would do. He swung back, clocking the detective square in the jaw.

Henry stepped back, holding his sore face. All eyes in the room turned to Arthur. It was only then, a few seconds later, that Arthur became aware that he had just assaulted a police officer.

"Men," said Edward Henry quietly, "place the darbies on Dr. Doyle, if you will." Two detectives approached Arthur from behind. They were considerate of Arthur's comfort, as they placed his hands inside a pair of metal cuffs and clamped them around his wrists. As they stood to Arthur's sides, each with a hand on one of his shoulders, they stared down at their own boots, as if frightened of making eye contact.

Arthur was too stunned to speak. What had he done? He looked to Inspector Miller for support.

"Don't you worry, now, Arthur," said Inspector Miller, "we'll straighten this all out."

Arthur did not say another word as the two bobbies led him down the stairs and out into a waiting carriage, bound for Newgate Prison.

CHAPTER 32

The Library

"Watson insists that I am the dramatist in real life," said [Holmes].
"Some touch of the artist wells up within me, and calls insistently
for a well-staged performance. Surely our profession, Mr. Mac,
would be a drab and sordid one if we did not sometimes
set the scene so as to glorify our results."

—Sir Arthur Conan Doyle,
"The Valley of Fear"

January 11, 2010, cont.

The outside of the British Library, at St. Pancras, was the color of terracotta. Architecturally, it resembled a set of misshapen rectangles that had been laid on top of one another without quite fitting together. Harold was reminded of a broken Lego kit.

Harold and Sarah passed through the public gate, under the tall portico on which the words "British Library" descended in pudgy letters from the ceiling. Harold quickly glanced at the mammoth statue of Isaac Newton as they made their way inside; he didn't have much of an eye for sculpture, but he did think that the bronze figure's meaty calf muscles were surprisingly large for a mathematician's.

They filled out their paperwork in the cramped registration office. They claimed to be bird scholars and presented their driver's licenses. Harold had thought that getting access to the stacks of the British Library would be difficult, time consuming, and horrifically bureau-

240

cratic, but within twelve minutes he and Sarah had made it through security and into the first of the private reading rooms.

A quick search of the electronic card catalog revealed that the nature section, on Shelf 7852, was located on the fourth floor. They went up the elevator and through the stacks, finally making their way to a low shelf on which sat dozens upon dozens of bird-watching guides.

The idea of coming to the British Library had been Harold's. He was certain that the missing copy of *British Birds* from Alex Cale's writing office could not be an accident. So where would it be?

"Remember what Jennifer Peters told us about Cale's research?" Harold had said. "He did most of it in the British Library. It sounded like he spent much of his final weeks there. And if I had to pick one place in London to hide a book where it wouldn't be accidentally disturbed..."

As soon as Harold saw the birding section on the fourth floor, he felt more confident in his suspicion that some clue might be waiting for him there. The whole natural-sciences area was devoid of visitors. Dust covered every book on the shelf. It looked as if no one had been there in months, at best. If Cale had left something here to be found after his death, there was every indication that Harold would still be able to find it. He dropped to his knees, yanking the books off the shelves with excitement.

"Is there a specific book we're looking for?" said Sarah as she joined Harold on the floor.

"Not really," replied Harold. "Anything with 'British' and 'birds' in the title. In the story the book is just called *British Birds*, but nothing with that exact name exists. But there are a bunch of similar options. Here." Harold pulled out a book called *Bird Song: A Field Manual for Naturalists on the Songs of British Birds*. "Hmm," he continued as he flipped to the book's copyright page. "From 1925. Too recent. He would have used a book that had been in print when Conan Doyle was alive. Something Sherlock Holmes could have read. Something printed in the 1880s or 1890s."

Sarah picked up a thick picture book called *The Varieties of British Birds*. She looked at the date—1975. No good. Over the next few minutes, they peeled book after book from the shelves. Both were surprised with how thoroughly the subject of England's birds had been covered in naturalist literature.

With a gleam in his eye, Harold settled on a squat little volume, torn at the edges. He removed it from the shelf. *Bacon's Guide to British Birds*, read the faded cover. He opened it up. The book had been first published in 1876. This edition had been printed in 1894.

Harold separated the covers eagerly. Before he'd even held the book to his face, a single sheet of white paper fell from between the pages. Harold looked down. The white paper had been folded in half. It looked new.

Sarah saw the paper on the floor and shifted over next to Harold. As he picked up the sheet, she tilted her head over Harold's shoulder so that she could read alongside him. He could feel her breath on his earlobes.

When he opened the paper, he found a typewritten note.

To Whom It May Concern,

If you are an amateur ornithologist and have come across this note in the course of looking up information on the wing coloring of the pied wagtail, then please dispose of this paper forthwith. Its intended recipient was slow in finding his way here and is no longer in need of the information below. If, on the other hand, you are a player in the Great Game and have found this note by way of a dead body in a New York hotel room, then congratulations. Your journey is ended. Almost.

So, fellows, which one of you is it sitting in the British Library reading these words? Is that you, Jeffrey Engels? Were I a betting man, I would have placed my money on you. Or Les, my dear friend Les... I would have thought you were too sane to go traipsing about the globe in search of a dead man's final message. Or Ron? I wouldn't have believed that you had the faculties to have made it this far, but if this is you, Ron Rosenberg, then congratulations are in order. You've surprised me to the last. If this is Sebastian Conan Doyle—well, if this is you, Sebastian, then I have failed. Which one of them did you get to help you? I assume that you would try to throw your money at the problem and hire one of my fellow Sherlockians to figure out the mystery of your own family. Which one of them was stupid enough to agree? I can only hope you'll both join me in hell soon enough.

Which segues rather nicely into what you're doing here, whoever you are. As you know, I am dead. I was strangled in my room at the Algonquin Hotel in New York, on the early morning of January 6. Do you know who killed me? If you've made it all the way here, then I'll wager you probably do. I'm the murderer. I killed myself.

Oh, yes, I'm sure that you're wondering why. But have no fear. You'll figure it out. Well, that is, if you're smart enough!

Have you deduced where the diary is yet? My guess is that you haven't. That's a trickier problem, and it took me over a decade to work it out myself. But as soon as I did, I knew I'd have to take the secret to my grave. However, I thought it wouldn't be fair to go off to my doom without giving someone else a hint—just a little push in the right direction. And so I devised this devilish little puzzle, to live on after my passing. In my life, I was the greatest Sherlockian scholar in the world. Whoever can solve the mystery I've left behind deserves the title of second place. Now that I am gone, you can feel certain that you are the most accomplished Sherlock Holmes scholar alive. Congratulations. You have earned it.

So where will you be off to next, Detective? You must know by now that I did not have the diary with me in New York. And you know that it is not in either of my London flats. So where is it? It is a delicious little puzzle, is it not? I can only hope that Arthur Conan Doyle would have been proud.

My father died on January 6. Did you know that? I'm positive that he had no idea, when the aneurysm in his brain burst, that it was Sherlock Holmes's birthday. I don't think Jennifer ever made the connection either. My good Jennifer—she was a wonderful sister, I assure you, no matter what she says about me now. And now I have died on January 6 as well. Was I a better man than my father? My God, I hope so. You, Detective, you'll be liable to think the worst of me after you've read this. You'll think I was vain and self-centered, you'll believe me to have been unbalanced. You'll psychoanalyze me with such ease—obsessed with Holmes, unbalanced after the death of my father, unable to ever lift myself from the burden of his disapproval, etc. You'll need to get inside my head, won't you? You'll need to feel that you can explain me, because that's what a great detective does: He explains. Well then, have at me.

The old centuries had, and have, powers of their own, which mere modernity cannot kill. I believe that's all the explanation you're due.

Farewell,

Alexander Horace Cale

Harold held his arms stiff, and the letter outstretched, until Sarah had finished reading. She nodded gently, breathing more warm air onto his earlobe. Harold shuffled forward, giving himself a few inches. He turned to face her. The silence that enveloped them was like many of the silences they had known over the past week. Neither wanted to sully the moment by saying something obvious. And so, neither of them having anything to say that wasn't obvious, they were silent. He passed her the note, and she read it again. Harold leaned back against the largely empty shelf and closed his eyes.

There was mostly sadness, now. Even Alex Cale's suicide note was well written and coursed with his wit, with his charm, with the strength of his personality. Even his suicide note made you want to know him. And yet it seemed to Harold as if no one really did. He had held himself back from everyone.

"You knew him," said Sarah after she'd read the letter a second time. "I'm sorry."

Harold said nothing. He couldn't help but notice that Cale had not mentioned his name among the list of Sherlockians who might have made it this far. Cale didn't even know who Harold *was* before he died. And yet Harold was the one who had made it here. For a moment he felt vindicated and victorious—and then in an instant he was ashamed at the thought. Cale hadn't died so that Harold could prove himself—though, in some perverse way, he had.

"*Dracula*," Harold said suddenly.

Sarah was confused. "What? Look, I know that you and Alex weren't *best* friends, but you knew him, and—"

"No. *Dracula*. The last part of the note is a quotation. 'The old centuries had, and have, powers of their own, which mere modernity cannot kill.' That's from *Dracula*. He's telling us something. It's the next clue."

"Oh," said Sarah. There was hesitation in her voice. "That's...very quick, good work. I'm really sorry about Alex. I just...whatever. I wanted to tell you that I'm sorry. I never met him. In person, I mean. Just a few e-mails back and forth. And I read his book, the copy of it we found. It's funny how much sense you get of a guy's personality from his suicide note."

"Is it okay if we don't talk about it?" Harold couldn't handle thinking about Alex right now. He wanted to move on. He wanted to investigate.

"Yes," said Sarah reassuringly. She squeezed his hand. "But when you're done investigating and this all hits you, I want you to remember that you did a great thing. You did what Alex wanted. You followed his clues. You've solved his puzzle, almost. There's no better way you could honor his memory."

"Thank you." He squeezed back.

"So whatever happens, however this ends, you should feel proud."

"I will."

"Promise?"

Harold smiled. "Yes."

"Good. So, what's *Dracula* have to do with all of this?" Sarah asked as she began putting some of the birding books back on their shelves.

"That's the question," replied Harold. "We know that Conan Doyle was good friends with Bram Stoker. Everybody knows that, it's public knowledge. But what if Stoker is the key to finding the diary? Is that what Cale was getting at? If Cale somehow found the diary through Bram Stoker..."

Rather than respond, Sarah elected to continue sliding the books back into place.

"Cambridge!" Harold exclaimed.

Sarah smiled. She knew he'd get it, of course. All she had to do was wait. Harold did feel proud, and he had her to thank for it.

"What's in Cambridge?" she asked.

"Didn't Jennifer Peters say that her brother had been on a trip to Cambridge just before he died?"

"I think so," she said after she'd thought about it. "But so? He probably went to half a dozen universities for research."

"Right. But Cambridge is the university that houses all of the original letters of Bram Stoker." Harold's face brightened.

Sarah took the letter, folded it back up, and put it in her purse.

"All right then," she said. "Let's go get the diary."

CHAPTER 33

Newgate

I sometimes think we must be all mad and that
we shall wake to sanity in straight-waistcoats.
—Bram Stoker,
Dracula

November 13, 1900, cont.

The stench of Newgate Prison wet the tiny hairs on the inside of Arthur's nose. Given his social stature, the prison's governor had granted him a private cell. The knowledge that this must have been the largest and best maintained of all the cells in Newgate only served to further horrify him. The room was eight feet by twelve, with a barred window at the far end, facing the central yard. Yet as Arthur was on only the second floor, not much light got through the thick bars. A water tank and a washbasin lay beneath the window, accompanied by a rolled-up set of bedding. There was no table in the cell, but merely a single shelf, on which rested a plate, a mug, and a Bible. On the opposite side from the window, Arthur could see out the cell doors to the gallery. When he pressed his face against the bars, he could see cell after cell in neat little rows, like hedges stretching into the distance. Arthur could not see the end of the cells, or any of the floors above or below his. There was a skylight at the roof of the prison gallery, and yet little light from that made it to Arthur either. The gallery smelled like a rotting corpse and sounded with the wails of men halfway to death themselves.

Arthur thumbed through a Bible to pass the time. It was the King

James Version, and so stained with filth as to be barely readable. He wondered if it would provide him some comfort in this moment of need. Might he open the page to a trenchant aphorism that would buoy his soul from the crushing iniquities of the prison? The first words he saw, when he let the Bible fall open, were these: "I am a victem of yer sweet smell'd cunt." Some previous inhabitant of these quarters had scrawled the words into the margins, as if they were a scholar's commentary upon the text. Arthur glanced down at the cheaply printed verses. He was treated to the bit in Joshua where the children of Israel are circumcised for the second time. "And Joshua made him sharp knives, and circumcised the children of Israel at the hill of the foreskins," Arthur read. He was unsure as to whether the misspelled commentary was supposed to refer to this specific verse or whether it was more a general statement of the man's attitudes on the day he'd written it. After thinking upon this matter for a minute, Arthur realized that he did not much care. For the Bible or for his fellow prisoner.

The day wore on, and he did not speak to a single inhabitant of the nearby cells. When the men were released into the yard, for some sort of recreation, Arthur was purposefully kept inside his cell by the guards. "You'll find it safer here," a guard told him as he unlocked the cell beside Arthur's while leaving his door untouched. Arthur was not in a position to disagree.

While the other prisoners frolicked in the yard, the governor of Newgate came down to see him personally. "Terribly sorry about all this," the man said. "Inspector Miller sent word, and he'll try to have you out by nightfall. Can we fetch you anything to help you pass the time?" Arthur thanked the man for his sympathies but said that he had all that he required. The governor offered to assist him in sending a message to his family—"I'll take it down to the GPO myself," he said—but Arthur wouldn't hear of it. He would rather that Touie and the children not learn about this particular adventure. The governor said that he understood.

"I've a family, too, Dr. Doyle. My good wife, Shelly, and my boy. Terrific lad. His name is Arthur, too. Funny that!"

"Yes. I appreciate your discretion," said Arthur, well aware of where this discussion was headed. He had learned, over the years, that as soon as any man made even the briefest mention of his "terrific lad," Arthur should begin to search around for a pen forthwith.

"If you don't mind, sir," said the governor. "He's a great admirer of yours, my boy is. And...well, of course I am, too. If you wouldn't mind, if it's not too much of an imposition..."

"Oh, just give me the bloody book," said Arthur. He signed a copy of *The Memoirs of Sherlock Holmes* for the governor and then signed a copy of *The Sign of the Four* as well. Elated at his good fortune over having Arthur Conan Doyle as a day prisoner, the governor left Arthur alone with a firm handshake for a farewell. As the man strode through the galley of his prison, Arthur could hear him whistling.

The sun had just set when Arthur was released. Though the guards were surprised to loose a prisoner at this late hour, they quickly fell into line upon receipt of his release papers. One even bowed to him as the man opened the sturdy central gate and let him out onto the noisy streets.

Bram Stoker and Inspector Miller were waiting together on Newgate Street to greet him. Both embraced Arthur warmly, and Bram had even brought a flask of gin for the occasion.

"If the inspector here doesn't mind, I thought you might be in need of a drink," said Bram as he passed the silver flask into Arthur's dirty hands.

"Most certainly," said Inspector Miller. "Please. You've been through a great ordeal." Arthur was not the sort who was prone to public drunkenness, nor had he been craving the taste of liquor. And yet, as he felt the cool flask in his hands, he became instantly grateful for Bram's considerate forethought. Arthur drank deeply and felt warm as the chilled gin tinged his gullet.

"Assistant Commissioner Henry has been reprimanded for his hasty actions," continued Inspector Miller when Arthur had finished. "This should set back his takeover of the CID at least a year, if I have anything to say about it. The commissioner himself asked that I pass on to you his deepest sympathies and his solemn promise that no record of this...incident shall be kept in the Yard's records. We had to generate a bit of paperwork for Newgate, but I'll see to it that it's burned by the week's end."

"Inspector Miller here has been most helpful on the matter of your release," said Bram. "He contacted me this morning, and has been working tirelessly for your benefit."

"Thank you both," said Arthur. He took another swig of gin.

"Where shall I take you?" offered Bram. "I'd suggest your home for a hot bath, or mine for a hot toddy. But knowing you, I suspect you'd like to get right back to your case. To sniff out the murderer of Emily Davison and all that."

Arthur smiled. Bram was such a dear friend, and he knew Arthur's mind as if it were his own. And yet, right then, Bram could not have been more incorrect as to Arthur's wishes.

"Thank you, no," said Arthur. "The late Miss Davison, and her dead friends, can rot away in their graves as they please. It's no business of mine. But, Bram, I think this gin was the best idea either of us has had in months, and I will require some more of it before I retire. Come! To the nearest public house! We'll drink ourselves to sin and stumble home when we start seeing double."

Both Bram and the inspector made curious faces.

"Arthur, this is most unlike you," said Bram. "I vaguely remember your giving me some long-winded speech a few weeks back: Justice something something, or truth something something, I don't quite recall the details. But it was awfully earnest."

Arthur laughed bitterly and dove snout-first into the flask.

"You know, they say that gin is the curse of the poor," he said. The alcohol had somehow already made it to his stomach, and he seemed drunk. "But I think it may be the other way about—the poor are the curse of gin!" Arthur laughed, only to himself, and finished the rest of the flask in one gulp. He dropped it onto the street.

"Well then," said Inspector Miller politely, "I'll leave you two gents be. Good evening."

Arthur bowed regally to the inspector, while Bram grasped him in a sturdy handshake. When the inspector had gone, Bram turned to his drunken friend.

"Arthur, this is embarrassing enough as it is."

"Is it? Are you embarrassed?" Arthur lurched in the general direction of St. Paul's. "I've been near blown up, I've been to the Sodom of Whitechapel and the Gomorrah of the docks, I've had a revolver pointed at my head, I've been arrested by the Yard and sent to waste away in the mire of Newgate Prison. And what have I to show for it all? Three dead girls. I looked into the bloody, beaten face of Emily Davison, and do you know what was there? Nothing. Not a damned thing. There is nothing at the bottom of the rabbit hole, do you understand? She wasn't killed for a reason, Bram. None of them were. She wasn't murdered for love, and she wasn't murdered for coin—she was murdered for the sake of murder itself. What am I to do with that? How does one investigate that? And what would I hope to find? From dead girl to dead girl, I can trace the sins of London, but to what end?" Arthur's eyes had swelled. He sat down in the dirt and let his head hang between his knees.

"Look up there," said Arthur, pointing at the southern sky. "We're fifty paces from St. Paul's Cathedral. And we could have our veins overfilled and bursting with medical opiates in a quarter of an hour if we chose to. There was a civilization here, once. There were a thousand years of progress, building from the muddy soil to that spire. There were rules. There was order. There was Britain. I had actually believed that I was helping, can you imagine that? With those stupid stories. That we lived in an age of transcendent reason. That the pure and brilliant light of logic was on its way, to shine over the pallid city and sweep us into the white future of science." Arthur spit forcefully into the dirt. "*Horseshit.* You were right from the beginning, you always are. This has been a great mistake. And now I am finished with it. All of it. No more playing detective, I promise you. The dead can keep their secrets. We the living wouldn't know what to do with them anyhow."

Bram Stoker said nothing, but merely placed a hand on Arthur's shoulder, and squeezed as tightly as he could.

CHAPTER 34

Only Those Things
the Heart Believes Are True

*"There had been a time when the world was full of blank spaces, and
in which a man of imagination might be able to give free scope to
his fancy. But... these spaces were rapidly being filled up; and the
question was where the romance writer was to turn."*
—Sir Arthur Conan Doyle,
from an address given in honor of Robert Peary, May 1910

January 12, 2010

The 9:15 train from King's Cross to Cambridge was a five-car express.
In the first-class cabin, Harold and Sarah sat beside each other in warm
silence. Harold had become, over the past week, a connoisseur of
silences. He was an expert at differentiating their particulars; was this a
Tranquil Silence, marked by slow sighs and peaceful smiles? Or was it a
Tired Silence, marked by ornery chair shifting? Or a Tense Silence, full
of tight breaths and cautious glances? He and Sarah had experienced
them all, and yet this one was different. It felt conclusive. If Harold
were a sommelier of unspoken moods, then this would be his recom-
mended *digestif.* This was an After-Dinner Silence, where both parties
could digest the meal they'd had and contemplate the approaching end
of their evening.

When she spoke, Harold was surprised but not startled. There was
something gentle in her voice.

"You're not reading," she said.

"No," Harold replied, "I don't have anything left to read. All the books I brought with me are stuck in that first hotel room. But it's nice, staring out the window."

"What do you see?" she asked.

He felt like he was a child and she was playing a game to pass the time on a long drive. Harold looked out the window.

"Mmmm...Some wet, gray trees. Some wet, gray train tracks. A few wet, gray trains passing us on the opposite track. A few towns in the distance, and even though they're just specks on the horizon, I'm pretty sure they're wet and gray, too."

Sarah smiled. "In other words, Britain."

"It's funny," he said. "I'm so much more familiar with Britain a hundred years ago than Britain today."

"Yeah? I'd imagine that's true of all Sherlockians."

"There's a poem by Vincent Starrett. He was one of the first Sherlockians. What is it? 'Here dwell together two men of note / Who never lived and so can never die / How very near they seem, yet how remote / That age before the world went all awry. / But still the game's afoot for those with ears / Attuned to catch the distant view-halloo; / England is England yet, for all our fears— / Only those things the heart believes are true...' The ending is great, it always gets me. 'And here, though the world explode, these two survive, / And it is always eighteen ninety-five.'"

Harold paused. "Isn't that beautiful?" he added.

"Yes," she said. "It is. But it's odd, when I hear you say that...There's something really conservative about you Sherlockians, isn't there? I don't mean in a political sense, but in an aesthetic one. Always wishing to return to this rose-tinted vision of the world as it existed a hundred years ago. 'England is England yet...' Well, this is England, too, right? Only now women can vote and racial discrimination is at least on the retreat. As a woman, I'll tell you flat out, I wouldn't want to live in 1895."

"I understand," said Harold. "There's something...incomplete about our vision of Holmes's time. I know it's not real. I know that in the real 1895 there were two hundred thousand prostitutes in the city of London. Syphilis was rampant. Feces littered most major streets. Indian immigrants were locked up in Newgate on the barest suspicion that they had committed a crime. So-called homosexual acts were crimes, and they were punishable by years in prison. It was a racist culture, and a sexist one, too."

Harold took a breath while he thought of how to proceed. "Look, I get it. I'm a white, heterosexual man. It's really easy for me to say, 'Oh, wow, wasn't the nineteenth century terrific?' But try this. Imagine the scene: It's pouring rain against a thick window. Outside, on Baker Street, the light from the gas lamps is so weak that it barely reaches the pavement. A fog swirls in the air, and the gas gives it a pale yellow glow. Mystery brews in every darkened corner, in every darkened room. And a man steps out into that dim, foggy world, and he can tell you the story of your life by the cut of your shirtsleeves. He can shine a light into the dimness, with only his intellect and his tobacco smoke to help him. Now. Tell me that's not awfully romantic?"

Sarah laughed. "Sure," she said. "That definitely sounds romantic." She looked out the window at the gray countryside sweeping by. "But maybe this is romantic, too."

Harold looked at the passing trees, noticing how they were stooped over with water from a recent rain. He saw an expanse of grass, a damp heath pocked with yellow bursts of dandelion. He turned from the window to face Sarah, and as he did so, his elbow touched hers on the armrest between their seats.

"I see your point," he said.

"Is that why you love the stories so much? For the romance?"

Harold considered this. He realized that he'd never before had to put into words his reasons for loving the Holmes stories. Did this sort of obsession even have reasons? If she had asked Harold why he loved his mother, there wouldn't be any answer he could give. How could he then explain his love for Holmes?

"I think I love the idea that problems have solutions. I think that's the appeal of mystery stories, whether they're Holmes or someone else. In those stories we live in an understandable world. We live in a place where every problem has a solution, and if we were only smart enough, we could figure them out."

"As opposed to . . . ?"

"As opposed to a world that's random. Where violence and death are happenstance—unpreventable and unstoppable. Of all the conventions of mystery stories, the one that's impossible to break is the solution at the end. Conan Doyle has writings in his journals about it. And plenty of novelists since have tried. Can you write a mystery story that ends with uncertainty? Where you never know who really did it? You can, but it's unsatisfying. It's unpleasant for the reader. There needs to be something at the end, some sort of resolution. It's not that the killer even needs to be caught or locked up. It's that the reader needs to *know*. Not knowing is the worst outcome for any mystery story, because we need to believe that everything in the world is knowable. Justice is optional, but answers, at least, are mandatory. And that's what I love about Holmes. That the answers are so elegant and the world he lives in so ordered and rational. It's beautiful."

"The romance of a rational world," Sarah said. "Do you still think there are answers at the end of all of this?" she asked.

"Yes."

"Satisfying ones?"

Harold watched the rain. He wasn't sure how to answer that question, and he wasn't sure that he wanted to.

CHAPTER 35

A Plea for Help

*"One should put one's foot to the door to keep
out insanity all one can."*
—Sir Arthur Conan Doyle,
unpublished journal entry, 1912

November 23, 1900

A week after Arthur had stumbled free from the gates of Newgate, life
in Hindhead had returned to normal. Or as close to normal as anything in Hindhead ever achieved. From the early-morning clanking of
the chambermaids with their pans to the evening *thunks* of the butler
as he closed the chimney flues, the house was alive with noise at every
hour of the day and night. The stable master was having some difficulty with a new mare that had just arrived from Spain. Somehow little
Roger had managed to break his arm when he toppled out of a wheel-
barrow being pushed around by his older brother, Kingsley. Roger
got a cast for his forearm, and Kingsley got a stern talking-to about
excess roughhousing with his brother. Touie rested comfortably in her
bedchamber, and one morning Arthur went so far as to bring her the
breakfast tray himself, wearing one of the servants' uniforms as a little
joke. Touie had giggled like a girl when she realized that it was Arthur
holding her tray of oatmeal. Arthur hadn't been out to see Jean yet, so
concerned was he with the affairs of the house, but he would be into
the city to see her soon enough. He was happy—happier, really, than

he could remember being in some time. It takes a shock to the system, doesn't it, to make a man realize what good things he has.

What a dark and sinister madness must have overcome him, to make him think that he should be a detective himself. It was a miserable vocation taken up by miserable men. But, thankfully, that fog had lifted from his brain, and Arthur saw his life anew, as the days of middle age glimmered resplendently before him. He was a father. He was a husband. And he was a writer. He was neither detective nor criminal, and he would leave them both to chase each other around in circles as they saw fit. "The scarlet thread of murder"—he had written that phrase once, many years ago, as if it were something lovely, something vibrant. Well, he would let the thread drop. He would fashion his life—his true life—from another cloth.

Of course, a certain lingering curiosity was only natural. Who had killed Emily Davison and her friends? There was no shame in an occasional moment of wondering, so long as he didn't give himself over to it. Arthur had never properly learned the name of the second girl to be murdered. She had signed the false name "Morgan Nemain" to the boardinghouse book, but Emily had referred to her as "Anna." The Yard might have found something among Emily's possessions that would reveal this Anna's family name. He could send a quick word to Inspector Miller and—

But no. Down that way lay madness. When Arthur felt that inkling in his brain, that involuntary twitch, he would remind himself of the world right before his eyes. Arthur would feel his feet press against the hardwood floors of his half-reconstructed study, and a sensation of lift would buoy up his spine. From his neck to his tail to his heels to the floor and into the deep soil, Arthur was home. The twitch would pass.

Realism ruled his work. Oh, how good it felt to dive into something sensible for a change! No more of that nonsense about chasing archvillains down foggy alleyways with the aid of scent-sniffing hounds. No more magic, no more fantasy, no more romance. What frivolity was detective fiction, compared to the hard-nosed reality of true literature!

Since putting Holmes to rest those years ago, Arthur had tried his hand at historical epics, scientific adventure, and even horror. There had been gallant knights on grand quests, damsels under hypnotic spells, and an evil sorceress of the occult. But now he had found his calling: war stories.

Using his experiences in the Transvaal for inspiration, he began a series of stories about the brave men who fought in the jungles against the Boer raiders. They were rough boys, most not yet twenty years of age, and yet as they battled in the stifling heat, they earned their manhood. The stories were bloody, they were graphic, and, most importantly, they were true.

It occurred to Arthur, as he sat for his tea one afternoon, that in a full seven days the name Sherlock Holmes had not once been uttered in his presence. Nor had it once crossed his mind.

The bell rang the following day. Arthur was in his study when he heard it, finishing up a brief piece about a young Scottish soldier who is snared by an Arab sheikh's ambush in the Nubian Desert. The clank of the bell sounded foreign. It had been so long since Arthur had last heard it that it took him a moment to place the noise. He lifted his head from his new writing desk when he heard the bell ring a second time. This was odd. Arthur was expecting no visitors. And any deliveries would have gone straight in the back way. The house's staff were scattered on myriad chores, but a known guest should have been let in instantly. He would have been hard pressed to explain how, but even the jingle of the bell seemed off.

He thought he heard the front door open, and then some hushed conversation at the entryway, but from this distance it could have been whispering from anywhere in the house. He put down his pen and waited for the knock at his study. It was a full minute before his waiting bore fruit, and he attended the gentle rap-rap-rap of the butler's knuckles on his door.

"Yes?" called Arthur.

"Pardon, sir," said the butler, Barrow, "but there's a stranger at the door. She...demands an audience with you."

"Demands?" And then he added, after a moment, "She?"

"Yes, sir. She gave her name as Janet Fry." Barrow entered Arthur's study and handed him a sheet of white paper. "She had no card, but said to give you this instead, and that you'd know to what it referred."

Arthur took the paper from the man's hand and glanced at the top of the sheet. Before his eyes even landed on the image printed there, he knew what he would find. He looked down upon a three-headed crow.

"Show her in," said Arthur. He laid the paper on his desk and pushed aside his fiction. "And, Barrow," added Arthur as his butler was on his way out, "stay close, if you will."

Barrow nodded and went to grant Janet Fry entry into the study.

Arthur quickly ran to the floor-to-ceiling bookshelf along the north wall of the study. On one shelf a wooden box lay at the end of a row of books. Arthur took the box down, flipped open the latch, and removed an old revolver. He had never served in the military himself, except as a medic, but he had seen many a man perform his weapon inspection. Arthur looked over his pistol. There was a bullet in every chamber. The barrel was unobstructed. The hammer was pliant to his thumb.

He sat back at his desk and placed the revolver under his mostly finished story. He returned his hands to his lap just as Barrow opened the study door and introduced one of the most beautiful young women Arthur had ever seen.

"Miss Janet Fry," said Barrow as he left, closing the door behind him.

Arthur blinked, as if trying to shake off the false sight of a mirage. But no, there she was. From her dark hair to her dark, sunken eyes, her face was seductive and sinister. She was the polar opposite of the mousy, expressive Emily Davison. Janet carried a broad frame, and her expression was like a reflective pool of blackness, shining back at Arthur whatever he brought to it. He found himself immediately drawn to this young woman, while at the same time his right hand reached out to rest on his revolver.

"If you've come to kill me," said Arthur, "I can assure you that you'll never get away with it."

Janet dismissed Arthur's suggestion with the smallest movement of her eyebrows. When she spoke, her voice was calm, measured, and—to Arthur's great surprise—weary with sadness.

"Is that why you think I'm here?" she said. "To kill you?"

"It wouldn't be the first time you've made the attempt. Your friend Emily Davison told me all about your involvement in the letter-bomb plot."

Janet's eyes opened wider, and she gave Arthur a pleading look. "So it's true you found her?"

"Yes."

"She sent me a letter. The night she died. She said that you'd made contact with her and that you were hesitant, but she thought you would help."

Arthur would have laughed, were the situation not so dark. This would not be how he would have described the state of affairs when he'd left Miss Davison.

"I *caught* her, Miss Fry. I caught her right in the act of building another bomb. The only reason she's not in Newgate at present is that she's in the ground."

Janet became rigid, as if she were holding a great well of emotion back behind the stone dam that was her face. She sat slowly, gingerly, like an invalid. Arthur felt that she was using every ounce of strength she had not to give herself over to grief, and so she had none left to spend on the simple task of sitting.

"Did she..." Janet pressed her hands together in her lap. She was unable to look into Arthur's eyes. "Did Emily say anything about me? Did she tell you that we...Did she mention my name?"

"She said that you were the most beautiful girl she'd ever seen. She said that you were fast friends. She said that the two of you had been inseparable, that you shared every secret of your lives together."

Janet Fry became short of breath. She looked to be choking on the air in her throat. In a moment, she leaned forward, folded herself over her knees, and vomited.

Arthur called for Barrow, and, based on the speed with which the butler entered, it was clear that he'd been waiting behind the door. He brought water and damp cloths. Janet was too stunned to speak as Barrow wiped the bile from her black dress and rested a warm cloth against the girl's forehead. She rocked back and forth in her chair while Barrow tended to her, as if her grief were a stone in her belly, the only thing weighting her to the ground while a great wind blew her broad frame to and fro.

Stabbed girls. Shot girls. Drowned girls. Strangled girls.

Crying girls. Grieving girls.

Arthur watched the colorless dribble of bile drip from Janet's lips to her skirt, but the sight did not horrify him. What horrified him was not the stomach-churning grief of the beautiful girl before him, but rather the resolute indifference in his own heart. All he felt was a bit of gas from breakfast, burping up into his throat.

He knew then that the ugly engine of murder had done its work on him as surely as it had on Sally Needling, or Anna, or Emily Davison. The damage was done. And now he, too, was tainted with blood, drowned into a lifeless indifference. He had not been wounded by the violence—he had been callused. And that, he now realized, was worse.

When Miss Fry had been tidied up, Barrow left her with a clean washcloth and a cup of hot tea. The click of the closing door, as the butler exited, introduced a long silence to the study.

"Pardon me," said Janet Fry after a good while. "I loved her, too. She was impulsive and so deeply angry, and she could never be mollified by reason. But she was brilliant, and she was passionate, and she would giggle sometimes—I can't begin to describe it—as if life itself were some dirty little joke and only she had heard it. When she'd begun all that talk of the bombs...well, that's when we split. I wouldn't be a part of that. 'No one will be hurt, you dummy!' That's what she'd say to me. But she was wrong, of course—someone always gets hurt. That's what bombs are for, aren't they? Hurting people. We had an argument. I left her there, took a train back to my parents' home in Norwich.

You have to understand, I was angry. She was going to ruin everything we believed in by sending you that bomb. It's a blessing she didn't kill you. It was so stupid...But I'd written letters, before. To you. Do you remember receiving them?" Arthur said nothing, but his silence was clear. He received many letters.

"Yes," Miss Fry continued, "you must get so many. We needed your help...We simply couldn't think of any other way to get it! I'm just glad that her stupid bomb didn't hurt you, that's all. But yes, I was angry. I didn't respond when she wrote me. What else was there to say? I mean, there was no *convincing* Emily when she had her mind on something. I couldn't have stopped her, even if I'd tried. You must believe me."

Arthur absorbed this monologue with only a few blinks by way of response.

"I don't care," he said when he was sure that she was finished. "Please leave my home."

Janet stared at him in disbelief. "I'm in desperate need of your help," she pleaded.

"I don't care."

Janet gave Arthur a look of such horror and revulsion as he had never before seen in his life. "She was neither saint nor angel, that I will grant you, but she was a human being. And I loved her. And she is murdered."

"I don't care." The words had become a catechism to Arthur, a chant that was equally ritual and revelation.

"I already know who killed her, Dr. Doyle. I only need your help to prove it."

"I don't care."

"It was Millicent Fawcett. It must have been. She must have found out about our group, the Morrigan. I can't say how she found us out, but she must have. And so she killed us off, one by one. She would have done anything to halt a schism in the NUWSS. She was the only one with the motive. Who else would have wanted us all dead? And she certainly had the means. Our names, our addresses. Have you ever met her? Have you ever looked into that woman's eyes? I don't believe she's felt a single emotion in her entire life. Everything to her is tactics, the whole world merely rationed out by politics. She wouldn't have spent a tear on killing us off."

"I don't care."

"The police know you. They trust you. They have to, don't they? You're a man of the realm. You're a *man*. You're the only one of us that's fully a citizen. For you, they'll catch a killer."

"I. Do. Not. *Care*."

Janet Fry stared deeply into Arthur's eyes. She saw the anger that had welled up within him, as well as the implacable determination he had to keep it back.

"You're lying," she said. "You do care. You're just too bloody cowardly to do anything about it." Janet stood. She laid the now-cool washcloth across her wooden chair. She bowed and, with one hand on the doorknob, turned back to Arthur.

"So damn you to hell regardless," she said. "I'll see myself out."

It was only after she'd been gone for a minute that Arthur managed to turn to his desk. Laying his hands on the desktop, he felt a bulge of steel underneath his papers. *The revolver.* He'd forgotten about it entirely.

Arthur returned the revolver to the wooden box on the shelf. He would certainly not be requiring that again. Back at his desk, he breathed deeply. He banished all thoughts of Janet Fry and Emily Davison from his head. He focused himself completely on his war story, on the sheikh's trap and on the brave strategies of the small Scottish regiment, committing his day to realist fiction.

CHAPTER 36

A Problem Without a Solution

A problem without a solution may interest the student,
but can hardly fail to annoy the casual reader.
—Sir Arthur Conan Doyle,
"The Problem of Thor Bridge"

January 12, 2010, cont.

Dr. Gwen Garber was easily among the smallest women Harold had ever seen. She sat behind her desk, in her office at St. John's College, and seemed dwarfed by the book stacks in front of her. She angled her chin upward in order to place her elbows on her desk, and looked up to Harold and Sarah like a penitential child to a cross.

"Yes," she said after they had been in her office for a few minutes politely explaining their purpose at Cambridge. "Alex Cale was here. Just a few months ago. He came to read the Stoker letters, so of course he stopped by to talk with me. I'm the only one about who's done much work on them at all."

"Did he say what he was looking for, specifically?" asked Harold.

"I don't recall," said Dr. Garber, searching her memory with a series of finger taps to her chin. "But I'm sure he'd be more than happy to assist you with your research. He's the friendliest man. He truly is."

"He died," said Harold.

Despite all the inquiries he'd conducted into Alex's death, he realized that this was the first time he'd ever had to break the news to someone. Dr. Garber took it well, though perhaps that was only because she barely knew him. She blinked a few times, as if waiting for Harold to correct himself and admit that he'd been talking about someone else. When no correction or addendum came, she gave a shiver and looked down at her shoes.

"I'm so sorry," she said. "I had no idea. Were you...friends?"

"We were friendly."

"We're continuing his research," added Sarah. "Finishing up his work."

"*In memoriam*," said Harold.

"Oh, my, that's so good of you," said Dr. Garber. "Please, any information I can provide, I'd be quite happy to help. It's so sad. Can you... can you tell me what happened? Was he sick?"

"He was murdered," said Harold, more quickly than he might have liked. It was only in hindsight that it occurred to him that he probably should have lied. And yet, ironically, even the truth was more complicated than this. "Well, possibly," he added lamely.

"Hell." Dr. Garber seemed to recede into her chair as she digested the news. If possible, she looked to be growing even smaller.

"The more you can tell us about the letters, and what Alex Cale might have been looking for in them, the better we can help finish his book," said Sarah.

Dr. Garber looked at her for a moment. As always, Sarah seemed utterly convincing.

"All right then, let's head down there. I'll explain what I can along the way." Dr. Garber put on a bright yellow winter coat. "Our collection of Stoker's letters," she began, "is quite exhaustive. But, of course, Alex was only interested in his correspondence with Arthur Conan Doyle. They were good friends, you know. And Conan Doyle wrote a number of plays which were put on by Stoker's client, Henry Irving, at his theater. Since Stoker managed both Irving and the theater, he of course had plenty of business to discuss with Conan Doyle. There's a fine book of correspondence down there concerning only the details of the various payment schemes that Bram had devised. Hard to tell, from only one end of the conversation, but it rather looks like Stoker was cheating Conan Doyle out of some chunk of the box office. Funny, really. But I don't think that's the part of the conversation you're interested in, is it?"

"Under normal circumstances I would be," said Harold. "But right now... Well, do you have any sense of what period Alex was looking at? Was it the fall of 1900?"

"Yes... yes, I think that's it. Cale was trying to piece together what Conan Doyle and Stoker had gotten up to during the fall of 1900. Stoker had been working on a production of *Don Quixote* at the Lyceum, and he was at work on a few short stories as well. But I believe that Cale was interested in what Stoker knew of Conan Doyle's activities in those months. October, November, December."

"That's the period covered by the missing diary," Harold explained to Sarah. She returned a look indicating that not only did she not require his explanation, she did not particularly appreciate it.

"Oh, yes," said Dr. Garber. "That rings a bell. Cale said something about a missing diary of Conan Doyle's, how he'd been after the thing for ages. 'Since I first began my study of Sherlockiana,' I think that was the phrase he used. He was such a character, that one."

"Do you know if he found anything about the missing diary in the letters?"

Dr. Garber pushed open the double doors of the library building and stopped. Her hands continued to hold open the doors in front of her, as if she were announcing the entrance of royalty.

"To be honest, I don't know," she replied after some thought. "He did not seem pleased with what he'd found. I can tell you that. He left in rather a hurry, when he'd finished. He didn't even stop by to say goodbye—it was only that I happened to pass him on the footpath back there as I was on my way to give a lecture. He was all mumbles, very twitchy. I'd have thought it was rude, but I've had my share of researchers around over the years, and I know how they can get. Like a bunch of actresses, always overemotional about some crisis or another."

Harold did his best not to appear twitchy himself. The more

Dr. Garber said, the more promising these letters seemed. Clearly, what was in them had meant a great deal to Cale's investigation. Harold's tongue fluttered inside his mouth. He bit down on his lip. As soon as he saw these letters, he felt, the whole of the mystery would reveal itself to him...

And yet when, ten minutes later, Dr. Garber left Harold and Sarah alone in the underground rare-manuscript reading room, little was instantly revealed. Locked in the moistureless, climate-controlled room, Harold laid two cardboard boxes on the small wooden table. Both boxes were fastened shut with white string and marked with lined index cards. "STOKER, BRAM," read the cards. "COLLECTED LETTERS." The years of Stoker's life contained within each box had been marked as well. Harold ran his hand underneath the string. It felt like lingerie against his stubby forefinger.

He couldn't get the string untied, so Sarah, with her long, thin nails, stepped in to help. She scratched at the string with a catlike playfulness, and it fell apart from the box at the stroking of her nails. At the same time, both Harold and Sarah dug their hands into the cardboard box hungrily, pulling out thick stacks of plastic-protected papers. Each page was filled with Bram Stoker's own narrow and nearly illegible handwriting. Flipping through them left Harold both excited and awestruck. Millimeters from his fingers, behind the clear plastic sleeves, lay the dirty pen marks of Bram Stoker himself.

Where had Stoker been when he wrote these letters? In the study of his home in...Kensington? Yes, that's right, Stoker was living in Kensington in 1900. Harold remembered from Conan Doyle's diary—that is, in one of the volumes that hadn't been lost—about how Stoker had had his house outfitted for electric lights in that year; it had been one of the first private houses in London to have them. Conan Doyle talked about the shocking experience he encountered each time he'd visit Bram under those electric bulbs. Harold held the plastic sheets up very close to his face, communing with the pen strokes. What did they say?

Everything, Harold soon learned, and yet nothing at the same time. He and Sarah divided up the letters from the fall of 1900, trying to find any written to Conan Doyle. They found short letters to Stoker's entire extended family, they found obsequious letters to every well-known theater professional in London, and they even found repentant letters to the writer Hall Caine, to whom it seemed that Stoker owed a considerable sum of money. But they found none written to Conan Doyle, except the carbon-copy receipt of a single telegram Stoker had sent. On December 1, 1900, Stoker had sent a telegram to Conan Doyle that read, in its entirety, "Come at once. Please. B.S."

It was equal parts thrilling and infuriating. What did Stoker need to see Conan Doyle about so urgently? Where was Conan Doyle's reply? What were those two up to, after all?

Harold felt sure that Stoker held the key to everything that was happening, but he couldn't think of what Stoker and Conan Doyle had gotten into together. His first thought was that they had composed a story together, and yet that failed to explain any of the mystery surrounding Cale's final clue. Why not just make that story public, however poor it might have been?

Harold tried to imagine Stoker's involvement in Conan Doyle's other known activities at the time. Had Stoker joined him in one of his brief, unsuccessful investigations for Scotland Yard? None of the newspaper reports at the time mentioned anything about Conan Doyle having discovered anything particularly noteworthy. Scholars had even checked the Scotland Yard records, which were quite thorough. Whatever Conan Doyle had gotten up to there, it hadn't amounted to much.

Curiously, Harold did find a letter in one of the piles addressed to one "Inspector Miller, Scotland Yard." Bram had written him a brief note thanking him for his assistance. "Your kind help at Newgate was very much appreciated," read the letter. Harold thought this odd but didn't know quite what to make of it. Why would Stoker have been writing to Scotland Yard? And Newgate...Did that mean someone had been in prison?

After an hour of poring over the semi-legible letters, most of Harold's excitement had faded. In all the letters Bram Stoker had written in the fall of 1900, and into the winter of 1900–1901, there was nothing addressed to Conan Doyle and nothing that seemed like it could have sent Alex Cale into a depressive stupor.

"Nothing, right?" said Sarah as she set down a handful of letters.

"Right. Nothing." Harold wasn't sure what to do next.

"That's about it for these boxes."

Harold could do nothing but nod. There was something here, he was sure of it. But where? He turned the words of Alex Cale's final message over and over in his head. Then he spoke them aloud.

"'The old centuries...have powers of their own...'" He let the *Dracula* quote drip from his lips. "The old centuries..." It was a beautiful phrase, Harold thought. "...'Which mere modernity cannot kill.'" How poignant and poetic that last bit was as well—"mere modernity." There are some things, some evil things, so old that not even a little thing like modernity can stomp them out.

"What was Cale trying to tell us about Stoker? Why was he pointing us to Stoker's letters? What did Stoker know that Cale discov..." Harold trailed off midword. The flash of inspiration in his head was sudden and discrete. It was like the moment he'd had in the hotel armchair. There had been a period of not-knowing, and then this moment, and now Harold had entered a period of knowing. He simply knew.

"The diary is gone." As Harold spoke the words, their truth became even more manifest.

"What do you mean?"

"The diary is gone. Destroyed. That's got to be it. What other news would have upset Cale so much? Remember, in the hotel, he didn't have the diary. In his two flats, he didn't have the diary. In the suicide note we found in the British Library, he didn't even *say* he had the diary, only that he knew what had happened to it."

"So what happened to it?" Sarah asked.

"It's gone. There never was a diary to find."

"I don't understand. Everyone agrees that Conan Doyle had *written* the diary, right? He'd written dozens of other volumes of the thing."

"Yes. Conan Doyle wrote it. But then it was destroyed."

"Why would he have destroyed it?"

"He didn't."

"Then who did?"

Harold smiled and gestured to the letters at their feet. "Bram Stoker."

Sarah made a sour face. This news was not making her happy. But Harold was exhilarated. The thrill of inspiration overtook him, the pleasure of a problem solved. As Harold's face brightened, Sarah's darkened in equal measure.

"How did Cale know that?" she said.

"It must be in the letters. But not these letters. Later ones. Do you get it? Conan Doyle wrote the diary. Bram Stoker stole it, or threw it out, or something like that. And then he and Conan Doyle must have exchanged letters about it. That's how Cale knew. 'Mere modernity' didn't destroy Conan Doyle's old diary. Bram Stoker did."

Harold was up in a flash, ringing the bell for the library attendant to come back. He hurriedly asked her for the volume of letters chronologically after the ones they were currently looking at. She made him fill out a new request form, which he did impatiently. His own handwriting became quickly more smudged and illegible than even Stoker's.

It was an agonizing fifteen minutes for Harold while the attendant was off to fetch the letters, and he and Sarah were forced to wait in the rare-manuscript room. He paced back and forth maniacally, hands behind him. When he looked over at Sarah, he found her lost in her own thoughts. Yet something on her face—some shadow of concern and disappointment—gave him the impression that her thoughts were very different from his own. He couldn't imagine what she was feeling, and he didn't know how to ask.

Finally the attendant returned with another box, tied with the same white string.

It was less than five minutes before Harold found what he was looking for, though it felt a lot longer to him. His sweaty fingers slipped across the smooth plastic as he shuffled through the pages. "Dear Arthur," began the letter he held. "Your anger is understandable, but unfounded. Anything I have done—no, everything that I have done— has been done in the spirit of friendship and goodwill that exists between men such as you and I. If you will not thank me now, then I trust that one day you will thank me from the gates of heaven, when St. Peter alone whispers the truth from his lips. Let us discuss this in person, shall we? I can call on you anytime you like. B.S."

The next letter in the stack continued the argument.

"Dear Arthur," it read. "These bitter insults do not become you. But there is no reason for us to exclaim our opposite views in these missives. Let us sit in your study with a bottle of brandy, as we have so many times before, and hash out this affair. B.S."

The third letter conveyed even more anger and ill will between the men than the first two.

"Dear Arthur," read the third letter. "Please stop this childish behavior. I'm afraid that what you want from me I cannot give. It's been burnt in your own fireplace, from the first 'elementary' to the bitter end. And your rude and unseemly letters have been burnt up in mine. Please, I beg of you, let me come to your house and discuss this matter with you. Allow me the chance to explain myself, and I will allow you the same chance as well. B.S."

And that was it.

Harold flipped through further letters but found no more written to Conan Doyle in the box. Sarah flipped through the same piles, achieving the same result. Neither spoke until they'd both satisfied themselves that this was it, that this was the end of the trail.

"I was right," said Harold when his mind had settled enough to speak. "Stoker stole the diary and burned it in Arthur's fireplace. That's the secret that's been hidden for a hundred years. There never was a diary to find."

"But," Sarah replied, "but that's so... What was in the diary? Why did Stoker burn it?"

"I don't think we'll ever know," said Harold. "And that's why Alex Cale killed himself. Because at the end of the mystery, at the conclusion of the story he'd been living for his entire adult life, there was no solution. So he built a new mystery above his grave. Something that someone else could investigate. He wrote the word 'elementary' at the scene because he read these letters and wanted us to know when we'd found them. 'Elementary' wasn't the beginning of the mystery, it was the end. It's ironic, I suppose, but it seems so obvious when you think about it now. The most upsetting truth that Alex Cale could have figured out wouldn't be whatever ugly, dark secret is hidden in the diary—it's that there *was* no diary. That the secret that had been inside it would be hidden forever."

"That's sick."

She was right, Harold knew. But he also understood Cale's reasoning completely.

"There's a quote from Conan Doyle," Harold began. "'A problem without a solution may interest the student, but can hardly fail to annoy the casual reader.'" Harold gave a small laugh. "But I think Conan Doyle was wrong. In this case the problem without a solution upset the student, too."

"He killed himself to preserve a mystery? Then why leave all these clues?"

"He killed himself because his life was a failure. His great work was never going to be completed. It couldn't be. He would never be able to be the success that his father wanted, he'd never be able to toss his thick, award-winning Conan Doyle biography on his father's grave. His life was over. So he figured if he was going to kill himself anyway, why not plant a seed? He couldn't just tell everyone that the mystery was over... So he left behind a gift. For us. For me."

Harold could not place the look that Sarah gave him then. It was not disgust, exactly, and it was not despair, but it was a kind of sadness.

"Are you mad at me?" he asked finally. He didn't know what else to say. He was still exhilarated, but it was starting to wear off.

"No," she said. "Of course I'm not." She stood up from her chair and gave a long stretch. She arched her arms over her head and then folded them across her chest, curling herself inward. "So that's it, then? You're sure? The diary is gone? Burned up by Bram Stoker in Conan Doyle's own house. We'll never be able to find it, or what it says?"

Harold took a few seconds and ran through the chain of events in his mind that had led him to this conclusion. They were so orderly, so logical, and so flawless.

"Yes," he said. "This is it." An awful thought occurred to him.

"You're not going to tell anyone?" he asked. "Your article. I don't think Cale wanted anyone to... Well, look, he wanted to leave a mystery. He wanted someone to follow the clues, but only one person. Only the best. That was me. He didn't want everyone to know. You can't write about this. I know how much this article means to you. But you can't write about what Alex did. Please."

Sarah squeezed herself tighter. "Sure," she said. "I understand. I won't tell anyone." She put on her coat. "Your secret is safe with me."

Harold stood as well. It had felt so good to share his victory with someone. With Sarah. There was a puzzle, a test, and he'd solved it. But now his elation was somehow giving way to a hollow sensation. Why wasn't she enjoying this with him? Why had he been left to experience this alone?

"Are you leaving?" he asked.

"Yes. I think... Well, it's over now. There's no diary. There's nothing to write about. It was a pleasure to meet you." She reached out her hand, and before he could process what he was doing, Harold gave it a polite shake.

"What's going on?"

"Good-bye," she said. "You're really, really smart." Sarah picked up her purse and knocked on the door. The attendant answered quickly and asked Harold if he was coming along as well. He had nothing to say besides no. The attendant led Sarah out, and Harold was left alone with a jumble of thoughts more confusing than the scribbled letters of Bram Stoker before him.

It was only minutes later, as he sat in the bright, quiet reading room, that he remembered the car chase in London. The handgun. The Goateed Man. Was he still looking for Harold? For Sarah?

Harold knew then that a problem without a solution was not an annoyance, but the most maddening and horrible sensation in the world.

CHAPTER 37

A Death in the Family

*"The things which we do wrong—although they may seem little
at the time, and though from the hardness of our hearts we pass
them lightly by—come back to us with bitterness, when danger
makes us think how little we have done to deserve help,
and how much to deserve punishment."*

—Bram Stoker,
Under the Sunset

December 1, 1900

"Come at once," read the telegram. "Please." It was signed simply "B.S."

Arthur was angry, but he went all the same. It was the sort of message that Holmes was always sending to Watson in his stories, and Bram knew it. What gall! To drag Arthur back into this horrible affair without even the courtesy of an explanation. It was conduct unbefitting a man of Bram's stature, and especially a friend of Bram's caliber. "*Come at once.*" For heaven's sake. Arthur would have liked to think that Bram was a better man than to commit such skulduggery.

Arthur received the message a little after three in the afternoon and managed to make the 3:55 for Waterloo. From there it was but a twenty-minute ride in a two-wheeler to get to Bram's home along St. Leonard's Terrace, Kensington.

He couldn't imagine what Bram had found that was so urgent that Arthur had to drop his day's cricket and head into the city. It was assuredly nothing, of course. Bram most likely just could not accept Arthur's refusal to further engage in detective work. But to tantalize him like this... to tease him with the promise of clues! It was like holding cheap gin under the nose of a recovering dipsomaniac. Arthur would not forget this.

Nor, obviously, would he take the bait. He would go to St. Leonard's Terrace, yes, and he would see what Bram was making such a fuss about. And then he would explain, calmly and resolutely, that he was of an age too advanced for such follies. If Bram wanted to continue his investigations, Arthur would not stand in his way. But for Arthur there would be no more interviewing of witnesses and no more sniffing of rancid blood-stains. The circus had left town, and Arthur would not travel with it.

Number 18, St. Leonard's Terrace was rather larger than Arthur had remembered. Four years previously Bram had moved here from Number 19—he'd moved all of one house over in order to acquire an extra floor. The new house was re-created like the old one, almost down to the positioning of the vases in the drawing room. It was a move so very like Bram—expensive, a touch indulgent, and yet meticulous in its labors. There were rumors that Bram had been forced to borrow around town in order to pay for the new furnishings. Some said six hundred pounds from Hall Caine alone, while others said as much as seven hundred. But there were always rumors, and Arthur paid them little mind. And it was not as if it were Arthur's place to ask. He and Bram knew enough about each other's sins and shortcomings at this point. There was no cause for adding weight to the scales.

The butler recognized his face, and before Arthur had a chance to speak, the man issued a polite, "Right this way, Dr. Doyle.

"Mr. Stoker has been expecting you," added the butler for effect.

"Yet I suspect he'll be disappointed when he finds me," said Arthur.

The house was both dark and ornate. It received little light from the street outside, despite the fact that it was buttressed to the south by the open parks of the Royal Hospital. The windows were too small, thought Arthur, and there were not enough of them. The drawing room seemed sodden with a princely and expensive gloom. The golds and silvers of the exposed tea set were transmuted into bronze by the pervasive dim. The lush reds of the oil paintings on the wall were darkened into bloody browns.

As Bram turned from his desk, Arthur saw that he was in the midst of lighting his cigar. The match burst orange light into the room and then was squashed out quickly with a blow from Bram's lips. Cigar smoke trailed into the darkness above.

"I don't care what you have to tell me," Arthur began. "I haven't the faintest interest in knowing who killed Emily Davison."

Bram simply stared.

"Very well," he said at last. "Thank you for making me aware. But that's not why I asked you here."

"Oh," was all Arthur managed in reply. It had not occurred to him that Bram could have asked him over to discuss anything other than the murders.

"Oscar is dead."

It took Arthur a long moment to understand what Bram was saying.

"... Wilde?" asked Arthur lamely.

Bram nodded. Who else would it have been?

Arthur sat down on a plush chair. He allowed his body to tumble into it as if he were diving bottom-first off a cliff.

"Where?" he asked. "When?"

"Paris. Did you even know that's where he's been? I didn't. He's been two years in the Hôtel d'Alsace. I never sent him a letter, or even a bloody note. Did you? Well, no. Of course you didn't. He died sometime yesterday. Florence, of all people, got a telegram this morning, and she informed me." Bram sighed. "Since he was released from prison, we didn't offer him so much as a kind word, did we? We left the poor chap to drink and bugger himself to death on the Continent."

Arthur didn't take kindly to the implied accusation in Bram's tone.

"And what were we to do?" he said. "Oscar had ... proclivities. He was drawn inexorably to sin. It is a tragedy that such a great man was brought so low by vice. But the villain here is the vice, not you and I."

"Vice?" said Bram. "Do you think that's what killed him? No. A vice is a thing which may be applauded in moderation but becomes horrific in overuse. Morphine is splendid by the ounce, but it's a vice by the gallon. A healthy desire for one's wife, that's a virtue. But a compulsive desire for another, however . . . well, that's a vice that will do a man ill."

Bram looked Arthur dead in the eyes. Arthur wondered if he was referring to Jean, if Bram was judging him. Well, so what if he was?

"No," Bram continued. "It wasn't the vice that killed Oscar. It was the loneliness."

"Do you remember that night we met, he and I?" said Arthur. "At that dinner in the Langham Hotel? Wait, no, you weren't there. It was hosted by Joseph Stoddart, of *Lippincott's*. Oscar was so deliriously funny, and he was a towering figure. It was a golden evening for me. Oscar told me he admired my work. Stoddart commissioned novels from us both, did you know that? On the same evening. Oscar wrote his *Dorian Gray*, and I wrote *The Sign of the Four*."

"And then," added Bram, "he went to prison. And you to an audience with the queen. Oh, say, I've simply forgotten to ask—has your knighthood come through yet?"

"Look here, it's not so simple as you make it seem, all right? It's not as if they locked him up in jail over *Dorian Gray*, and it's not as if *The Sign of the Four* were the proximate cause of this knighthood everyone says I should be expecting. There was a series of intermediate steps. We took two different paths, do you see?"

"Yes, Arthur. I do."

The men sat in silence for long minutes as Bram puffed on his cigar and Arthur let his mind recede into the fantasia of recollection. With Oscar it was the dinners one remembered most. With some men it was the afternoons at sport or late nights before the brandy bottle. But Arthur would always remember Oscar at dinner. At the head of a long table, six guests laid out before him on either side of the centerpiece like wings. Every head turned to face him hungrily, waiting for the next jest, the next outrageous and delicious proclamation. Arthur would remember the words that Oscar spoke, but he would also remember the way that Oscar fed off the attention and the laughter. Oscar was merely witty one-on-one, but he was uproarious in a group of twelve. It was as if, for Oscar, if there were no audience, then it was not worth the effort to try.

"It's getting dark," said Bram suddenly.

Arthur had to admit that it was. Little remained of the sun's light outside the windows. Bram stood and approached a small switch near the door. He flicked it upward, and the room exploded.

Or so it felt to Arthur, until his eyes adjusted to the searing glare. When the blinding whiteness had subsided and Arthur's eyes began to perceive color again, he noticed that on the sconces of the walls beside him, and on the arms of the miniature chandelier above, were electric bulbs. The six-inch tubes of glass burned a light of such whiteness as Arthur had never before seen.

"Oh, have you not seen my lights yet?" said Bram. "I had these put in over the summer. You've seen the public ones they're putting out on the streets, but these are smaller. For private use. Dreadfully expensive, I don't mind telling you, but look at them! I feel like I'm blowing cigar smoke into the clouds of heaven itself!" To illustrate his point, Bram puffed a hearty cloud of smoke at one of the wall sconces. The smoke seemed to be incinerated by radiance.

Arthur blinked his eyes, trying to stamp out the red and orange spots he hallucinated before him. When he had done so and his vision was fully restored, he surveyed Bram's drawing room again.

The colors were those of medieval pageantry. All red was pure red, and all blue was pure blue. The shadows of the chairs cut sharp black lines on the golden Persian rugs. All was clean, visible, and still. Arthur thought that the room used to look like a Michelangelo and now it more resembled a medieval panel work. The luscious and spooky gray-browns of gaslight chiaroscuro had been stripped clean off by the sharp razor of electricity.

"They are a marvel," said Arthur. A twinge of hesitation remained in his throat.

"Quite," said Bram. "And yet I hear it in your voice. Something bothers you about them."

Arthur looked around and felt adrift in the nova glare of progress.

"I can't explain it, precisely," he said. "But they make me sad, somehow."

"You feel it, too, then?"

"I'm not sure what you mean."

"It's the end of an age," said Bram. "And the beginning of a new one. The twentieth century. It sounds odd on the tongue, doesn't it? The calendars have already changed. And now we've lost Oscar. Not even Victoria can last forever, though she's certainly of a mind to try."

"Hush! Don't speak that way."

"Oh, come now. Edward won't be so bad. You wait and see."

"Perhaps," said Arthur, "what saddens me is not the passing of time but the curious sensation of being aware of it as it happens. We're used to demarcating our histories in hindsight—we draw the lines afterward. It's the scholars who separate one period from another. Did Constantine know that he was presiding over something more than the natural tumult of empire? Did Newton know that he'd arrived upon a wave of revolution, like Aphrodite on her clamshell? And moreover, did anyone *else* perceive the change in the air around them? Were they 'self-aware,' as we are?

"But you're right, I think," Arthur continued. "I don't know how any man could feel his eyes burn in the electric light and not also feel the sudden palpability of history."

Bram smiled. "The 'palpability of history,'" he said, rolling it over his tongue. "I like that." He paused, looking Arthur up and down curiously. "You've been writing again? At work on more stories?"

"Yes," said Arthur, unsure of where Bram was headed with this line of inquiry.

"You always get a touch more poetic in conversation when you've just been writing. It's something of which I've taken notice over the years. Quite charming, really." Bram held his breath and scratched his beard. Arthur felt that Bram was preparing to broach a delicate subject. And when Bram next spoke, Arthur's suspicions were confirmed.

"Holmes?"

"Oh, hell, not you, too!" said Arthur. "I get enough bullying about him from my publishers. No. I have not been writing about Sherlock Holmes."

"As you say. I just had the thought...well, how shall I put this? There was no man who felt your 'palpable history' more than Sherlock Holmes."

"I will not write more Holmes stories, do you understand? I would have thought I'd made that perfectly clear at this point."

"I don't care whether you do or not," said Bram. "But you will, eventually. He's yours, till death do you part. Did you really think he was dead and gone when you wrote 'The Final Problem'? I don't think you did. I think you always knew he'd be back. But whenever you take up your pen and continue, heed my advice. Don't bring him here. Don't bring Sherlock Holmes into the electric light. Leave him in the mysterious and romantic flicker of the gas lamp. He won't stand next to this, do you see? The glare would melt him away. He was more the man of our time than Oscar was. Or than we were. Leave him where he belongs, in the last days of our bygone century. Because in a hundred years, no one will care about me. Or you. Or Oscar. We stopped caring about Oscar years ago, and we were his bloody *friends*. No, what they'll remember are the stories. They'll remember Holmes. And Watson. And Dorian Gray."

"And your count? What was his name? From that little province..." Arthur trailed off. He searched his mind for the name of that backwater kingdom but couldn't find it.

"Transylvania," supplied Bram when it became clear that Arthur did not recall the name. "He was from Transylvania. No, they won't remember him. He didn't inspire the imagination of a people as did your Holmes. He was my great failure." Bram laughed bitterly. "Count What's-His-Name."

"I'm sorry, Bram," said Arthur. "I'm so very sorry. I know well how much of your own blood was in that novel. And I thought it was a grand thing, I truly did." He paused. "Is that why Oscar's death has you so battered up?"

"Yes, I suppose it is. We treated the man himself as scrap paper; to be used for a while and then discarded. But the stories we will treasure forever. At least Oscar will have his tales in posterity. What will I have?"

"'The man is nothing. The work is everything.' That's what you're getting at?"

"Yes." Bram paused. "That's Flaubert, isn't it?"

"Yes."

"And we still remember." Bram laughed bitterly again.

"My stories," said Arthur. "The science of deduction. The reasoning detective. The solution delivered patly in a satisfying *dénouement*. They're all horseshit."

Bram smiled. "I know," he said. "That's why we need them."

Arthur considered this. "I've moved on," he offered after a long pause. "I've been working at realism. History."

"Realism," Bram repeated. "Realism, I think, is fleeting. It's the romance that will live forever."

"And what about me? Will my name live on?"

Bram's face turned sour and grim. "I do not know, my friend. All I'll say is this: The world does not need Arthur Conan Doyle. The world needs Sherlock Holmes."

"No!" exclaimed Arthur quite suddenly. "No. I am better than he is, don't you see? I will not be shamed by him. I will outlive him, and I will outshine him."

"Arthur—"

"Wilde is dead and already forgotten, you say? We're all bound for the grave and bitter obscurity? Damn it, no. I will not let Holmes win."

"He doesn't even *exist*!" pleaded Bram, but it was no use.

"And the killer of Emily Davison?" Arthur said. "He exists. And

I'll see him to his grave before I unearth that blasted Holmes from his. Holmes won't save Emily Davison—I will."

"Arthur," said Bram quietly. "No one will save Emily Davison. She's dead."

Arthur paused, momentarily speechless, as he blinked under the electric lights.

Chapter 38

The Pickerel

"Any truth is better than indefinite doubt."
—Sir Arthur Conan Doyle,
"The Yellow Face"

January 15, 2010

Harold sulked through the next three days, swimming through glass after glass of bourbon and damp Cambridge mist. He should leave, he knew. He should leave Cambridge, because there was nothing else for him there. But leaving Cambridge meant returning to London, it meant boarding a plane at Heathrow and flying west, past the murder scene in New York all the way to a one-bedroom apartment in Los Angeles.

The second he left Cambridge, real life would return, minute by minute, until he found himself on his own doorstep, standing on top of a dirty welcome mat that actually read "Welcome." He would turn the key, lock himself inside, and none of this would ever have happened. The thought was more horrible than Harold could bear.

He should send Sebastian Conan Doyle a message—he knew that, too. As far as Harold was aware, he was still working for the man, and so he might as well let the guy know that the investigation he'd paid for was over. The diary had burned up a hundred years before, and now no one—not even Sebastian Conan Doyle—would be able to profit from it. Harold waited, however. Because if he gave Sebastian a call, if he sent him an e-mail, then he would be one step closer to facing the end of all of this.

But the end was there whether Harold admitted it or not. It couldn't be held off even with liquor, or long and aimless walks through the university gardens. The end would not be held off by checking his messages, by wondering every few minutes whether Sarah might have called.

So he read through the letters again. Not because he thought there was anything pertinent left in them—he was more than sure that there wasn't, and he was proved right the more of them he read. Harold read the letters because it was the only way not to leave. For now he could still sit in the same claustrophobic reading room, between the same moistureless walls where he'd been with Sarah. He thought about her standing up, getting her coat, saying something polite, and leaving.

Harold didn't know where she had gone, or even where she had come from. He knew so little about her, really. And he would never learn more. Like the rest of this adventure, Sarah would be a secret he kept alone. A point of pride, in some small way, that he could never share with anyone.

The Pickerel, an old pub on Magdalene Street, became his home away from his hotel room. It was close and relatively free of shouting, flirting undergrads. It was dark, it kept its "football"-tuned televisions down, and it would do. For three nights it did. Harold kept to himself, and to some books he'd picked up from a shop down the street. They weren't Holmes. They weren't even mysteries. Harold wasn't sure when he'd be able to read anything from the Canon again, but he thought it might be a while.

Strangely, the uncomfortable thought that he would never know the secret within the diaries bothered him less than the thought that his investigations were at an end. He wasn't plagued by grief over the lack of answers—he was plagued by melancholy over how quickly the answers had come, and how final they appeared to be. Harold found himself pining not for solutions, but for questions. For *more*. He realized that even after all the stories he'd read, he'd been left completely unprepared for this moment—for the quiet days after the climax when the world ticked onward. He'd read thousands upon thousands of moments of revelation, of grand gestures of explanation in which the torn fabric of life had been stitched tightly shut and patted over. He'd read thousands of happy endings and thousands of sad ones, and he had found himself satisfied with both. What he had not read, he now realized, were the moments after the endings. If Harold believed in the stories because they presented an understandable world...well, what happens when the world is understood and that understanding means nothing to anyone but you and the empty tumbler of bourbon nestled in your palm? Harold had understood that not finding a solution would have been awful, but he had never before thought that finding one, and then having actually to go on living with it, might be worse.

One phrase kept flickering across his drunken sorrows. "The penny dreadful." Having no one else to laugh to, Harold laughed to himself. It was a term so much more apt than he'd known. For the story he'd been living in had now been revealed to be fleeting, shallow, and cheap. A brief flash of petty magic that entertained only the dull and the naïve. A penny tale, and not even worth so much as that.

The taps on his shoulder came while he was reaching for more pretzels, his arm dangling across the long wooden bar in search of the tiny plastic bowl. They were an insistent series of quick taps—one-two-three on his back, just at the bottom of his shoulder blade. He turned, swiveling on the stool, and saw no one behind him. Strange.

Harold heard a cough and looked down. There he found some manner of black-helmeted gnome staring up at him. He swallowed, blinked, and recognized the face of Dr. Garber. With Harold high on his stool, the top of her head came up only just above his navel. She smiled.

"Harold!" she said, as if she were genuinely happy to see him.

"Hi there," he replied. He really wasn't in the mood for conversation right now. He turned himself a half inch farther back toward his drink, trying to be subtle.

"Where's your friend? Sarah?" The subtlety didn't seem to be working.

"Gone. She...she had to leave." He was too tired to come up with a good lie. Plus, he was such a shitty liar anyway.

Dr. Garber frowned. She gave him a concerned look.

"Lovers' quarrel?" she asked, in a tone equally playful and sympathetic.

"Not exactly."

"Well, I'm sure you'll patch it up," Dr. Garber said as she hopped up on the adjacent barstool. Harold was not aware of having invited her to join him. "I like the sight of you two together. You're a lovely couple."

He offered no response, save a few nods. He sipped more bourbon. Dr. Garber sipped at her own drink, something clear and carbonated, most likely gin and tonic. He realized that she wasn't going to leave, and he determined that his best bet was to change the subject, so at least he didn't have to talk about Sarah anymore.

"Thanks for your help with the letters," he said. "I think we found everything we needed."

"Terrific! You're on your way to the missing Conan Doyle diary that Cale was on about?"

"Well…no." It was going to involve more effort not to talk about this than to talk about it, Harold realized. Might as well just give in. "The diary was burned up. Stoker did it, in 1900. He tells Conan Doyle about it in one of his letters."

"Hmmm," Dr. Garber pondered. "Is that what he wanted to meet about, then?"

"Meet about?"

"Yes. The meeting Stoker kept trying to arrange. I've always wondered about it myself. Did you see the notes from Stoker's business secretary at the Lyceum? Even she kept pressing Conan Doyle for the two to have a meeting, for a few months, on some pretense of financial concerns."

Harold frowned. He hadn't seen any correspondence between Stoker's business secretary and Conan Doyle in the collection. "Are those letters down there as well?"

"Oh, I suppose not, now that you mention it. They weren't from Stoker personally, you know, so they're kept elsewhere. I forget which university they've run off to, but they're in some lesser Stoker collection somewhere. Maybe Austin, actually. The messages are all from Stoker's

secretary to Conan Doyle's secretary, so they're really not of much interest. Mostly about Conan Doyle's unpaid cut of profits from his plays,
about making sure various seats of good quality are available for various
of Conan Doyle's friends. But if memory serves, all that fall and winter
there's some harping about scheduling a meeting between the two men."

"A meeting?"

"Yes."

In that moment Harold become intensely aware of all the bourbon
in his system. He found himself, for the first time in days, fighting
against it. The liquor had done its job of subverting and nullifying all
rational thought for the past forty-eight hours, but now Harold desired
very much to think. And to think clearly.

"Where?" he asked, his lips moving slowly. He was afraid of the
answer she might give.

"Where did Stoker want to meet?"

"Yes. In the letters I read, Stoker made a reference each time to wanting to come to Conan Doyle's house, his study. It didn't occur to me
as noteworthy at the time, but...Oh, Jesus...Did I seriously just...?
Okay, try to remember: In the letters between Stoker's secretary and
Conan Doyle's, did Stoker's secretary suggest any particular spot he
wanted the two to meet in? Like, say, Conan Doyle's study?"

Dr. Garber made an odd face. She seemed startled by Harold's
sudden bout of intensity.

"I'm not sure," she said, taking a sip of her clear cocktail and trying
to brush Harold's seriousness off with a smile. "Does it matter?"

"From the letters we have, we know that Conan Doyle was missing his
diary. He always wrote in his study, and we know, from the found volumes,
that that's where they were kept. We know that Stoker was involved in the
diary's disappearance, or else why was Conan Doyle so sure that Stoker
had taken it? But Conan Doyle wasn't aware of its being destroyed, of its
being burned, before Stoker told him in the letter. So Conan Doyle hadn't
walked in on a fire in the study, for instance. Stoker must have been left
alone in the study, where he stole it. But what if he didn't actually burn it?"

"Why wouldn't he burn it," asked Dr. Garber, "if he was trying to get rid of it?"

"I don't know," said Harold. "Maybe he didn't have time. Maybe Conan Doyle was on his way back into the room. Something might have stopped him."

"What would he have done with it, if he hadn't burnt it?"

"Hidden it," said Harold. "Hidden it in Conan Doyle's own study."

"The letters!" Dr. Garber exclaimed, her face brightening. She took up her role much faster than Sarah had, for sure. "That's why you think Stoker wanted so terribly to meet Conan Doyle in person! So that he could get back into the study."

"Yes," said Harold, impressed with Dr. Garber's reasoning. "Did the secretary-to-secretary correspondence talk about meeting at Conan Doyle's house as well?"

"I don't know," she said after some thought. "They very well could have. I just don't remember."

Excitement percolated through Harold's body, tingling every inch of his skin. Was he deluding himself? Was he tricking himself into thinking that the mystery wasn't over, that there was more to do? He realized it didn't matter. Whether the clue was real, or whether it was simply a half-remembered fragment of an utterly uneventful business note from a hundred years past that had been divulged in idle conversation, it was a reason to keep going.

He swallowed the rest of his bourbon easily in one gulp. "Sounds like enough to go on," he said.

"But where will you go? Even if Stoker did hide the diary in Conan Doyle's study in 1900, how does that help you find it now? Where would you find it?"

Harold stood and collected his coat.

"I think first I'll try Conan Doyle's study," he said, grinning from ear to ear.

CHAPTER 39

The Printer

*"I don't think you need have any fears about Sherlock.
I am not conscious of any failing powers, and my work is not
less conscientious than of old... You will find that Holmes
was never dead, and that he is now very much alive."*
—Sir Arthur Conan Doyle,
in a letter to his mother, Mary Doyle, April 1903

December 3, 1900

The chain of reasoning which led Arthur from Bram's house on Saturday to the storefront of Stegler & Sons Printing House, along the Strand, on Monday was quite simple. Indeed, by the time Arthur stepped up onto the small front stoop of the printing house, he was genuinely surprised that it had taken him this long to arrive.

To be sure, there had been detours in his investigations. When Arthur decided, after leaving Bram's study, to reopen the case, there was an initial period of uncertainty and of concern over his powers of deduction. Now that he had resolved to find Emily Davison's murderer... well, how did he intend actually to go about it?

He laid the facts at hand out before him. They were as follows: A gentleman, described only as being tall, in the possession of a long black cloak, and speaking in a high-pitched voice, proposed marriage to, and then married, and then murdered, two members of the Morrigan, Sally Needling and the mysterious Anna. He committed these crimes months apart, and both marriages were conducted in secret. One had to assume, and Arthur certainly did, that these marriages must at first have been secrets even between the young women in question. Some months later this man had snuck into Emily Davison's home and savagely beaten her to death. Odd, Arthur thought, that this crime did not fit the pattern of the others. Did he first woo Emily Davison as well? Arthur could not imagine the girl he'd met having fallen under the spell of this man, whoever he might be, as her compatriots had. So who was he?

Arthur spent a morning entertaining Janet Fry's suspicions about Millicent Fawcett, but the more he thought about it, the less convincing he found that argument. First, there was the issue of the bridegroom who'd accompanied the girls to their death. Yes, she could have employed an accomplice, but even if Arthur were to grant that Millicent Fawcett had a murderous bone in her body—and he certainly did not feel comfortable doing so after her performance at the suffragist lecture—would she have chosen bloody violence?

A man had composed these murders, Arthur was sure of it. He knew something that Janet did not. He had looked upon the bloodied, beaten corpse of Emily Davison, and he had seen the anger that had been inflicted on her body. Only a man who hated women with a passion that Arthur could just barely fathom could wreak such violence.

Arthur possessed few clues as to the man's identity, if any. But, he reasoned, perhaps more than clues, more than evidence, reason itself could see him through.

The murderer would have had to know all three girls, which meant that he would most likely have known about their secret organization. Two could have been coincidence, but not three. He could not have known the group well, however, or else they could hardly have kept their respective engagements to him a secret. He could not have been their friend, exactly, but he was someone who had some contact with them.

It took only a few brief hours of concentration upon the subject before the answer revealed itself to Arthur, when he glanced down at his one memento from his investigations—the pamphlet, printed on cheap paper, of the three-headed crow.

The paper was still in his pocket when he marched down the Strand and ascended the front steps of Stegler & Sons Printing House. To be fair, this was the sixth printing press Arthur had visited that day. But from the moment he opened the door and entered the noisy shop, he had a feeling that he'd found what he was looking for. The large presses clanged metallically, grinding out books and pamphlets and posters on sheet after sheet. Arthur regarded the massive machines and thought of Blake's "dark Satanic mills." Funny, to think of them serving the distribution of information, of sending out the written word. There was something menacing about each slap of the press upon the flat papers. The unyielding smacks called to mind the image of Emily's body, beaten blow by blow into the floor.

But Arthur's incubating sense of suspicion did not become full grown until he was greeted by the shopkeeper. A boy of no more than twenty, he stepped from behind one of the presses, lifting his head to the light to reveal the handsomest face Arthur had ever seen on a man. His blond hair fell delicately over his brow, toward his shimmering blue eyes and a small, evenly sloped nose. Even Arthur, no expert on the subject of men's faces, was taken aback. The boy raised his hands in greeting, and Arthur saw that he wore two ink-stained gloves. Blotches of ink had spread to his shirt, and when Arthur stepped closer, he could even make out a sprinkle of purple ink on the boy's unshaven chin.

"Help you, sir?" said the lad in a delicate voice. "Pardon my hands. I'd give you a shake, but I'm afraid it'd ruin your suit."

Arthur was charmed. And, upon recognizing how charmed he was, he became terribly frightened. He knew that he'd have to be very cautious about how he proceeded. His eyes on the boy's dirty hands, Arthur removed the flyer from his own coat pocket.

"Good afternoon, then," Arthur said. "We'll exchange a proper handshake at a later date." He gave his friendliest smile. "I'm here to find the printer of this sheet. Might you have printed this here? It would have been some months ago."

Arthur held the image of the three-headed crow up to the light. The boy looked at it expressionlessly. If he recognized it, he gave no indication of doing so.

"What's that, then?" said the boy.

"Hell if I know," said Arthur.

"Then why're you inquiring about it?"

Arthur paused. Yes. The boy was playing dumb, but he was not particularly good at it. Arthur considered how next to approach the matter. Not like a detective, he reasoned. Not like a member of the Yard. What this boy needed, Arthur guessed, was a sympathetic ear.

"Bunch of bloody dollymops have been leaving them around my shop," said Arthur. "I run a butcher's, down in the East End. I put up some literature in the windows, and it seems they didn't take kindly to it. So wherever I turn now, these infernal pictures keep popping up in my property. They even found my flat and left some papers there. It's frightful, don't you think? I want to see these cunnies punished." These last words left a bitter taste on Arthur's tongue after he'd spoken them. But he knew of the rage within this boy, and he knew that he needed to tap into it. They would be brothers in misogyny before the evening fell.

The boy smiled again and removed his gloves. He placed them atop one of the printing machines and held out his clean hand for a shake.

"My name is Bobby," the boy said. "Bobby Stegler. This is my pop's shop, I just help out."

Arthur reached out and shook Bobby Stegler's hand.

"Andrew," Arthur said. "Andrew Greenleaf. Pleased to meet you."

"You know these girls, then?"

"Afraid I do," said Arthur. He let go of Bobby's hand and gave him a look of playful suspicion. "Say, I'm willing to bet that you know a little more about them than you're letting on, don't you?"

Bobby Stegler lowered his head sheepishly. "If I was to say that I printed those papers, sir, and know a thing or two about these girls' organization, would you hold it against me?"

"Not if you could tell me who they are," said Arthur.

"Bunch of rabble-rousers, really. They're part of a group, those girls, agitating for—can you believe this?—granting woman suffrage."

"Yes, I know. They told me as much. Can you imagine?"

"The downfall of the empire, it would be," said Bobby Stegler.

Arthur gave the boy a hearty pat on his shoulder. "Finally!" Arthur exclaimed. "A man who understands reason! I'm afraid their cause is growing frightfully popular of late."

"That's why something needs to be done about it," said Bobby.

Arthur looked the boy dead in the eyes. It was time to see what he was made of.

"And will you?" Arthur asked. "Will you do anything about it?"

The boy smiled mischievously. "When was the last time those girls came around your 'shop' anyway?" The lad had accented the word 'shop' strongly; Arthur was not sure what he was getting at.

"I'll admit, they haven't come around recently. Might you have had anything to do with that?"

"Not sure what you mean, sir," said the boy. He paused. He looked as if he were waiting for Arthur to say something.

"If you've a mind to take care of these girls," said Arthur, "I might have a pair of hands that could help you."

"What'd you say your 'shop' was, again?"

"Just a simple butcher's, like I said."

The boy returned Arthur's pat on the shoulder. But this one was harder, sharper. There was a lot of strength in the boy's arm.

"Oh, come off it," said Bobby Stegler. "I know who you are! What did you say, Andrew Something-or-Other from the East End? Really now. Don't think that the great Arthur Conan Doyle could walk into my printing house and I wouldn't put the name to the man's face!"

Arthur blanched. He had not expected to be so well known among the murderers of London.

"You've made a mistake, boy," he said lamely.

Bobby Stegler was having none of it.

"It's all right, Dr. Doyle. You can come level with me. You don't know what an inspiration you've been. Your speeches against the suffrage. Tops. And your stories. They'll show a man what his place in the world is, won't they? Sherlock Holmes wouldn't have listened to any of that feminine mewing."

For the first time in a great while, Arthur felt truly ashamed. Is that really what people took from his stories? Is that what they said?

"Please, take a seat, sir," said Bobby. "We have a lot to discuss. You see, you and I are on the same side. And I think we could help each other out quite a bit."

CHAPTER 40

The Old Centuries

"If you will find the facts, perhaps others may find the explanation."
—Sir Arthur Conan Doyle,
"The Problem of Thor Bridge"

January 16, 2010

As Harold's cab passed from under the great pines, he gazed up at Undershaw for the first time. Most of the windows were shattered. Empty husks of jagged glass hung from the peeling panes, like the teeth of a dying animal. The windows that weren't empty were boarded up with cheap, rotting wood. The grass out front was tall and unkempt, sprouting mangy vines that scratched at the bricks.

Harold had never laid eyes on Undershaw before, though he'd seen it in photographs. He could only imagine what it must have looked like in its prime. To think that behind those faded walls the entire second half of the Canon had been written. Holmes had been resurrected from the Great Hiatus not a hundred feet from the spot along the driveway where Harold's cab pulled to a dusty stop. For once he might actually be days—or even moments—away from knowing why. Who knew how many scholars had made this trip before him and come away empty handed? Harold would not be among them. He felt awed, he felt humbled, and yet a part of him was glad that he was going to first enter this house now, and not earlier in his life. Because now, Harold felt, he was worthy of its secrets.

An elderly woman sat on the stone steps leading to the front door.

Only there was no front door, just a series of broken wood planks that had been nailed together. The woman was hunched over, hair pulled back in a bun, her bent frame wrapped in the sort of heavy, dark coat that would have been equally at place in any decade of the last six. She kept her head buried in a thick volume of photographs on her lap.

The woman—broad-boned, heavy-cheeked, rosacea pink—was named Penelope Higgins, and Harold had spoken with her late the previous day. Her mother had been Conan Doyle's maid, and Penelope had lived in Hindhead her entire life. The Conan Doyle family had sold the house a generation ago, and for most of the century it had been a small country hotel. Now it was abandoned, and developers were fighting with various preservationist societies over the property's future. As the battles dragged on, Undershaw languished in disrepair. Penelope lived close by and was one of the most vocal preservationists in the cause. She kept an extensive collection of photographs, plans, and other records of Undershaw's history. It was these documents—open across her lap, growing brittle in the January air—that Harold had come to see.

When he'd called the day before, he had explained his Sherlockian credentials and his relationship with Alex Cale, whom she knew well. He had even called Jeffrey Engels to have him put in a quick word. Jeffrey had been surprised to hear Harold's voice on the other end of the line, but registered Harold's urgency and dutifully made the call to Penelope Higgins as requested. Harold realized that at some point he'd have to tell Jeffrey, and everyone else, where the hell he'd been for the past two weeks, but he figured he could work his story out when the time came. He was back on the trail now, and that was all that mattered. Without Harold's needing to say so, Jeffrey had seemed to understand as much. He'd sent Harold on his way with barely a question.

Penelope gave Harold a once-over as he ascended the crumbling stone steps to the foyer.

They discussed their mutual Sherlockian acquaintances, and how Harold had always meant to visit Undershaw but had never gotten the chance. It was a banal and perfunctory conversation, but somehow both seemed to feel that a little chitchat was necessary. Ms. Higgins was clearly suspicious, but she had the good grace not to ask Harold about it directly. He'd been vouched for by the biggest names in Sherlockian studies, so she couldn't very well deny him a look at her collection. But she must be aware of the strange circumstances of Alex Cale's death, Harold realized, and so she must know that his visit was somehow connected to the murder. Harold repeated the same story he'd given her the night before: He was finishing Cale's work, because they were friends, and he just needed to see Undershaw for himself, because Cale had been there. It was a weak story, and both of them knew it. But she nodded when he repeated it, offered a polite and accepting "I see," and then stood. This woman did not trust him at all.

"Like to take a look at the house?" she said.

"Can we? It's all boarded up."

"No one in there now but rats and pigeons," said Penelope drily. "If the likes of them are allowed in, I don't see why we shouldn't be."

They entered through an empty window. Harold felt like a burglar, and yet there was nothing to steal. Everything of any value had been stripped from the house years ago. Nothing remained here save history and insects.

The house was smaller than he'd imagined. The hallways were narrow, and though the windows let in a lot of light, they seemed miniaturized. Dainty. Silence nestled into the dirty wooden floors, and into the paint-peeled walls. As they walked, Harold's and Penelope's footsteps echoed like typewriter clicks down the long, still halls.

"Anything in particular you'd like to see?" offered Ms. Higgins.

"Yes," replied Harold. "The study."

When she showed him in, past the heavy wooden door creaking on its single functioning hinge, Harold's breath caught in his throat. He was a grown-up, thank you, and so he wasn't afraid of ghosts or monsters or any sort of ghoul that Stoker might have written about. And yet to walk into this house...into this room...who wouldn't be spooked by the rotting, abandoned mansion of the greatest mystery novelist of all time? Harold felt as if something were present here—something old, something worn, something dead.

"I was told that you have photographs of this room?" he said. "From when Conan Doyle was living here?"

"Yes. I have many of them. Conan Doyle was fascinated with photography, as you know. He had this whole house documented, from the first stone to his last days here."

She dutifully flipped through her books and produced the photographs. Harold stared down at the black-and-white shots and then up at the same space, ravaged by the century since. The bookshelves along the walls no longer held their dusty volumes. The oak desk, which once sat heavy against the far wall, was long gone. The armchairs had been taken away, the lamps, the case in which Conan Doyle had kept his revolver. Gone, gone, gone.

Harold stood in the spot where Conan Doyle's desk had been. Where his chair had been set back. Where the stories had been composed, where they had been written down in longhand. Where Sherlock Holmes was resurrected.

The old centuries had, and have, powers of their own, which mere modernity cannot kill. Stoker had been right. So had Alex Cale. There was something alive in this house. Not even modernity, not even the horrible rinse of history, could kill what had been born here.

Harold formed his hand around an imaginary pen. He placed it on his imaginary paper, on top of his imaginary desk. He wrote, imaginarily, with a wide flourish.

Penelope Higgins coughed. She seemed used to this sort of behavior from visiting Sherlockians.

"What are you looking for, Mr. White?" Her tone was firm. She wanted a real answer.

"The diary," said Harold, absentmindedly. "I'm looking for the diary."

Ms. Higgins smiled. "Best of luck to you, then," she responded. "You've an illustrious set you're following. Since 1930 we've had chaps like yourself in and out of this room looking for that diary. How many times do you think they've paced around here? How many times do you think they've pulled at the floorboards? Tapped at the walls for hollow spaces? Unscrewed the light fixtures? They must have gone over this room...what, now? A hundred times? A thousand? That's more than eighty years of Sherlockians that've been in here. I don't think there's much left for you to search."

Now it was Harold's turn to smile. And he smiled bigger and wider than Penelope Higgins ever would. Here he was in Conan Doyle's own study, in his own house, and here before him was a mystery worthy of his efforts.

"Elementary," Harold said, because he simply could not resist.

Penelope Higgins shook her head.

"I'll leave you to it, then. Here are the photos. Just don't poke yourself on a rusty nail, give yourself tetanus."

Penelope Higgins left, though she did not close the door. It seemed she would wearily give Harold the benefit of the doubt.

He settled in. He sat on the broken floor. He closed his eyes. He pressed his stubby fingers together in his lap, and he devoted his mind to the task at hand.

The diary would not be found by searching. It would be found by thinking. All problems have solutions, even if they've evaded a generation of inquisitors.

The diary was here. It had been hidden here a hundred years before. But how? But where? He had no doubt that scores of Sherlockians, of scholars both professional and amateur, had combed over every inch of this room. What would they have missed? What hiding place was obvious enough that Bram Stoker was able to quickly stash a leather-bound book in it, without plan or preparation, and yet was ingenious enough that both Conan Doyle and a thousand literary detectives had missed it? What spot had remained untouched over a century of icy winters, summer storms, and ravaging descendants?

Harold thought of "The Purloined Letter." No. In this case, the diary had not been hidden in plain sight. That would be too easy.

What was the twist? If Conan Doyle had hidden the diary himself, where would he have hidden it? Or, better yet, if Conan Doyle had hidden the diary for Holmes to find and Holmes were strolling through this study right now, where would he look? If Harold was sure that the diary was hidden here, and he was...well then, he was only more sure of one thing: that there would be a twist. Because there always was.

He thought of all the great twists he'd read at the ends of all the great mystery novels. Some were small shifts of focus, others were radical shifts of plot, such that everything you thought you knew turned out to be false. Harold wasn't certain what sort of twist he hoped for. But all the best twists he'd read shared one key feature.

The well-written twist always preyed upon the reader's assumptions. Something the reader had simply assumed to be true—because how could it not be?—turned out to be false. Something unquestioned was questioned. Something that had never felt worth examining was examined, and an answer was found in the most unlikely place.

What did Harold assume? That Bram Stoker had hidden the diary so that he could come back later and destroy it. That Bram Stoker had hidden the diary within this room. That no one had ever found it. That the room had been emptied, destroyed, turned over a thousand times and that the diary wasn't here.

That the diary had been here. That the diary wasn't here.

Harold stopped breathing.

The diary had been here. The diary wasn't here.

And it was all so stunningly, embarrassingly obvious.

He flipped through the pages of photographs quickly, looking hard at the gray-on-gray images.

"Have we found the diary yet?" came the voice of Penelope Higgins.

He looked up to find her stocky frame in the doorway.

"Yes," said Harold, in no mood for games.

Ms. Higgins laughed at him through her nose. "Right then! Well, where is it?"

Harold earnestly turned back to the photos, plowing through her sarcasm. "The diary was hidden here in 1900. But it's not here anymore, and it wasn't here after Conan Doyle died. So at some point between 1900 and 1930, someone took it out of this room."

"So somebody stole it?"

"No. Somebody took it out of this room. But I don't think they knew what they were taking. I think somebody removed the diary *by accident*, not realizing what it was. So what I want to know now is, what was taken out of here in those years? What was big enough, and obvious enough, and hollow enough, that somebody could have quickly shoved a diary in it but that no one would have looked inside? It's not a vase, it's not a chest... Maybe the empty base of a lamp?"

"The lamps all went to Conan Doyle's daughter, I believe. And there weren't many of them. Fairly little, too, if I remember. Probably kept them in her attic. But I don't think you'd be the first to search Conan Doyle's daughter's attic for the diary, Mr. White."

Harold turned the page and laid his eyes on a small, dark photograph from 1899. It was of the study, of a liquor table in one corner, festooned with clear decanters and a strange, tall object. He squinted and looked closer. It was bigger than any of the liter-size decanters, wider around the bottom and rising a good two feet into the air. Both the base and the balloon-shaped body were made of opaque glass. A series of what looked like tubes ran around it, and something like a nozzle poked out from the top.

He flipped the pages quickly, finding a later photograph of the same space. It had been taken in 1905. The angle was different, and the liquor cabinet was in a slightly farther spot along the wall... But the object was gone. In its place was something similar but smaller. Much smaller.

He pressed his finger against the first photograph. "What is this?" he asked. "It's hard to make out."

Penelope Higgins bent over the photograph book herself, squinting past her thick, round glasses.

"Oh!" she exclaimed. "The gasogene!" Harold remembered reading about gasogenes over the years, but he didn't think he'd ever seen one. They were early carbonators, used privately to put the bubbles in a gentleman's seltzer. They were expensive and rather unwieldy, and they were found only among the bar sets of the wealthy.

"It's huge," said Harold.

"Yes, rather. It was an early gasogene, I think. Conan Doyle received one of those monstrous nineteenth-century ones early on and got rid of it when the newer ones were developed a few years later. This one was a gift, if I recall."

"From who?"

"Bram Stoker. They were friends, you know."

Harold froze again.

"He got rid of it? To where?"

"Hell if I know," said Ms. Higgins. "Conan Doyle would have sent the thing away long before he died. 1901? '02? '03? Must have been."

"Did he toss it away?" Harold asked, worried that she might say yes. If Stoker had been able to stuff the diary in the wide base of the gasogene and then Conan Doyle had carelessly tossed it in the trash a year later...

"I don't think so," said Ms. Higgins, doing her best to recall. She sighed. "If I must, I can check my books. We have lists, you see, of all of Conan Doyle's possessions and where they've gotten off to."

"Please," said Harold. "Please."

"I think I've one in my car. The thing is dreadfully heavy. Hold on." With an irritated sigh, she left him alone while she went outside. Harold sat, tapping his fingers, waiting for her to return.

He flipped through the photograph book listlessly. He was so close now. So miserably close... He skimmed through the end of the book, where he saw portraits of the Conan Doyle family. Harold looked over the faces of Conan Doyle and his wife, his second wife, his children.

Generations of Conan Doyles had been in this house and had never known the secret that Harold was about to uncover.

He stopped at the very last photo in the book. It was bright and colorful, modern—clearly taken only a few years past. It must be of the great-grandchildren of the Conan Doyle family. It was unlabeled, but Harold recognized a few of the faces. He even saw Sebastian, grinning out at him from the photograph. If only Sebastian knew where Harold was now. Harold grinned back at the photograph. He felt as if he'd beaten them all.

His eye caught on a young woman standing next to Sebastian in the photograph. She was a solid foot shorter than Sebastian, with curly brown hair and a bright yellow scarf wrapped around her neck.

As Harold's eyes went wide and every muscle in his body tensed in shock, Ms. Higgins came back in holding a folder full of papers.

"Lucerne," she said. "It looks like Conan Doyle's first gasogene, miraculously, made its way to the collection in Lucerne."

Harold didn't look at her. He couldn't take his eyes off the photograph. He mumbled something about Switzerland.

"Yes," said Ms. Higgins, not expecting this level of indifference from Harold. "It's at the Sherlock Holmes museum in Lucerne, in Switzerland. You know it?"

"Yes," muttered Harold. "It's at the base of the Reichenbach Falls, where Holmes died. They have a complete re-creation of Sherlock Holmes's study. It's made up with all items from the period, including a number from Conan Doyle himself. I'm sorry, who is this?"

Ms. Higgins stepped toward him. "What?" she asked. "Who?"

"This woman. In the photograph." Harold pointed, his hand shaking in the air. He felt as if he were pointing straight at a ghost.

Ms. Higgins approached the photograph. She followed his outstretched fingertip to the beautiful face of the young woman.

"Oh," she said. "That's Sarah."

"Yes," said Harold. "I know that. What the hell is Sarah doing in a Conan Doyle family photograph? Why is she standing next to Sebastian?"

Ms. Higgins laughed. "Well, I think she's done a bit more than stand next to him," she said. "That's Sebastian Conan Doyle's wife, Sarah." She paused, regarding Harold curiously. "Sarah Conan Doyle."

Harold felt the bitter bile well up in his throat, and he did everything in his power not to collapse.

CHAPTER 41

Whatever That Cost Might Be

"If the law can do nothing we must take the risk ourselves."
—Sir Arthur Conan Doyle,
"The Adventure of Wisteria Lodge"

December 4, 1900

Arthur threw the rock as hard as he could against the gray stones of Scotland Yard. With a sharp clack, the rock bounced off the new Yard building and landed ineffectually at the feet of a nearby constable. Seeing the stone below him, the constable looked up to find its source. He saw Arthur backing away along Victoria Street, and as the constable opened his mouth to shout at the strange rock thrower, Arthur turned his back to the Yard and sped off. The brisk walk was a good outlet for his anger, and so he kept trotting west until, just before Westminster, he slowed and began to pant.

No one had believed him. No one had listened. Arthur's name was more synonymous with the art of detection than any other in London, save that of Sherlock Holmes, and yet still they had not had the slightest interest in a word he'd said. Inspector Miller, in particular, had been the worst offender, given his recent dealings with Arthur. When Arthur had marched into Miller's office and announced that he'd found the murderer of Emily Davison, Sally Needling, and their friend Anna, the man had calmly set down the report he'd been reading, awkwardly adjusted the pens on his desk, and then launched into a series of polite platitudes which overwhelmed Arthur in their obsequious banality.

"We do so appreciate your help," Inspector Miller had said, before thanking Arthur for all the time he'd devoted to the cause of justice. The Yard knew that Arthur must be terribly busy, what with all of his novelistic work. His generosity in taking so much time away from his writing had been noticed and appreciated. If he wished, a formal letter from Commissioner Bradford himself could be written, signed, and even framed for placement in Arthur's home. "We value your assistance more than any other man of the realm," continued Miller's flattery. Arthur tried to hush him, tried to concern Inspector Miller with the case at hand rather than this disgraceful sycophancy. His ego did not need burnishing, he explained, but his findings deserved a public hearing. And one Mr. Bobby Stegler, of Stegler & Sons Printing House along the Strand, deserved to be clapped in the inspector's most uncomfortable darbies and led forthwith to the gallows.

Inspector Miller had sighed. He'd told Arthur that after his recent trip to Newgate, it was best for Arthur to abstain from further involvement in this matter. No one wanted another mistake, after all. Why, careers that had taken a lifetime to build might be rubbed out with a single compromising word! If Arthur ended up in Newgate again, Inspector Miller's own position of influence within the Yard might be shaken. Wasn't it better for everyone if Arthur simply let the matter slide?

Arthur insisted that he did not know what would be best for himself or for the inspector or for the imbecilic muffs who ran this ragtag institution, but surely the world would be better off with a murderer placed properly behind bars! The man had killed three women. He would doubtless kill more.

Yes, very well, Arthur had been forced to admit that he had precious little in the way of actual evidence. In fact, he had none at all, save the man's indirect confession, which only Arthur had heard. Moreover, Arthur did grant that the boy had not actually *admitted* to having killed those girls—but he certainly alluded to having done so. And that must count for something, mustn't it? Arthur would stake his own life on this boy's having been the murderer they'd been hunting for.

Inspector Miller had not been convinced. He had not believed. And, so Arthur realized with a growing anger, Inspector Miller seemed to be harboring suspicions elsewhere as to the identity of the killer.

"You went to the home of Sally Needling's family?" Miller had asked. "You've made contact with this other girl—what was her name? Janet Fry? How do you know these young women so well?"

"I don't," Arthur had insisted. He'd tried to explain again. But the inspector's questions revealed something dark and unspoken about the man's thoughts—he thought he already knew who had killed Emily Davison. And, Arthur realized to his own horror, the inspector thought it was Arthur.

"What are you insinuating?" Arthur had finally asked him.

"Nothing, Dr. Doyle. As I said, it was my pleasure and my privilege to free you from the chains of Newgate the once. But I think no good would be served by my having to do it again." The sympathetic nod which Inspector Miller had then given Arthur was the most aggravating part. As if Arthur were a co-conspirator in this corruption.

"If you think I killed Emily Davison," Arthur had said furiously, spitting the words wetly from his mouth, "then you had better lock me up this very instant. Do not dare let my station in life deter you from bringing the full weight of the law down upon my back, do you hear me?"

The inspector had demurred. He'd defused the situation quietly and then had a constable show Arthur to the door. Arthur had been sputtering with rage when he grabbed the rock from the dirty cobblestones along Victoria Street and pitched it at the ugly stone face of British justice.

He found Bram less than three-quarters of an hour later in one of the Lyceum's basement dressing rooms. Arthur entered to find Bram polishing the mirrors himself, wiping them clean with an old rag and a stick of Lever Bros. Sunlight Soap. Bram's sleeves were rolled past his elbows as he scrubbed the soap streaks from the brilliant surfaces. The electric bulbs which surrounded the mirrors were reflected in the newly clean glass, doubling their brightness and making it appear, for an instant, as if the entire mirrored wall were constituted only of bursting flame.

Bram turned to face Arthur, setting down his rag.

"I'd know that face anywhere," said Bram. "Welcome back, Mr. Holmes."

Arthur did not smile. Rather he unburdened himself upon his friend, sharing the events of the past few days in detail, and in a rueful tone. When Arthur had finished, Bram scratched at his bushy red beard thoughtfully.

"The boy," said Bram. "Bobby Stegler. He just let you leave? After he'd near confessed to you? He let you walk out of there in one piece?"

"Yes," said Arthur. "Don't you see? Once he knew who I was...well, he'd thought he'd found a fellow in his cause. And for my own part, I didn't see much point in disabusing him of that notion. Strange, damn it. Everyone thinks I'm on his side. Inspector Miller thinks I'm trying to help him cover up my own crimes. And Stegler thinks I'm working to help him cover up his own."

"So then, whose side are you on really, Arthur? That of justice? That of law?"

"No. Emily's. Sally's. Anna's. I'm on the side of the *girls.*"

"Well then, what do you think your girls would have you do now?"

Arthur considered the question, turning to face both men's reflections in the dressing-room mirrors. He noticed how well his own mustache had grown back, how quickly his visage had again taken on the form of a proper man's. A strange image appeared in his head. It was of his own wedding day. Except that Arthur was not wearing his black tuxedo. Rather he was wearing a sparkling white wedding dress. He imagined himself stitched all in white silk, a flowing train following behind him as he walked blushingly down the aisle toward his betrothed. He imagined the smile on his face, the exuberance of a bride on her wedding day.

Arthur noticed Bram regarding him curiously, and he shook himself from this vision. What a queer thing to imagine!

"I think," Arthur said at last, "that these girls would have us see to it that their killer was brought to justice. At any cost. Any cost at all."

Bram stood and began unrolling his sleeves. He fastened the buttons on his cuffs one by one before he spoke again.

"Very well," said Bram. "Then I am with you." He took his coat and slid it over his outstretched arms. "Whatever that cost might be."

———————

December 6, 1900

Arthur and Bram stood on Bridge Street, just across from the Jews' Burial Ground. Though it was quite dark, they could still make out a few of the tallest headstones, chipped and ragged, illuminated by the lights of the workhouse behind them. They heard the groans of drunks from somewhere beyond, and from the large road they heard the faint pitter-patter of prostitutes' feet along the dirt. Arthur had not planned this return to the East End, to be sure. But now that he was here, and had been venturing here for the past two days, he realized that of course there was nowhere else for this matter to properly end.

Arthur regarded the Stegler family's staunch two-story in front of him. He and Bram had found the house easily, by a simple search of the public records regarding the Stegler printing business. Over the last two days, they had kept watch over the property. In a small black notebook, they had kept track of the identities and schedules of each resident of the house. First there was Bobby, who left the house early every morning to attend to his duties at the family press. Bobby's father, Tobias, left each day a bit later in the morning, stopping in on the press and then on other errands in regard to his business. Bobby's sister, whose name they learned was Melinda, lived in the house as well and seemed to be at home most of the day, watching after the various servant girls who came by and attending to some of the chores herself. In the evenings she would dine out with friends. These three characters made up the sum of the house's residents—a search of the death notices revealed that Bobby's mother had passed many years ago, when he was just a boy.

Arthur had followed Tobias Stegler the day before, and to Arthur's shock he learned that the man owned a number of houses on Watney Street, near Whitechapel, including the one that had been rented out secretly as a boardinghouse by its caretaker—the one behind which the body of Sally Needling had been found. When he'd seen Mr. Stegler give a few raps on the outside of that house's door and then saw the lady of the house answer, Arthur had almost lost his wits with surprise. The last time he'd seen this woman, she had been disconsolate, sitting on the narrow staircase of her black-market boardinghouse and crying over the body she'd found and robbed. And here she was calmly opening the door for her landlord, the father of the boy who had done that very murdering. Arthur remembered her fear, he remembered that she'd been keeping the business she ran from this house secret from the landlord—from the man he now knew was Tobias Stegler. Arthur watched as she passed Mr. Stegler a clump of bills and sent him on his way. He never entered the house, as he was seemingly content to have collected his rents and saw no need for further inquiry into the state of his property.

Clearly, this was no coincidence. But it took an hour of talking through the situation with Bram, later that night, before Arthur figured out what it meant. Tobias Stegler did *not* know about the boarding-house being run out of his property, they reasoned. If he did, then the woman of the house would have had no cause to respond to Arthur's threat, all those weeks ago, that he would tell her landlord of her secret. But, they also reasoned, somehow Bobby Stegler *did* know, and he'd used this to his advantage. He knew that he would need an out-of-the-way place, a quiet boardinghouse without a lot of guests, to bring his first victim. When he learned, probably through some simple accident, that one of the women his father rented to was secretly keeping lodgers, it only made sense for him to make use of it. He would not, however, have risked a second trip to the same house, for his second victim.

He had gotten lucky enough that the woman hadn't recognized him once—though as far as Arthur and Bram could tell, she might not even know the boy's face.

If Arthur had harbored any doubts as to Bobby Stegler's guilt in the murders, this revelation eliminated them. Bobby had particular means to have committed these crimes, he had the opportunity, and he certainly had a motive, however perverse it might be. What the boy had done was more evil, Arthur knew, than simple murder. He had toyed with his victims first; he had seduced them, he had said he loved them, he had made them feel love, and then he had strangled them in dirt-flecked bathtubs. He had not simply slaughtered these women; he had first violated their womanhood. He had cruelly struck each woman at the core of her female being. It was worse than murdering a man. And it was worse even than simply murdering a woman. He had struck at the entire womanly sex.

Arthur and Bram waited until the house was empty. At 8:30 p.m., as expected, Bobby's sister, Melinda, left the house for an evening rendezvous with her girlfriends. Bobby had not yet returned from the printing house; the past two nights, he had not returned until after ten. Tobias was out at this hour as well, dining with another neighborhood landlord. The house was dark, and perfectly still. This was as planned. As Arthur and Bram watched Melinda Stegler turn the corner on to Harford Street, they each finished a final cigarette of the evening and stepped across Bridge Street, toward the house.

They had discussed their plan at length, and so as the men stepped around the house, to the back, neither needed to speak a word. The back door was cheap and thin, probably held shut with only a small lock, but they went for the window next to it. As Arthur raised his booted foot and kicked straight through it, the glass broke easily. Amid the squalid noise of the East End, the sound of shattering glass blended into the din. One more violent crash hardly added to the neighborhood's clamor.

Arthur stepped through the window, and Bram followed close

behind. Their boots crunched the glass underfoot as they walked through the kitchen. Their earliest reconnaissance had told them that Bobby's bedroom was on the second floor, and they wasted no time in heading straight for it. They knew what they were here for. They had abandoned all caution to get it.

The staircase creaked with the weight of two bodies on it. The house was of poor construction, and the wooden boards felt as if they might snap at any moment. Arthur's boots left a trail of tiny glass shards as he walked, a line of glinting sparkles from the kitchen to the second-floor bedroom and into the mouth of hell itself.

When both men had entered Bobby Stegler's quarters, they shut the door and lit the single gas lamp upon the wall. A narrow four-poster bed rested, unmade, in one corner of the room. Two broad chairs sat across from it, as if ready to entertain guests. But, judging from the messy piles of clothes which covered them, Arthur found it unlikely that many guests came up here. The sloppiness of the boy's room pointed to a loneliness within him—as if he could allow his private quarters to be in disarray because he would never, at any point, need to share them. Did this raging child have friends? Did he have cricket with the other boys his age? Had he ever felt love? Had he ever looked into the face of a woman and known that tender feeling, that warmth which spread from belly to beard? Had his hands ever quivered as they touched a young girl's glove? Had he ever bit his lip to keep from crying out with joy as he bent over to kiss a woman's hand?

Arthur looked at the messy sheets of printing paper on the small desk, he looked at the ink-stained clothes strewn haphazardly across the floor, and he knew that Bobby Stegler was not a man. He was a beast. And Arthur would see that he was put in a cage where he belonged, to live out his miserable days until his death, when his heart could be cut from his chest by a doctor's scalpel and that black, wrinkled organ could be placed in a jar for the edification of future generations. "This is the cold heart of a dead man," the typewritten sleeve on the bell jar would read, "and this is what it looks like when a heart dies years before its owner." In the bright twentieth century, when reason ruled the world, this boy would serve as a reminder of the dark years that had passed, and of the generation—Arthur's generation—which had led them all from superstition into the brilliant rationality of science.

But first he would need to be caught. And so Arthur and Bram got to work, silently and methodically. They searched the clothes, the bed, the desk, the chairs, and into the tight closet. They searched for evidence. Arthur hoped to find the wedding allegations—this boy would be arrogant enough, proud enough of his villainy, to have saved them, Arthur suspected. And with the allegations in hand, the Yard would have to listen to him. Failing that, they hoped to find letters from any of the dead girls written to Bobby Stegler. Or perhaps proofs of the girls' pamphlets, which would at least prove that he knew them. There were a dozen possible pieces of evidence they might find here, and they needed only one.

When the first sweep of the room produced nothing of interest, they searched again. The minutes wore on, and Bram began to express concern about the hour. At some point one of the inhabitants of the house was bound to return. And it wouldn't do for Arthur and Bram to be caught ransacking their home.

But Arthur would not leave. He would not think of it until something useful had been discovered. He had followed his scarlet thread of murder too far to stop here, or even to come back and try again at a later date. This would end tonight, and by the morning, so help him, Bobby Stegler would be in the care of Inspector Miller and his men.

The search continued.

"We must leave, Arthur," said Bram as his impatience grew. "What if Tobias returns? Or the sister?"

Arthur pulled back his coat, showing off the revolver strapped to his waist.

"Then we will explain the situation fearlessly and be on our way. What are they going to do to us? Call the Yard? I'm sure Bobby Stegler would appreciate having the Yard men sniffing about his quarters."

"I have no natural aversion to breaking and entering, don't misunderstand. But we have to be discreet about this, don't you think?"

"I think," said Arthur, "that we have to find something that we can use here. And this jabbering is not going to help us do it."

He turned from the desk before him to the windowsill. A few used, broken pens lay on the sill, and one had even dripped ink onto the white paint. Arthur touched at the pens and then raised his head to the window, where he found himself inches away from the smiling face of Bobby Stegler.

Arthur froze and caught his breath. For a second he was motionless, watching what could only be a specter in the window. But as the boy's smile widened and the window was pulled open from the outside, Arthur realized that there was no ghostly presence at work. The boy was sitting on a tree branch outside the window. For all Arthur knew, he might have been watching them the whole time.

Arthur stepped back as Bobby Stegler stepped into the bedroom through the open window.

"As soon as I saw the light on, from the street, why, I knew it was you!" said Bobby. "I just knew it!" He closed the window behind him and looked at Bram.

"And you would be Mr. Stoker, wouldn't you?" continued the boy as he moved the blond hair from his eyes. "I've been looking after you two. It seems you've been looking about for me, too!" Bobby laughed then, and the sound was hideous.

Arthur drew the gun from his waist and held it in front of him.

"Be quiet," said Arthur, "and be very still, do you understand? Or I will shoot you here and now."

The boy smiled again and looked over at Bram.

"If Arthur doesn't," said Bram as he pulled a revolver from his own coat, "then I most certainly will."

"Oh, ho," said Bobby, "my two detectives! You've really taken your roles quite seriously, haven't you? But come off it. You don't want to shoot me, not after everything I've done for you.

"Why, Arthur, don't look at me so! I've saved your life! Frankly, don't you think we should be sharing a pint o' bitters and laughing over our good fortune? Those bleeding cunts were going to kill you. I know about the letter bomb. Didn't find out till I'd already had my way with that last one, mind you. I can't give myself *too* much credit. I didn't kill them to save your life, but by the by, as I've killed, so I've without a doubt saved you!"

"They weren't going to kill me," said Arthur. "Not really. And I won't defend them, all right, I won't defend the horrible things those girls were planning. But you... What you've done is infinitely so very much worse. You murdered three innocent women."

"Innocent?" Bobby Stegler's face lit up with incredulity. "You can't mean that. Innocent? Three queer dollymops with a boxful of dynamite? You must know they were... well, I think they loved each other. I mean, I think they *loved* each other, as if one were a man! Emily Davison and Janet Fry most certainly did. My God, can you imagine? They were horrors, those hairy cunts. And they were out to remake the world—our world—in their hairy-cunted image."

As Arthur held the revolver in his hand, he felt a shaking in his arm. He felt himself twitching. He imagined the faces of those dead girls—sweet, pale, and mutilated. More than anything else he had ever wanted, he wanted at this moment to pull the trigger. To see this ugly thing before him smitten from the face of the earth.

"Arthur," said Bram. "Don't."

As usual, Bram could read his thoughts exactly. Bobby Stegler looked back and forth between the two men, and something new registered on the boy's face. Curiosity. As if it had never before occurred to him that Arthur might actually fire the revolver.

"Oh!" Bobby said. "Are you going to shoot me? I mean, you're honestly thinking about shooting me? I just can't... My!" He pressed his hair away from his face again and scratched at his scalp. "Seems rather unlike you, doesn't it, Dr. Doyle? I mean, I don't have a weapon on me. Unarmed and all that. Not a threat to your person. You'd be killing me in cold blood like, wouldn't you? The storyteller has a gun, and he's fit to use it. Well then. All right. It's up to you then, I suppose. What are you going to do now, Dr. Doyle? Are you going to shoot me? Or are you going to tell me a story?"

Arthur looked deeply into the boy's clear blue eyes and scanned the contours of his handsome face. Arthur could hear something, faintly, in the distance. A rushing sound. A crash of water against rock. He wasn't sure if it was real or not, but he heard it all the same. Torrents of water rushing over a cliff. He tuned his ears to the noise and recognized the tone. He steadied his hand and listened to the sound, from the back of his mind, of the Reichenbach Falls.

CHAPTER 42

The Sherlock Holmes Museum

[Holmes] pushed to an extreme the axiom that the only safe plotter
was he who plotted alone. I was nearer him than anyone else,
and yet I was always conscious of the gap between.
—Sir Arthur Conan Doyle,
"The Adventure of the Illustrious Client"

January 17, 2010

From the base of the mountain, below the Reichenbach Falls, Harold stared across the Hauptstrasse at the Sherlock Holmes Museum. He shivered and pulled his thin coat tighter against the Swiss air. At just after six in the evening, the final spots of orange sunlight were disappearing to the west, behind the museum. The unlit streets were getting darker, and with every passing minute they were getting darker faster. From his perch on the other side of the wide road, Harold could see two museum guards locking up for the night. It would only be a few more minutes now. He clenched his fists in his pocket. He could not remember the last time he'd been so cold.

As he watched the two guards mill around the entrance to the museum, laughing at a joke that Harold couldn't hear, he turned and looked behind him to the east. The Swiss Alps broke clear of the earth not fifty yards from where he was standing. Snow blanketed the top third of the range like a white silk shawl.

Harold shifted his weight, feeling the bulky bag slung across his shoulder. The steel tire iron inside pressed against his back. The guards laughed again and began a slow wander in the direction of the parking lot. The museum was dark. Empty. The last morsel of the sun vanished into the distance, and Harold stepped from the shadows into the nighttime.

There was nothing left for him to lose anymore. He had no life he wanted to return to, and the life he knew he wanted, the life of these weeks in which he'd for the first time come truly alive, had been revealed as a fraud. And not even a complicated fraud at that. The twist had come so easily, and bowled him over with such self-evident obviousness, that Harold couldn't even muster up anger at Sarah, or at Sebastian. He'd known he shouldn't have trusted her from the beginning, hadn't he? Her whole story had been just as improbable then as it was now. Harold knew enough to blame himself.

At first he couldn't believe that she'd gotten away with her lie. Sebastian Conan Doyle's wife—or soon-to-be-ex-wife—had walked into the world's largest Sherlockian convention under a fake identity, and no one had known who she was? But *of course* they hadn't, Harold realized. Most of the attendees spent their days pretending that Sherlock Holmes was real and that Arthur Conan Doyle was just Watson's literary agent. They didn't care about Conan Doyle or his descendants. Harold was even aware, when he searched the recesses of his memory, that Sebastian Conan Doyle was married, and he might even have known that his wife's name was Sarah, though it was hard to remember now. But of course he hadn't made the connection. She'd lied so obviously, so plainly, that no one would ever have thought to question her. "You're really, really smart," she'd said to him when she left.

Harold couldn't understand why she had deceived him. What were she and Sebastian planning? Were they actually getting a divorce? The lawyer she'd called was real, but had the story she'd told him been utterly fake? And who the hell had been chasing them in London? Was that all for show? Harold had realized, over the past day, that he simply didn't care. He didn't care who the men with the guns were, he didn't care what Sebastian was after, and he didn't care who Sarah Lindsay, or

Sarah Conan Doyle, really was. Alex Cale's "murder" had been solved, his trail of clues followed to perfection. But the pursuit gave Harold no joy anymore; it granted him no peace. All he wanted now, all he craved, like a drowning man's last gasp of oxygen, was the diary.

But he knew that the diary wouldn't make him happy either. When he put his sweaty palms on its cover and peeled open its parched pages, he would hear no choir of angels in his head. There would be no swelling of his heart; no sense of contentment would fill his panting lungs. He understood that in just a few minutes, when he laid his hands on the leather-bound book and learned its secrets, things would only get worse. But that would not stop him. He would see this through to its awful conclusion, because he had to. Because he had to *know*.

His footsteps felt quick and firm as he marched through the snow. He came through the blackness to the front of the museum. The building had once been a church, and a humble spire still poked up from the angled roof of the simple two-story. Even in the dark, Harold could make out the reddish hues of the bricks and the beautiful glasswork in the windows.

There were many ways that Harold could have snuck into the museum. He could have entered during the day and hidden in some forgotten storage closet. He could have learned to disengage the alarm system. He could have learned to pick locks. But even if those methods worked, they would take an impossibly long time to accomplish. He didn't have the heart. He couldn't bear this anymore. He was going to know *now*.

Harold was home, at the base of the Reichenbach Falls. The place where everything ended.

He removed the tire iron from his bag and stared at the antique stained glass in a low-hanging window. The image was of Jesus raising Lazarus from the dead. A golden halo surrounded Lazarus's head as he stepped from his cave, toward the beckoning hand of Jesus. A legion of apostles and followers stood behind, marveling at Christ's divinity and soaking up the comfort of his presence.

Harold raised the tire iron above his head and smashed it down on the glass. The sound of the window shattering was much louder than he'd anticipated, and yet he didn't flinch at the noise. Tiny shards of glass sprinkled back at him from the broken window, covering his coat sleeves and muddy shoes. He flicked the tire iron around the open window a few times, knocking out the remaining hunks of sharp glass. He dropped the iron back into his bag and placed both gloved hands on the windowsill, pressing himself up and through the window. In a moment he was inside.

Harold heard no alarm but assumed that one must have been activated. He didn't have much time, but he didn't think he needed it. And if the Swiss police found him smashing a priceless gasogene in the private museum? Well, then they could tell the New York police they'd found him, and the various authorities could figure out which jail they'd want him in. Harold didn't care. All he wanted was the diary.

He walked quickly through the museum, and as it was small and Harold's destination was its main attraction, he found what he was looking for in no time at all. He entered the carefully prepared study of Sherlock Holmes, flicked on the lights, and looked around. Of all the places to end, this one made as much sense as any.

The room was cramped with objects. The fireplace was adorned with sharp pokers and a long singlestick, with which Holmes had stalked Moriarty in "The Final Problem." Drawings of various Holmes adventures littered every available surface. On a small table lay Watson's stethoscope, as well as Holmes's violin. Another table held Holmes's chemical kit, with which he would test bloodstains, tobacco, and the other assorted residues of murder. A deerstalker hat, just like Harold's, rested on a hook. First editions of all of the Holmes stories covered the bookshelves. A tea set was laid out on a breakfast table, spoons and knives set in their places as if Holmes and Watson were midmeal. Newspapers of the period sat beside the cups and saucers. And along the far wall, in what Harold couldn't help but notice was the darkest corner of the darkened room, a small desk held an antique gasogene up to his gaze.

Without hesitation Harold walked to the gasogene and raised it from the table. He shook it. The base was easily wide enough to hold a diary, and, for a piece of hollow glass, the gasogene felt quite heavy. He twisted at one of the screws on the base, but it wouldn't budge. He tried the other, with no better luck. It occurred to him that besides a steel tire iron something along the lines of a screwdriver would have been a pretty smart addition to his collection of break-in tools.

He set the gasogene back down on the table, went to the fireplace, and lifted the poker. It was heavier than the tire iron. Longer. It was perfect. Harold gripped it with both hands and could see his knuckles whitening around the hilt. He raised the poker over his head. Was he sure that the diary was in the gasogene? Yes. No. It honestly no longer mattered. He'd smash it to pieces, or he'd smash something else to pieces, or he'd break every heirloom in this entire museum if that's what it would take.

He kept his eyes open wide as he squeezed the poker in his palms, arched his back, and drew the poker down on the gasogene with every bit of strength he possessed. Glass shattered, the steel poker clanged violently against the metal base, and the force of the contact sent Harold stumbling back across the study. His wrists hurt.

"Harold White." When he heard the voice behind him, his mind went instantly blank. The words themselves sounded foreign. Harold? White? *Oh, yes*, Harold realized, as the color drained from his face. *That would be me.* He prepared himself for jail, placating his natural terror with the thought that it wouldn't be for more than a few years. It's not as if he'd killed anybody, after all. It was only as he was turning around to face the voice addressing him that he realized that whoever was calling his name *knew his name.* And that was when Harold became scared.

He completed his turn to see the Goateed Man staring back at him across the study. The man held a gun in front of him. Harold's vision danced between the top of the pistol and the goatee on the man's face. The gun looked like the same one he'd seen in London. And the goatee was no more attractive than he'd first thought.

Despite the fear that squeezed on his muscles and contracted his breath, Harold realized that the man in front of him hadn't yet pulled the trigger. Harold could handle this. He stepped forward, right foot and then left, toward the Goateed Man.

"Stop there," said the man.

"No," said Harold. He stepped forward again. He couldn't be more than six feet from the man now. The man drew the gun higher, aligning its barrel directly across from Harold's scalp.

"Take another step and I'll bloody kill you," said the man.

"No," said Harold as he took another small step. "You won't." He stepped again. Four feet separated them now. "Because you want the diary. And you know you need me to get it."

The man gave Harold a strange look.

"You mean that?" he said, glancing ever so quickly to the floor behind Harold's feet. Harold turned his head, shifting his eyes down to the floor. A few feet behind him, amid a pile of broken glass and poking out from the metal base of the gasogene, sat a two-inch-thick, leather-bound diary.

"I don't think I need your help anymore to find the diary," said the man, grinning.

So much for that. Harold had accomplished everything he'd been asked, and then some. He was done now. So much for being just a little bit smarter than everyone else. Being clever had gotten him far, but now it didn't seem like it would get him any further.

"Not yet," said Harold. Only now was he truly scared. But it wasn't the gun that terrified him—it was the thought that the gun would kill him before he could hold the diary in his hands and peel open its dusty pages.

"I wasn't supposed to kill you," said the man. "But now I don't have a bloody choice. I just need the diary, but I can't have anybody knowing where it came from. And if you're alive when the Swiss police get here..."

"Fine," said Harold. "Kill me. I don't care anymore. But please. Five minutes. Give me five minutes to read the diary. I can read really fast. Really, really fast."

"Step back and kick the diary toward me."

"No, please. Three minutes. That's it. You can't let it..." Harold was pleading now, begging. He was mere feet away from the diary. He imagined that he could smell its must, that he could taste a century's grime on the back of his tongue. "You can't let it end like this. I just need to read it."

Staring into the man's eyes, Harold saw something he thought was pity.

"Look," said the man, "I didn't sign on to kill nobody. I'd rather not. I'll make you a deal, all right? You get out of here, and you never tell a word of this, and I say I found my way here on my own. But you need to leave. Now."

"No," said Harold. He wanted to explain his desperation, to somehow make clear to this man why he couldn't walk away. But he couldn't explain this.

"Are you bloody crazy? Go away. Leave me the book and go."

Harold wanted to cry, but he didn't. He tried to speak, but all that came was a soft panting. He looked with wide, begging eyes at the man, and he stepped forward again. If he could not leave here with the diary, then he could not let himself leave here at all.

"Right then," said the man. "You win." His finger curled around the trigger. Harold did not close his eyes but held them open. He felt no need to shield himself from this.

"*POLIZIA!*" came a loud cry from elsewhere in the building. The sound snapped both Harold and the man loose from their diabolical pact. They heard footsteps and the noises of a body shifting around. Harold thought he heard the crunch of broken glass under a boot.

The man kept his gun aimed at Harold, and for his own part Harold didn't move.

"*POLIZIA!*" came another shout. The voice was Italian-speaking Swiss, and female.

"Please," said Harold to the man. "Shoot me, take the diary, and run. Or give it to me. But I'm not leaving."

The man continued staring at Harold, gauging his seriousness. The man's face grew tight, as if acknowledging that Harold would not bend. As the footsteps approached the study, the man turned his body toward the door. That was all the time Harold needed.

He swung the poker through the air, aiming for the man's head but landing it across his left arm. There was a crunch, and Harold felt the recoil of contact through his own arm. The man doubled over to his left side, instinctively protecting his wounded forearm with his right hand. He still held the gun, but it wasn't pointing at Harold anymore.

Harold swung again with the poker, ramming it into the man's shoulder. He howled in pain. As Harold stepped back for another swing—would he aim for the man's head? Would he kill him?—Harold saw a figure in the doorway. It was the woman who'd yelled "*polizia*" from the hallway, but she was not, so far as Harold knew, a member of the Swiss police.

It was Sarah.

He dropped the poker and was only vaguely aware of the clank it made against the floor. Sarah held a small gun in her hand, and she was aiming it at Harold. The man, given a moment to catch his breath, used the opportunity to lash out with his own gun, punching it into Harold's belly. Harold felt all the air leave his body. He dropped to his knees, holding himself up from the floor only by pressing both hands into the floor. He had moments ago prepared himself for death, but now he felt like he was actually dying. It was more horrible than he'd imagined. He opened his mouth for air, but none entered. His mouth hung open as if in a silent scream.

The man didn't waste an instant. He pistol-whipped Harold about his brow, swinging the arm that held the gun against his temple. Harold felt the hard steel batter into his head, once and then again. Everything went blurry.

Harold lost the next few seconds to shock. When he finally became aware of the world around him, he was on the floor, staring up at the Goateed Man. He felt something wet on his forehead. Blood, most likely, trickling between his eyes toward his nose. The man raised his gun to Harold's face. Strangely, Harold felt some small measure of instantaneous joy at the thought that when he died, Sarah would watch. If a bullet was about to enter his brain, blowing gray matter and bone particulates into the floor of Sherlock Holmes's study, he wanted her to see it.

Harold heard the gunshot. It was the loudest sound he'd ever heard, and his ears screamed from the volume. It sounded more like static than like any of the gunshots he'd heard on television or in movies, but it still sounded like a gunshot. And Harold heard it. Which meant, he quickly realized, that he wasn't dead. Dead people didn't hear the bullet as it entered their brain, he was pretty sure of that. So he hadn't been shot. Who had?

"Step back," Sarah said. Her tone was insistent but calm. Harold looked over at her and at the gun she held before her. She'd fired the shot. But as he turned his head to the Goateed Man, he saw that neither of them had been hurt. The man obeyed Sarah, stepping back away from Harold. When he moved, Harold could make out the hole that had been ripped by her bullet in the wall behind him. She hadn't been trying to kill anyone, Harold realized. Just to make a point.

If the bullet hadn't done the job, the look on Sarah's face certainly did. The man stepped back farther, and he even lowered his gun without being asked to.

"The bleeding hell are you doing?" the man said to Sarah.

"I'd ask you the same thing," she responded. "No one was supposed to die."

"I don't see how it's your problem whether I kill this bastard or not."

"It is my problem," Sarah said. "And it's yours, too. 'Cause if you kill him, how much longer do you think I'll let you live?"

Harold had no doubt whatsoever that she was serious. He felt himself growing light-headed. He was coughing, choking, trying to get some air into his lungs but finding himself unable to take a breath. He was suffocating—and growing panicked.

Sarah glanced at him quickly.

"Breathe *slowly*, Harold," she said. "Calmly. Slow, deep breaths. You just had the wind knocked out of you. That's right. Very slow. Don't try to take in too much air at once or you'll choke more. There you go. There you go."

Harold did as she suggested and felt the oxygen warming his lungs. He tried to press himself up to his feet but stumbled. He was still light-headed, and he doubted that the wound on his head was helping. He looked down and saw a line of blood that had dribbled to the floor. He raised his hand to his head and, bringing it back down in front of his face, saw that it came back stained with red. The sight of his bloody hand made Harold nauseous.

The man held the gun to his side but didn't drop it. Sarah tensed herself, preparing to fire again. This time she would not aim for the wall.

"Please drop the gun, Eric," she said. "Or I'm going to shoot you."

Harold looked up at the Goateed Man. *Eric*. It seemed odd for him to have a name, a real name, a normal name. He didn't look like an Eric.

Between the wooziness in Harold's head and the blurriness of his vision, he was never clear about the exact order of the events that unfolded next. Everything moved very fast, and the actions taken by Sarah, Eric, and even himself seemed not so much to happen in response to one another as all at once. At the very same instant Eric raised his gun toward Sarah, Sarah lowered hers and pulled the trigger. Two more violent gunshots blared across the study, rattling Harold's senses.

The next sound he heard was far off—sirens. The actual Swiss police were finally on their way.

Screaming. Male screaming. Eric was alive, and screaming. Cursing.

Harold could see nothing. Thanks to the deafness he was tempo-rarily experiencing due to the gunshots, all he could hear nearby was some sort of scuffling. He felt a hand on his shoulder, pulling him up. A voice said something to him, but he had no idea whose it was or what message it conveyed.

He struggled to his feet. He was in no position to fight back at any-one right now, whoever happened to be pulling at him.

There was more screaming, but Harold couldn't make any of it out. And a moan. The hand on his shoulder pulled him across the room, and he went as it directed. He felt himself tripping over things, stumbling, but he managed, somehow, to put one foot in front of the other as he tumbled through the museum. The hand was pulling him faster now, yanking more insistently. Whether he was headed toward salvation or summary execution, he didn't know. He was not sure which outcome he'd prefer.

It wasn't until he felt the freezing Swiss air on his cheeks that he looked up. It was darker now than when he'd broken in. The street they were on, whichever one it was, was lit only by stars and the sliding, shifting red-blue of distant police lights. Harold felt the air stab at his head and became aware of the cold nipping at his open wound. There was no way to know how much blood he'd lost. The hand kept pulling at him, however, and for the first time Harold brushed it aside. He used a sleeve of his coat to wipe the blood from his forehead. The owner of the hand, still a blurry shape, paused for an instant and turned back to face him.

"Come on," she said. It was Sarah.

"The man...Eric...Is he...?" Harold had only the faintest idea of what he was saying.

"No, he's alive," she said quickly. "Bleeding, but alive. Which is about where you're at right now. Time to run away. We have what we need."

Harold looked down, wiping the blood from his eyes.

Under the crook of Sarah's left arm, she held the diary.

CHAPTER 43

The Murderer

"What you do in this world is a matter of no consequence,"
returned my companion, bitterly. "The question is, what can
you make people believe that you have done?"
—Sir Arthur Conan Doyle,
A Study in Scarlet

December 4, 1900, cont.

The bullet tore off Bobby Stegler's left cheek. Blood and skin sprayed against the window behind him and then slid down the glass, down onto the dirty sill.

There was screaming. The boy wailed, still very much alive. He bellowed like some demon, and he looked the part, half-faced and grotesque.

Arthur watched the boy tear at his face and the blood spurt onto his blond hair. The bullet, Arthur's single bullet, had transformed him into something monstrous. His true form was now revealed.

Still wailing, Bobby lashed out at Arthur, grasping at the gun in his hand. They struggled. Arthur strained every muscle in his arms to hold on to his revolver, while his nose was pressed up against Bobby's open jaw. Arthur could see the bones poking out from behind what once was a cheek.

Arthur heard Bram fire as well, but Bobby was undeterred by the shot. Arthur fought, pushing and pulling, trying to get hold of his pistol for one more shot.

He was faintly aware of a sound at the door. A single breath, caught in someone's throat. Arthur could not turn to look.

He struggled against Bobby. The boy was so much younger than Arthur, and he was clearly stronger, despite his injuries. Arthur felt his own biceps strain to the point of bursting. He ground his teeth as he pulled, and he thought he might bite through his own molars.

The revolver in Arthur's hand went off again. When he would think on these moments, later, this is how he would think of them: The gun simply went off. No one fired it. Certainly not he. It was simply fired. The passive voice was there for Arthur, and it understood. The gun was fired. The bullet was loosed. And yet Arthur and Bobby still struggled with all their might. The bullet had not hit either man.

Bram fired again. This time Arthur saw the metal ball carry what was left of the boy's brains out the other end. He felt the boy's grip slacken. With a dull, wet thump, Bobby Stegler's corpse smacked against the wooden floorboards. He was dead.

It took Arthur a few moments to hear Bram's voice. Arthur's mind was pure white snow, clean and uncluttered by thoughts. He regarded Bram, his friend, his Watson, dazed and dreaming.

"What have you done, Arthur?"

There was another sound, from the doorway. A gasping and gurgling, like a country brook. Arthur turned, and saw Melinda Stegler, Bobby's sister, slumped in the doorframe. Her neck had been opened wide by the stray bullet.

Arthur did not kill her. This point would become of paramount importance to him, later on. He did not pull the trigger. Bobby must have done it. Arthur would have remembered pulling with his forefinger. In the struggle, amid the blood and the noise and the all-consuming shock of violence, Bobby had shot his sister.

Melinda's body did not fall as easily as her brother's had. She did not die. At least not at first. As her blood spouted into the thickening air, she clutched at it, trying to hold it in. The sickly red liquid gushed through the cracks between her fingers before falling onto the front of her sky blue dress. A stream of blood rushed into the fabric between her breasts, soaking through her corset and then down toward her waist. From her throat came the gargling noise, as her lungs took in deep swallows of blood and coughed them back up again.

When Melinda fell, she fell only to her knees. There, while she knelt on the floor, her eyes went wide as she gripped tighter at her throat. The look on her face, as Arthur watched her die, was not of horror or pain but of wonder. She beamed at Arthur, her eyes shining a brighter blue than even those of her brother. She looked like a baby, staring at the new world for the first time. She held her mouth open, but Arthur knew that she did so out of awe for the lights dancing across her vision. Yes, Arthur noted to himself later on, she was happy when she died. She saw something beautiful before her, and she went to it. She did not suffer.

In another moment her heavy head tugged her body over to the side. She slumped there on the floor, blood still flowing freely from her wounds. He watched it come toward him across the room until it mingled with her brother's, right between Arthur's feet. Arthur thought about Emily Davison's brutalized corpse. This was so very different. The passing of these two children so much more gentle than Emily's would have been. Arthur was no monster. A killer, perhaps. But he was no monster.

He felt a hand on his shoulder. It was Bram. And he was squeezing firmly.

"Let's be off, then," said Bram.

CHAPTER 44

Is It Your Turn to Kill Me Now?

*"It is of the first importance," he cried, "not to allow your
judgment to be biased by personal qualities. A client is to me
a mere unit, a factor in a problem. The emotional qualities are
antagonistic to clear reasoning."*

—Sir Arthur Conan Doyle,
The Sign of the Four

January 17, 2010, cont.

Harold and Sarah sat down, finally, on a small outcropping of rocks.
The stones were cold against his thin pants. The wind was blowing fast
and cold across his face.

They looked down at the valley below. In the distance they could
just make out the museum, illuminated by the flashing lights of a few
police cars. Officers, little black dots scampering between the light
beams, seemed to be approaching the scene.

"We should be safe here," Sarah said. "Eric's the only one who knows
we were even in the museum, and he didn't see where we went. The
cops didn't follow us. No one knows where we are."

Harold nodded but didn't speak.

"How's your head?" she asked.

"Bleeding."

Sarah took the bright yellow scarf from her neck and wrapped it
around his head, covering the wound. She pulled the scarf tight, tying
it off, and Harold winced. She had been wearing this scarf the day he

met her, he realized. He watched now as the bright yellow of the scarf was blotted black by the red blood gushing into the fabric.

"You'll be okay," she said. "It's not a deep cut. Head wounds just bleed a lot."

He gestured toward the gun she'd placed on her lap. "Is it your turn to kill me now?"

She smiled. "No. It was never my turn to kill you. Nobody was ever going to kill anyone."

"Eric?" Harold said, pronouncing the name with particular bitterness.

"Eric wasn't supposed to kill you either, all right? I promise. Look. I'm sorry. Okay? I know I have a lot to explain, and I'm going to, but before I start, I just want to say I'm sorry."

"Do you want me to forgive you?"

"Yes, I do. But not right now. I know that you won't. At least I wouldn't. But please, believe me, I'm sorry."

"Yeah," said Harold after a sizable pause. "I'm sure."

"Here." Sarah took the gun from her lap and handed it to Harold. It felt cold and heavy in his hand. "You take this. If you want to shoot me, then shoot me."

Harold felt the weight of the gun, turning it over curiously between his hands. He regarded it as he would a mysterious relic dug up from a lost civilization.

"No," he said. "I don't shoot people." He wound up his arm behind him as best he could, and pitched the gun over the ledge. They heard no sound of its landing, though it most likely fell into the river at the mountain's base.

"Were you following me?" Harold asked after another long silence.

"I wasn't. Eric was. I followed him, which was easy enough. He works for my ex-husband." She looked at Harold, trying to gauge how much of this he already knew. His expression did not register much in the way of surprise.

"I used to be married to Sebastian Conan Doyle," Sarah continued. "*Used* to be, okay? Everything I said about the divorce was true. He's a bastard, let me just say that straight out. But I seem to have a long history with bastards. I don't know. They find me, I guess."

"Why do I care?" The harshness in Harold's voice surprised even himself. As he felt calmer, and safer, he also felt angrier.

"Because none of this was my idea, okay? At least not the worst parts. You have to think I'm a terrible person, don't you?"

"Yes."

Sarah sighed. "I understand. But listen. I really am a reporter. Well, I really was a reporter. That was all true, too. Sebastian and I separated six months ago. We did. You can look it up. It's a long story, and you don't care. After we split, I wanted to write again. And I had all these Sherlockian connections, because of him. Or at least I knew a lot about Alex Cale, and about all of your organizations, because Sebastian followed them religiously. He hated you all so much, I can't even begin to tell you. But he wanted that diary. And I'll tell you right now, I think he *would* have killed Alex to get it. He didn't, I know. But I think he would have.

"When Alex announced his discovery... I wasn't there, but I can only imagine how furious Sebastian was. When I heard about it, I knew this would be my opportunity to write again. That's when Sebastian called me. I honestly don't know how he found out about the piece I was working on. He said we could combine forces. We could work together to find the diary. I could write whatever I wanted, as long as I helped him. And we were finalizing our divorce... He offered to make things easier. A lot easier. There were some complications that didn't make me look very good, and he was offering to be very generous, and... I said yes, okay? I said yes. I accept responsibility for that. It was complicated, and I said yes. I'd play the reporter, and I'd help him get the diary."

"Where the hell did Eric come from?"

"He works for Sebastian. He has for a while. But that's all I know."

"If Sebastian got you to help him find the diary," said Harold, "and then he got me to help him find the diary, then what was Eric doing?

Why did Sebastian need Eric running around with a gun if he had me and you?"

Sarah paused for a moment. This was a problem she'd thought about before.

"Because he didn't trust you," she said. "And God knows he didn't trust me. It's just like Sebastian, really. You have a problem, so you throw as much money at it as possible. Hire three different people to work on it, but don't tell them about each other, keep everyone in the dark, and if they kill each other . . . well, whatever. At least one of them will find what you're looking for. I told you, Harold. He's really, truly, totally, and completely a bastard."

Harold looked up at the glittering stars. They barely lit the side of the mountain. Even Sarah's face was disappearing in the blackness. He believed her. But believing her didn't make him feel any better.

Sarah reached behind her and took the diary, placing it on Harold's knees.

"We can use the light from my phone," she offered, "if you want to read it."

Harold swallowed. "Yes," he said. "I do."

Sarah removed a cell phone from her pocket and opened it, using the face of the phone like a spotlight as she pointed it at the diary. Harold gently pried open the covers. The pages were fragile and yellow, but he could make out the words written in Arthur Conan Doyle's broad hand.

Harold held the diary between them, and together they read.

CHAPTER 45

The Missing Diary of Arthur Conan Doyle

"Come, come, sir," said Holmes, laughing. "You are like
my friend, Dr. Watson, who has a bad habit
of telling his stories wrong end foremost."
—Sir Arthur Conan Doyle,
"The Adventure of Wisteria Lodge"

December 8, 1900

Arthur wrote it all down.

That's what he did—he wrote things down. Writing was both his occupation and his calling. He was celebrated around the globe because was so very *good* at it. When he wrote, when he put events into words, into clear and tidy sentences, they were understood. Things made sense when Arthur wrote them down. And so, terrible as these events were, they demanded to be chronicled. They demanded to be wrought onto paper, to be sculpted from raw feeling into refined language. That's what writers did, wasn't it? They named that which needed naming, they enunciated that which had previously been unspoken.

The night of the deaths of Bobby and Melinda Stegler, Arthur stayed up till dawn, describing everything that had happened in as much detail as he could recall. When a particular moment escaped his memory, he embellished upon what he knew. He wrote the story as it existed for him. He did not glorify himself. He did not make it seem as if he were blameless, as if he bore no responsibility for the evening's tragedy. He did, and he would not deny it. But nor would he gloss over the villainy of Bobby Stegler. That the boy had deserved to die was really beyond debate, and Arthur had to be sure to be clear on that point. It did not justify the tragedy of his sister. Nothing would. But then, in these weeks, in all this time since that bomb had exploded, no tragedy had ever been justified. None of the violence that had stained Arthur's life had ever been explained. Death, murder—perhaps in the end they were never explainable. They simply were.

Arthur and Bram did not see each other again for a few days. Neither man, it seemed, wanted to talk about what had happened. They read the reports in the newspapers, and when no culprits were found—and no bobbies came knocking on either of their doors—they knew that it was over. They would never see Tobias Stegler again, and the burden of his children's death would live with him and him alone. For that they were quite sorry. Arthur did wonder whether Janet Fry would call on him again—she knew the name Bobby Stegler. She must have been in his shop. If she saw the notice of his death in the papers, would she make the connection to the deaths of her friends? Or would she chalk it up to odd coincidence? She had been so convinced of the guilt of Millicent Fawcett, after all...

But as the days went by and Arthur heard nothing from her, he became satisfied that he wouldn't. And so he was free. If Inspector Miller suspected anything, which he probably did—well, what would he do about it? Inspector Miller had, at least so he thought, helped Arthur cover up one murder already. He would do the same for another two. Was Inspector Miller at work, pulling strings to keep Arthur's name in the clear? Or was Scotland Yard really incompetent enough not to be able to trace the murders back to Arthur's doorstep? He would never know. He was free, whether through corruption, incompetence, or dumb luck.

On December 8, 1900, Bram Stoker made his last visit to Undershaw, and to Arthur's study. He came to talk. It was time for them to consult about what had occurred and to properly bid farewell to this period in their lives.

For two men of such intimacy, the meeting felt curiously formal. As Bram entered and Arthur put down his pen, he felt awkward for the first time in his friend's company.

Silence followed.

"What are you writing?" asked Bram, after the strangest quiet in their friendship.

"It's . . . Well, you wouldn't believe it if I told you," said Arthur, oddly embarrassed by the words on the page before him.

"I'll be the judge of that."

"It's Holmes. I haven't told a soul yet. You're the first to hear. But it's Holmes."

Bram simply nodded, as if somehow he had expected as much.

"The other day," Arthur continued, "I had an idea. Have you been to Dartmoor? Those frightful heaths? They're quite terrifying. I thought it would be a great setting for the old fool. I had this notion of a plot, after my friend Robinson described to me this story about a gigantic hound terrifying the countryside. Ha. Sherlock Holmes on the trail of a terrific hound . . . Well, maybe it's too far-fetched. But perhaps it would be a good yarn, wouldn't it?"

"Yes," said Bram. He appeared content. "It would be an excellent yarn. And the world is short, nowadays, of good yarns."

Arthur described the plot to Bram, and both men went over the pages. Bram was more than approving; he was ecstatic. He described the tale as a return to form—Arthur was delighted.

The conversation took an odd turn when Arthur told Bram about what else he had written.

"You've kept a diary of all . . . of all that happened?" asked Bram, stunned.

"I needed to put it all down. Oh, don't give me that look, man! I'm no fool. It's not for anyone to read. I won't share it with a soul. But I needed at least to share it with my diary." Arthur smiled then, his face turning wistful. "Perhaps one day when I pass into the next world, if someone finds the book and reads what happened...well then, what do I care if people know the truth? And what do you? Perhaps the truth deserves to go free at last, one day."

"You cannot be serious, Arthur," said Bram angrily. "Your reputation...your worth to generations...It's not just your name you're tearing down, don't you see? It's Holmes's. This is about more than just you."

"Please, calm yourself. Sherlock Holmes will be fine with or without my help."

"No," replied Bram. "He'll be nothing, Arthur, for heaven's sake, if you don't destroy that thing. Do you hear me? For your own good. For my good. And for Holmes's good."

"Lord, Bram," Arthur began, before he was cut off by a noise from upstairs. It sounded like a crash. One of the children had done something improper with a table lamp, and the sound of yelling followed. "Excuse me one moment," said Arthur as he wandered from his study to see what the matter had been.

By the time he came back, a few minutes later, Bram had the most curious look on his face.

"What is it?" Arthur asked.

"Nothing," said Bram. "Nothing at all." He was sweating, Arthur noticed. Bram so rarely perspired.

Neither man had any idea at that moment that in those few short minutes a mystery had been laid. And that after the diary had been hidden, it would take more than a hundred years for it to be found.

CHAPTER 46

The Reichenbach Falls

"Wear flannel next to your skin, and never
believe in eternal punishment."
—Mary Conan Doyle, to her son Arthur,
as recounted in his memoir *Memories and Adventures*

January 17, 2010, cont.

When Harold closed the diary, he realized that he was crying. His tears were dripping onto the hard leather cover of the book, mingling with a hundred years of dirt, dust, and a few specks of blood.

He'd read slowly, making sure that Sarah could follow along with him. Now they both sat freezing on the rocks, and they both knew everything. Sarah placed a hand comfortingly on Harold's knee, and he found himself crying harder. He pulled the diary to his chest and let his tears fall on the dirt. He didn't have the energy to conceal them. Neither Harold nor Sarah said a word.

After a few minutes, Sarah stood. Without speaking, she gestured along the path through the mountains. She wanted to walk. Harold didn't object. He brought himself to his feet, feeling aches forming in his thighs and knees. He followed her in the darkness, up the path, higher into the snowy Alps.

He had no idea how long they walked. It could have been twenty minutes or two hours. They walked under the cover of starlight, through the snow, higher and higher. The exertion warmed Harold a little, and after some time he thought he was close to regaining feeling in his fingertips. Sarah sensed his cold, and despite her own she removed her coat and wrapped it around his shoulders. He didn't thank her but only walked farther, higher and higher through the thinning air.

He wasn't sure where they were going, and he didn't care. He began to appreciate the cold in his bones, the cold freezing the tears on his face. The chill quieted his racing thoughts. He could only feel so much in his head, in his frayed and slow-beating heart, when the rest of his body was frozen. The thought occurred to him that if he lived here, if he set up camp in the mountains and never came down, he might be able to avoid all future feeling altogether. The plan sounded as reasonable as any other.

Before they came upon the clearing, Harold heard the sound of rushing water. Because of the darkness, they didn't see the waterfall until they were only a few feet away from it. Harold felt the mist from the racing falls spray his face at the same time that he saw the cascading torrent of water through the trees. He could hear the water crashing against the rocks below, slapping against the hard side of the mountain every hundred yards until, somewhere far in the dark distance, the water landed in a churning pool and fed into a lake deep in the valley.

The Reichenbach Falls. They both stopped walking and stared silently off into the distance at what little of the falls they could see.

"I'm sorry," Sarah said.

"Me, too." Harold didn't have an ounce of anger left inside him. He wasn't sure how much of anything he had left inside him anymore.

"Are you happy?" she asked. "Are you glad you found the diary?"

Harold did not need to think in order to answer truthfully.

"No."

Sarah reached across his body and took the diary from his hand. He loosened his fingers and gave it to her without argument or complaint. She stepped back from the ledge. She pulled the diary behind her, curling her arm like a pitcher, and overhand she threw the diary as far as she could into the darkness. They could almost hear the diary collide with the falls, as it was rocketed downward toward the cragged lake by the force of the water.

And then silence. Stillness. The hum of the waterfall and two sets of breaths, puffing in unison.

"Thank you," Harold said.

Sarah reached for his hand and held it warmly in her own. There, staring into the night sky, they stayed, fingers intertwined. Harold squeezed as hard as he could, and Sarah squeezed back, each gripping the other's hand until they felt their fragile bones were about to shatter.

CHAPTER 47

Farewell

*And so, reader, farewell to Sherlock Holmes! I thank you for
your past constancy, and can but hope that some return has
been made in the shape of that distraction from the worries
of life and stimulating change of thought which can only
be found in the fairy kingdom of romance.*
—Sir Arthur Conan Doyle,
preface to *The Case Book of Sherlock Holmes*

August 11, 1901

The workmen were tired. They had been at it all day, sweating through
the August heat and dampening the armpits of their navy blue uniforms. Two days ago they had finished laying the twenty-foot-long
main electrical cables from the Marylebone Station to Baker Street.
The mains were thick and quite heavy, two copper tubes placed one
inside the other and layered with brown wax. The whole thing was
encased in heavy iron, and every time the men lifted a long section of
cable between them, they'd grunt and feel the strain in their bulging
necks. Yesterday a larger team had come to help raise the cables above
the houses, laying them between the lampposts and over the two-story
roofs. It had taken twelve men to spread their web of wires outward
through Marylebone, slowly west to Paddington. Today only two
workmen were left to remove the gas lamps atop each pole along Baker
Street and replace them with electric bulbs. Late in the afternoon, as
the sun melted into the taller buildings along Montague Square, the

two sweaty, exhausted men took turns mounting their one ladder and unscrewing the tops of the gas lamps. One would stand on the ladder's lowest rung, weighting it down, while the other would climb to the top. The poles had been connected to the nascent grid already, so all that remained was to connect the sockets to the positive and negative lines and then replace the bulbs. The wires kept slipping through their damp fingers, and when they would try to brush the sweat off on their work suits, they would leave finger-shaped stains of wax and dirt on the navy cloth. They were getting very tired.

Just after sunset, a few hours behind schedule, they came to the final lamppost, right before the corner of Igor Street and the park. The shorter of the two held the ladder from below, because it was his turn to do so, and the taller man ascended the eight vertical steps to the bulb. It took him only a few minutes to rewire the fixture, and by the time he came back down the ladder, every lamp along Baker Street had been wired for electricity.

After returning the ladder and tools to the back of their wide-bedded carriage, they walked to the Marylebone Station to complete the connection. Once they had connected the Baker Street line to the system, from the transformer room deep underneath the station, they made their way back to examine their work.

They turned the corner as ten thousand volts surged from the Deptford Power Station, nine miles away, through the Ferranti cables underneath the city and onto the shining expanse of Baker Street. It was a brilliant sight, and though they had worked for the London Electric Supply Company for a few years now, the first glance at a street illuminated solely by the searing electric bulbs still caused a brief shock. Every building, every alleyway, every dark and fetid cobblestone had been washed clean in the radiant light.

"Oi," said the taller workman. "That's it, then."

"I'd say so," replied the other.

"Lord, but it's sure bright, isn't it? I can't hardly see the fog anymore."

His partner simply nodded in agreement. It was as if a layer of gloom and dread had been stripped from the streets, leaving the city white and clear. But the vision of this white and sparkling street was odd, too, and neither man possessed the words to explain why. So much that had been hidden was revealed in the electric light, so much had been gained. But perhaps something had been lost as well. Perhaps, both men thought but did not say, a part of them would miss the romantic flickering of the gaslight.

The first workman fished around in the pocket of his coat.

"You have any coin on you?" he said.

His friend patted his own pockets and heard a comforting jingle of metal.

"A few pence, I'd say. Why?"

The first man gestured toward the park.

"There's a boy 'round the corner selling the papers. I've got a couple bits on me as well. You feel like a story?"

The second man thought about it, and smiled.

"Yes, I dare say I do. Something you have in mind?"

"There's that new *Strand* out this morning. 'The Hound of the Something-or-Another.' A new Holmes one."

"Oh! Yes, I think I could go for a good one of those."

As they walked, both men removed all the coins they could find from their pockets. They presented the meager change to each other sheepishly. It wasn't much, they knew. But based on a quick count, they found they had exactly enough for two pints of bitter ale and one paperback mystery.

Author's Note

Romance writers are a class of people who very
much dislike being hampered by facts.
—Sir Arthur Conan Doyle,
from an address given in honor of
Robert Peary, May 1910

So, then, what *really* happened?

Not to disappoint you, but the only honest answer I can give is this one: It's a bit of a mystery.

While *The Sherlockian* is a work of historical fiction, the emphasis needs to be placed on the word "fiction." Many of the events described here did not happen, and many of the characters rendered did not exist. But since a number of them did exist, and since the work in front of you is a collage of the verifiably real, the probably real, the possibly real, and the demonstrably false, I thought a few words of explanation might be in order.

So here goes. The following is all true:

After Sir Arthur Conan Doyle died in 1930, a collection of his papers went missing from among his effects. This collection—some letters, some half-finished stories, and a volume of Conan Doyle's diary—remained mysteriously vanished for over seventy years and was the holy grail of Sherlockian studies for most of the twentieth century. Generations of scholars attempted to locate it, but none met with any success.

Finally, in 2004, Richard Lancelyn Green, the world's foremost scholar of Sherlock Holmes, announced that he'd found Conan Doyle's lost papers. However, Green claimed that a distant relative of Conan Doyle's had stolen these papers from Conan Doyle's daughter and was planning to sell them at auction rather than donate the documents to charity as Green—and Conan Doyle's immediate heirs—had wished. A dispute emerged between Green and this relative, and their argument over the rightful ownership of the papers grew increasingly bitter, and increasingly public. By March of 2004, Green had begun to tell his friends that he was worried for his own safety. He claimed that he received threatening messages and that he was being followed by a shadowy American. He told one close friend that his home was bugged, and he demanded that some visitors speak with him only in his garden. Green's friends in the Sherlockian community became concerned.

On March 27, Richard Lancelyn Green was found dead in his South Kensington flat. He had been strangled—garroted—with one of his own shoelaces. His sister, Priscilla, discovered the body. The coroner returned an open verdict, and as of this writing the case is still considered unsolved by the London police.

Immediately thereafter Sherlockians around the globe began to search for Green's killer. Grand theories quickly emerged, as some Sherlockians believed that the feud within the Conan Doyle family over the author's estate had grown violent and taken Green's life, while others thought it more likely that Green had committed suicide in order to cast suspicion on another party. The character of Harold, in this novel, is a composite of a number of real-life Sherlockians—all of whom, I can assure you, outshine Harold in both brilliance and social grace.

For more information about the death of Richard Lancelyn Green, I highly recommend the article "Mysterious Circumstances" by David Grann (*New Yorker*, December 13, 2004). Or, for a shorter introduction, try "The Curious Incident of the Boxes" by Sarah Lyall (*New York Times*, May 19, 2004).

All the information in the novel about modern Sherlockian societies—the Baker Street Irregulars and their many scion groups—is accurate, to the best of my knowledge, as are the descriptions of their meetings and rituals. That said, meetings of the Irregulars are not open to the public, and so I have relied upon public reports and interviews for a glimpse into their secret world. A very special thanks to Leslie Klinger—world-class Sherlockian and editor of *The New Annotated Sherlock Holmes*—for his help on these points and many others. And thanks also to Chris Redmond—creator of Sherlockian.net, which is an invaluable Sherlockian resource entirely unaffiliated with this book—for teaching me the long and not particularly sordid history of the Irregulars. As both of these men have forgotten more about Sherlockian studies than I will ever know, please note that all errors in this work are entirely my own.

As for the turn-of-the-century story line, all of the biographical information about Arthur Conan Doyle contained here is true. Many wonderful biographies of Conan Doyle exist, though I recommend Daniel Stashower's *Teller of Tales* in particular. Stashower also edited *Arthur Conan Doyle: A Life in Letters*, a masterfully compiled collection of Conan Doyle's personal correspondence. Additionally, Julian Barnes's novel *Arthur & George* presents a beautifully rendered—and accurate!—portrait of Conan Doyle working on one of the real-life crimes he investigated. Over the years Conan Doyle assisted Scotland Yard on a number of cases; *The Real World of Sherlock Holmes*, by Peter Costello, contains a terrific list of all of the crimes with which Conan Doyle became involved. The particular case he investigates in *The Sherlockian* is fictional, though it is a composite of a number of non-fictional ones, especially the infamous "Brides in the Bath" murders of the period, a mystery that Conan Doyle himself did help to unravel.

One major fictional leap has been taken in the Arthur Conan Doyle story line, however: A group of angry suffragists did not place a letter bomb in Conan Doyle's mail in 1900. They did so in 1911. *The British Women's Suffrage Campaign: 1866–1928*, by Harold L. Smith, has been a fantastic resource on the subject of the NUWSS and its leader, Millicent Fawcett.

The portrayal of Bram Stoker in this novel is also as accurate as possible and is based chiefly on *Bram Stoker and the Man Who Was Dracula*, a brilliant biography written by Barbara Belford. Though Oscar Wilde is not quite a character in *The Sherlockian*, his presence looms large over both Conan Doyle and Stoker. *Oscar Wilde*, by Richard Ellmann, remains the final word on Wilde biographies, as it has been for over twenty years.

All locations featured in this novel are real. If you can manage it, I highly recommend a trip to Switzerland to see the Sherlock Holmes Museum. Take a stroll between the chairs, lamps, and gasogenes from Arthur Conan Doyle's old study. Who knows what you'll find there?

GPM

2010

Acknowledgments

My deepest thanks—

To the great friends who read early drafts of this work and whose editorial insights are worth far more to me than any lost diary: Alice Boone, Kate Cronin-Furman, Amanda Taub, Rebecca White, Janet Silver, Richard Siegler, Helen Estabrook, Leslie Klinger, Sara McPherson, and Johnathan McClain.

To the professionals—the very best in the business—who through their creativity and acumen turned this book into something far grander than I could ever have imagined: Jennifer Joel, Niki Castle, Jonathan Karp, Colin Shepherd, Cary Goldstein, Maureen Sugden, Dorothea Halliday, Tom Drumm, Vanessa Joyce, and Max Grossman.

To the loved ones who made sure that I kept writing when I was awfully convinced that I would stop: Lily Binns, Ann Schuster, Avinash Karnani, Matt Wallaert, Tony O'Rourke, Christine Varnado, and the Plaid Shadow.

To my family. All of you.

And an extra special thank-you to Ben Epstein, who is the best writer I know and the reason I started writing fiction in the first place.

About the Author

GRAHAM MOORE is a twenty-eight-year-old graduate of Columbia University, with a degree in religious history. He lives in Los Angeles.